THE BIRDS
OF THE AIR

L.H. ARTHUR

Copyright © 2022 L. H. Arthur
All rights reserved
ISBN: 979-8-9865895-0-3

For Greg and Noah.

They know why.

PART 1: PULLMAN

CHAPTER ONE

THE NIGHT BEFORE everything began, Libby dreamed about the scarecrow in the vegetable garden.

In the dream, her mother had sent her to the garden, but she couldn't remember why, because the scarecrow kept looking at her. It hung on its tall stick like always, an old set of straw-stuffed clothes that had once belonged to her father, with a potato-sack head coming out at the top. But instead of the black button eyes Grandma Barnett had sewn on, it had pale-gray human eyes, set into the rough-woven burlap. The eyes followed her – no other part of the scarecrow moving except for the little flapping of its clothes in the wind – and she felt that it wanted to tell her something, but all it had for a mouth was a line of black-yarn stitching.

"I dreamed about the scarecrow last night," she said at the breakfast table.

Her mother, scooping oatmeal into her little sister's bowl,

tightened her lips. "*That* useless thing. I don't know why I let your grandmother talk me into wasting time on it. It doesn't do a darned bit of good; the birds still eat us out of house and home."

"I dreamed it had –" Libby began, but her mother gave the wooden spoon a sharp rap on the edge of the pan, to unstick the oatmeal that clung to it.

"We have a lot of washing to do today, Libby, so I don't want you dawdling over your breakfast all morning. Finish up there and clear the table, and then you can strip the beds."

After the dishes were done, Libby gathered the bed linens as her mother had asked, then fetched the big metal washtubs, set them on the kitchen floor, and filled them with buckets of hot water from the sink. Her mother added soap flakes to one, set the washboard in it, and began scrubbing their clothes and sheets, along with the washing she took in for pay. Libby carried the heavy baskets outside to the wringer and ran the wet laundry through, struggling to turn the stiff crank; then she carried the baskets to the clothesline.

It was a brilliant morning, noisy with birdsong – a Friday, and still only April, but Libby and her sister Maisie had no school: in this fourth year after the Crash of '29, the town had run out of money to pay the teachers, and had ended the term early. Maisie missed her little friends, and often talked wistfully about her second-grade teacher, Miss Gardner. But Libby was happy to be outdoors – even helping her mother with the wash – instead of stuck in Mrs. Mitchell's musty eighth-grade classroom all day.

A boisterous wind harried drifts of white cloud across the sky, and snatched at the damp, clean-smelling clothes as Libby hung them on the line. Maisie – who was supposed to feed the chickens, gather the eggs, and then start ironing the pillowcases – followed Libby around, chattering.

By mid-morning they ran out of soap flakes, and Mama had to walk to the five-and-dime. "I'll be back in an hour or so," she told Libby. "Keep an eye on your sister, and get the rest of those sheets on the line."

At the clothesline, Libby fought the wind, using half a dozen pins to hold each flapping sheet. From time to time, when a gust opened spaces between the snowy expanses of cloth, she saw Maisie kneeling in the grass, playing with a paper doll Mama had made for her. After a while she called to her: "Maisie! Did you get the eggs yet? You're gonna fool around all morning, and not get the pillowcases ironed! Lazy Maisie: that's what we should call you."

When the sheets parted again, she looked to see whether her sister was listening, but the patch of grass was empty. "Maisie?" she called, pushing through the billowing laundry. A bright flash of pale, wind-whipped hair caught her eye, way down at the far edge of the yard, near the irrigation ditch that separated their property from the fields beyond. Maisie teetered there like a small blown-away kite, smiling up at a ragged-looking man who stood on the ditch bank, talking to her.

Libby hurried across the yard, grabbed Maisie's arm, and hauled her back a few steps from the stranger. The man stayed where he was, smiling in a way that looked almost friendly, but not quite. He was short for a man, and stocky; his face was red, with threads of darker-red veins worming beneath the skin of his nose and cheeks. An odd construction of sticks and wire hung on his back; it looked like a homemade birdcage, but it was empty except for a vacant twig perch. Libby thought he must be one of the drifters who sometimes came to the back door to ask their mother for food. Mama always gave them something. "They're just ordinary men, out of work from the hard times," she said. "It could happen to anybody." But the hint of a smirk in this man's smile made Libby uneasy, and she didn't think Mama would want them talking to him when she wasn't at home.

Maisie looked up at her with an impish smile. "*He* says I don't have to *mind* you, Libby. He says I don't have to mind *Mama*, even!"

Libby ignored her. "Mama's busy in the house right now," she said to the man, raising her voice so her words would carry over the wind. "If you come back in an hour or so, she could talk to you." She backed away a little farther, pulling Maisie with her.

The man didn't answer; instead he began to unstrap the stick-and-wire cage from his back. Maisie gaped at Libby with gleeful shock. "You told a *fib!*" she cried, loudly enough for the man to hear. "Mama's not back from the store yet!"

Libby let out an irritated breath and started toward the house, towing her sister behind her; but before they had gone five steps, Maisie dug in her heels, pulling her arm free. "Look what he *gave* me, Libby!" Beaming, she lifted her hand and opened it, revealing a tiny, perfect miniature bird, white except for a round brownish spot between its outspread wings. It was no bigger than a bumblebee, and all made of hard sugar, like the cherubs on the cake at their aunt's wedding.

"Maisie, don't you *dare*! You give that to me, right now." Libby held out a stern hand, but Maisie only giggled and scampered off a little way toward the clothesline.

The man had the cage in his hands now, and was fumbling at the latch of a small door in its side. "That there candy was s'posed to get delivered to *another* little gal here in town, for her birthday," he said, "but your sis is lot nicer an' purtier'n *that* little gal, so I just asked her would *she* like to have it instead." He looked up from the cage, straight at Libby. "An' your sis, she says yeah, she would."

Libby's heart was beginning to speed up. She turned and darted across the lawn toward Maisie, reaching for her, but Maisie skittered away. "He says I'll be able to *fly*, Libby!" she said; and before Libby could get near her again, she popped the sugar bird into her mouth.

After that, things began to be hard to understand.

Libby, shocked to a halt, cried, "*Maisie!* You spit that out, *right now!*"

"Too late for that, girlie."

The tramp's voice sounded closer; Libby turned, and saw that he had left the ditch bank and come into the yard. He was stumping quickly toward them, holding the cage in one hand, his smile no longer even almost-friendly.

Libby wheeled to grab Maisie, meaning to run with her to the house, to get inside, lock the doors. But it seemed she had turned too quickly and made herself dizzy: the house and yard kept rotating around her for an instant after she stopped, and she had the extraordinary feeling that her feet jerked to one side, as if the lawn beneath her had been yanked like a rug. She staggered and half-fell, having to catch herself with one hand on the ground; an underwater-sounding rumble muffled her hearing.

When the sound and the dizziness passed, she straightened quickly to look for Maisie, but her sister was nowhere in sight. A mound of sky-blue cloth lay on the grass a few feet away; she recognized it as one of Maisie's dresses, and for a heartbeat she thought it must have blown off the clothesline.

Then she remembered.

It was the dress Mama said matched Maisie's eyes – the dress she had been wearing just a moment before, when Libby had turned away from her.

"Out a' the way, sister," the tramp said – gruff now, right at her shoulder. She jumped, and stumbled back, but he pushed past her without a glance. A strong smell of stale sweat trailed after him, along with a pungent, sweetish odor Libby didn't recognize.

He hurried to the dress and squatted beside it. Libby saw something moving in its folds, as if a mouse were trapped beneath it. Setting the cage down, he carefully gathered the fabric around the moving thing and picked it up; then he pushed the dress against the open cage-door. He loosened the cloth a bit, and a little brownish bird flew out and fluttered against the twig bars.

Quickly the tramp pulled the cloth away and snapped the door shut. He stuffed Maisie's dress into the front of his shirt, and bent to pick up other bits of cloth that had fallen. Libby saw that they were Maisie's underthings; he stuffed those in as well, then lifted the cage and slipped the straps over his shoulders again. The little bird fluttered wildly inside, its wings making frantic flapping sounds.

The tramp resettled his battered felt hat, pulling it down tight against the wind, and squinted at Libby. "Best keep quiet about this, missy. Ain't nobody gonna believe ya, anyhow." He gave a brown-toothed grin, winked at her, and started off toward the fields.

And Libby knew.

A jolt like a surge of electricity ran through her, and she bolted after him. She grabbed the flimsy homemade cage, yanked as hard as she could, and felt something give; but the tramp growled out a curse and, with one swing of his arm, knocked her to the ground.

The second she hit, she rolled onto her stomach to scramble

to her feet. But there, on the ground before her, lay the cage, wrenched off its straps by the pull she had given it, broken wide open. Its twig bars slanted at crazy angles; perched on one of them, the little bird cocked an eye at Libby – an eye the same sky-blue as the dress the tramp had stuffed into his shirt.

The tramp lunged at the bird, grunting as he fell onto his belly, reaching out with both hands. But the bird was gone before he thumped to the ground, and Libby watched it fly across the fields and disappear into the woods beyond.

The tramp made a sound between a snarl and a howl, lurched to his feet, and snatched up the broken cage. He paused, glaring down at Libby. For a moment he looked ready to kick her, but then he slapped a hand to his neck as if a mosquito had bitten him, and scowled briefly back over his shoulder. He cursed again, turned, and shambled off, disappearing behind the tall choke-cherry bushes that edged the yard behind the henhouse.

Libby struggled to her feet and stood still for a few ragged breaths, trying to shape some idea of what to do. She turned and raced to the house, in case she was wrong – in case the impossible thing she thought had happened really hadn't. She called her sister's name; she made a swift circuit of the empty rooms. Then she burst out again to search the yard, whipping aside the hanging sheets, scattering the chickens when she slammed open the henhouse door. A noise in her head began to rise, as if the fitful wind had gotten into her skull and was swelling and moaning against the insides of her eardrums. She caught a glimpse of color in the lilac bush and dove at it, pushing branches till they snapped, but it was only the paper doll Maisie had been playing with, blown in among the twigs and trapped there. Libby pulled it loose and stared at it; its blank, opaque eyes stared back at her, accusing. The wind-sound in her head became a howl and burst out of her mouth, and she ran past the house toward the road, screaming "Mama! Mama!"

THAT NIGHT, SOME of the neighbor women stayed with Mama, while their husbands and the men from the sheriff's office searched the fields and woods nearby.

From her dark room, with Maisie's empty bed across from her, Libby could hear the women murmuring in the kitchen, trying to comfort Mama. When she heard heavier steps and deeper voices – men coming in to get coffee and rest a little, before going out to search again – she was struck by the strangeness of it: there had been only women and girls in the house for almost as long as she could remember. She could feel the concern she heard in the men's voices threatening to draw something up in her, something huge that filled her chest and pushed up into her throat, dense as poured sand.

The women's voices were quiet, and only once did Libby hear words she could make out: her mother, crying over and over, "Why did I leave her? Why did I leave her *alone?*" Her voice rose in a moan that sounded almost like singing, and it made Libby's heart pound as if she were being chased by something. She pressed her pillow over her ears so she wouldn't hear if her mother said what everyone knew she was thinking: *why did I leave her with Libby?*

The next day, Grandma Barnett came on the bus from Ashland. She and Mama clung to each other's hands and wept together, the slight, icy brittleness Libby usually sensed between them thawed by the flow of their tears.

Libby told what had happened over and over: to her mother, to Grandma Barnett, to the neighbors, to the sheriff's men. She described the tramp and pointed out the direction he had gone. She could tell they all thought she had seen it wrong – that she was a foolish child imagining things, though she would be fourteen in July – and she kept running over the memory in her mind, trying to figure out whether they could be right. The men from the sheriff's office asked for a picture of Maisie to add to the small, faded drift of other children's faces on the wall of the post office. "Don't worry, Mrs. Barnett," they kept saying to Mama. But three days went by – three days in which there seemed to be vast, vacant stretches of time between each two ticks of the parlor clock – and nobody brought Maisie home.

Libby had trouble sleeping at night. She lay on her bed and stared up at the dark, forgetting to blink until her eyes stung. She wondered if Maisie knew how to find food to eat, and thought about snakes and hawks, owls and cats. When she did finally sleep, her dreams were filled with the panicked flapping of wings.

In the deep hours of the fourth night, she jolted awake from such a dream and lay staring into the dark, thinking. As soon as the first robin began its tentative, chirruping call, she got up, dressed quickly, and set out across the spring-scented fields.

Mr. Robertson, who owned all the farmland behind Libby's house, lived about a quarter-mile away; he was already up, milking his cows, when Libby arrived. Libby offered to clean out his mules' stalls, in exchange for a piece of the fine netting he spread on his fruit trees in summer to keep the birds away. Mr. Robertson wouldn't let her clean the stalls, but he gave her the netting – a square about the size of a bedsheet – just the same. He didn't ask what she wanted it for, and Libby didn't try to tell him.

She took the netting home and hung it at the back of the chicken pen, where the sparrows flew through the wire from the chokecherry bushes to steal the hens' food. She hung it about a

hand's breadth inside the fence, taut like a sheet on the clothesline, and anchored the lower edge with stones. Then she scattered
chicken feed, and left the pen so she wouldn't keep the sparrows
away. All day long, every half-hour or so, she crept to the corner
of the henhouse and peered around it. When the feed was all
gone, she scattered more. She saw sparrows pecking among the
hens, but they flew away if she tried to get closer, and the net
remained empty.

The next morning she woke early again, and crept into the
chicken pen before the sun had edged over the eastern hills. The
chickens straggled out, mumbling sleepily. She scooped feed
and scattered it, then backed away and crouched beneath the
low eaves of the henhouse, trying not to sneeze from the prickling smells of dust and straw. The chickens pecked and squab-
bled, and after a while, as she watched motionless, the sparrows
appeared. They flew out of the chokecherries, which stood a few
yards from the back of the pen, and landed in the little rectangles
of the fence wire. They cocked wary eyes at the netting. First one
and then another turned away and flew to the top of the fence. A
flick of tail and wing, and they were down among the chickens,
snatching seeds and dodging the hens' huffy pecks. Others followed, and soon there was a little flock of them, darting in and
out, all having avoided the net.

Libby waited until they were intent on their feeding. She
took a deep breath, then burst away from the henhouse wall,
straight toward the birds. She waved her arms, making the noise
she always made when Maisie forgot to latch the gate and she
had to chase the hens out of the vegetable garden: "PSSSHHH!
PSSSHHH!" There was an explosion of wings and a deafening
chorus of cackling from the hens. For a few seconds, birds filled
the air in front of her; then there were only bits of down swirl-

ing in the eddies they left behind. But one sparrow remained, fluttering helplessly, caught by a leg in the fine mesh of Mr. Robertson's net.

Libby held her breath for a moment, perfectly still except for her heart, which beat as if a second bird were trapped inside the cage of her ribs. When the sparrow hung quiet in the net, exhausted, she moved forward softly. It began to flutter again, and she waited until it stopped, tiny bill open and breast heaving; then she gathered it into her hands. It didn't peck at her, or scratch with its claws; it crouched as if stunned, fearfully fragile. Carefully she freed its leg – thin and brittle as the stem of a dried leaf – and cupped the light, soft body against her chest, making a covered nest for it with her hands. She bent her head and opened her hands enough to look into its eyes. The bird lay still, blinking now and then, turning its head in little jerks. At first, its eyes looked as shiny and opaque as two drops of black paint; but when she looked more closely, she saw tiny black pupils surrounded by irises of deep brown. She let out her breath, opened her hands, and let the bird fly away.

Over that day and the next she caught three more sparrows in the same way, and after examining them, let each one go. But soon the birds became wiser. No matter how suddenly she sprang at them, how she hissed or yelled, they always managed to avoid the net. She tried spreading it over the chokecherries, where the sparrows liked to hide, but it caught only dead leaves and loose chicken feathers, so she gave up on it. Instead, she spent her days prowling the brushy edges of the fields, or pushing through the green tangle of the nearby woods. She crept along little streams, or crouched beneath bushes humming with foraging bees, but she never saw the blue-eyed bird.

Grandma Barnett had gone back to Ashland, and Mama

didn't seem to notice Libby's absence. When Libby came home at sundown, she would find her mother sitting in the kitchen with a bowl of unsnapped string beans on the table before her, or in the chair by the front window, staring out at nothing, some forgotten piece of mending on her lap. "Oh – there you are," she would say, and her glance would slide across Libby's face but just miss meeting her eyes. "I suppose we'd better get supper."

One day, almost two weeks after Maisie had gone, Libby spent the afternoon on a grassy stream-bank, beside a miniature waterfall where the birds came down to bathe and drink. The birds flitted up to nearby branches when she approached, peering down at her and calling warnings to one another. But she lay down on her stomach beneath the bushes, staying silent and still, and soon they seemed to lose sight of her, as if she had become invisible. They fluttered down again to splash in the stream, to hunt for insects in the leaf litter and gather stalks of grass for their nests, sometimes within a few feet of her.

She watched them for a long time, chin on her crossed arms, straining to see the tiny beads of their eyes; but sometime during the warm, insect-buzzing afternoon she slipped into a doze. When she woke, it was nearly sundown. The birds were gone, and the only sounds left were the crickets and the murmur of the stream.

She was about to raise herself up when a movement caught her eye: a solitary buff-and-rust sparrow, alighting in the grass on the near side of the stream, not three feet away. Libby froze, holding her breath, but she must have made some tiny sound, and the bird cocked an eye to look at her. The eye was as blue as a sky freshly washed by rain.

Without moving her gaze from the bird, Libby began to inch

The Birds of the Air | 15

her hand forward – slowly, slowly, so as not to frighten it – until her arm was outstretched toward it, palm upward, pleading.

"Maisie?"

The bird cocked its eye down to her hand, then back up to her face. After a few seconds it took a single hop toward her. She held her breath. It peered at her again for a long moment, then took two more hops; but at that moment the raucous call of a crow sounded overhead. The little bird tensed, cowering, and tilted an eye skyward; then, with a flicker of wings, it disappeared into the trees.

A small, anguished breath burst from Libby, but even as it came out she was slithering backward from beneath the bushes. She sprang to her feet and looked around wildly, making sure she would remember the spot. Then she ran, shoving aside branches and crashing through undergrowth. When she reached the edge of the fields, she cut straight through Mr. Robertson's green wheat. Even so, the sun had dropped behind the trees by the time she pounded into the yard, sweaty and out of breath. She didn't slow, but headed for the rear of the henhouse. She rounded the corner, her hands already reaching for her net – but then she stopped.

There was a bird in the net.

It was a sparrow, like the others she had caught, but this one didn't struggle or flutter its wings. It only stirred a little, like a withered leaf, in the evening breeze, because this time Libby hadn't been there to release it – hadn't checked the net for days.

She pulled the net down and dropped to her knees, cupping the dead bird in her hands. Its beak was slightly open; one brown eye was half-closed, the other wide but crumpled, its smooth surface dented in places. The ants were busy about the body, coming and going along the threads of the mesh, which wound tightly around the leg above one curled foot.

Without warning, pain exploded inside Libby, as if some sort of machine were slamming everything in her body upward, crushing her heart and lungs into her throat. She doubled over, her mouth open but silent. For the first time since Maisie had gone, she wept. After a while, a sound escaped her, and it was like the sound of her mother's cry from the kitchen: unbearable.

CHAPTER TWO

"WHAT'S THE MATTER, kid?"

Libby straightened with a jerk at the sound of the unfamiliar voice, and saw a boy, maybe three or four years older than she, standing a little way off where the chokecherries ended. She scrambled to her feet and backed toward the henhouse, peering at him through the twilight, her face still wet with tears.

"Reckon you're worried about your little sis, huh?"

The boy flicked the stub of a cigarette far out into the field beyond the ditch. He wasn't one of the teen-aged boys from around town, but a lean, black-haired youth Libby had never seen before, his eyes narrow under dark, knitted brows.

"Whatcha foolin' with that for?" He asked, nodding at the dead bird, and she felt again the light stiffness of the tiny body in her hands. She looked down at it, then jerked her hands back, letting it fall, and turned to run for the house.

"Hold on a second!" the boy said. "It's your little sis I come about. Fella named Pullman sent me."

The words halted her, and she turned back, eyeing him warily. He was tall – a good foot taller than she – and as rangy as a young timber wolf, with the same intent, watchful gaze. She edged to the corner of the henhouse, where she could see – glancing over her shoulder – the lit window of the kitchen. When he made no move to follow, she hovered there, uncertain. "What do you mean, you came about my sister?"

"Fella I work for, Pullman, says he can help you find her."

"What?"

With no recollection of decision or movement, she found herself standing right in front of the boy, staring up into his face and holding a fistful of his sleeve. "Someone knows where Maisie is? *Who?"*

The boy grabbed her wrist, none too gently, and shoved her hand from his arm. He frowned down at her. "You deaf? *Pullman.* He's down Seifert way. Says to come on with me, an' he'll help you. But we gotta go soon."

Libby frowned back, suspicious. She didn't know exactly where the town of Seifert was, but she knew it was a long way off, somewhere to the south. "Why do I have to go *with* you? Why can't we just tell my mother, and –"

The boy shook his head. "Can't nobody else know. I don't aim to get mixed up with no kinfolk or cops. You tell your ma, or anyone else, you won't see me again."

"But... *why*?" Libby thought of the tramp with the birdcage. "Is... is the man that sent you the one who came here? The one who tried to take Maisie?"

The boy looked scornful. "Course he ain't. Didn't I just tell you he's gonna help you get 'er back? But we gotta catch out before midnight. You need to meet me out here, soon as your ma's asleep."

"Catch out?"

"Catch a train." He looked her up and down. "You got any britches?"

"I – I have some blue jeans, for when I –"

"Wear 'em; and some kinda dark-colored shirt, if you got one. An' bring somethin' warm – a jacket or somethin'." He moved toward her, and she shrank back, but he only slipped past to look around the corner of the henhouse at the light in the kitchen window. The expression on his face as he looked at it gave her a strange feeling. "You got any food in the house?" he asked.

Libby nodded. "Some."

"Get you a gunny sack or somethin', an' bring what you can carry easy. You got any money?"

Libby shook her head.

"Can you snitch some from your ma?"

Libby stared at him, shocked.

"All right," he grumbled. "Just askin'." He pulled back behind the henhouse, out of view from the windows. "Pullman says bring a picture a' your sis, if you got one."

"But *how* does that man – Pullman –"

"Don't know nothin' about any a' that." He didn't look at her. "You just gotta decide if you're comin'. If you come, you can ask 'im yourself."

Libby regarded the boy, doubtful. His clothing was worn but not ragged, and his hair, pushed back from his forehead in dark, oiled waves, was not particularly unkempt, yet he seemed somehow undomesticated, as if his presentable appearance was an imperfect disguise. Her voice came out suspicious when she spoke again: "What's your name, anyway? How'd this Pullman come to send *you*? I bet you're still in high school. You're just a kid."

He snorted. "Look who's talkin'." He moved deeper into the shadows, which were now hardly darker than the dusk around them. "They call me Scab. I'll be around till the moon comes up; then I'm headin' out. You decide you wanna come with me, get yourself out here before then." Squatting down with his back against the boards of the henhouse, he pulled a tobacco pouch from the pocket of his jacket and began to roll another cigarette, dismissing her.

LATER, IN HER bed, Libby nearly vibrated with agitation; the thought of the boy waiting in the dark outside made it impossible to lie still. If what he said was true, the grownups must have been right: she must have been imagining things. She didn't see how a man way down in Seifert — or *anywhere*, for that matter — could know where Maisie was, if she had been right about the blue-eyed bird. But what if the boy was making the whole thing up? What if it was some kind of trick?

The light from the kitchen cast a dim glow down the hall outside her room; she could hear the occasional creak of her mother's chair at the kitchen table. She sat up and looked out the window, trying to see if the sky to the east was brightening with the coming of the moon, but she couldn't tell. She threw back the sheets and slid off her bed.

Her bare feet made no sound in the hall. She paused at the open kitchen door; her mother sat with her back to the doorway, elbows on the table, face buried in her hands. All at once, Libby made up her mind: she would tell her mother about the boy. Her mother would call the sheriff's men; they would catch the boy before he got away, and make him tell what he knew about Maisie.

In spite of her determination, her voice came out small and hesitant: "Mama?"

Her mother whipped around with such a ferocity of joy and astonishment in her face that Libby took an involuntary step backward. Then, just as quickly, the joy and astonishment fell away, replaced by bitter disappointment, and Libby realized that, for a moment, her mother had mistaken her voice for Maisie's.

Her mother put her hands over her face again; then, abruptly, she slammed them onto the tabletop, making Libby jump. *"Elizabeth,"* she said, her voice deep and choked-sounding with a fury that sounded to Libby like hatred. "Will you please give me one moment's *PEACE?!"*

The unfairness of the words, as much as their force, seemed to knock Libby off balance so that she had to steady herself with another backward step. She gaped stupidly, then turned and fled back to her room. She closed the door and stood beside it, her chest heaving as if she had run much farther than the few steps down the hallway. Then she yanked her nightgown over her head and started to dress herself, quickly and silently, in clothing from her bureau: blue jeans, a dark shirt, and a navy-blue sweater.

THE ROAD OUT of town passed between wheat fields silvered by moonlight, and rose gently from the river toward the eastern hills. The boy, Scab, walked a little ahead of Libby, with the moon in the sky beyond him, illuminating a thin drift of clouds that looked like ripples on water. The pillowcase Libby had taken from her bedroom bumped lightly against her back with each step.

She had slipped the case from her pillow once she felt sure her mother was asleep, and had crept down the hall to the kitchen. Mama had left the porch lights on every night since Maisie had gone, no matter the cost in electricity, and the light from the back porch shone in through the kitchen window. By its glow Libby had found some biscuits, and taken leftover fried chicken from the icebox. She had tied these up in a dishtowel, and shoved them into the pillowcase. After some hesitation, she took her father's small folding knife, which had been in the top kitchen drawer ever since he died, and slipped it into the pocket of her jeans.

The picture of Maisie that the sheriff's men had returned still lay on the table; Libby slid that into a pocket as well. Then, by the light of the porch bulb, she wrote a note and left it where the picture had been: *Dear Mama, please do not worry, I will be back soon. I have gone to get Maisie as I have met a boy who knows where she is or at least knows someone who does. Please do not be sad anymore and please shut Jezebel out of the henhouse every morning as she is broody. Your loving daughter, Libby.*

Now, following Scab up the dusty road, she tried not to think about her mother finding the note in the morning. To distract herself, she studied the boy as he walked ahead of her. A large canvas knapsack hung on his back, and he carried a bedroll slung over one shoulder by a leather strap. These made him look more tramp-like than he had before, and she felt a twinge of misgiving.

"Where do you live?" she asked.

He glanced back, then faced forward again. Libby thought he wasn't going to answer, but after a while he said, "No place special," clipping the words short as if he begrudged her the effort of talking.

She trotted a few steps to keep up with his long stride. "How old are you?"

He shrugged. "Maybe seventeen, eighteen."

"You mean –" she frowned, trying to take it in – "you don't *know?*"

He didn't answer, and after a bit she said, "I've never seen a tramp young as you before."

"Prob'ly ain't seen much of anything, hick town like that."

"It's not a hick town," she said, but on the empty road under the wide black sky the words sounded unconvincing.

"If you say so." His tone made it clear he meant no such thing. "I ain't no tramp, anyhow. A tramp's the same as a bum – won't do a day's work for nobody. I work for Pullman."

He didn't sound insulted, only matter-of-fact, but Libby wasn't sure how to respond, and they walked for a while in silence. She looked across the fields, breathing the scent of green wheat and the rain-on-dust smell of irrigated earth. She was surprised at how clearly she could see in the moonlight, and tried to remember if she had ever been this far from a lit-up house at night before. "What's *that?*" she asked suddenly, pointing.

In the distance, off to their left, the silver of the field was broken by a dark line. Where the line ended, a figure moved, thigh-deep in the wheat, heading on a path roughly parallel to theirs, and in the same direction.

Scab glanced in the direction she pointed without slowing. "Nothin' to do with us," he said. "Hurry up. Freight's due through before long, and I don't aim to spend the whole damn night waitin' on another one."

"But – it's somebody *walking*, isn't it?" Libby kept staring at the dark figure, fascinated and a little uneasy at the thought of someone else out walking in the night. "Wonder where they're going?" she murmured, more to herself than to Scab.

"Ain't your concern," he said, not turning again. "Don't look at it."

The figure moved steadily, lengthening the dark line behind it. As Libby stared, it began to look as if it was slowing down. She squinted to try to get a better view, but a sharp smack knocked her gaze from the figure: Scab's hand, whacking the back of her head.

"*Ow!*" She rubbed her head and scowled up at him.

"I *said*, don't *look* at it."

They walked until the fields gave way to woodland, and the road rose more steeply into the hills. The air was still, the woods full of the sounds of little night-living creatures. Libby tried to see up into the shadowy branches, thinking of the birds, each one sitting in its nest or clinging to its twig through all the long dark hours. She felt a stab of apprehension about leaving the little blue-eyed bird behind. But she must have been mistaken; why had she ever thought it was possible? *Because I saw it*, a stubborn voice in her mind said, but she pushed the thought away.

She was almost sleepwalking, almost thinking she was dreaming the faint mournful sound of a train whistle rising from the valley off to their left, when Scab grabbed her by the wrist. "Come on – *run!*" he said, and took off up the climbing road, towing her along so fast she could barely keep her feet under her. After a while the road bent away to the left, but Scab pulled her straight on, through trees and undergrowth and then up a steep slope, their feet slipping in soft dirt. He let go of her wrist, and they both scrambled upward using hands as well as feet. Then all at once the ground angled downhill sharply, and Libby found herself half-running, half-sliding down the side of a steep railroad cutting.

Scab came to an abrupt halt, throwing out an arm to keep her from pitching forward as the slope leveled suddenly. She squatted down, gasping; at her feet, the dirt gave way to the rough, irregular rocks of the rail bed. Lifting her eyes, she saw the steel rails glinting in the moonlight. She could smell creosote from the ties.

"She's gettin' close," Scab said, squinting down the tracks. "She's gotta slow down here on accounta' the grade." With his outstretched arm, he pushed Libby back into the scraggly bushes at the edge of the rail bed, and crouched there beside her. "Stay hid back in here till I tell you; then follow me, and get ready to run like hell."

The whistle blew again. Libby's heart was still pounding; she leaned to peer down the tracks, and saw the trees beginning to glow with a ghostly light. A deep rumbling and humming grew louder around them every second, and the rails gleamed brighter and brighter.

At last the train came into view, laboring a bit up the grade, but not moving nearly so slowly as Libby would have hoped. When the engine passed, it crowded out everything else in the world: nothing was left but light and noise and vibration, steam and rushing air and the smells of hot metal and smoke. Scab had to grab her and yank her to her feet before she remembered what they were doing. He pulled her out beside the tracks, so close to the deafening rattle of the cars that it seemed the mere noise of them would somehow suck her under. Scab was looking down the line, tensed to run. "*Now!*" he yelled suddenly, and, shoving her ahead of him, he began to race along beside the train. He passed her, looking back over his shoulder, and Libby ran hard, trying to keep up with him. She glanced back as well, and saw an open boxcar door, overtaking them so quickly she was sure they would never make it. Then it was past her, and Scab was grabbing onto the doorway and swinging himself up with a smooth, practiced motion. He turned and leaned out, stretching an arm toward her. He was yelling, but she couldn't hear him over the clatter of the train. She ran even harder, reaching out her free hand, the pillowcase swinging wildly in the other. She gained on the train, and got near enough to Scab to hear him yell, "Throw the bag in!" Even as she threw it, she wondered crazily for a second if he had done all this, brought her all this way, just to steal a bag of food from her mother's kitchen. Then her left hand caught the edge of the door, and she planted her right hand on the sill. The forward motion of the train yanked at her instantly, threatening to pull her off her feet. Half-panicked, she pushed herself up as hard as she could, her belly sliding onto the sill as her feet left the ground. Her arms, quivering with the train's vibration, felt too weak to pull her the rest of the way up, and she suffered a moment of terror; then she felt strong hands grab her under the arms, and Scab hauled her up and dumped her unceremoniously onto the boxcar floor.

She lay on the vibrating planks, trying to catch her breath. The wood smelled heat-baked even in the middle of the night, and the rough rattle of the car jarred her cheekbone against the floor. "We made it!" she gasped finally, but her words were swallowed by the noise of the train.

"For as skinny as you are, you sure are slow," Scab said. She saw his silhouette against the rectangle of night that showed through the boxcar door; he was bending to reach for something on the floor. "Whatcha got in that bag?"

THEY RODE ALL the rest of the night, Scab wrapped in one of the blankets from his bedroll, sleeping through all the noise and jouncing of the train. He had given Libby a blanket, as well, and she was glad to have it; the spring nights were still cool, and the doors on both sides of the car were open, allowing the wind to whip through. She wrapped the blanket around her, and sat staring out at the passing woods and fields, feeling a little sick as she took in the reality of what she was doing. Sometimes the train would stop – sidetracked to take on water, or to let another train pass. Scab never stirred, even when it banged and rattled into motion again, making a tremendous racket.

Libby tried not to think about how many miles the clacking wheels were putting between her and her home. She had never even left their property after dark without her mother's permission, and now here she was on a train, speeding into the night with a boy she'd never met before. *I have to find out,* she kept telling herself, trying to calm the waves of panic that swept over her. *I have to see if this man Pullman really knows where Maisie is.* She thought about where Maisie might be, and what might be happening to her, but these thoughts made her heart pound and her head feel light and dizzy, so she pushed them away.

At last she wrapped herself in the blanket, curled up in a corner and must have slept, because the next thing she knew Scab was shaking her, and daylight was shining through the boxcar doors.

"Comin' into a yard before long," he said, leaning close so Libby could hear. "Soon as she slows down enough, we gotta jump off and get out a' sight, quick as we can."

He rolled up the blankets, and slung them and the knapsack on his back, then went to the door opposite the one they had come in by and squatted down, looking out at the land rolling toward them. Beyond him Libby could see wooded hills and, among more distant trees, the roofs of a town approaching.

As soon as they reached the outlying houses, Scab moved farther back into the car, pulling Libby back also. The train blew its whistle and began to slow. "Not long now," Scab said.

They stayed out of the doorway until the train slowed to a crawl and swerved off the main line into the yard. Libby leaned forward to look past Scab at the vast landscape of parallel tracks. Strings of waiting cars stretched along the lines, and up ahead she could see the peaked hulk of the coal tower, and the conical roof of the stilt-legged water tank. Scab edged back to the doorway and peered out. "Come on," he said after he had squinted up and down the train. "Run straight for them bushes there." He pointed through a break in the sidelined cars, toward a wall of green far off at the edge of the yard. The boxcar jolted; the brakes hissed and the couplings banged as the train tried to heave itself to a halt. The hugeness of the sounds daunted Libby, but Scab crouched in the doorway and, with one hand on the floorboards, dropped easily to the ground. He ran across the siding tracks, toward the tall brush beyond. Libby slid off the edge of the car, clutching her pillowcase, and raced after him. She glanced toward the front of the train as she ran. A man was walking way off near the engine, but his back was toward them and he didn't look around. At the edge of the yard Scab slipped into the bushes with barely a rustle, and Libby followed.

She stayed hidden there while Scab did some kind of scouting to find out when the next train was leaving the yard. "We got a while before we catch out," he said when he came back. "I reckon we'll hit the stem, see what we can pick up."

Libby wondered how he had found out about the train, and what "the stem" was, but she felt too tired to ask. The short, uncomfortable night's sleep hadn't done much to remedy her exhaustion from the day before, and the noise of the yard workers shunting cars around had kept her from sleeping in the bushes while Scab was gone.

The town was called Gilson, Libby saw from some of the signs they passed. Like Seifert, it was a town she'd heard of but never been to before. It was a long way from Schillerton, she knew, and she had to push down the panicky feeling again.

Scab led the way to the main street and pulled her into an alley between two shops. He fixed a stern gaze on her. "Now I want you to walk up an' down along here, and any folks you see, you go up to 'em and tell 'em your family's passin' through, your ma's sick, and you got little brothers and sisters, and ask 'em could they spare you some money for food."

Libby stared out toward the empty street. "What about my dad?"

"Wha'd'ya mean, what about your dad? He's *dead*, ain't he?"

"But *they* don't know that!"

Scab rolled his eyes. "Well if they ask, tell 'em. Now you stay on this street here, and I'll find you when I get back."

Libby had been about to ask him how *he* knew her father was dead, but his last words startled the question from her mind. "Get *back*?" she asked, turning to look at him, but he was already slipping off toward the back of the buildings.

She went to the mouth of the alley and looked up the street. Dead leaves rattled along the gutter. A block or so away, a man sat on a bench outside a barber shop, turning the pages of a newspaper. A dog sauntered across the street farther up, and after a while, the man closed his paper and went into his shop. Finally Libby gripped her bag tighter and started off, her feet dragging a little along the cracked sidewalk.

Many of the shops were out of business, their doors locked, their signs faded, dust and dead flies in their windows. She wandered up and down for an hour or more, looking in through smudged glass, or out into the street at the old, rattling cars that drove by from time to time. She stole glances at the faces of the few people who passed, but they all looked guarded and careworn, their eyes focused inward on their own troubles, and she didn't dare ask them for money as Scab had told her to do.

Down one side road she could see a little overgrown park, and the second time she passed it she noticed a small flock of sparrows, darting like mice through the leaf litter near some tangled bushes. She turned the corner and edged nearer, stopping some distance away so she wouldn't frighten them. She eased herself down onto the grass and watched them – their swift, sudden movements, their enthusiastic rummaging through the dead leaves and their brief, energetic squabbles over whatever they found. She strained to see the color of their eyes, staring so intently that she had no idea how much time had passed when a sudden sting on the side of her neck broke her concentration. As she clapped her hand to the spot, she saw the pebble that had struck her bounce onto the grass, and turned to find Scab, frowning at her from the sidewalk. "Thought I told you to stay on the main street."

CHAPTER THREE

"I BEEN LOOKIN'" for you for half an hour," Scab grumbled as they started toward the freight yard. "You get anything?"

Libby shook her head. "I just –"

He made a disgusted sound, cutting her off. "What the hell you been *doin'* all this time?"

"Well, why'd you tell me to ask for money anyway? What if a policeman or somebody saw me, and sent me home?"

Scab let out a scoffing breath. "You know how far we come from that little hick town a' yours? Ain't nobody 'round here lookin' for you."

Libby kicked at a pebble. "Well… anyway, if this Pullman *sent* you, how come he didn't give you money to travel on?"

Scab shrugged. "He did. Ain't no point spendin' it till we see what we can pick up for free." He paused to squint along a tree-lined lane, then turned into it. "Could need that money later. Might get put off a train, might get pinched. Sometimes you run up against a bull that'll let you ride if you give him a few bucks, but like as not, if you got no money, he'll beat the shit out a' you."

Libby, alarmed at this information and a little abashed, said nothing more. Scab led the way into a small stand of woods, pushing through new-leafed buttonbush and wild honeysuckle to a little clearing, where a ring of blackened stones circled the ashes of old fires. He squatted down, and Libby noticed for the first time that he was carrying his jacket under his arm, bundled as if it was wrapped around something. He set it on the trunk of a fallen tree and opened it up. Inside was a fat red hen, her neck broken.

Libby stared. "Where'd you get *that*?"

"None a' your concern." He picked the hen up by its flopping neck and held it out. "You start pluckin' while I get a fire goin'."

Once the fire was dying down to coals, Libby watched with interest as Scab pulled a long, sturdy jackknife from his pocket and cut a slim green branch to spit the hen on, and two forked sticks to lay the spit across.

"Scab – who *is* Pullman?" she asked as they waited for the chicken to cook.

Scab, lying in the grass with his head on the bedroll, shrugged. "Fella I work for."

"But – how does he know where my sister is?"

Scab shrugged again and drew on his cigarette, his eyes on the thin canopy of new leaves above the clearing.

Cicadas whirred noisily, and small birds flitted about, catching Libby's eyes. "You got any brothers or sisters?" she asked.

Scab's habitual scowl grew darker, but he gave a curt nod. He sat up to turn the chicken, and poked at the coals with a stick.

"Where do they live? In Seifert?"

The Birds of the Air | 33

Scab only continued his fire-tending, so after a moment she went on. "My dad? ...he was a railroad dispatcher. He died a long time ago, right before Maisie was born." She paused, remembering what Scab had said earlier. "Scab... how did *you* know my dad was dead?"

"Pullman."

Libby frowned, perplexed, but went on. "Well... my mama's been sad a lot, ever since he died – even before Maisie..." a tightness came to her throat, and she had to stop and swallow. "Anyway... you think maybe, if we find Maisie... do you think you could help me and her get back home? I know Mama would want to thank you – *and* Mr. Pullman."

Scab stood up slowly and took the cigarette from his mouth, frowning down at the fire. When he raised his eyes to Libby's, they were narrow and stern. "Look," he said, "you're a nice enough kid, but you gotta get this through your head: I ain't here to answer no questions, and I ain't here to make friends."

Libby dropped her eyes, her face growing hot.

"I work for Pullman, and I'm here to take you to him – that's *all*. Got it?"

Libby nodded, keeping her eyes down. "Yeah. I got it."

WHEN THEY HAD finished eating, Scab led the way back to the freight yard, where the little switcher engine still shunted cars noisily back and forth. Libby must have looked as exhausted as she felt, because he tossed her the bedroll when they reached their hiding place in the brush. "Might as well see if you can get some sleep. I'll wake you when it's time."

She was so tired by now that even the racket of the yard didn't keep her from sleeping. When Scab shook her awake, the sun was setting beyond the lines of cars. He led the way into the yard, and then along the side track nearest the main lines, using the sidelined cars for cover. A long way behind her, toward the yard's main buildings, Libby could hear an engine huffing, but the train on the mainline still sat motionless. Scab scanned it for a car that met with his approval. "There," he said at last; Libby looked where he pointed and saw a boxcar with its door only partly open. Scab eased forward, watching, his hand out to tell Libby to wait. Finally he whispered, "Come on," and darted out, silent as a shadow. Libby followed, crossing empty tracks; they reached the boxcar door and Scab vaulted in, then helped her up.

The door was open about halfway; the one on the far side was closed. It was dark inside, but Libby could make out a few huge spools wound with cable, sitting on their ends in the front of the car. Scab nodded in satisfaction when he saw them. "She'll ride quieter'n the last one." He steered Libby to the wall nearest the open door – where, she realized, anyone looking in would be least likely to see her – and then jumped back off and was gone for a few minutes. He returned with a loose sleeper spike, which he used to wedge the door in place, hammering it in with a rock. He tossed the rock out and came to sit beside her. "That door half-shut like it is, it coulda slid shut all the way, it got jolted just right. Prob'ly be dead before they found us."

The engine's whistle let off two long blasts, and the train shuddered into motion, couplers banging. Bars of illumination moved inside the car from back to front as they passed the lit buildings at the edge of the yard. Libby watched the door uneasily, hoping Scab had wedged it tight.

Suddenly something flew into the opening. She jumped, and felt Scab stiffen beside her. She just had time to see, by the passing town lights, that the thing on the floor was a grubby bedroll;

The Birds of the Air | 35

then a hand grabbed the edge of the door and the large figure of a man scrambled into the car, growling and cursing. Another man followed him, and then one more, the last one helped in by the cursing man.

"Damned if we wasn't almost rid of you that time, Smiley!" The cursing man said. The man called Smiley bent over to brush dust from his baggy pants, giving a chuckle that sounded like gravel in mud. Libby saw, when the light slid across his face, that his two front teeth were missing.

"What we got here?" the cursing man said, his eye on Scab and Libby. "Well, well, boys! Looks like we got us a couple a' lambs."

Libby glanced up at Scab, but he sat with his head leaned back against the vibrating wall, eyes closed, as if he hadn't heard the man.

The men settled across the car from her and Scab, against the far wall and ten feet or so closer to the front of the car. The bars of light were moving faster now, and as one flashed past, Libby saw the glint of a bottle. The men talked and laughed loudly, but she couldn't make out most of what they said over the noise of the train. She huddled against the wall and hoped they would pay no more attention to her and Scab.

For a while, it seemed that was how it would be. The men sang songs that made no sense to Libby; they passed the bottle around and appeared to have forgotten there were any other riders in the car. Scab looked as if he were sleeping, but she could feel alertness in him, even from a half a foot away.

The train left the town lights behind, and Libby slipped into a doze, from which she was jarred half-awake now and then by the whistle of the train or a loud burst of laughter from the men. At last she was fully awakened by the far-off hiss and squeal of the brakes, and the successive banging of the couplings, each one closer and louder than the last. "Are we there?" she shouted up toward Scab's ear, but he shook his head.

"Water stop."

When the train had finally lurched to a halt, the man who had gotten on second – a bald man with his eyes squeezed in close to his nose – struck a match and lit a makeshift tin-can lamp. The flame on its rag wick danced and trembled in the breeze drifting through the open door.

"So, little sis," the cursing man said suddenly, thumping the bottle down and raising his voice, making Libby jump. "What brings a little bitty gal like you out on the road?" His two companions chuckled as if he had made a joke, but he ignored them. "Sure does make a fella wonder, seein' a nice little gal like you keepin' company with the likes a' *that*." He gestured toward Scab with a grubby finger. "You know, if I was you, I'd be mighty careful. You surely could get yourself into trouble."

Libby glanced at Scab again, but he remained motionless, his arms folded loosely across his ribs, his eyes still closed.

"You know, little sis, there's all kinds a' trouble a body can get into on the road." The man was looking into the flame now, and his voice sounded like he was telling a story. The other two seemed to think everything he said was funny, and kept chuckling to themselves. The tin-can lamp sent up a skein of black smoke, and the smells of burning grease, the men's sweat, and whatever was in the bottle lay heavy on the air.

"There's a lot a' hungry folks in the world, sis. Maybe you ain't never seen 'em yet, but they're out there. And I tell you what, I don't care who he is, if a man gets hungry enough, why, he's gonna do whatever it takes to hush up that hunger." The cursing man raised his eyes to look at her again, and Libby could see the flame reflected in them. "It ain't no other creature in this world can bite like a hunger. And not every kinda hunger is the kind you feel in your belly." He shook his head slowly, his eyes fixed on hers and his mouth bending downward at the corners. "But even all a' that – all them hungry folks, an' what-all they might do to get what they need: that's just what's on the *top*, if you take my meanin'. Like weeds, little sis, a-growin' on a grave without no stone; and most folks walk right on over and don't never know what's underneath." He showed yellow teeth in a smile that made her want to close her eyes. "Didn't your mama never tell you about the bogeyman?"

Libby looked at the other two men to try to see if he was making fun of her, but they were both staring at her now, their faces expressionless, the lamp flame moving in their eyes. "You'd best watch where you're walkin', little sis," the cursing man said. Then he reached out his hand and seized the rag wick between his thumb and forefinger, snuffing out the light. "Sweet dreams," she heard him say, and the sound of his voice was like the look of his smile.

The darkness was so thick it seemed to make it hard to breathe; Libby's heart beat fast, and felt higher in her chest than it should have been. They sat there in the dark, the train not moving, for what seemed like a very long time. Libby heard no more talk from the men, and after a while she thought they must have gone to sleep. Her heart slowed and the tension in her muscles eased a little. Finally the train began to hiss and clank again, and it jerked into motion and quickly picked up speed.

The rhythmic sound of the wheels had just begun to make her drowsy when she heard a loud *clunk*, coming through the blackness from where the men sat, as if one of them had knocked over the bottle. A shuffling, sliding noise gradually became audible above the sounds of the train, as if whatever was making it was moving closer. A hand gripped her shoulder and she jerked in fright, but it was only Scab. "Stay *right here*," he hissed in her ear, and when she reached out her hand, she felt nothing except the plank floor where he had been. Her breath grew ragged, and she jammed frantic hands into her pockets till she found her father's knife. She pulled it out and fumbled with it in the dark until she got it open, then slid sideways and wedged herself into the rear corner of the car. Her spine vibrated with the jolting of the train; her eyes were so wide they felt stretched, but she could see nothing. Holding the little knife out in front of her, she yelled, "Scab!" – but there was no answer.

Sounds came out of the blackness; Libby heard frantic scuffling and thumping, not far away. She tried to crush herself even farther into the corner. She heard loud cursing from one of the men, and then a terrifying sound like someone screaming through closed teeth. "Scab!" she cried again, and then, after more scuffling, light flared in the boxcar as someone lit a match.

At first she saw only Scab, standing with his back to her several feet away, his legs braced wide against the swaying of the train. He was a shadow against the weak glow of the match, but the light glinted on something in his hand. She looked past him to where the three tramps crouched, glowering, in a knot near the far wall of the car. The big one, the cursing man, had a hand pressed to his cheek, and blood oozed from between his fingers; the sight of it made Libby feel lightheaded and distant, as if nothing in the boxcar were real.

The man called Smiley held the match. He bent, shielding the flame with his hand, and lit the tin-can lamp. The flame danced wildly in the wind from the half-open door, the light wavering upward to make monster-masks of the three men's faces and set huge misshapen shadows dancing on the wall behind them.

The cursing man bared his teeth like an animal. "Oh, you have bought your ticket now, boy," he snarled. He took his hand from his face, revealing a long slash down his grimy, stubbled cheek, and looked down at the blood smeared across his palm. Then he reached behind him, his red, glaring eyes on Scab's face, and felt around until his hand found the bottle. He hefted it by the neck and stood up unsteadily. He seemed to have trouble keeping his balance, and Libby realized, with a jolt of shock, that she was looking at a drunken person – something she had heard about but never seen before.

The man lurched across the vibrating floor and made a lunge toward Scab, swinging the bottle. Libby cried out, but Scab sidestepped the man's staggering charge easily, and sliced the air with the glinting thing in his hand. The man's sleeve was laid open, and a red line appeared across his arm; looking down, Libby saw that the thing Scab held was an open straight-razor. The man recoiled, almost falling, then regained his balance and lifted the bottle again.

"You wanna stop right there," Scab said, his voice raised hard and clear above the train-noise. Holding the razor ready in his right hand, he reached up with the left and jerked at the collar of his shirt, sending two buttons pattering to the floor as he pulled the cloth toward his left shoulder. "You mess with us, you're messin' with Jaeger."

Libby couldn't see what it was the shirt had covered, but she saw the man flinch back as if Scab had thrust at him with a redhot poker. He ducked his head to one side, and the hand not holding the bottle jerked upward, as if to shield his eyes. The other two men, who had risen to come to his aid, sank back down again. Libby saw the flush of belligerence drain from their faces until they looked pale as dough, even in the ruddy glow of the grease lamp.

The cursing man held out both hands, palms toward Scab, fingers spread except for the thumb and forefinger of his right hand, which still circled the neck of the bottle. With his head ducked and his eyes cast down, he crouched slowly, teetering, and set the bottle on the floor, where it trembled a bit with the vibration of the train. "All right – all right," he said, his voice slurred and sullen. He shuffled unsteadily backward to the far wall, and sank down beside his companions, but he dared one more glance at Scab; the hatred in it chilled Libby. "There's some'd be mighty interested, though," he said, in a tone between a whine and a snarl, "in what the likes of *you's* doin' with a little gal like that."

Scab made no reply. He jerked his shirt straight and backed away from the men, the razor still open in his hand. When he got near the open door, he turned his head to glance out, then fixed his gaze on the men again as he moved along the wall to sit down beside Libby. Libby realized her whole body was shaking, and clutched her arms tightly around her middle to try to hold herself still.

"When she slows down outside Seifert, I reckon we better jump for it," Scab said, his voice so quiet that Libby could barely hear him. "I don't trust those goddamn rummies to stay as scared as they oughta be." He reached across Libby to grab the bedroll, and thumped it down in front of her. "You try an' get some sleep. I'll keep an eye out, an' wake you when we're gettin' close."

Libby couldn't imagine sleeping, but she unrolled the blankets and lay down. The man called Smiley had doused the lamp, but whenever the lights of some town or outlying farm slanted across the inside of the boxcar, she could see the white gleam of the men's eyes keeping wary watch on Scab. The only sound was the rhythmic clack-clack of the wheels; it went on and on, lulling Libby's fearful mind, until all at once Scab's hand was shaking her, and she opened her eyes to see a faint hint of approaching dawn outside.

Scab rolled up the blankets, tied them, and slung the strap over his shoulder, then pushed Libby wordlessly toward the door. The clack of the wheels was much slower now. Looking out, Libby could see the shadowy curve of the train bending to the left up ahead, the engine hidden from her view by woodland bordering the tracks. The inside of the car still held the night's darkness; peering over her shoulder, she thought she could see the forms of the men, but she couldn't tell whether they were asleep, or awake and watching.

"You gotta hit the ground runnin'," Scab said as they crouched in the doorway. His voice sounded tired. "She's movin' faster'n you think. You ready?"

Libby looked at the ground passing next to the train. In the blue predawn light she could just make out the sharp-looking rocks that made up the railroad bed. She nodded.

Scab sat in the doorway, legs hanging out, and Libby copied him, setting her pillowcase-bag beside her. Keeping his forward hand on the floorboards, he jumped, landing light as a cat, running alongside. "Come on!" he called over the clack and rattle, keeping up with the train easily. But she couldn't take her eyes off the rocks skimming by below, couldn't seem to make her body obey. "Come *on*!" Scab yelled again. "You wanna stay on there with *them*?" She clenched her jaw and jumped, trying to hit the ground running as Scab had said. Immediately she pitched forward onto the gravel, frighteningly close to the wheels, scraping her hands and knees a bit but unhurt otherwise. Scab grabbed the back of her sweater and yanked her up, pulling her farther from the tracks.

Libby looked down at her scraped hands and realized they were empty.

"Oh no – my bag!"

"Don't matter."

He was right; there wasn't even anything *in* the bag anymore, except the dishtowel. But the thought of losing that familiar dishtowel from home, and the pillowcase from her room, embroidered with daisies by her mother, was suddenly more than she could bear. Tears filled her eyes and spilled down her cheeks. She wiped her face with her arm and stood staring at the receding boxcar.

"Come on," Scab growled. "You wanna find your sister or not?" He shot one murderous glance after the train, and stalked off into the dawn mist. Libby stood on the edge of the railbed for a moment longer, then let out a shaky breath and turned from the tracks to hurry after him.

CHAPTER FOUR

THEY PUSHED STRAIGHT into the woods, Scab leading the way and shoving the springy green underbrush aside. "We got a long walk ahead," he said, his face grim. "Maybe twenty, thirty miles. Coulda rode almost all the way if it wasn't for them sons a' bitches."

Libby, a bit awestruck by his handling of the tramps, struggled along in his wake without talking for a half-mile or so. Eventually, though, curiosity overcame her newfound shyness, and she trotted to catch up with him. "Scab... what did you show those men that scared them so bad?"

He scowled, not looking at her. "None a' your concern." Pausing for a moment, he fished in his knapsack and brought out some leftover chicken, wrapped in a handkerchief. He gave half to Libby; it was cold and leathery, but she wolfed it down as they moved on.

"Where'd you get that razor?" she asked after a while.

"Bought it."

They drank from a small stream they crossed in the forest, and Scab filled a tin water-bottle that hung from his knapsack. They walked in silence through the woodland for a long time as the sun climbed in the sky.

"Scab," Libby said at last, her voice sounding strange and small in the lonely woods, "what... what was wrong with those men on the train?"

"What d'ya mean, what was wrong with 'em? They're a bunch a' damn kid-fiddlers."

"What's *that* mean?"

"It means if I ever come across one of 'em passed out drunk somewhere, he ain't never gonna wake up again," Scab said, and the way he said it seemed to block all the rest of Libby's questions in her throat.

The woods were very like the ones near her home, and she kept an eye out for birds, and listened for their songs. "Scab, I..." she began, then hesitated and rubbed at her sweaty face, embarrassed. "I... thought I saw something kind of... crazy... on the day my sister got lost." Scab said nothing, so she went on, telling him all that had happened on the morning Maisie disappeared. "Do you think..." she finished, panting a little from talking and pushing through the brush at the same time, "do you think I maybe *imagined* all that? Like I was having some kind of a spell or something?"

Scab flicked a dark glance down at her, then turned his gaze forward again. "You can talk to Pullman about all a' that. I told you once, I ain't here to answer no questions."

"Well you must know *something*," she said, nettled. "I *listened* to you, didn't I? I came along with you. Can't you tell me *anything* about what this man Pullman knows? What he knows about my sister?"

Scab kept pushing ahead through the undergrowth. "I told you everything Pullman told me. You can ask him about the rest when we get there."

Libby scowled at his back. "When's that? I'm *tired*. And I'm *starving*."

Scab gave an exasperated sigh, but stopped and moved his right arm in an arc to the south, pointing. "That train woulda taken us in a big ol' loop, 'round the edge of Seifert down there, an' on to the far side where the tracks cross the river; that's where Pullman's jungled up." He shrugged. "Now we gotta cut across."

"Well how long's *that* gonna take?"

"I reckon we're gonna find out."

BY SUNDOWN IT seemed to Libby they had walked more miles than she ever knew there were in the world. They had crossed fields, more woodland, streams, and even an out-flung edge of the town of Seifert. At last, when their shadows stretched far out in front of them along the ditch bank they were follow-ing, Libby halted abruptly and sat down. "I'm not going *any farther*." She drew her knees up and buried her face in her arms, fighting tears of exhaustion. "I don't think you even *know* where we're going."

"Damned if you ain't the biggest bawl-baby I ever seen in my life," Scab grumbled; but he slipped off his knapsack, rolled his shoulders back, as if to unstiffen them, and dropped down beside her in the rough, weedy grass. He looked almost as exhausted as Libby felt, and she remembered with a twinge of remorse that he hadn't slept the night before.

He scanned the broad stretch of farmland in the direction they were headed, and she followed his gaze; the gold evening sunlight made the patchwork of greens and browns look powdered with pollen. He pointed toward a distant line of trees. "We just gotta get to the river there, an' then we can follow it on down." He sighed and ran a hand over his face. "Looks like it's gonna be a ways yet." He sat silent for a while, then glanced down at her. "I seen a house back there, with a garden. Nothin' much growin' this early, but we'll rest here awhile till it gets dark, and then I'll go back an' see if I can't get us somethin' to eat. Later on, when the moon's up, we can get on over to the river."

Libby let out a grateful sigh and lay back against the ditch bank, the sun-warmed earth and prickly grass feeling as welcome as a feather bed.

When she woke, a lopsided moon was just topping the far-off hills behind the line of trees Scab had pointed out. She sat up to look around. Scab was nowhere in sight. She looked back in the direction they had come, and saw only the moonlight lying silver on the fields and picking out the little thread of water in the bottom of the ditch. Crickets chirped noisily, and somewhere along the ditch frogs croaked. Without Scab there, it seemed suddenly unbelievable that she was out in the night alone, maybe hundreds of miles from home. She thought about her mother, then quickly pushed the thought away when tears prickled behind her eyes.

She'd been peering down the ditch for what felt like a long time, hoping to see Scab returning, when all at once the crickets stopped chirping. She looked around, a bit startled by the sudden quiet, and saw something moving, so far off in the moonlit fields that it looked no bigger than her thumb. Squinting, she made out a dark figure, like the one she had seen the night she and

Scab had caught the first train. It looked to be walking, heading toward the river. *Maybe it's Scab,* she thought. *Maybe he forgot where I am.* She stood up to see better, trying to make out details, but all she could discern was the figure and the shadowed line left in the moon-silvered wheat where it had passed.

She was wondering whether she should call out and wave when the figure suddenly stopped. It stood still for a few moments, and though Libby stared hard, she couldn't tell what it was doing. Then it started walking again – this time straight toward her.

It must be Scab then, she thought, but somehow she didn't feel relieved. There seemed to be an oddness about the way the figure moved. *Stop being stupid,* she told herself. *Who else would it be?* She was raising her hand to wave when some slight noise off to her left caught her attention, and she turned to see Scab, running toward her so fast that his shirt was whipped back by the still night air.

When he got to her, he grabbed her arm without stopping, dragging her along behind him. "Come on, you damn idjit," he growled; *"run!"* He let go after a few steps, and she pelted after him, struggling to keep up, along the bank toward the distant river.

They ran for maybe half a mile – Libby's breath, by the end, ripping like a saw blade in and out of her throat – before Scab finally swerved to the right, over the bank and into the ditch. He flung himself down onto the sloping side, above the thin trickle of water at the bottom, and doubled over with racking coughs which he managed to keep almost silent. Libby followed and sank down beside him, clutching her side, gulping air that smelled of mud and stagnant water.

"God*damn* there's a lotta' them things out right now," Scab said when his coughing had subsided, muttering under his ragged breath as if he was talking to himself rather than to Libby.

"Why'd we have to run?" Libby's words came out in gasps as well. "Was that one of the men from the train?"

"Hell, no," Scab said, contemptuous. "That was one a' them field-walkers. What the hell's wrong with you? I told you before, don't *look* at them things. You *look* at 'em, you're gonna get their attention."

"Well... I thought..."

"You let *me* do the thinkin'; you just do what I tell you."

Libby glanced toward the top of the ditch and wrapped her arms around herself. "What happens if you get their attention?"

"You saw. You ain't blind, are you?"

"But I mean... what would've happened if we *didn't* run?"

"Don't know. Ain't never been stupid enough to find out." Scab stood up and brushed dirt from his clothing. "We better keep movin'. That thing might've forgot about us by now, or it might not."

That thing. Libby shivered and stood up at once, wide eyes fixed on the top of the bank. Scab crept partway up to peer back the way they had come, but seemed to see no immediate danger. "Better walk down here for a while," he said, slipping back to the bottom. He dug in a pocket and pushed a couple of hard, roundish things into Libby's hands. Holding them up to the moonlight, she saw that they were immature raw potatoes. She rubbed one on her jeans and bit into it ravenously. Scab was already moving off along the ditch, toward the line of trees by the river; they looked a little closer now, and Libby hurried to keep up with him. "Scab – who *are* those... field-walkers?"

Scab shot a fierce glance back at her. "You ask too goddamn

many questions. You been trouble enough for one night; just hush up and keep walkin'."

SHE WAS ALMOST asleep on her feet when they finally reached the river. Scab had to grab the back of her shirt to keep her from stumbling out onto the dirt road that divided the fields from the thick belt of woods along the riverbank. He crouched among the weeds at the edge of the road and pulled her down beside him. "We ain't gonna walk on the road," he said, leaning out to scan left and right along it. "It's been two days; might be folks lookin' for you by now, even way down here."

Libby was too worn out to answer. She had no idea how long they had been walking, but the moon had climbed high in the sky above them. When Scab's words sank into her foggy mind, she felt in a distant way that she doubted them. She had a brief image of her mother, sitting blankly at the kitchen table all those nights after Maisie had gone, and couldn't imagine her rousing herself to much action when she discovered Libby was missing as well. The realization made her feel even more exhausted, and she slumped down to sit cross-legged in the weeds, propping her head with both hands.

Scab glanced at her, then settled back and raked a hand through his hair, looking worn out himself. "I reckon we better find a place to hole up for the rest of the night. Come daylight, we can hike on down the riverbank, keep out a' sight of the road."

They crossed the road and entered the woods, Scab warning Libby to walk directly behind him while he pushed his way through the undergrowth, jabbing at the ground ahead with a long stick. "Don't wanna get bit by no damn cottonmouth," he grumbled, but Libby was too weary even to be nervous. He found a small clear spot among the scrub-willows, tramped down the tall grass, and spread the scratchy blankets over it. Before he would let Libby lie down, he shoved her to the river's edge, where he plastered mud over his face, neck and hands, and made her do the same, to discourage the voracious mosquitos.

Lying on the blanket at last, gazing at the little well of stars visible above the clearing, she murmured drowsily, "Scab?"

"*Now* what?"

She turned toward where he lay on his back, a few feet away, his hands laced behind his head. "Thanks for all this. I mean, for getting me here and – and looking out for me, and all."

There was no sound but the buzzing of the river insects for so long that Libby thought he must have fallen asleep. But then the grass rustled as he turned abruptly onto his side, his back toward her. "Hush up and go to sleep," he said. "We still got a long way to go tomorrow."

Libby rolled over also, then thought she should take off her shoes. She pulled a knee up toward her chest and started to reach down to untie one, but she was asleep before her hands touched the laces.

She woke to a boisterous clamor of birdsong, and the sharp, fresh scent of dew-soaked grass. The sky above the clearing was pale shell-pink. Scab was nowhere in sight, but he appeared before long, dangling a line from which four shining brown catfish hung. She helped him gather dead branches for a fire, and when the fish were cooked, she wolfed hers down and thought she could have eaten two more. If she hadn't been with Scab, she realized, she would have been half-starved by now.

No wonder he called me a bawl-baby, she thought. She wondered if hauling her all this way was as exasperating for him as looking after Maisie often was for her. *No more acting like a baby,* she vowed to herself. *I have to be smart. I have to be brave. I have to get Maisie back.*

It was hard to keep her resolution. The day was a seemingly endless trek downriver, along a narrow path that Scab said had been made by drifters who, for one reason or another, didn't want to be seen on the road. The path wove through the scrubby trees and underbrush along the river's edge, and was often so overgrown that they had to push through tangles of branches. Libby was hot and tired and covered with scratches before they had gone a mile; the fuzzy new leaves clung to her damp skin, reminding her of Maisie's sticky little fingers when she had been a baby. Scab had washed the dried mud from his hands and face that morning, so she had done the same, but she soon wished she hadn't; the mosquitos never stopped biting in the humid shadow of the riverside trees. Scab walked ahead of her, constantly scanning the dense green tangle to either side of the path for cottonmouths, and the thought of them kept Libby tense and jumpy.

At last, in the late afternoon, the trees thinned, leaving the trail more passable and letting narrow shafts of sunlight through. A breeze rose, filtering through the branches from the direction of the river, and from time to time Libby thought she heard a faint clinking sound drifting from someplace up ahead. She followed Scab around a bend in the trail, and all at once they emerged into sunlight: a strip of grassy open ground stretched before them, and Libby could see the river, glinting through reeds off to their left. Across the belt of meadow, the trail disappeared into dense woodland made up of older, taller trees.

Scab paused when they stepped into the sunlight, and ran a sleeve across his forehead. "When we get in there," he said, squinting at the woods, "just follow me, and don't say nothin' to nobody." Libby nodded, but she felt a nervous constriction in her stomach as she followed him across the meadow, as if her insides were shrinking back even as her feet carried her forward.

The clinking grew clearer, and when they drew close to the trees Libby saw that a cord had been strung across the path, high above. Its ends were tied to branches on either side, and bottles dangled from it, hung by wires twisted around their necks, clinking against one another like wind chimes in the breeze from the river. Other things had been strung from the cord as well: bird and rodent skulls, and other bones Libby couldn't identify; flattened spoons that chimed together softly; strips of torn cloth spotted with dark stains.

"What are *those* for?" she asked in a hushed voice, peering up as they passed beneath the odd collection.

Scab made a scoffing sound, not bothering to glance upward. "Some a' these ign'rant lumpheads figure they can scare things off with 'em."

"What kind of things?"

He shrugged. "Evil spirits and the like."

The shade beneath the trees was as deep as twilight, and it took Libby's eyes a few moments to adjust to it. When she could see more clearly, she realized the path was taking them past small clearings in the undergrowth, many half-hidden from the trail. Soon she began to see ragged men in the clearings, sitting by smoking campfires, or lying open-eyed in crude shelters made of broken-up crates. Some of the men exchanged nods or brief greetings with Scab as he and Libby passed; others only stared, their faces weary and vacant. Scab never slowed.

When they came to a narrow stream that cut across the trail, Scab turned right, onto a path that led up the streambank. They passed under a bridge where the road Scab had avoided crossed the creek; then they passed a few larger clearings, where groups of men lounged around cookfires, some of them laughing, some passing bottles. Libby saw no women at all. The men stopped talking and watched as she and Scab passed, the ones with their backs to the path turning around to see what the others were looking at. A few lifted hands to Scab, and he nodded but said nothing, quickening his pace as the path climbed the gently rising ground. Libby was glad he didn't talk to them; they reminded her of the men in the boxcar, and she thought she caught a whiff of the same heavy, sweetish smell that had come from the bottle they had drunk from.

After a half-mile or so, the path curved away from the creek, bending to the right. Scab followed the bend, leading the way into a good-sized clearing where the path came to a dead end. Libby stopped to look around.

A dense growth of young willow and ash surrounded the clearing, with a wall of taller trees behind them, and a thick, brilliant-green jungle of brambles and brush interwoven between them. On the far side of the clearing stood a wooden shack, sturdily constructed – unlike the ramshackle shelters she had seen in the camp – with a solid-looking corrugated tin roof. A similar shack, a little smaller, stood off to her left.

In the middle of the clearing a wizened little man grinned at her from beside a campfire, over which a large stew pot was steaming. Four thick logs were ranged like benches in a square around the fire.

Scab went straight to one of these and, dropping the bedroll and knapsack on the ground, sat down. He pulled his tobacco pouch from his pocket. "He inside?" he asked the little man.

"Yep." The man kept grinning at Libby. "Talkin' to some fellas. Y'all hongry? I got some stew ready." He motioned to

Libby to sit. Feeling timid and ill-at-ease, she slipped across to Scab and sank down beside him.

The little man ladled some of the stew from the pot into a tin cup, stuck a speckled blue enamelware spoon into it and passed it across the fire to Libby. "Careful – better let it cool down a mite!" he said as Libby, half-starved after walking all day on nothing but that morning's catfish, was about to gulp a spoonful down immediately. She stopped and blew on the grayish, watery stuff in the spoon, then swallowed it gratefully.

"Good, huh?" The man seemed never to stop grinning. It was hard to guess his age; his face was so leathery that its many creases looked like deep grooves carved into wood, but his wispy hair was just beginning to gray. "We ain't been innerduced yet. They call me Roach – I won't say why!" He gave a wild giggle. "Not right now, anyways – you'd be a-scared to eat my mulligan!" He scooped another cupful of the soup from the pot and settled on the log opposite, slurping noisily.

"I'm Elizabeth." She gave him a shy smile. "But everyone calls me Libby."

"Yep, I know." Roach winked and pointed a finger at her, bouncing it playfully. "I know all about *you*. Don't you worry, sis: ol' Pullman'll set things to rights."

Scab had finished rolling his cigarette, and was lighting it with a stalk of dry grass he had stuck in the fire. He took a long drag, leaning forward with his elbows on his knees. "How long they been in there?" he asked Roach, smoke streaming out with his words.

"Maybe a half-hour or so. Rusty, an' some new fella from out Springfield way."

Scab nodded, then rose and scooped out some of the stew with another tin cup.

It wasn't until Libby had finished her second cup of stew, and was trying to get up her courage to ask Roach if he knew anything about Maisie, that the door to the shack scraped open. Two men filled the doorway, battered felt hats in their hands. The man in front held the door handle; the other was stuffing a small package wrapped in brown paper into a knapsack. Both looked dusty and travel-worn. They stood for a moment, nodding deferentially to someone speaking inside. Though she couldn't make out the words, Libby could hear the deep voice of the man speaking: *Pullman*, she thought with a mixture of excitement and nervousness.

The two men each gave a last nod – almost a little bow, Libby thought – then came out, shutting the door behind them. They put their hats on, nodded to Roach, Scab and Libby, and left without saying a word. Libby thought they stole curious glances at her as they passed.

As soon as they had gone, Roach went to the door and knocked gently. The deep voice rumbled again inside, and Roach opened the door and leaned in to speak a few words. Libby heard a chair scraping, and a gray-haired man appeared in the doorway, beaming at her. "Elizabeth, my dear!" he said; "I'm so very happy to make your acquaintance. They call me Pullman."

CHAPTER FIVE

PULLMAN WAS BETTER dressed than any of the men Libby had seen in the camp; he wore a dark suit-jacket and pants, with a clean-looking white shirt, though his collar button was undone and he wore no tie. He was a stocky, pleasant-looking man with shrewd, smiling blue eyes. He looked to be older than Libby's mother but younger than her grandmother, and he spoke a bit oddly, as if he was from another country – maybe England, Libby thought, or Ireland. He crossed to stand behind Scab, though Scab neither spoke nor looked up at him. "I'm so pleased you were able to come, Elizabeth. And so very relieved that our young friend here has brought you to us safely – at last."

He dropped a hand onto Scab's shoulder with the final two words and gave it a shake, gripping so hard that Libby saw Scab wince a little. "Had some trouble on the road," Scab said.

"Trouble, eh?" Pullman crossed to the log opposite Scab,

The Birds of the Air | 57

moving, Libby noticed, with a slight limp, and extending his left leg stiffly when he sat down. "No one hurt, I hope?"

"Not us, anyway," Scab said, and glanced at Libby with a faint half-smile – the first one, she realized with an odd little shock, that she had ever seen on his face.

"Well, perhaps we'd better discuss all that tomorrow." Pullman's sharp gaze fell on Libby and softened. "Our poor little visitor appears to be about done in."

It was true. Now that her stomach wasn't knotted with hunger – and even though the spring sunlight was still a couple of hours from fading – Libby could hardly keep her eyes open. Still she protested: "But, Mr. Pullman – my sister –"

"Time enough for all that tomorrow, my dear," Pullman said, his deep voice reassuring. "I'll need you at your full capacity. Roach?"

The little man popped up immediately, his ever-present grin widening. Pullman swept an arm, with a wry flourish, toward the larger shack. "Show young Elizabeth to the guest quarters. You'll have the chateau to yourself for the duration of your stay, my dear." He nodded toward the smaller shack: "I'll bunk in the carriage-house with these two savages. Sleep well; we'll make our plans tomorrow."

Roach grinned his way to the door of the shack and opened it, bobbing his head to indicate that Libby should go inside. The interior was rough but surprisingly clean, with a floor made of wood rather than earth. The space was just large enough to contain a wooden chair, a little table, an old army cot with a battered suitcase beneath it, and a trunk, locked with a padlock. A kerosene lantern stood unlit on the table, and thin, moving shafts of late-afternoon sunlight slanted through a small window opposite the door. Shelves on the wall held a few books, some folded clothes, soap and shaving supplies. "I warshed the sheets for ya," Roach said, pointing with bashful pride to the cot, where two stiff-looking sheets lay folded, along with a pillowcase, on top of a bluish wool blanket and the striped ticking of a bare pillow.

"Thanks, Mr. Roach," Libby said, feeling a warm rush of gratitude toward the little man through the haze of her exhaustion.

Roach gave his nervous-sounding laugh. "Just Roach, little sis. No call to fool around with no 'mister'." He backed away from the doorway. "'Night, now."

"Goodnight."

As Roach retreated, Libby paused before shutting the door and called shyly to Scab and Pullman, "Good night. And... Mr. Pullman?"

Pullman, filling a pipe from a bag of tobacco, paused and turned to her, smiling, and she gave him a hesitant smile in return. "They call me Libby."

The sheets were as stiff as they looked, and the cot was so narrow that Libby wondered how Pullman ever stayed on it; but the shack was such an improvement over the hardships of the past few nights that, when Roach tapped on the door to call her for breakfast, it seemed she had just that second laid her head on the pillow.

Her fingers fumbled with excitement as she pulled her jeans on. Today, at last, she would discover what Pullman knew about Maisie – and perhaps, with his help, get her back.

Scab and the two men were seated by the fire, eating from tin plates. The air was heavenly with the scent of frying bacon. "Help yourself, sis," Roach said, pointing with his fork toward a grease-encrusted skillet where the bacon still steamed, along with a small mountain of scrambled eggs. Roach's gleeful good-humor was already in full force. "We live a lot more comfortable than the rest a' these 'bo's," he told Libby through an eggy grin, "on accounta' bein' pardnered up with Pullman here!"

Scab and the men were drinking brawny-smelling coffee, but Libby shook her head when Roach offered the pot to her. "Mr. Pullman," she said, scooping eggs onto a tin plate, "can we talk about my sister now?"

"Of course, my dear. Do you feel more rested? Did you sleep well?"

"Yes, sir; thank you very much," Libby said, and Scab snorted softly into his coffee – the closest thing to a laugh she had ever heard from him.

"Quiet, you young hyena," Pullman growled, eyeing Scab with affable scorn. "Even in days like these, some few people remain more human than beast." He set aside his empty plate and, taking his pipe from a jacket pocket, gestured with it toward Scab. "Our youthful warrior here was just favoring us with an account of your conflict with those miscreants on the train." He turned to Scab. "I do commend you for your handling of the situation once it arose. However, before you jump your next freight, *wunderkind*, perhaps you had better check the under-growth for degenerates."

Roach cackled quietly, but Pullman became serious, looking down at Libby where she had seated herself beside him. "Now: your little sister, my dear." Lines that looked to be etched by pain deepened around his eyes. "I'm afraid it's as I feared from the first." He glanced at Roach, as if for confirmation. "Fuller."

"Yep," Roach said. The smile was completely gone from his face for the first time since Libby had met him. It made him look like a different person.

Libby looked from one to the other. "*Please*, Mr. Pullman," she said, touching his sleeve. "Scab said you could help me find my sister. Won't you just tell me where she is?"

He laid a hand on hers, gently. "I'm afraid I don't know that, Elizabeth. Not yet, at any rate."

"But –" Libby gaped at him, stunned.

"What I told Scab to tell you is that I believe I can help you to *retrieve* your little sister. In point of fact, I mean to attempt to draw her *here*, to us. I'm confident that I can do this, if she's still at liberty, but I need your help; that's why I had Scab bring you here. I'm deeply sorry for the hardship and danger to you, Libby, and for adding to your mother's anxiety. But I was unable to send Scab as soon as I wished, and there's been too much delay already. It's imperative that we retrieve your sister *quickly*; and your mother, other adults – they would never have listened, and wouldn't have believed if they had."

"*Retrieve* her? But – how? And…" Libby sank back, trying to sort through the swarm of questions that boiled up all at once – and, she felt queasily, a little late – into in her mind. "If you don't know where my sister *is*… how did you know about us at *all*? How did you know what happened to us?"

"I make it my business to know about such cases – at least in this region. As to my methods, I fear no amount of explanation would render them comprehensible, child. Suffice to say I have certain – abilities. I know a great deal about this man who tried to take your sister. I know what he is, I know what he is doing, and I've dedicated myself to opposing him. Don't be deceived by what anyone says: you *did* see what you thought you saw. Fuller has abilities as well. He's trapped your sister in a form which will prevent anyone from recognizing her. He captured her, and he would have her still, imprisoned along with the many others he has stolen, had you not possessed the perceptiveness to realize

The Birds of the Air | 61

what was happening, and the courage to act. Because of your action, we have some hope that she's still free, and can be recovered before she falls back into Fuller's hands."

Pullman's approval warmed Libby: no matter what her mother, the neighbors and the sheriff's men thought, she *wasn't* just a foolish little girl. Hope began to rise in her again, but his last words sent an icy splinter through it. "Mr. Pullman... *why* does this man -- Fuller -- want Maisie? Does he... does he want kids, and not have any of his own?"

Pullman looked at Roach again, and Roach returned his gaze with an expression Libby couldn't read. When she looked at Scab, his dark glance flicked up at her for a second, then back down to the fire.

"Libby," Pullman said, "I'm going to ask you to excuse me from answering that question. Some knowledge is simply too heavy for children; I only hope we are able to spare your *sister* such knowledge, as well as yourself. It's enough that *I* know about John Fuller. But I'm afraid that until -- and unless -- I'm successful in drawing your sister here, you'll have no way to test the veracity of my claims. It's up to *you*, Libby, to decide whether you're willing to invest a little more time to discover whether what I say is true. But you'd best decide soon." He looked at her, the lines around his eyes etched deeper than before. "There isn't much time."

All the warmth that had risen in Libby moments before drained away just as suddenly, and she shivered.

"BLOOD CALLS TO blood when you're kin."

Roach gave Libby his gap-toothed grin. They stood beneath a lone hickory tree, in the center of a small, wild meadow outside the hobo jungle. Roach squinted wistfully in the direction of the river. "Still think we shoulda done it on the bridge, though. Runnin' water." He winked at her. "Washes away any hinderin' sway."

"And half the efficacy of our *own* operation, as likely as not," Pullman said. "Hold this." He pulled from his pocket the small wooden figure of a girl. He had spent half the morning carving it, using the photograph Libby had brought as a reference, and it bore a rough but striking resemblance to Maisie, with its heart-shaped face and straight bobbed hair. He handed the figure to Roach and began to pace the meadow, his sharp eyes scanning the ground. At intervals he stooped, stiff in his bad leg, to pick something up. Once it was a stone, once a dead branch, and several times he uprooted small plants. He carried these to the edge of the meadow and tossed them into the woods, then turned and nodded to Scab, who was lounging in the shadows at the border of the woods. Scab slipped off; Libby turned to see where he was going, but she found Roach at her elbow, squinting at the sky so hard that his grin pulled up into a comical near-snarl. "Easterly breeze," he said when Pullman rejoined them beneath the tree. "Y'wanna hold off a while?"

Pullman shook his head. "It'll do." He snapped his fingers and held out his hand; Roach gave him the little wooden figure, and he turned to Libby. "All right, my dear – let's get started." He too squinted at the sky, toward where the mid-morning sun was just topping the branches, and took Libby by the shoulders, adjusting her position until her back was toward it. "You stand right here. Don't move or speak until I tell you what to do next." He looked her in the eyes, cocking an eyebrow. "Do you understand?" Libby nodded and wrapped her arms around herself; her eyes kept being caught by the flitting of birds among the leaves.

The Birds of the Air | 63

Pullman drew his knife from his pocket and unfolded it, then went down, with a grimace, onto one knee. He held the little wooden figure on the other knee and, murmuring words Libby couldn't make out, rested the point of the knife above where its heart would be. He began to turn the knife back and forth, pressing down, drilling into the wood. For some reason this disturbed Libby; she almost raised her voice to protest, but caught her tongue behind her teeth.

After a few moments Pullman rose, pushing hard on his good leg with one hand. He limped to four different points on the edge of the meadow, at each point scattering a pinch of the shavings he had dug from the carved figure. Libby watched him, twisting her neck and body but not moving her feet from where he had told her to stand, until he came back and stood in front of her again. "Are you ready?" he asked, smiling down at her.

Libby nodded and held out her right hand with the index finger extended.

"Other way round, my dear," Pullman said. Pulling her right hand open, he laid the carved figure on her palm, face upward. "Right: now the other." Libby extended the finger of her left hand, not looking at it but staring down at the wooden figure. Her breath sharpened only a tiny bit when Pullman pricked her finger with the point of the knife. Holding the finger over the carving, Pullman squeezed gently until a single drop of blood fell into the hole he had dug in its chest. He closed Libby's right hand around it. "Now: speak to your sister, my dear. Tell her why you want her back. Say it out loud."

Libby closed her eyes. "I want – " She stopped and swallowed. She felt nervous and blank-minded; she felt stupid. "I want Mama to be happy again." A small, bitter something – like a poisonous worm – seemed to twist in her chest when she heard herself say the words. Her mind filled with the picture of her mother, staring out the window after Maisie had gone, her hands like dead birds in her lap, as if there was nothing left in the world worth caring about – and no one. Her eyes stung and she squeezed them shut tighter. "I – I want things to be like they used to be."

"No, no, Libby – that's no good." There was a touch of the impatient growl in Pullman's voice with which he sometimes spoke to Roach and Scab. "Come on, girl! Why do *you* want Maisie back? What do you miss about *her*, herself? Here –" he pulled from his pocket the picture of Maisie he had borrowed as a reference for the carving, and pushed it into her free hand. "Look at this and try again."

Libby looked down at the picture: the little-kid roundness of Maisie's cheeks; the bright, open smile she had given the school photographer.

"I... I miss –" she began, but her throat clenched like a fist. She *knew* she loved her sister, and wanted her back; why couldn't she think of the words? When she tried to pull up her feelings for Maisie, they came in a twisted mass, like a dark clump of roots torn from the dirt, all snarled and knotted with feelings about her mother. She felt the threat of the horrible slamming pain she had suffered when she held the dead bird. "I can't!" she cried, and hid her face in her hands, wetting the picture and the little wooden figure with tears.

"Ah, well." Pullman spoke softly, the growl gone from his voice. He pulled her hands from her face gently, and looked at the carving. Its wood was stained dark in places from Libby's tears; the drop of blood had soaked in, leaving a darker stain. "Don't fret, child. Where words fail, blood and tears may suffice."

He took the carving and, looking past her, nodded sharply.

She turned to see that Scab had returned, carrying a small wire cage with an odd-looking spring mechanism attached to its door. He and Roach approached, and secured the cage with baling wire to the trunk of the solitary tree. Libby saw a perch inside, anchored at one end to a latch that would release the spring and close the door.

When the cage was secure, with its floor at about the level of Libby's eyes, Pullman limped forward. He propped the little wooden girl inside and set the latch, leaving the door open. Libby noticed that something had been carved into the bark of the tree, just above the top of the cage: a triangle, its point turned downward, with a circle around it and the rough representation of an eye inside it.

"Very well, my friends." Pullman said. "Now we simply wait."

THAT AFTERNOON, LIBBY helped Roach with the cooking, cutting up onions on a board laid across two buckets.

"Reason they call me Roach?" he said gleefully. "It's 'cause I used to eat *bugs*. Not *all* the time – just if I had to. Learnt it when I was a kid. I says to myself, when I was just a little shaver, I says: 'the world's *full* a' bugs – why go hongry?'" He gave his wild cackle. "I was so good at findin' 'em, I'd have extra to give to my brothers and sisters! And I tell you what, even now I'm growed up, I'd *still* rather dig me up some grubs than have a empty belly. Yessir –" He stirred the soup, beaming into the pot – "if times ever gets too hard, I'll just do like the ol' bear does: I'll just cree-eep 'round the woods, lookin' o-ver all the leaves, lookin' un-der all the rocks, findin' a-ll the little bugs – and then I'll EAT 'em!"

"And one day, you daft bastard, they'll return the favor," Pullman rumbled good-naturedly. He rose from the wooden chair, which he had brought out into the clearing, and tapped the ashes from his pipe; his face looked drawn. "I believe I'll lie down for a couple of hours before supper. I'm feeling a bit done in."

"Takes a lot out a' him, stuff like he done this mornin'," Roach said, when Pullman had retreated into the smaller shack. Libby glanced at the door he had disappeared through, warmed by a surge of gratitude.

She hadn't seen Scab since they had left the meadow. When she asked where he was, Roach shrugged. "He's off rangin' around half the time, don't nobody know where he's at. No tellin' what he gets up to. Brings us a lotta good stuff back, though!" He held up the rabbit he was skinning, one Scab had snared.

Libby had finished the onions, and was cutting up spotty potatoes. "Roach? If Maisie *does* come, what do we do then?"

"Oh, I reckon ol' Pullman'll have a plan for all that. Might be he can undo the hex hisself. Might be if he can't, he knows somebody who can."

She frowned, puzzled. "How did Mr. Pullman know about Maisie in the first place? Did he see her picture in the newspapers or something?"

Roach shook his head. "Naw, nothin' like that. Ol' Pullman, he can get a fix on things, like."

"What do you mean – a fix?"

"Well – it's like a way of *seein*', but not with your eyes. I don't mean like just imaginin' things; I mean like seein' things that's *real*, but far away, or hid. Not many folks can do it. It's hard on him, though – gives him godawful headaches sometimes."

"Do you think what he did will really work? You think Maisie will come?"

Roach nodded. "Oh yeah – we'll get 'er. Don't you worry 'bout that, sis. Course, now, this here's the first time one a' them kids has got *loose*, far as I know, so I ain't seen him call one a' *them* before. But I reckon he's plenty able for it; I seen him do harder things." Roach flopped the rabbit carcass onto another piece of board and started to cut it up. "Ol' Pullman's a *educated* fella; he ain't no ign'rant stiff like Scab or me. This here jungle's just his headquarters, like."

"Headquarters for what?"

Roach paused in his cutting and his glance flickered up at her, then away. "Well – to hinder John Fuller, sis, like he told you. Try ta stop him hexin' kids, and runnin' off with 'em, like he almost done with your little sister." He waved the knife toward the hobo camp. "Place like this, you keep your ears open, you can find out a lot. This here's one a' the biggest jungles in the whole U-nited States. These 'bo's 'round here, they go everwhere, all acrost the country. They see a lotta things, hear a lotta things reg'lar folk don't. It's like they live in a whole differnt world, kinda down under the reg'lar world, like."

Libby felt a chill at the back of her neck, remembering the cursing man's yellow-toothed grin. *Like weeds, little sis, a-growin' on a grave without no stone; and most folks walk right on over and don't never know what's underneath.*

"You think that was John Fuller you seen hex your little sister?" Roach shook his head, his expression grim. "That was just some stiff that works for him. Ol' Fuller's got a whole *army* a' 'bo's out there, stealin' kids from all over the country. They know how ta ride the rails; they don't buy no tickets, don't leave no trail, don't let nobody see 'em in the towns where they take the kids from. So Pullman, he got the idea he'd get him people of his *own*: find bo's that'd be his eyes and ears, like, for all the things he can't get a fix on hisself, and that'll travel 'round and do things for him, like Scab done when he come to get you."

Libby stared at him, stunned. For the first time since she had seen them, she thought of the other pictures tacked up around Maisie's on the bulletin board in the post office back home. So many mothers and fathers, sisters and brothers grieving; so many kids missing from their homes. Had John Fuller taken them *all*?

She looked at the small shack again. "If Maisie's the only one that got loose, how does Mr. Pullman help the other kids?"

Roach gave his nervous-sounding laugh. "I reckon you better ask *him* about that, sis. I don't wanna talk out a' turn."

A sudden idea made Libby's stomach knot. "And this man Fuller... can *he* do what you said – get a fix on things – too? Could *he* maybe... 'see'... where Maisie is now?"

"Well..." Roach avoided her gaze and scrubbed the back of one hand over his forehead. "Yeah, sis, likely he could. But ol' Fuller, he must have a lot on his mind. Long as we get hold of your little sis soon, I reckon we'll be all right."

"Do you think she *will* come soon, Roach? How long do you think it'll take?"

"Aw, not more'n a couple days. Don't you worry, sis. All we know, maybe Fuller ain't even heard what you done yet. Maybe he don't even know your sis got away! Don't you worry. We'll get her all right. Now are you gonna finish cuttin' up them 'taters, or do I hafta do it myself?"

THE THICK BELT of woodland that camouflaged the camp was upriver, Roach said, from the railroad bridge, and some little distance from town. "It's good to have you a lot a' trees an' bushes," he told Libby, "so's the town folks don't see you too easy. That's why they call it a hobo *jungle*, see?"

Libby couldn't get much idea of how many people were

camped in the jungle. Roach said hobos were always coming and going, mostly men but an occasional woman, hitchhiking or catching freight trains in and out. When she asked him if he ever rode the freights, he cackled and said, "Not me, sis! Not no more. Since I pardnered up with Pullman, I'm just a ol' jungle buzzard!"

From the clearing where the shacks stood, surrounded by their dense wall of foliage, Libby couldn't see the faintest gleam of any other campfires at night. She had seen other parts of the jungle only when she first walked in with Scab and, later, on the walk to the meadow where they hung the cage. Pullman and Roach wouldn't let her wander alone. "You better stick close to ol' Pullman, or to Scab or me," Roach told her, his grin for once absent. "Some a' these stiffs ain't no damn good."

Scab went into town for supplies the day after they hung the cage, buying beans, bacon, eggs and tobacco with money Pullman gave him. On that day, also, Roach put the big washtub inside Pullman's shack, and filled it with water heated over the fire, so Libby could take a bath. She never would have dreamed before how wonderful it could feel, just to bathe, wash her hair and put on clean clothes. Pullman gave her one of his shirts, which came down nearly to her knees, to wear while Roach washed her grubby clothes and hung them in the trees to dry.

Another day passed, and then another. Scab went frequently to check the cage in the meadow, but always came back with the same report: empty. Every time this happened, the knotted feeling came back to Libby's stomach, and each time the knot grew tighter; yet aside from her fear for Maisie, she was oddly content. Pullman and Roach were kind to her, and Scab, though he paid little attention to her, didn't seem to mind her being there. She'd hardly been around men since almost before she could remember, and she watched with furtive fascination as they talked to one another, did chores around the clearing, shaved in the mornings at the little mirror nailed to the outside of Pullman's shack.

As Roach had said, Scab was gone most of the daylight hours, checking and setting snares, fishing, scavenging, or doing whatever mysterious things he did for Pullman. In the mornings after breakfast, Pullman often talked with him for a short time in the shack; after that Scab left the clearing, carrying his knapsack, and usually didn't return until suppertime.

Pullman spent much of each day inside his shack, and occasionally men from the camp came and disappeared inside to talk with him. When Libby asked Roach who they were, he waved a hand vaguely. "Aw, just some a' them that work for ol' Pullman."

Libby spent most of her time with Roach, helping him to cook, wash the tin dishes, scour the pots with sand in the creek, gather firewood and wash clothes. He was cheerful and congenial in his odd way, and Libby felt less lonely in his company than she had at any time since Maisie had disappeared.

Roach was also the easiest of the three to coax into answering questions, and Libby was overflowing with them. Only about things having to do with Maisie's situation was he a bit close-mouthed – at Pullman's insistence, she suspected – but on most other topics he was endlessly voluble.

"Roach, how did Scab get that name?" she asked on the fourth day, as they gathered kindling in the woods.

"Well, it ain't nothin' to do with no line-crossin', like how the union fellas use it." He was striking low branches with a stick, knocking down dead wood, and he panted a bit as he spoke. "He was banged up purty bad when Pullman first brought him around – that'd be three, four years ago now. He'd got in a fight with some fellas on a train; got pitched off while it was movin'. He was all skinned up on one side, an' some a' the bo's kidded him he looked

The Birds of the Air | 71

like one big ol' scab walkin' around. That just kinda turned into his moniker."

"Moniker? What's that?"

"Well –" Roach stopped whacking the trees and leaned on the stick. "Your name – I mean your *real* name – it can give folks sway over you, you're not careful."

"What does *that* mean – 'give them sway'?"

"Well – give 'em a hold over you, like. Could be just a reg'lar, outside hold, like findin' out where you come from, or who your folks are. Or, if the person has the know-how, it can give 'em a differnt kinda hold, a hold over your *inside*. And if somebody's got a hold over your inside, purty soon they're gonna have a hold over your outside too. You see, sis?"

"I... guess so."

"Well, you tell folks your name – your *real* name – you could be givin' 'em sway over you like that. So out on the road, most folks don't use their real names. You get you a moniker: somethin' you call yourself, or other folks start callin' you."

Roach returned to knocking down sticks, and Libby was quiet for a bit, gathering them, before she spoke up again. "When I asked Scab how old he was, he didn't know."

"Yep." Roach's wrinkled, cheerful face became serious. "Ol' Scab 's had a rougher time than most."

"Why? What happened to him?"

"Well, the way I heard it from Pullman, Scab's folks was some no-'count drifters, ended up in some little backwater in Arkansas. Had themselves a whole litter a' young'uns they dragged there with 'em, an' Scab was the oldest. Purty soon his ol' man owed money all over town, so he started sendin' Scab to work for some a' the folks he owed, tryin' to work off some a' the debt." Roach shook his head. "Scab wasn't but around ten, eleven at the time, but he'd go stay with some strangers or other, workin' for 'em just like a slave, while them low-down folks a' his was a-layin' 'round their shack, drinkin' 'shine and pilin' up more debts." Roach's face hardened with disgust. "Well, this one place Scab was workin' at, the ol' farmer got to knockin' him around a little too rough, so Scab run off and went back home. When he got there, what do ya think he found?" He spat on the ground. "Nothin' but a buncha' trash an' empty bottles. Them worthless folks a' his, they up an' took off with the rest of them young'uns and left him; didn't leave no word or nothin'. Scab never seen hide nor hair of 'em again. Been on his own ever since."

Libby swallowed, not knowing what to say. What would it be like, to discover that no one in the whole world cared the least bit about you? But inside her rose the picture of her mother's eyes sliding away from hers. *I know what it's like,* she thought – but felt guilty, even as she thought it, for comparing her troubles to Scab's.

When they returned from gathering kindling, Roach gave Libby the key to the lean-to – a small structure behind Pullman's shack, used to store cooking pots and food supplies – and told her to fetch the lard and flour. Pullman was still shut up inside the shack, but Scab had come back and was sitting on one of the logs, plucking some large bird. Gray-barred feathers drifted at his feet; Libby saw that the bird was another chicken, and wondered if he had stolen it. She felt suddenly a little shy around him, now she had heard about his past, and was relieved that he paid no attention to her.

It wasn't until she rounded the back corner of Pullman's shack that she realized something about the clearing had changed. She stopped, frowning, in the narrow space between the lean-to and the underbrush that marked the edge of the woods, trying to figure out what it was. The forest there had an odd, waiting feeling, as if everything were holding its breath, but she couldn't seem to make out why. She had given up and was struggling with the rusty lock, when she suddenly realized that, though the insects around the rest of the clearing – the crickets, the katydids, the noisy cicadas – were droning on as usual, the ones in the woods behind her had fallen silent. In the instant after she realized it, there was a rustle in the bushes at her back, a hand clamped over her mouth, and strong arms grabbed her and pulled her into the forest.

CHAPTER SIX

SHE WAS DREAMING of the scarecrow again.

This time she was lying on her back in the garden, with her head right beside the post that held the scarecrow up. The straw-stuffed figure towered above her, looking as tall as a house. It was staring intently toward the east, and above it dark clouds ripped apart and tumbled, racing across the sky.

Something was wrong; she couldn't move. She tried again, in rising panic, but her body wouldn't obey. The scarecrow shifted its gaze, its gray, human eyes looking down at her. Its face, too, looked more human now, and when its eyes met hers the burlap brow furrowed – whether in anger or sorrow she couldn't tell. It fisted its work-glove hands and flexed its arms, breaking the broomstick that held them like a toothpick. With its left arm it made an expansive gesture, its open hand starting low at its side and sweeping in an arc, across its body and upward, as if it was scooping something up and flinging it into the air.

With a harsh, deafening burst of noise, the ground all around them appeared to lift and swirl in a great spiral, following the sweep of the scarecrow's arm. The rising ground was black as tar and, following it with her eyes, Libby saw it begin to break apart into ragged shapes. Just as she recognized the sound assaulting her ears, some link between vision and brain seemed to click into place, and she saw it was not earth rising, but a multitude of black-winged bodies, barbed with sharp beaks and talons: crows. They swirled up in a tornado around her; they seemed to be on the verge of shattering the substance of reality with their clamor. Then, just when she thought she couldn't bear it any longer, they flew off toward the south in a raucous, inky torrent across the tempestuous sky.

As she watched them go, Libby began to get a queasy, vertiginous feeling that she wasn't seeing things correctly. The crows diminishing in the distance, the dark, riotous clouds, the scarecrow standing over her – all of them began to look wrong, as if each was becoming transparent and something behind it was showing through. She made an effort to focus her vision; there was another click, a shift in perception, and she found herself awake.

She was still lying on her back. Instead of clouds, a wind-blown ceiling of leaves churned above her; instead of the scarecrow, the trunk of a tree towered over her head. The deafening tumult of the crows had diminished to the urgent, stifled sound of men's voices arguing in half-whispers.

"Well I ain't *got* no goddamn pliers. How can I bring what I ain't got?"

"Well what *did* you bring?"

Libby turned her head toward the voices, and saw that she lay in a more open part of the forest than she had been in before, surrounded by tall trees with column-like trunks. Late-afternoon sunlight slanted between the branches. The voices were coming from three men, strangers, squatting in a huddle a few feet away. Their faces were stubbled, their clothing grubby. Her queasiness uncoiled into sick fear as she remembered standing at the lean-to door, and what had happened afterward.

She hadn't seen the man who grabbed her: his hand, as huge and suffocating as a bag of meal, had covered her nose and mouth, not only keeping her from turning to look at him, but making it impossible to breathe. Small branches had whipped and scratched her as he pushed through the underbrush. She had tried to cry out, but even from inside her head her voice sounded tiny and muffled. She had tried to struggle, but her legs had only flailed uselessly against the air, until the edges of her vision had begun to shimmer, and everything had faded away.

"She's awake. Hurry up."

Seeing the men move toward her, Libby tried to roll to her hands and knees and scramble away; but as soon as she moved she realized her ankles were bound tightly, and her hands tied behind her. Before she could get to her knees, the men had hold of her. Though they weren't the three men from the boxcar, they had the same sour-sweetish smell of sweat and alcohol; their hands were hard and merciless.

The largest man knelt astride her body, his hands like vises on her arms, pinning her down. As she opened her mouth to scream, one of the others – a wiry, leathery-faced man – shoved a stick between her teeth, sideways like a horse's bit. With some kind of cord, he tied it tightly around her head so it kept her mouth from closing; it stretched her lips painfully and muffled her cries. She exerted every ounce of strength she had, trying to thrash away, but she could no more budge the man who held her than she could have budged one of the great trees around them, if it had fallen across her chest.

The wiry man knelt and wedged her head between his knees, holding it motionless with both hands. The third man, his lips peeled back in a grimace of concentration, knelt beside Libby and leaned over her, between the other two. He held things in his hands; Libby's rolling, terrified eyes couldn't at first register what they were. He was sweating profusely, and as he leaned over her, a drop of his sweat fell onto her cheek. "Hold her still," he panted. With his left hand, he pushed something metal beneath Libby's upper lip. Straining her eyes to focus, Libby saw it was a screwdriver, the wooden handle clenched in his fist and the tip resting against one of her front teeth. She could feel the cold metal touching her gum. Unable to close her mouth, unable to move her head even a quarter-inch to either side, she watched, nearly senseless with horror, as the man raised his other hand.

In it, he held a hammer.

He bounced it in the air a couple of times, as if to get the feel of it. Then he raised it into position to strike the screwdriver, and Libby's voice rose to a gagged, frenzied shriek as she realized what he meant to do.

"Don't let her swallow it," he said. As he cocked the hammer back to strike, Libby longed to close her eyes, but she couldn't: they were riveted on the hammer; the hammer filled the whole world.

And then, suddenly, a blur of incomprehensible motion swept across her field of vision, knocking the hammer away. She heard a confusion of noises, and the man kneeling astride her toppled sideways, his knee dragging across her ribs, rolling her roughly onto her stomach. She found that no one was holding her anymore. She turned to look to her left, where some sort of commotion was going on, and saw the hammer, only a couple of feet from her face. A hand still gripped its handle, but a man's heavy work-boot stood on it, crushing the fingers against the wood. She heard someone howling in pain, and felt someone grab her arms. She struggled, thinking it was the man who had been pinning her down, but then she heard Roach's voice close to her ear: "Quiet, sis, it's jest me. Be still so I can cut ya loose."

She went limp, and lay with her cheek prickled by damp, earth-smelling dead leaves, while he sawed through the cord holding the stick in her mouth, and then began on the ones binding her wrists. At first her eyes wouldn't stay still, and kept darting around more quickly than she could register what they were seeing. Then, like pieces of a jigsaw puzzle, the things happening around her came together and began to make sense.

The big man who had been pinning her lay groaning, face down on the ground, the back of his head covered with blood. Scab stood scowling over him, one hand gripping a heavy piece of tree branch the size of a baseball bat, ready to club him again if he tried to get up. The man holding the hammer continued to howl and writhe on the ground, dirt and blood streaking his face. It was Pullman's boot she had seen crushing his hand; Pullman still stood with his full weight grinding down on the fingers clasped around the wooden handle. As Libby watched, the man raised the screwdriver in his left hand and stabbed savagely at Pullman's leg. Libby cried out, but Pullman appeared unaffected. Still standing on the hand that gripped the hammer, he drew back his other foot and kicked the man in the head, so hard that it looked to Libby as if his neck should have broken.

Roach finished cutting her loose. She struggled to her feet and tried to walk, but the ground reeled and tilted, as if she were on a sinking boat; her legs felt like rubber, and she only managed to half-stumble, half-fall to the foot of a nearby tree, where she vomited up the soup she had eaten at noon.

After that, for some time, things were disjointed and unreal. She was aware of Roach beside her, handing her a handkerchief and helping her to get to a sitting position against another tree, and of Pullman barking out questions to him, asking if she was all right. She was shaking so hard that Pullman took off his jacket and tossed it to Roach, who wrapped it around her shoulders, and in some far-off part of her mind she thought this was funny, because she wasn't shaking from cold.

Then Roach was no longer beside her, because she saw him with Scab, dragging one of her abductors across the ground. It was the large man Scab had clubbed. Blood ran down his face, and his shirt tore halfway open as they dragged him to where Pullman stood over the man who had held the hammer. Libby lost track for a while then, but when she could focus again, she saw both men slumped with their backs against the base of a thick tree. Someone had used the cords they had bound her with to tie their ankles together. She looked around for the wiry man who had jammed the stick into her mouth, but he was nowhere in sight.

Pullman was talking to the men, asking them questions, Libby thought, though he didn't speak loudly enough for her to make out on his words. The men didn't seem to be answering, and Pullman, without turning his icy blue gaze from them, held out a hand toward Scab, who was standing a little behind him. Scab drew the folded razor from his pocket and handed it to Pullman.

Libby thought distantly that she should look away, that she didn't want to see what Pullman was going to do to the men with the razor. But then she thought maybe she was dreaming again, because Pullman, his lips moving, unfolded the razor and drew the blade across his own palm. He fisted his hand around the blood, and nodded to Scab. Scab stepped forward, grabbed the hair of the man who had held the hammer, and wrenched his head back so his face was tilted up toward Pullman. Pullman touched two fingers to the blood in his palm and drew them across the man's forehead, leaving two red parallel lines there. Libby saw his lips move again, and then he spoke in a louder voice, his words carrying to her clearly: *"As to the servant, so to the master."* The man slumped in Scab's grip seemed dazed, only half-conscious, but when Pullman held his fisted hand over the upturned face, Libby saw the man's flesh sizzle and smoke where Pullman's blood dripped onto it, blistering like bacon in a hot skillet. The man shrieked, and Libby flinched back, her eyes squeezing shut and her hands flying to her ears, feeling as if she might vomit again.

She must have made a noise, because when she opened her eyes, Pullman was looking toward her. He rapped out a command to Roach, who crossed to her and helped her to her feet. He put an arm around her and half-steered, half-supported her, leading her through the woods, away from the intermittent screams of her tormentors.

It was only later, when she lay wrapped in the scratchy blanket on the cot in Pullman's shack, that she remembered the mark. She had seen it on the large man's chest, when Scab and Roach had torn his shirt open dragging him across the ground: some sort of drawing or tattoo, a little larger than a silver dollar, dark against the man's pale skin. She hadn't been close enough to see it very clearly, but as the scene replayed in her memory she was almost sure the mark had been in the shape of a circle surrounding a crude eye inside a triangle: the same mark she had seen carved into the tree where they hung the cage to catch Maisie.

SHE WOKE SOME time later to Scab's voice, raised angrily outside the shack. When her mind cleared enough, she caught the last of his words: "— coulda got *killed!*" There was an equally angry-sounding answer in Pullman's low growl, but she couldn't make out his words.

Scab's mad I got them into that mess, she thought miserably. *He doesn't want me around.* The shock of her abduction, the violence on both sides, the fearfulness of what she had seen Pullman do – all of it rushed back with wakefulness; tears sprang up and she wept quietly into the pillow. "I wish I'd never come here, Mama," she moaned into the rough cotton case. "I want to go home."

But I've got to find Maisie, she thought with an inward burst of desperation. *I don't care what happens to me; I don't care what Scab thinks. I'm the one who lost her, and I have to find her.* She rolled over and stared at the tin roof. *It's my fault she's gone.* It was the first time she had allowed the thought to form clearly into words, even inside her head, and as soon as it did a fierce anger blazed up: anger at the men who had tried to steal Maisie; anger at herself, for failing to protect her; anger at her mother, for a vague, dense snarl of things she couldn't disentangle enough to name.

Her tears, if not her shock and fear, evaporated in the heat of her anger. She rubbed her eyes with her sleeve, wincing at the sting of the scratches on her face. Remembering Roach's hand-kerchief, she pulled it from her pocket and blew her nose. Then she wrapped the blanket around her and went outside.

It had grown dark while she slept, and Scab and the men

were sitting around the campfire. The fire was low, but even by its fitful glow Libby could see that they looked exhausted. Pullman sat bent over, his forehead resting on his bandaged left hand, which shaded his eyes as if even the dim firelight bothered him. No one was speaking, but when Scab took a drag from his cigarette, the glow from its tip lit a scowl more fierce than usual. Even Roach looked grim, but when he saw Libby his lined face softened.

"Have a seat, sis! How ya feelin'?" He gestured toward the stewpot. "We saved some supper for ya."

Pullman lifted his head to give her a tired smile, but Libby, unsettled by a mixture of gratitude and something close to fear, quickly dropped her eyes from his, and sat down on the log across from Roach. She shook her head. "No, thank you. I'm not hungry."

"Are you all right, my dear?" Pullman's voice was gentle, and it almost started Libby crying again. "Did they hurt you?"

She swallowed hard. "I'm all right. Did... my sister...?"

Pullman shook his head, the lines of weariness deepening in his face. "No sign of her yet, I'm afraid."

She glanced at Scab. "I'm sorry I've been causing you all so much trouble."

Pullman gave a harsh bark of a laugh. "And how is it that you imagine *you've* been causing us trouble, my dear?"

She shrugged a bit, not letting herself look at Scab again. "Who... who *were* those men? What did they want? Why did they ...." But her voice failed her when she thought of the hammer and the screwdriver, and she felt a bit of the shakiness and nausea returning.

"Tooth," Scab said, and she turned toward him, almost startled that he was the one who had answered. "Works like the

The Birds of the Air | 83

blood," he said, lifting his dark gaze to Pullman, his eyes like hot coals in the firelight. "Even better, some ways."

Libby looked to Pullman, and he nodded. "Yes, Scab is correct. Those men were after Maisie. They knew that if they got hold of your tooth, they could use it to send a calling to her, as we did with your blood. You see, Libby, the way these things work..." but he broke off – too exhausted, Libby thought, to search for the words to explain.

"It's *payment*, like," Roach chimed in, taking over for him. "When you fool around with the natural way a' things, there's gotta be a reckonin'. Could be tears; could be skin or bone or blood. Some folks have even given eyes, or –" he paused and glanced at Pullman – "or hands and the like. The bigger the payment, the more pull you get out of it." He waved his cup toward the woods. "Them fellas, if they'd got ahold a' your tooth, or say, one a' your fingers or toes, somebody coulda used it to draw your sis to 'em, you bein' close kin an' all. It's sorta' like what we done with your blood, but –"

"But it would have been *coercion*, not a call like the one we sent." Anger momentarily sparked through the weariness in Pullman's face. "It's a barbarous, crude method they meant to use. It would have brutalized your sister's mind, and might even have damaged it beyond repair." He looked at Libby, his expression grim. "Elizabeth, we can't afford to wait any longer: we must get your sister back, *quickly*. Not only for her sake, but for your own protection: once we have Maisie safe, a calling will be of no more use, and Fuller's people will have no more reason to trouble *you*."

"So – those men who took me worked for Mr. F-Fuller?" Libby felt horrified, but not surprised. Her thoughts had been scattered and fragmented after the incident in the woods, but in some part of her mind she had known who the men must be. Now that the realization came into full focus, though, she was struck by an implication that jerked her upright and rigid on the log. "Does that mean Mr. Fuller knows where we *are?*" Her eyes darted around the edge of the clearing as if she might see Fuller crouched there, watching them. "Should we get *away* from here?"

Pullman looked at her, a touch of surprise in his face. "Ah... no, no; I apologize, my dear," he said. "I... I didn't mean to frighten you." He paused for a moment, fishing absently in his pockets until he found his pipe and tobacco, seeming to gather his thoughts. Across from Libby, Roach leaned forward and prodded studiously at the fire; she had the feeling he was trying not to look at Pullman – or at her.

Pullman spoke up finally: "I'm afraid, Libby, that there are many things I cannot go into detail about. We're not alone in trying to stop John Fuller, and secrecy is the best protection for us, and for our allies. But you can trust me when I tell you that, for the time being, it will be safest for us to remain here."

Libby didn't feel much reassured by this non-answer, but before she could press Pullman further, a new idea struck her with a force that seemed to stun all other questions out of her brain. "But... what about *afterward?* If we *do* get Maisie back, and we go home, what would keep Fuller's people from coming after her *there?*" She felt hollowed out by shock – not only at the question itself, but at her stupidity in not having thought of it before.

Pullman lifted a soothing hand. "Don't *worry*, my dear; we have a *plan* for all that. But..." he sighed... "I'm very tired tonight; time enough to discuss these things *after* we get your sister back. Let's just take one thing at a time, shall we? First and foremost, we *must* retrieve your sister before Fuller's people get her; we'll have to use whatever method necessary, so long as it does no lasting harm to either of you. First thing tomorrow morning, we'll go back to the meadow, and send out a *proper* call."

Libby felt a quiver of apprehension: what would constitute a "proper" call? She thought of what Roach had said about toes and fingers, skin and bone. *So long as it does no lasting harm,* Pullman had said... but what did he mean by "lasting harm"? *No matter what it is, I'll do it,* she thought. *I'm the one who lost Maisie, and I have to find her.*

Pullman struck a match to light his pipe, and she was startled out of her thoughts by the sight of his face in the flame's glow: half the white of his left eye had turned blood-red. "Mr. Pullman!" she cried, her hand rising involuntarily to her own eye.

"Oh, this?" he said, gesturing toward the eye. "Don't worry, my dear, it looks much worse than it is. Just the price of finding you so quickly, after those misbegotten wretches carried you off." He rose stiffly from his seat. "But... I do have a bit of a headache, so I think I'll say goodnight. Scab will take a look about; and I've asked him to sleep outside your shack tonight, just in case." He gave an approving nod toward Scab, who didn't look up from the fire. "The boy can sleep through a train whistle, but let a cat set one paw into the clearing and he'll be awake before it sets down another."

He started toward the small shack, but his faint limp struck Libby with a sudden recollection. "Mr. Pullman!" she cried, ashamed she hadn't thought of it sooner; "Is your leg all right? I mean, where the man stabbed you with the screwdriver?"

Pullman stopped, turning to smile at her. "Oh! Well – see for yourself, my dear!" Bending over, he pulled his left pant leg up nearly to his knee. Libby squinted, confused, until she realized what it was that looked so odd in the flickering firelight: the leg beneath the lifted cuff was made of wood.

Pullman dropped the pant leg and turned back toward the shack. "Good night, my friends. Get some sleep; we'll start early in the morning."

As the door of the shack closed, Scab made a wordless sound of disgust. Libby looked at him, surprised. She thought he might say something, but he only spat into the fire, which hissed briefly, then went back to its quiet crackling.

"Roach," she said, "what... what *was* that... what Mr. Pullman did to those men in the woods?"

Roach poked at the fire, then gave a small, rueful tilt of his head. "Well, sis... he needed to send a message." He hesitated, glancing at Scab as if for help; but Scab only gazed into the fire, his face impassive, so Roach continued. "Sorry you had to see it. Not that they didn't have it comin', but it ain't too pleasant to watch." He frowned. "Had to be done, though. See, them fellas, they was just the *tools*, like. What ol' Pullman done there, he sent a message to the one *usin'* the tools. The way that works, what he done to those *men*, well, it gets passed on back to whoever *sent* 'em. What he done to them, it happened to *him*, too."

Libby looked up, startled. "You mean – it happened to *Fuller?*"

Scab gave a short, scornful exhalation, and Libby glanced at him, confused.

Roach shook his head. "No, sis – 'fraid ol' Pullman don't quite have the horsepower to get all the way back to... to John Fuller hisself. It'll be someone workin' for Fuller – someone about on a level with Pullman, I reckon." He grinned. "Whoever it is, though, he's sure gonna think twice before crossin' ol' Pullman again!"

The Birds of the Air | 87

Libby frowned. "Level with Pullman? So, you mean... Mr. *Pullman* works for someone?"

Roach darted another nervous glance at Scab. "Aw, there I go, shootin' my mouth off again," he clucked, fidgeting with the stick he'd been using to stir the fire. "I reckon ol' Pullman'll wanna tell you about all that hisself, sis." He tossed the stick into the fire and drained his coffee cup. "Guess I'll get some shut-eye. See ya in the mornin'." And he too disappeared into the small shack, closing the door softly behind him.

Libby turned her puzzled frown toward Scab, but he stood up and flicked the butt of his cigarette into the fire with Roach's stick. "Don't look at *me*," he mumbled, and started to move away; but then he paused and turned a level gaze on her. "Tell you one thing, though. Wasn't nothin' *Pullman* did helped us find you so quick." He scanned the dark treetops, which swayed and whispered in the night breeze. "Somethin' come in from the outside. Hit 'ol' Pullman' like a mule-kick to the head; just about put 'im on the ground." He looked back down at Libby. "Don't know where it come from, but one thing I *do* know: it scared the *shit* out a' Pullman." He gave his ghost of a smile, then turned and headed toward the path into the forest, the firelight picking his form out faintly until he slipped into the trees and became a shadow among all the others.

THAT NIGHT, SLEEPING in Pullman's shack, Libby dreamed she was there in the daytime, sitting on the cot. Leaf-dappled sunlight slanted through the window, and she noticed some tiny thing moving through the shifting circles of light it made on the floor. She blinked, and found herself lying with her cheek against a floorboard, one eye almost level with the thing that had made the movement: a miniscule spider, smaller than a grape seed, translucent in the sunlight.

The minuteness of the spider made the floor beyond it look like a vast plain, and Libby worried about what would happen to it there. She wanted to move it to safety, but she couldn't imagine how she could pick up such a tiny creature without crushing it. She sensed a presence beside her and looked up to see a tall man, someone she had never seen before, smiling down at her. She feared he would take a step and inadvertently crush the little spider, but instead he rolled back a sleeve of his faded work-shirt, and pulled a thread from the frayed seam inside. He bent down beside Libby, and lowered one end of the thread to the floor in front of the spider. At first the little creature ran away, but the man continued patiently until at last the spider was coaxed onto the thread. Rising, he carried the thread, with the spider clinging to it, to the open window, and laid it on a leaf of the lilac bush from back home, which now dangled its heavy blossoms just outside.

The man turned an easy smile on Libby. He had sand-colored hair and a weather-worn face. When Libby looked up into his eyes, she saw without surprise that they were the pale-gray eyes of the scarecrow. He reached to the shelves on the wall and took down one of Pullman's books. Opening it, he turned the pages toward Libby, and she saw there was something wrong with it. It took her a few moments to figure out what it was, but then with a beat of recognition she saw it: it looked like a book in a mirror. Every sentence, every word, every letter – all were printed backwards.

CHAPTER SEVEN

THE NEXT MORNING, they were in the meadow before the sun had fully risen. The woods around them rang with bird-song, and the tall grass had soaked their pant legs by the time they reached the hickory tree. The cage hung just as Libby had seen it last: empty, door open, the little wooden figure propped inside. She saw the mark carved into the tree, and almost spoke up to ask Pullman about it – to tell him she had seen it on one of the men in the woods – but he turned to her and spoke first. "All right, Libby. Take the figure out of the cage."

She stood on tiptoe and reached in to retrieve the little image, lifting it out carefully. Roach and Scab had hung back a bit, but Pullman beckoned them, and they crossed through the grass to where he and Libby stood. "I want the two of you to check the woods around the edge of this clearing," Pullman told them. "Make sure we weren't followed, and that no one is watching. Be thorough. We can't have Fuller's people knowing where our terminus is."

As Roach and Scab headed off toward the trees in opposite directions, Pullman turned to Libby. He laid a hand on each of her shoulders, his expression grave. "Libby, I must speak to you now as if you were an adult. I had hoped to spare you the more disturbing details of... well." He looked down for a moment, then raised his eyes to hers again, his bloodstained gaze unsettling. "Libby, something is standing in the way of our call to your sister. Something in *you*." Libby took in a sharp breath, startled, but he held up a hand to stop her from interrupting. "A calling like the one we're attempting here – it's not like the crude, brutal methods those men who took you were planning to employ. A procedure like this – well, its power stems from *desire*, from *longing*: the longing of the caller for the person called. I'm acting as your proxy, or... your *transmitter*, you might say. But it's *you* who are sending the call – or *should* be. So I need you to tell me, honestly, now: what is standing in the way of your desire to have your sister back?"

Libby began to splutter a protest, but Pullman stopped her short, giving her shoulders a sharp shake. "Elizabeth, there is *no more time* for the comfort of self-deception. Fuller's people are *upon* us. And have you for one moment considered the anguish your *mother* must be suffering, while you fritter the days away, nattering on with Roach and playing at camping?" He shook his head. "I've spared you full knowledge of the danger your sister is in, but I can do so no longer."

Libby dropped her eyes and tried to pull away, but Pullman held her fast and spoke more gently. "There are a certain few people, very rare, who possess an inborn... *ability*, I've called it, or you could say... capacity, or gift. They are born with the power to bend the laws of nature to a greater or lesser degree. It's what you saw me do in the forest yesterday. Libby –" he gave her another little shake and waited until she lifted her eyes to meet his – "your sister is such a person."

Of course, Libby thought bitterly, and was immediately ashamed that this should be her first reaction. But defiance sprang up, contending with the shame. *Of course: Maisie is* always *the special one. No wonder my mother..."* but she stopped herself short, her cheeks blazing. What a horrible person she must be. She forced herself to meet Pullman's gaze, to focus on what he was saying.

"John Fuller is a predator; he preys upon the weak in order to satisfy his own appetite for power. He's discovered a way to tap into the capacities of children like your sister; to steal their power and use it to amplify his own. He *drains* them; he *enslaves* them; he prevents them from living, yet will not allow them to die – until, that is, he has used them up, which happens very quickly. He is always searching, Libby – always looking for new victims, new fuel. As I said, such children are extremely rare, and Fuller is so greedy, so immoderate, so profligate in his use of their power, that he is continually desperate to find more. He'll do *anything* to regain possession of your sister, Libby – and if he does, believe me, it would be better for her if she were dead."

All the blood that shame had brought rushing to Libby's face seemed suddenly to drain away, leaving her dizzy and light-headed, unable to fully take in what Pullman was saying. She swayed, and his hands on her shoulders steadied her as she sank to her knees in the grass, Pullman going stiffly to one knee with her.

Maisie.

Maisie.

Her impish smile, her flyaway corn-silk hair. The silly little jokes she made, her eyes shining up at Libby, eager to share her enjoyment. The way she trusted Libby, idolized her, wanting to know what she thought about everything. And how often Libby had been impatient, unkind, irritable, selfish – jealous.

Anguish came slamming up inside her, just as it had on the day she found the dead bird; it felt solid as an upheaval of rock, as if it would crush her heart and lungs. She doubled over, gasping for breath, and the awful animal moan she hated escaped from her again.

Pullman's grip remained steady on her shoulders. "I don't fault you, my dear. It's natural to try to hide from pain. But, for Maisie's sake –"

"*Please*, Mr. Pullman," Libby broke in; "I'm sorry; I'm so sorry. Please, *please,* help me. I want my little sister back." Tears came, washing away the last of her flimsy barricade of indignation.

Pullman relaxed visibly. He pulled out his pocketknife and unfolded the blade, but instead of reaching for Libby's hand to prick her finger again, he put his own hand gently to the back of her head and raised the knife toward her face. Libby flinched a bit, Roach's words about the sacrifice of eyes flashing wildly through her head, but Pullman held her steady: "Stay still, child; I won't hurt you." He lifted the small blade to her face and slid it, blunt side toward her skin, up her cheek beneath her left eye. She looked down at the blade as he lowered it, and saw that it was wet with her tears. He took the hand in which she held the little wooden figure. "We had tears before," he said, "but only the meager tears of frustration and anxiety." He tilted the blade so the moisture ran down to form a droplet at its point. "These are the much more costly tears of grief confronted, of heartfelt contrition." He pressed the point to the hole in the figure's chest, and the droplet soaked in where Libby's blood had gone before. He raised his eyes and smiled. "I don't believe we'll fail this time."

BACK IN THE clearing, Pullman gave Roach some money, and directed him to go into town and buy clothes to replace Libby's old ones, which had been badly torn in her ordeal with the men in the woods. "Mind you buy *boys'* clothes, not girls'," he said. "We don't want your man at the shop becoming curious."

Scab had stayed near the meadow to keep an eye on the cage – just in case, in spite of all precautions, some of Fuller's people had discovered where it was. Pullman looked haggard and exhausted, but he brought the chair from the shack out to sit with Libby where she perched on one of the logs. "I'll lie down for a bit when Roach gets back," he said. "I don't feel quite easy leaving you on your own just yet."

"Do you think those men will come *back*, Mr. Pullman?" Libby peered into the shadows beyond the edge of the clearing, queasy at the thought.

"I don't think so, my dear." He gave her a grim smile. "I believe those particular fellows have been sufficiently discouraged. But the fact that *they* knew you are here means others may, too. Fuller offers substantial payment to any degenerate who can deliver a child like Maisie to him, and *you* have become the easiest route to that money. I suspect rumors of your presence have begun to circulate, perhaps from some who saw you arrive here, or those miscreants you met on the train." He sighed, his shoulders bowed. "Fuller's parasites are everywhere. But don't worry, my dear: we'll keep you safe. We'll keep a much closer watch from now on."

Libby didn't feel completely reassured, but the mention of

the men on the train brought a recollection that caused curiosity to push up through her uneasiness. "Mr. Pullman," she said, "when we were on that train, and those men were bothering us, Scab said a name that made them stop. He showed them something inside his shirt, and said a name." She frowned at a dandelion she was idly twirling between her fingers. "It *scared* them... but I can't remember what it was." She looked up at Pullman. "Do *you* know?"

Pullman's brows twitched together for an instant, and he patted his pockets. "Now where did I – ahh." He pulled out his pipe and tobacco. "A name... a name." He filled the pipe and lit it, sending out smoke in quick puffs that reminded Libby of a train engine. "Well," he said finally, shaking out the match, "there's no telling, my dear. These hobos are steeped in superstition." He chuckled. "Our young Scab is a wily one. He probably just used the name of some bogeyman these ignorant men tell stories about, to frighten one another."

She dropped her eyes back to the dandelion. "Mr. Pullman," she said hesitantly, "I'm – I'm really sorry about all the trouble I've caused you, and Roach, and Scab."

Pullman turned toward her, about to protest, and she hurried to make her meaning clear. "I'm sorry I made – everything – take *longer* than it should have." She wrapped her arms around her ribcage, holding herself tight and still, as if her words were pebbles that might trigger an avalanche. "It's not that I don't want my sister back. I *do*, Mr. Pullman; that's why I *came* here! It's just that... my mother... she sort of didn't seem to *care* about anything, after Maisie was gone. I know it was awful for her, but it was awful for *me*, too! I know I should have been thinking about Maisie, and I *was*, but I also couldn't help thinking –" her voice caught, and she paused to steady it – "I couldn't help thinking it seemed like Mama *only* cared about Maisie... like she didn't care about me at all."

"But you *mustn't* think that, Libby!" Pullman placed a hand on her shoulder, and bent to meet her eyes with a serious gaze. "Parents are often woefully blind to the needs of their own children, but that doesn't mean they don't *care*. They may love you with all their hearts, and still not have the remotest idea how to give you what you need. That's why it's not always *parents* who are the best—" but he broke off, shaking his head with a quick, dismissive jerk. "The point is, my dear, you can't judge your mother's love for you by her behavior under such dreadful circumstances." He patted her shoulder. "After all, now, you're not so proud of the way all this has affected your *own* behavior, are you?"

Libby looked up at him quickly, but his sad smile was not unkind. She gave him a hesitant smile in return, surprised to find that his words had made her feel a bit better.

He lifted his hand from her shoulder, and rubbed his eyes. "I'm sorry, as well, Libby – sorry that I spoke so harshly to you in the meadow. I hope you understand."

Libby smiled at him more resolutely. "I understand. *Thank you, Mr. Pullman* – thank you for *everything*."

Pullman blinked, his brows once again twitching together; then he rose abruptly from the chair and clamped his pipe between his teeth. "Well," he said around its stem, "let's get some wood and mend the fire, shall we? You'll be wanting hot water for a bath when Roach gets back with your new clothes."

WHEN ROACH RETURNED – bringing stiff new blue jeans and a boy's cotton shirt for Libby, and even, to her embarrassment, some boys' underclothing – Pullman went to rest in the small shack. He only stayed there for an hour or so, though, before coming out to relieve Scab from his watch in the meadow.

Roach had brought back stew meat and vegetables for supper, and Libby helped him to peel potatoes and chop carrots while they waited for water to heat for her bath. When the last heavy stewpot-full was steaming, Roach – lifting it off the fire to carry it to the washtub in Pullman's shack – nodded toward the water pail. "Run fetch me one more bucket to cook with, would ya, sis?" he said. "Bring as much as you can carry, now!"

Libby carried the bucket along the short path to the main trail, crossed the trail to the creek, filled the bucket, and turned to head back. As she emerged from the bushes edging the creek, staggering a bit from the weight of the bucket, she glimpsed movement some distance down the trail. Turning toward it, she saw Scab, his back toward her and his bearing tense. He was blocking the way of some shorter, stockier person, and his right hand chopped sideways in a gesture of fierce prohibition. The pair was far enough away that, though Libby could hear the angry tone of Scab's voice and the aggrieved bluster of the other's, she couldn't make out their words clearly. All at once, the shorter man made a clumsy attempt to push past Scab, and Libby felt a scalding jolt of shock flash through her: it was the stumpy, red-faced tramp who had given Maisie the sugar bird.

She dropped the bucket, dousing her legs and feet with cold water, and bolted down the path into the clearing. "Roach!" she cried; "It's *him*! It's that man – the one who tried to steal Maisie! He's out on the trail with Scab!"

Roach's cheerful face clouded. "You stay *right here*, sis," he said. Taking the knife he had been using to cut up the meat, he hurried off toward the trail.

The Birds of the Air | 97

Libby jittered at the edge of the clearing, straining her ears to catch any hint of what was going on. Her eyes darted around the borders of the forest; she feared the tramp might have accomplices, and had purposely drawn Scab and Roach away to leave her alone.

As she turned to scan the far side of the clearing, the wind rose abruptly, tossing the high branches, filling the air with a soft-edged roar. There was a change in the sunlight, as if the rising wind had blown away an unnoticed haze. At the corner of her eye she caught movement at the mouth of the path and turned quickly, expecting to see Scab or Roach. She was startled to see, instead, a woman approaching – a youngish colored woman in a travel-worn dress. The woman's expression was pleasant, but Libby was fearful now of any stranger; she backed away, stumbling, and called out to Roach.

"He couldn't hear you right now, honey, even if he was close enough," the woman said, in a calm voice as pleasant as her face. "You and me, we're in a kind of a bubble. Ain't nobody can hear you but me, and ain't nobody can hear me but you."

Libby kept backing toward Pullman's shack, but the woman stopped on the far side of the fire pit. Her quiet voice seemed to slip beneath the sound of the wind, reaching Libby's ears as if she were much closer than she really was. "Don't be scared, honey," she said. "I ain't gonna try to run off with you, or nothin' like that."

There was a hint of laughter beneath her words, and something about her voice – or about the sound of the wind in the treetops – seemed to lull Libby's fear. A bit of the tension eased from her body, and she stopped moving away.

"I just come with a message, is all," the woman went on. "And I got somethin' for you." She slipped a hand into the pocket of her dress, took out some small object, and placed it in a depression on the surface of one of the logs; then she backed away a few steps.

Curious, reassured that the woman was keeping her distance, Libby edged a bit closer to see what she had left. It was a tiny glass vial, like the ones her grandmother's eye-drops came in – only an inch or so tall, and about as big around as her little finger. It was filled with clear liquid that looked like water.

"Now you need to pay attention, honey," the woman said. "Your little sister's on her way. She'll be here before sundown."

Libby's heart gave a jackrabbit leap, but the woman lifted a hand to keep her from interrupting. "Now: when she get here, if it's any way you can, you get to her *first*, before any of these menfolk do. Either that, or you wait till it's no one around but her and you. Remember that: *no one else around*. Might be you'll have to wait till everyone's asleep. Then you gotta take her out of that cage. Be real careful, now – hold her gentle, but don't let her fly off." She demonstrated with her empty hands, holding an imaginary bird in one and cupping the other over it. "They don't always remember folks so well, once they been changed." She pointed to the vial where it lay on the log. "Then you need to put a drop of that on her. Just one drop's enough. You oughta have you a blanket or some spare clothes handy, too; she gonna be naked as a jay-bird when she change back." The woman lifted both hands, as if to hold Libby's attention between them. "Now this here part's real important, honey: the minute she change, the two of you gotta *get on out a' this jungle*, quick an' quiet as you can. Don't let none a' these men see you. Follow the creek on down to the river, then follow the river downstream a ways, and you'll see the town, right there by the train bridge. When you get into town, just walk right up to any grown person you see looks like they got any sense, and tell 'em who you are and what town you come from. They'll take you to the police station, and the folks there'll help the two of you get back home to your mama." She paused, giving Libby a searching look, as if to see whether her words had sunk in. "It's up to you, honey: you can believe what I'm tellin' you, or not. But if you decide to do what I say, do it quick as you can. You and your sister ain't safe here." She smiled. "You'll find you can't tell nobody about this, but everything else is up to you. John Fuller says, don't believe everything you hear. John Fuller says, if ever you need him, just call."

At Fuller's name, Libby started, as if she had been dozing and jolted awake. She blinked and looked around, but the woman was nowhere to be seen. The wind had died, and the clearing was still, except for the crickets and cicadas making their usual racket. She rubbed her eyes, wondering if she really had been dreaming, and had walked in her sleep. She looked down at the depression in the log, and her breath gave a little jerk. The little vial was still there.

She reached out a hand, but hesitated, nervous about touching it. She glanced around the empty clearing again. After a moment, she picked it up – the glass cool between her fingers – and slipped it into her pocket.

BY THE TIME Roach returned, the odd, dreamy calm that had come over Libby during the woman's brief stay in the clearing had worn off, and she was nearly vibrating with anxiety. Roach still looked troubled when he came along the path, but he assured Libby that he and Scab had sent the tramp on his way.

"But he'll come *back*!" Libby cried. She seized his arm, trying to pull him back down the path the way he had just come. "He wants to get Maisie! We have to tell Mr. Pullman!"

"Scab's over there lettin' Pullman know now," Roach said, patting her hand, soothing. "We'll keep your sis safe; don't you fret, now." He set down the empty bucket, which he had retrieved from the trail. "Now: let's get that bath for ya, so you can warsh up an' put them new clothes on. Reckon we'll hafta start all over heatin' the water; it'll be stone cold by now."

Libby wondered if she should tell Roach about the woman, but something inside her seemed not quite ready.

After she had bathed and changed, she sat watching Roach cut up onions. "Boy oh boy," he said, eyes watering, eyebrows peaked with worry. "They sure are comin' out a' the wood-work now."

He meant Fuller's people, Libby knew, and she fingered the little vial in her pocket. The woman who gave it to her hadn't seemed evil or frightening – hadn't seemed even to be of the same world as the men who had dragged her into the forest. How could they all work for the same person? But if the woman *didn't* work for Fuller, how had she known about Maisie? Maybe the woman didn't know what Fuller was really like; maybe he had fooled her somehow.

Scab came stalking into the clearing – hackles still up, Libby thought, from the clash with the tramp on the trail. She looked around at the woods with a shiver. Who knew how many there were like the tramp, or the men in the woods, or the men on the train, maybe watching them from the undergrowth right now? She felt suddenly exhausted to the point of tears. The cursing man had been right: there was a whole separate, terrifying world hidden beneath the one she had lived in all her life, and he and his companions had been only her first glimpse of it.

The afternoon dragged. Roach's chatter, usually comforting, today seemed to have a strained edge that grated on Libby's nerves. Scab had apparently been directed by Pullman to stick close to the campsite; he divided the time between prowling the edges of the clearing and throwing his jackknife, from five or six paces away, into the wall of the small shack. He had drawn the rough, life-sized outline of a man on the boards with a charred stick, and he sent the knife spinning through the air over and over – aimed at the neck, not at the chest as Libby would have expected. The knife struck with a loud *thunk*, its point sunk into the wood right where the throat would be almost every time. Watching from her perch by the fire, Libby was both deeply impressed and vaguely unnerved.

Her head ached from endlessly circling thoughts about what the strange woman had said, what Pullman had told her about Maisie, and what he had told her about John Fuller. She fervently hoped the woman had been right about Maisie coming soon. She had to guard herself against the horror that overwhelmed her when she imagined Maisie – who dearly loved the tiny yellow flowers of creeping wood sorrel, and the pill-bugs that lived beneath the stones at the edge of the garden; who still sometimes slipped into Libby's bed at night and curled up in a warm ball against her, as if she were a pill-bug herself – falling into Fuller's hands. Recoiling for the hundredth time from this idea, she thought instead of the cage in the meadow and the mysterious symbol above it. "Roach," she said, "what's that picture with the eye, that's carved on the tree in the meadow? I saw it tattooed on one of those men in the woods, too."

Roach darted a glance over his shoulder toward Scab, who paused, arm drawn back, to meet it briefly with his dark, impenetrable gaze, then returned his attention to the shack and sent the knife spinning to strike into the wood again, *thunk*, and vibrate there.

"Oh, that?" Roach turned back to Libby with his nervous giggle. "That ain't nothin' but a hobo sign, sis. Just means, like, 'keep your hands off, this don't belong to you.'"

"Oh..." Libby thought for a moment, jabbing at the dirt with a stick. "Then... why would that man have it tattooed on him?"

Roach shrugged, fidgeting with the rag he used as a hot-pad for cooking. "Maybe jest a joke, like. Or, kinda fella he was, maybe tryin' to act tough, like sayin', 'you best not mess with me.'"

Libby frowned. Something about what Roach was saying, or the way he was saying it, didn't sound quite right to her. And with a little quivering feeling at the back of her neck, she realized she had felt the same way about Pullman's answer when she had asked him about the name Scab had said on the train: both times, the answers had rung false. She wondered if there was something bad that Pullman and Roach were trying to shield her from, the way they had shielded her at first from the awful details about Fuller.

Just then, she heard Pullman shout a greeting from the path outside the clearing. She happened to be looking at Scab, and his reaction to Pullman's call struck her as odd: his head dropped and his shoulders sagged, as if all the energy had gone out of him. She might have thought more about it, but at that moment the words Pullman had said sank belatedly into her mind: "She's here at last, my friends! We've *got* her!"

CHAPTER EIGHT

THE DAY THE tramp had transformed Maisie, Libby had only seen her for a moment before she flew away. Now, looking into the cage, she felt unmoored. Her mind reeled between two certainties: the certainty demanded by a lifetime of lessons and experiences, that the little creature within couldn't possibly be her sister, and her own bone-deep certainty that it *was*.

Maisie looked just the same as when Libby had last seen her: a small buff-and-rust sparrow with extraordinary cornflower-blue eyes. She looked none the worse for her long journey, and perched brightly in the little cage, cocking first one eye and then the other at Libby. She behaved just like any little bird, and this shook Libby a bit. "Do you think she remembers me, Mr. Pullman? Do you think she knows what's happened?"

"Perhaps not at the moment, my dear. But don't fret: she's young and resilient. She'll be her own little self again, as soon as we restore her."

"Can we do it *now*?"

"In the morning, my dear." Pullman patted her shoulder. "I'll need a bit of time to prepare."

Libby felt ready to burst with impatience. She remembered the vial, and reached into her pocket, meaning to bring it out and show it to Pullman, ask him if they could use it. But somehow her mind wandered, her hand slipped back out of her pocket empty, and it was only several minutes later that she remembered what she had meant to do. She slid her hand back in to do it again, but the same thing happened. A few minutes later, when she realized with a little start that she had failed once more to draw out the vial, the woman's words came back to her: *You'll find you can't tell nobody about this... get on out a' this jungle, quick an' quiet as you can... don't let none a' these men see you... you and your sister ain't safe here.* Libby felt a shadow of disquiet slide between her and the joy of recovering Maisie, but it only lasted a moment. Why should she trust a stranger over Pullman – a stranger who all but admitted she came from John Fuller? Pullman had gotten Maisie back, just as he promised, and in the morning he would restore her. Libby would take her back to their mother; Mama would see that Libby had been right to go after her, would forgive her for losing her, would love her for returning her. Everything would be as it had been before – no; *better* than before, at least between Libby and her mother. Gratitude toward Pullman expanded in her chest, buoyant as a hot-air balloon.

As the evening sunlight slanted across the treetops, they ate Roach's stew, with biscuits he had baked in the skillet. Libby fed Maisie crumbs, and slipped a tin cup of water into the cage for her to drink from.

Dusk fell as Roach and Libby washed the pots and dishes in the creek. When they were seated by the fire again, Pullman went

The Birds of the Air | 105

into his shack and came out with a bottle. It must have been in the locked trunk, because Libby had never seen it before. It held clear liquid, and had no label. Pullman poured some into his tin cup, and some into Roach's; he offered the bottle to Scab, but Scab shook his head without looking up. The smell of the alcohol drifted toward Libby, raising awful specters of the men on the train, the men in the forest. Another twinge of uneasiness brushed her mind, but once again it passed quickly. Pullman and Roach were not villainous brutes like those other men. They were trusted protectors, rescuers of her and her sister.

Taking Maisie's cage with her, she moved to sit on the log beside Pullman. As Roach chattered on about something or other, she reached shyly and took Pullman's hand; when he turned to her, mild surprise in his face, she beamed up at him. "*Thank you*, Mr. Pullman," she said, with all her heart in the words. "Thank you *so much.*"

Pullman looked down at her hand holding his; the lines around his eyes deepened for a moment, as they did when one of his headaches came on, but he smiled. He looked as if he was about to speak, but Scab's voice cut in, stark as a slap to the face:

"When you gonna tell her?"

Roach's chatter ceased as if it had been chopped off with a knife, and the clearing was suddenly dead silent, except for the crackle of the fire and the whir of insects.

Libby, still looking into Pullman's face, saw him freeze. His smile vanished, but his voice was level. "What concern is that of yours?"

Scab made the scoffing sound that served as his laugh. "What you still pretendin' for? You got what you wanted." He nodded toward Maisie's cage.

Libby flinched as Pullman shot up from his seat. Scab sprang to his feet as well, and Libby, shocked, saw his hand rise reflexively to the pocket where he kept his razor. She was dimly aware of Roach's white face on the other side of the fire, his eyes, big as fifty-cent pieces, turned up toward Pullman. But Pullman made no further move toward Scab; he only fixed him with a bloodstained glare. "I do not need *you*, Stephen McCafferty, to remind me of my responsibilities." His voice was quiet, but the sound of it made Libby think of something that would send off sparks; at the use of the name, she thought she saw Scab brace himself slightly, as if against a strong wind. "I have every intention of speaking to Libby," Pullman said. "It was my *hope* – though I suppose now you have made it impracticable – to choose a time when it would be as easy on her as possible."

"Easy on *you*, you mean," Scab said. "I'll do what you want – I'll take her on home." He glanced at Libby briefly, and she recognized an expression she had never seen in his face before: pity. "But I don't aim to be the one stuck here answerin' all the questions."

Pullman glared at Scab for a moment longer; then his anger seemed, all at once, to desert him. His shoulders sagged; he laid a hand on Libby's shoulder. "You two watch Maisie for a bit," he said. "Libby, come with me."

Libby was shaken by the confrontation, but she rose to follow. After a couple of steps she paused, looking back at the cage. "Can't I bring Maisie with us, Mr. Pullman?"

"She'll be fine here for a few minutes, my dear. Come along."

Libby looked back again, reluctant; but Maisie seemed safe, guarded by Scab and Roach. She turned and followed Pullman into the shack.

Pullman lit the lantern, then pushed the door most of the way closed. He motioned for Libby to sit on the cot, moved the chair, and sat facing her, leaning forward with his elbows on his knees and his hands clasped together. "Well, Libby, I imagine you're wondering what all that was about?"

"Yes, sir." Libby felt a bit timid after witnessing his anger at Scab, and her voice came out a little shaky.

Pullman looked down at his hands; the lantern stood behind him, and his face was in shadow. "Libby... I'm afraid I haven't been completely honest with you." He paused and bounced his clasped hands up and down a couple of times, as if the words he was searching for might fall from them like salt from a shaker. "I have what I believe are good reasons, which I'll try to explain to you; and although I've little hope that you're old enough to understand just yet, I do hope that, someday, you will." He raised his eyes to meet hers, and Libby felt a seed of apprehension taking root in her, both at his words and at the sadness in his gaze.

"Libby, do you remember what I told you earlier today, about parents? How I said that they may love their children, yet still be unable to give them what they need?"

"Yes, sir."

"And do you remember what I told you about people like your sister, people with special abilities – how rare they are?"

"Yes, sir."

He sighed. "I know this is too much for me to expect you to take in, all in one day, my dear, but I'm afraid I've run out of time. These people – Fuller's people... they'll know Maisie is here soon, if they don't know already."

Libby felt a tightening in her chest. Pullman was right – Fuller's people *did* know. The strange woman in the clearing had said Maisie would be here soon, as if she knew exactly where she was.

Pullman was still speaking, and Libby pulled her concentration back to what he was saying. "The world is in a desperate state, Libby. There are storms brewing overseas that –" he broke off and shook his head, then closed his eyes for a moment as if to gather his thoughts. When he opened them again, they were lit with a fervor Libby had never seen in him before. "Children like your sister, Libby – they hold the potential to *change* things, to finally remedy the ills of the world that past generations have only managed to worsen. But in order to do that, these exceptional children need what past generations have failed to give them: guidance, education, enlightenment. They need to have their abilities *cultivated*, *disciplined*, by people who understand what they are. Does any of this make sense to you, Libby?"

Libby nodded, but her apprehension deepened. She wasn't sure why, but Pullman's words were beginning to stir a sense of dread in her, as if he had taken her hand and was leading her somewhere she didn't want to go.

"The difficult thing is, Libby, it's seldom the *parents* of these children who are best equipped to give them the upbringing they need – to liberate and perfect in them the qualities that will so benefit mankind. The old ways aren't working anymore, Libby – if indeed they ever did. And aside from all that, as *you've* seen all too clearly, it is not the *parents* of these children who are best equipped to protect them from John Fuller."

Libby found herself on her feet before she even realized she intended to move. She stared at him for a moment; then she turned and took hold of the door handle, driven by an urgent desire to get back to Maisie, though the reason for the urgency was still not quite clear to her.

Pullman was beside her before she could pull the door open, reaching one hand to slam it shut. She looked up at him, frightened, but his expression was pleading. "Elizabeth," he said, "just listen to me for a moment longer; just try for a moment to understand."

When he said her name, Libby felt an odd tingling behind her eyes, a feeling she had never experienced before. She shook her head and blinked, and the feeling faded. Looking around her, she realized with some surprise that she was no longer at the door, but sitting on the cot again. Pullman stood between her and the door, and she saw him fish in a pocket and produce a small metal box, like the tin pill-boxes they sold in drugstores. He stepped away from the door, and set the box on the table beside the lantern. "Elizabeth Jane Barnett," he said, his deep voice musical; "such a lovely name."

Libby felt the tingling again, more strongly this time. She thought about going back to the door – now that Pullman had moved away from it – and leaving the shack. Hadn't she wanted to do that? But why? She couldn't seem to remember. She wondered how Pullman knew her middle name; she thought she was asking him, but as the tingling faded she realized she wasn't speaking after all. She shook her head, but this time it only made her feel as if her brain was loose in her skull, and was lagging behind a bit each time she moved her eyes.

Pullman was speaking again, and she squinted, trying to concentrate. "I don't expect you to understand my actions," he said. "In fact, there are very few *adults* – even those who consider themselves sophisticated, open-minded...." He trailed off with a rueful shake of his head. Distantly, as if she were looking at him through a spyglass from a long way off, Libby noticed that he still looked unhappy. He was looking down; her gaze followed his, and after a second, when her belated brain caught up, she saw he had opened the little box, and was pressing the pad of his right thumb into it. When he took his thumb out, she could see it was covered with a thin coating of light-colored powder. He did the same with his left thumb, coating it also; then he moved to stand over her. "Suffice to say I'm deeply sorry for the pain I must cause you, and I hope – I truly hope, Elizabeth – that one day you'll see this was all for the best."

He bent and placed his hands gently on the sides of her head, tilting her face up toward him. "Goodbye, my dear," he said. He moved his thumbs toward her eyes and, when she closed them, spread the powder over her eyelids. Libby could feel the slight graininess of it; and then somehow she was lying down, and Pullman was covering her with the blanket.

She felt strangely far away from everything around her. It made her think of a time when she was very small, and had blown too long and hard on a paper pinwheel her father had bought her. Afterward she had had this same dreamlike feeling of unreality. Her father had said it was because she wasn't getting enough air.

She peered across the room toward the table, where Pullman was opening the suitcase. She didn't know when he had pulled it from beneath the cot. The distance between him and her was vast; she wondered how she could ever have imagined the shack to be small. She noticed he had unlocked and opened the trunk, and was transferring things from it to the suitcase. She had a feeling that, only a short time ago, she would have been very curious to see what those things were. Now she was just so tired, and Pullman and the things he was packing were so very far away from her, that it didn't seem important.

There was *something* important, though, wasn't there? Something she should stay awake for, take care of? Something terrible she had almost figured out? She felt so certain of it, and so alarmed by the certainty, that she tried to fight off the tide of darkness pulling at her mind, tried to will herself to sit up. Her body wouldn't obey her. She struggled, as she had against the men who carried her into the forest, but with no more success: she could still see Pullman, far off across the expanding room, but she couldn't speak to him, couldn't lift her hand to reach out. Yet there must have been some tremor in a finger or catch in her breath, because Pullman looked up at her, frowning. He skirted the table and took an immeasurable time crossing the floor between them; he bent to lay a hand on her forehead. Even then, it seemed to her she was looking up at him from a great depth, and his voice echoed down, faint, remote. He murmured some words she couldn't understand, and she heard him say, "Sleep now, Elizabeth" – and then she heard and saw nothing more.

PART 2: JAEGER

CHAPTER NINE

WHEN LIBBY WOKE, daylight shone through the little window. Her head ached, right behind her eyes, and her mind was foggy. She sat up on the cot, and saw the trunk standing open. She had *seen* Pullman open the trunk, hadn't she? She remembered coming into the shack with him, but her memories after that were hazy and strange. She thought she must have fallen asleep and begun to dream while he was talking to her.

She rose and went to look into the trunk. It held an untidy drift of papers, many of them maps, and a couple of empty tin boxes. She remembered Pullman putting the suitcase on the table, but it wasn't there now, nor was it in its usual place beneath the cot.

Looking up, she noticed that all of Pullman's books were gone from the shelves on the wall, along with his folded clothing. She felt a knot beginning to form in her stomach. What had Pullman been saying the night before? Something about parents not being the right ones to raise their children? Something about Maisie?

She shook her head. She must have dreamed all that. She must have been so worn out from everything that had happened yesterday that she had fallen asleep while Pullman was talking to her. She would go and apologize to him, and ask him what he had wanted to say.

She went to the door, but it wouldn't open. She pulled again, harder, then pushed and pulled alternately, as hard as she could. The door moved back and forth a bit, something on the other side making rattling noises, but it wouldn't open. "Mr. Pullman?" she called, pounding on the wood. "Roach?"

She heard the rattle of the bolt sliding back; the door opened, and morning light flooded in. Shading her eyes, she saw Scab's rangy form silhouetted in the doorway. He turned, not looking at her, and started back toward the fire, his face set in a frown that looked less fierce than usual, but more unhappy.

"What'd you lock me *in* for?" She demanded, stepping out, blinking in the bright sunlight.

"Didn't. Pullman done it."

She stared at him. "Why?" She looked around the clearing. "Where's Maisie?"

Scab didn't answer; he sat down and began scooping coffee from its blue tin into the battered coffeepot. Libby started toward the small shack, but Scab's voice stopped her. "She ain't in there." When she turned to look at him, he had stopped scooping and was just sitting there, eyes on the tin in his hand. "They cleared out, 'round midnight last night."

"What do you mean? *Who* cleared out?"

"All of 'em. Pullman, Roach – your little sis." He put down the coffee tin, and rubbed one hand hard over his eyes and

The Birds of the Air | 117

forehead, still not looking at her. "I'm takin' you back home. Pullman said to tell you, your sis'll be better off. He said don't bother tellin' no one, because they won't believe you. He said to tell you, you don't know his real name, and not to bother sendin' no one here, because we won't be 'round here no more." His voice was bitter, and when he finished this recitation he spat into the fire, as he had done on the night when she first heard him and Pullman arguing.

Libby felt as if his words were floating on the surface of her mind, unable to sink in. She stared at him, as baffled as if he had spoken in a foreign language, yet there was a voice inside her already saying, *you knew it! You knew last night! Why didn't you DO something? You've lost her – you've lost her AGAIN!*

Without a word she turned and ran, across the clearing toward the path that led to the stream. She would catch up with them. They would have gone down the trail to the river, then along the river toward town, wouldn't they? Pullman, with his bad leg, wouldn't take the sort of cross-country ways Scab had brought her. Maybe something had held them up; maybe there was still time. There *had* to be. She couldn't lose her sister again. There had to still be time to catch them.

Before she had even gotten to the path, Scab had caught up to her. He grabbed her, his arm around her ribs as tight as the hoop around a barrel. She thrashed and kicked her bare feet, screaming hoarsely, but he lifted her, holding her off the ground. "Ain't no use, kid," he said, panting a little, and the gruff pity in his voice brought it home to her at last that there was no chance of catching up to Pullman. She went limp, collapsing into hopeless tears.

Scab let her down, and she crumpled into a heap in the long grass, her face hidden in her arms. "Pullman's got a car," he said, close by, as if he had squatted down beside her. "Keeps it in town. They're long gone, kid."

She wept for a long time. Something inside her chest felt crushed, like a tin can that had been stepped on. For some reason, the thought of Pullman hurt her just as much as the thought of Maisie, and a fresh stab of anguish struck her every time a memory of him surfaced: his grave concern; his courteous manner; his rescue of her from the men in the woods; his miraculous retrieval of her sister. She had thought all those things were motivated by kindness, and maybe even a little fondness for her: fondness like a father might feel for his daughter. Now, every one of them scalded her, like Pullman's blood had scalded the faces of those men.

Scab said nothing more, and after a while she realized he had risen quietly and gone back to the fire. When the tears finally loosened their grip on her, she pushed herself up from the damp grass and rubbed her sleeve across her face. Scab sat by the fire, holding a coffee cup and frowning into the flames. He didn't look up as she crossed to the log opposite him and sat down. "You want anything to eat?" He said at last. The pity was still in his voice, giving it a clumsy, inexpert gentleness. Libby shook her head, and he nodded, stood up, and threw the last of his coffee into the fire. "Reckon we better head out then. We're gonna have to hike on back to that bend where we ditched the freight, an' wait there to jump one headed the other way. Pullman don't want us goin' nowhere near town. Roach seen pictures of you an' your sis in the post office there yesterday."

He picked up the coffeepot and took it, with the cup, into Pullman's shack. When he came out, he was carrying Libby's shoes and the blanket from the cot. He took the padlock that hung from a hook just outside the door, shot the bolt and locked

The Birds of the Air | 119

it. He picked up the bucket of water Roach kept in front of the shack, brought it over and tossed it onto the fire, which died with a furious hiss and a billow of white smoke. Then he crossed to the small shack, went in, and came out again with another blanket and the leather bedroll-strap. He locked the door of that shack as well, and Libby watched him roll the two blankets together, tie them with the strap and sling it over his shoulder. He picked up his knapsack, already packed and lying near the fire pit, slung it over his shoulder as well, then looked down at Libby, waiting.

Libby stayed where she was, hunched on the log with her arms wrapped around herself, staring at the smoke rising from the dead fire. "I'm not going home."

Scab looked down at her for a long moment, then unslung the knapsack and the bedroll, dropped them on the ground and sat down opposite her.

"I won't go home without Maisie," she said, not looking at him. Tears started down her face again. "I *knew* something was wrong when Pullman was talking to me last night. I *knew* I should go to her. But instead I just went to *sleep*." A sickening hatred of herself rose in her chest and seemed to lodge in her throat, closing it up so the last word came out choked-sounding.

Scab gave his short, bitter laugh. "He say your name? Your *real* name?"

Libby frowned at him, puzzled, and nodded.

"He put anything on you? Blood, or some kinda powder?"

She nodded again, a bit surprised by the hazy memory. "Powder – on my eyelids."

"Ground-up bone. He *hexed* you, ya dimwit." In spite of the scornful word, the clumsy gentleness was still in his voice. "Wasn't nothin' you *could* do."

Libby thought about this, and the choking feeling eased a bit. "Scab... where is he *taking* her?"

Scab dropped his head and shook it. "Don't matter where. You gotta go *home* now, kid. Ain't nothin' you can do to get your sister back. Pullman's been soft with you so far, but don't make no mistakes: you don't wanna cross him." He gave a sideways nod toward the forest. "You seen what he done to them sons-a-bitches took you off the other day."

Libby gaped at him. Pullman would never do anything like that to *her*, would he? But – and whatever it was that was crushed in her chest contracted even further at the realization – she wasn't sure. Wasn't what he had *already* done to her even worse? The tears threatened to start up again, but she steeled herself, blinking them back. "I don't care what Pullman does to me. I don't care if he kills me dead. I'm not going home without Maisie."

Scab stood up abruptly, making an exasperated sound. "What d'ya think you're gonna *do*? How you gonna track 'em down? And even if you *could*, how the hell you think you'd ever get her *away* from him? And what would you do with her if you did? Keep her in a damn birdcage all her life?"

Libby felt her confidence leaking away; in its place, anger at Scab rose up: *he* had deceived her, as much as Pullman had. Then recollection struck her: glaring at Scab, she rose, pulled the vial from her pocket, and held it out to show him. "A lady came and gave this to me yesterday, when you were all gone. She said it would change Maisie back!" She meant to keep the part about Fuller to herself, but when she saw disbelief in Scab's face, she added, "I think... well... I think it came from John Fuller. But it might still *work*, right? The lady wanted me to change Maisie back and take her home. Maybe Fuller sent it to me so I'd take her away from Mr. Pullman, and *he'd* have another chance to get

The Birds of the Air | 121

her." This thought came to her for the first time as she said it, and it made her deeply uneasy. *But first things first,* she thought; *that's what Mama always says.*

Scab looked at the vial in her hand, his habitual frown giving way to an expression of wary interest, almost of wonder. "What makes you think it come from Fuller?"

"Well... the lady said something about him, like he was the one that sent her."

Scab took a step toward her, holding out his hand in a wordless request to look more closely at the vial. Before she had a chance to think, she had taken a hasty step backward. Her hand jerked away and shoved the vial into her pocket – in fear, she realized a second later, that he might take it from her, to force her to give up and go home. She knew immediately she had been wrong – that she should have seen he had no such intention – but it was too late. The curiosity, the openness vanished from his face in an instant; he flushed, and in the half-second his eyes met hers, she saw a swift passage from surprise to comprehension that stabbed her with remorse. Then the hardness was back in his face as if it had never left, and he turned away and scooped up the knapsack and bedroll. She tried to stammer an apology, but he cut her off. "Do what you want," he said, not looking at her. "You wanna come with me now, I'll take you on home. You don't, you're on your own. I ain't stickin' around here." He slung the straps over his shoulders and strode off toward the path.

"Wait, Scab – I'm *sorry!*" Libby ran after him and trotted alongside, her bare feet swishing in the grass, but he didn't slow down. "I didn't mean –" she stammered; "I just—"

At last, on the trail, she grabbed his arm, but he whipped around, flinging it up to break free so forcefully that she stumbled back and almost fell. His black eyes slid past her, like her mother's used to do, and he started to turn away again.

Swiftly she dug in her pocket and, pulling out the vial, sprang after him. She grabbed his hand, pressing the vial into it. "I *said* I'm *sorry,*" she panted. "But – how do you *expect* me to –" Anger flared in her, breaking off her words till the first hot rush of it passed. She glared up at him, meeting his scowl with one of her own. "I trusted *Pullman;* I trusted *Roach*, and –" tears burned her eyes again – "I trusted *you.*"

She thought she saw him wince a bit – the tiny twitch of a muscle, like the recoil of some small creature from the prick of a pin. But his eyes slid over the vial as they had slid over her, and he shoved it back into her hand. "Well, you shouldn't'a." With a jerk, he unslung one strap of his knapsack; then he undid two buttons on his shirt and yanked it open. Libby stared: there, on the left side of his chest, was a crude tattoo. It was the same mark she had seen on the tramp in the forest; the same one she had seen carved into the tree above the cage-trap: a circled, downward-pointing triangle with an eye inside it. The memory of the night in the boxcar, when he had frightened the tramps, flashed across her mind: this must have been what he showed them. And he had said a name – what was it?

"That there's Jaeger's mark," he said, as if he had heard her thought. "I work for Pullman, and Pullman works for Jaeger: Pullman, Roach, that dimwit Stubby, that came to your place an' changed your sister – even Slater, an' them bastards that hauled you off into the woods. We *all* of us work for Jaeger. We track down them kids, we go get 'em, and we send 'em to him." He jerked his shirt closed again, his eyes hard as two chips of black porcelain. "So now you know. Whatever idea you got in your head about me, you'd best get it out. I ain't no different from the

The Birds of the Air | 123

rest of 'em." He slung his knapsack back on. "Pullman told me to take you on home, but I ain't gonna drag you. If you don't wanna go, I'm done with you. So: you comin', or not?"

Libby felt half-dazed; her mind floundered, trying to make sense of what he had told her. At his last question, though, one point of certainty surfaced. Grasping at it, she glared up at him. "I'm *not going home without my sister.*"

Scab's jaw tightened; he dug in his pocket and pulled out three keys, tied with a blackened leather thong. "Suit yourself." He tossed the keys onto the ground between them, unslung the rolled-up blankets, and dumped them on the ground as well. Then he turned and stalked away down the trail.

BACK IN THE clearing, Libby couldn't stop her tears, so she just tried to ignore them. They slid down her face as she unlocked Pullman's shack and searched through his trunk for some clue about where he was taking Maisie. They dripped onto the maps when she spread them on the table, and smeared the pencil markings drawn over the printed towns and counties. After a while she wondered how there could be any liquid left in her body.

Nothing was any help. The maps were all of their state, or neighboring ones, and were marked with arrows and circles, but none of the markings meant anything to Libby. The only other things in the trunk were a couple of stubby pencils and the two tin boxes, which were empty except for straw packing and a bit of grainy white residue that looked like sugar.

She searched both shacks and the lean-to for anything that might help her, but she found nothing, except for a label inside the trunk that said it had been made in St. Louis. She tried to think how this information could help her, but the attempt only started a fresh flood of tears. What could she do? Go to St. Louis, just in case the label meant that Pullman lived there? How would she get there? And if she did, what then? Start asking everyone in that huge city about a man whose real name she didn't know?

She went to the table and sat down. Her mind felt like a tornado, her thoughts useless bits of refuse swirling around, everything moving too fast for her to get a grasp on. She got up and fished a pencil and a scrap of paper from the trunk. She put the paper on the table, sat down again, and wrote:

1. *Who is Yayger?*
2. *Where is Pullman taking Maisie to give her to him?*
3. *Ask the men in the jungle if any of them knows where Pullman went? Or where Pullman kept his car so I could ask the people there?*
4. *If I find out where Pullman is, how would I get there? Ask one of the men here to help me? Try to ride the trains by myself? How would I know where they were going? What if I get caught?*

She looked at her list and felt the tears threaten again; sick of them, she bit her tongue savagely to try to head them off. The horrible memory of the three tramps holding her down in the forest rose up in her mind. She rested her head on her hands for a few moments, her eyes squeezed shut, trying to still the tremor in her breathing. Then she opened her eyes and firmly crossed out *ask one of the men here to help me*, and *ask the men in the jungle*.

But new thoughts kept battering at her, debris in the tornado: how would she eat until she found Maisie? And if she *did* run across more dangerous people, what would she do? And then there was the other question Scab had raised: how would she get Maisie away from Pullman, even if she could, by some unimaginable means, find him? Staring down at her list, she felt despair welling up as she realized it contained exactly nothing she could do. She turned the pencil around in her hand so the eraser hovered over the page, and sat there for a long time. Finally, she erased the crossed-out phrases and carefully wrote them back in: *ask one of the men here to help me; ask the men in the jungle.* She put the pencil down and went to the cot. Clutching the pillow to her stomach, she curled tightly around it, and in utter exhaustion fell asleep.

She woke stiff and sore, as if her sleep had been work. Stumbling out of the shack, she was a bit dazed to find the day already golden with the approach of evening. She sat on one of the logs for a long time, watching the light fade to orange on the treetops. A wood thrush alternated its simple three-note call with more melodious phrases. She felt numb, remote from the beauty of the song, as if she had used up all her life's allotment of feelings. *That's good,* she thought. *Then I won't be scared anymore.*

She roused herself at last, built a small fire, and heated a can of black-eyed peas she scrounged from the lean-to. By the time she finished eating, it was almost dark; the air buzzed with the noise of evening insects, and fireflies flickered at the edges of the clearing. She fetched the lantern from Pullman's shack and lit it, then took the padlock from its hook and locked the door. She slung the bedroll Scab had left over her shoulder. Picking up the lantern, she crossed the clearing toward the trail that led to the jungle.

Full night had arrived under the thick trees, and she walked in a little sphere of lantern light surrounded by darkness. The creek chattered noisily. Insects clicked and whirred in the undergrowth; a mosquito whined in her ear. Somewhere above, a barred owl gave its eerie call, the one Roach said was a question:

who cooks for you? Who cooks for you all? She had never been alone in the forest at night before, and every new sound made her muscles jerk tight.

Before she had gone far, the smell of wood-smoke began to overpower the sweet fragrance of swamp milkweed and the sharp, metallic scent of the creek. She heard men's voices laughing and talking, some low and gravelly, others raucous as crow calls; she glimpsed the glow of firelight through the trees, up ahead to her right on the far side of the creek. After a bit she saw a narrow side-path. It led to the creek, crossed it on a series of stepping stones, then curved out of sight into the trees, in the direction of the voices and the firelight. She approached the spot where the path branched off, intending to follow it; she didn't notice her steps slowing until she realized she was standing stock still, her hand gripping the strap of the bedroll so tightly that her nails dug into her palm.

Go on, she told herself. Her heart was pounding, her breathing shaky. Nightmarish images kept looming in her mind: the brutal faces of the tramps in the forest, the leers of the men on the train. She tried to shove them down, to get her feet moving again. Surely not all the men in the jungle were like *those* men. For a brief moment, reflexively, she tried to encourage herself by imagining the men around the fire up ahead to be like Pullman, Roach and Scab – but then the foolishness of the thought, after all that had happened, bore in upon her, and she tried to shove it away as well. *Go ON*, she told herself finally: *it's the only thing you* can *do.*

She turned onto the side-path and crept toward the firelight, careful of her footing on the slippery stones crossing the creek. The voices grew louder, the words punctuated by braying bursts of laughter. When she came to the curve in the path, she stopped

The Birds of the Air | 127

to take in a deep breath: another few steps, and the men up ahead would see her – she wouldn't be able to change her mind. She let the breath out and took the first step.

Before she could take a second, the nightmare visions in her mind seemed suddenly to grow bone and muscle: a hand clamped over her mouth, and another seized her lantern. The hand over her mouth pulled her head firmly back against the body of someone behind her, muffling her cry so it couldn't be heard above the boisterous noise of the hobos. The shock of it seemed to short-circuit her vision for a moment, and everything went dark.

"*Have you lost your damn MIND?*"

It was Scab's voice, hissing into her ear.

The sudden relief seemed to melt her bones like wax, so her legs threatened to crumple beneath her. Scab took his hand from her mouth, turned her sharply around to face him, then held a finger to his lips. She could see him only dimly by the firelight filtering through the leaves, and she realized the reason things had gone black was because he had tilted oil onto the wick to put out the lantern. "*Come on,*" he whispered. When she didn't move immediately, he grabbed her wrist and towed her along behind him, out of the side-path and back up the trail toward the clearing.

"What – what's –" she panted, but Scab hushed her with a motion of his hand. He paused where the path turned toward the shacks, looking back down the trail and seeming to listen, then pulled her on into the clearing. He stopped for a moment and re-lit the lantern, keeping the flame so low that it gave scarcely more light than one of the fireflies.

"Now listen," he said, bending down a bit so his eyes were level with hers, speaking just above a whisper. "Them sons-a-bitches that took you off the other day?" He said it like a question, so she nodded, feeling her eyes widen. "Well…" Scab jabbed a thumb toward the trail they had just left. "They're back, and they're comin'."

CHAPTER TEN

BEFORE LIBBY COULD fully register what Scab had said, he straightened, grabbed her wrist again and started across the clearing, pulling her along. When the shock caught up with her, it felt like something she had been expecting – as if the three men's awful faces, rising in her mind's eye minutes before, had been a premonition.

"They brought some a' their crew with 'em – maybe even Slater, their boss. So I want you to keep quiet and mind what I tell you." Scab let out his short exhalation of a laugh. "Guess ol' Pullman didn't scare 'em so bad after all. Pissed 'em off real good, though."

He led the way straight across the clearing, to the left of Pullman's shack and past it to where the woods began. He stopped where the dense foliage of a scrub willow grew down to touch the ground, then ducked under the branches and searched with his hands through the deep drifts of dead leaves underneath. Libby dropped to her knees beside him. She stared back across the clearing, her eyes fixed and unblinking, but there was no moon up yet, and beyond the dim sphere of lantern light everything was black.

"Come on! Get in!" Scab hissed, and when she turned it seemed, in the faint yellow glow, that he had somehow opened a trapdoor made of the ground itself. Before she could really get a look at it, Scab had put out the lantern and was pushing her forward under the door, or whatever it was, into an earthy-smelling space beneath it, lined with rough boards. Scab shoved the dark lantern into her hands, then dropped in himself. The hole was deep enough that, when she sat with her knees pulled up, her head was below ground level, leaned back against the boards; but she could feel Scab jostling her as he folded his long limbs into the cramped space. He seemed to have propped the door up with something, and he reached out from under it; she could hear his arms shuffling through the leaves and realized he was hiding the traces of their passage. When he had finished, he removed the prop and laid it sideways, so the door was closed except for a small crack, which he crouched to peer out of. "Topside's camouflaged," he whispered. "Pullman runs some rotgut once in a while; this here's where he hides it."

Libby didn't understand, but she was scarcely listening; the idea of the horrible men approaching crowded out all other thought. "They won't find us?"

"Sure as hell hope not," Scab said. She heard him slip off his knapsack and drop it to the floor. "You douse that fire before you left?"

"N-no." Libby couldn't stop shaking. She could feel her shoulder jittering against Scab's arm. After a moment she felt his hand grip it, reassuring.

The Birds of the Air | 131

"Don't worry. They ain't gonna find us down here."

He crouched for a while in silence, peering out of the crack. Libby unslung the bedroll from her shoulder and huddled beside him, her arms around her knees, holding her breath and listening to the buzz of insects outside. After a while, she heard him take in a long breath. He let it out in a whisper: "There they are."

She got to her knees to look out.

Her eyes had become accustomed to the blackness inside the pit, and she could just see, past the curtain of willow leaves, the corner of Pullman's shack, and beyond it the fire pit surrounded by its logs. Dark figures were gathered there; one of them picked up a stick and jabbed at the coals of her small fire, which flickered up enough to give off a sullen orange glow. With a hitch of indrawn breath, she recognized the fire-stirrer as the wiry man who had gotten away on the day the tramps had taken her.

Another man came into view from the direction of the woodpile; he carried an armload of kindling sticks, and when he threw them on the coals, making them blaze up, she saw he was the man who had held the hammer. The left side of his face was bright pink, a melted, blistered mess. She didn't realize she had let out a small moan until she felt Scab grip her shoulder again to quiet her.

She dragged her gaze from the hammer man and looked at the others. There were three of them, besides the hammer man and the wiry man; one crossed to the small shack and kicked its door until it burst open. He looked inside briefly. When he turned back toward the firelight, she saw he was the large man Scab had clubbed with the tree branch. His face was burned as well, but on the right side.

Scab cursed under his breath. "Slater's with 'em."

Libby looked back toward the fire. One man, better-dressed

than the others, stepped away from the group and turned slowly, scanning the clearing. Though he looked younger than Pullman, he leaned on a cane. When the light hit his face, she saw that it, too, was burned, both down the left side and the right, the burns the exact same sizes and shapes as the ones on the other two men's faces.

Scab breathed out a quieter version of his terse laugh. "Slater's gotta be steamed about that," he whispered. "*Used* to be kind of a ladies' man. You lock up both shacks?"

"Yes."

"Good. Any luck, they'll just figure we all took off out a' here once we knew they'd found the place. Better if them coals hadn't a' been hot, though." He shifted, moving closer to the crack beneath the trapdoor. "What's he doin'?"

Libby peered out of the crack again. The man called Slater had sat down astride one of the logs by the fire pit. He set something in front of him on the log, a small thing that looked, by the way the firelight glinted off it, to be made of metal; then he pulled a lighter from his pocket and held its flame to something that dangled from his hand. His lips were moving, and the other men stood back from him at a respectful distance.

"They take any blood from you before?" Scab's whisper held no trace of humor now.

"I... I don't think so." As Libby watched, whatever dangled from Slater's hand blazed up, and he dropped it into the metal thing, which looked to be some kind of bowl or cup.

She felt a stab of pain behind her eyes, where she had felt the tingling the night before when Pullman was talking to her, and when it faded a vivid thought rose in its place:

I shouldn't be here.

She turned and peered through the dark, trying to make

out the dimensions of the space. Disquiet began to grow in her. Why, she wondered, had she trusted Scab, following him through the dark woods and into this grave-like hole? What had he, or Pullman, or Roach ever done to deserve her confidence? They had lied to her, used her, betrayed her. They had stolen her little sister.

Why would they care what happens to me now?

The thought was accompanied by a sickening surge of incredulity at her own stupidity; and then, a second later, by a freezing jolt of realization: Pullman, Roach and Scab had *nothing* to gain by taking her home. It would be simply foolish for them to risk having her identify them. The truth leapt to clarity in her mind, turning her blood to ice: they had left Scab here to kill her – to bury her in this hidden grave so she would never be found. She thought of his razor flashing through the lantern light, slashing the arm of the tramp in the boxcar. She thought of his words afterward: *If I ever come across one of 'em passed out drunk somewhere, he ain't never gonna wake up again.*

"Shit – you were all scratched to hell, though," Scab was murmuring. "They coulda got some a' your blood on their clothes..."

The sound of his whisper seemed to break her terrified paralysis. With a choked cry, she sprang up at the heavy trapdoor, trying to heave it open. It was, all at once, blindingly clear to her that her only chance of escape lay with the men in the clearing. Slater would help her; Slater would save her from Scab.

But Scab was snake-fast; his arm shot around her before she could even budge the door. His hand covered her mouth again, clamped down like a vise, and over her smothered cries she heard his urgent whisper, close to her ear. "It's a callin'. A *callin'*, kid! Like the one we done on your sister!" She felt him rise a bit, still holding her, to look out of the crack. *To see if they heard me,* she thought in panic; *I have to make them hear me!* "Don't pay no attention," Scab was whispering urgently – trying to lull her into compliance, trying to keep her hidden from the men who could save her. She braced her feet against the wood planks of the floor and struggled for her life, screaming behind the muffling pressure of his hand, her fingers clawing upward toward the trapdoor. Scab tightened his grip around her skinny ribcage. "*Quit, kid,*" he hissed into her ear; "*Quit it!*"

All at once she felt an incredibly strange sensation, as if her brain, inside her skull, had been covered with sticky cobwebs and someone had just pulled them off. All her panic and terror disappeared on the instant, and her straining muscles relaxed.

"It's a *callin'*," Scab whispered again. "It's Slater doin' it." He relaxed his hold. "You gotta fight it." He straightened to peer out of the crack. "That wind come up, blew his fire out." Listening, Libby realized there was a new sound outside: a strong wind gusted through the trees, nearly drowning out the racket of the crickets and frogs. "Good thing, too," Scab murmured. "Don't think they heard you."

Libby got to her knees, panting, to peer through the crack as well. Slater still straddled the log. The flames in the fire pit were high now, dancing wildly in the wind that tossed the tree branches. By their light she could see Slater glowering, his blistered face bent over the metal bowl. He was struggling to relight the thing inside it, trying to shield it from the wind with his hand. His lips were still moving, but his expression made her think that now he was only cursing.

After a couple of seconds, though, Scab let out an unhappy breath. "Think he's got it goin' again." He turned toward Libby. "Now kid, you gotta *fight* it." There was a pleading note in his

The Birds of the Air | 135

whisper, but also, she thought, a note of hopelessness. "Just – try to think about somethin' else; and *keep quiet.*"

But the sharp pain stabbed through her head again, and the fear began to creep back. She turned to stare at Scab's shadowy shape, barely distinguishable in the faint glow filtering through the crack. She tried to push the fear away, but she could feel it seeping in, rising like cold water. Her body tensed and she shrank from him, her breath growing ragged. She had to get away – had to get to Slater. Her hands reached up toward the door.

Scab murmured another curse and grabbed her again, covering her mouth as she cried out. "Okay," he said, and the word sounded like a sigh, even as he panted with the effort of holding her. "Hold onto these – it'll just make it worse if they find 'em on me." She felt him press something into her flailing hands, and was surprised into stillness for a second, trying to feel what it was. "Just *stay right here,*" he whispered. "I *mean* it, kid. I wouldn't put *nothin'* past those bastards." Then, before she knew what was happening, he was out of the trapdoor, leaving it shut tight behind him, the prop gone and the tiny cellar completely dark.

"Slater!"

She heard his voice calling loudly from outside, already some distance away.

"Slater!"

At the second call, she felt the unspeakably strange cobweb-sensation in her head again; her terror subsided, only to rush back upon her for a different reason.

Scab!

She got to her knees and lifted her head as close as she could to the door, listening.

"If y'all are still after that Schillerton kid, you're wastin' your time." Scab's voice was moving farther away, heading into the clearing. "Pullman got ahold of 'er; took off out a' here this mornin'."

Libby became aware again of the objects in her hand. She turned them over, running her fingers along them, and realized with a sick feeling that they were Scab's jackknife and razor. A miserable sound escaped her; she shoved them into her pocket and pushed hard against the underside of the door, straining to lift it.

She could hear Scab calling, "Aw – come on, fellas!" To her amazement, he sounded as if he was almost laughing. "Nothin' personal." He sounded even farther away, and she managed to shove the door up a tiny bit, so she could see out.

The men had thrown more wood on the fire; it was roaring up from the pit, the gusting wind whipping it higher than she had ever seen it, so the whole clearing rippled with orange light. She could see Scab, beyond the swaying curtain of willow leaves, advancing toward the men. His hands were held up a bit, as if to show he meant no harm. The men were moving toward him as well, fanning out to both sides – except for the boss, Slater, who only rose and stood leaning on his cane near the fire, the light playing hideously on his ruined face.

The heavy trapdoor pressed on Libby's hands, hurting her wrists; she lowered it silently and felt around at her knees until she found the stick Scab had used for a prop. Using one hand and her shoulders, she eased the door up again, just a crack, and slid the prop out sideways as he had done.

Scab had stopped advancing. The wind whipped at him, and at the men closing in around him. Only Slater stood where she could see his face; his expression made her wish she couldn't.

Two of the men – the large man and one Libby had never seen before – grabbed Scab by the arms, shoving him toward

The Birds of the Air | 137

Slater. She heard Scab's voice rise for a moment – "Aw, come on!" – but he didn't resist. The wiry man and the hammer man followed and stood behind him, boxing him in. Libby could no longer hear his voice, but she could tell by the movement of his hands – restricted by the men's grip on his arms – that he was still talking.

Slater stood listening; his blistered face impassive. Scab seemed to finish what he was saying, and Libby saw Slater nod slowly. He gave a half shrug, tilting his head to one side, and made as if to turn away; then he wheeled back, raising his cane, and smashed it across Scab's face, the force of his whole body behind the blow.

Scab crumpled to the ground, and with horrible, brutal rapidity the men closed in around him, delivering half a dozen savage kicks in the time it took Libby to cry out. Slater stood back and watched, his face a grotesque mask in the firelight. Libby thought her cry would stop the attack, at least for as long as it took the men to turn and look for her; but the wind and the fire were roaring, the men jeering and laughing, and none of them seemed to have heard her. She braced her hands against the heavy door – meaning to fling it open, to race to Scab's aid – but the insanity of the idea stopped her before she had moved the door an inch. She lowered her hands, still peering out of the crack, but tears mercifully blurred the awful sight of Scab's limp form, battered back and forth by the vicious blows slamming into him. Her breath ripped through her throat; she caught herself whimpering like a small child, and clenched her teeth to bite back the sound.

After an unbearable length of time, the men stopped kicking. Slater gestured; Libby could see him giving some order, but the wind took his words. Two of the men dragged Scab's lifeless-looking body out of her view, toward the front of Pullman's shack. The other two went to the edge of the clearing and fetched five-gallon kerosene cans, which she hadn't noticed before. One of the two – the wiry man – headed toward the small shack, tilted a bit from the weight of the container he carried. The large man had the other container; he lugged it toward the south wall of Pullman's shack, heading straight in the direction of Libby's hiding place.

Libby sank down hastily, pulled in the prop, and lowered the door. Huddling in the pitch blackness, shivering and swallowing sobs, she could hear the men's rough voices shouting to one another across the clearing. It seemed to go on for a long time. The voice of the large man was very close. She registered snatches of his words – "if the kid ain't lyin'"; "catch up to" – but her mind seemed unable to take hold of the sense of them.

When his voice moved farther away, she raised herself up to listen. All the men's voices were growing more distant, so she ventured to lift the door a tiny bit, letting a glare of firelight in. She peered through the latticework of twigs and leaves.

The clearing blazed with orange light: both shacks were burning, flames snaking up the walls, already rising, in places, above the rooflines. Libby still couldn't see Scab, but Slater's men were all visible; they were moving toward the entrance to the path, where Slater stood. As they approached, Slater turned and disappeared down the path; the others followed, the large man pausing once to glance back at the blazing shacks and toss his empty container toward the center of the clearing.

As soon as they were out of sight, Libby pushed the door up farther and eeled her way from under it, clawing at the slippery drifts of leaves. Her eyes were fixed on the corner of Pullman's shack, where Scab had been dragged out of sight.

The Birds of the Air | 139

The air was thick with smoke and kerosene fumes, and heat blasted at her from the fires. She darted behind Pullman's shack to its north end, where she could get a better look down the path, hugging the forest edge to stay as far from the flames as possible. Slater and his men were nowhere in sight. She raced to the center of the clearing, choking back the impulse to scream Scab's name, in case the men were still in earshot.

She saw at once where Scab must be. The door to Pullman's shack had been kicked in, the bolt splintered loose from the wood, but then it had been closed again. A heavy length of baling wire, wrapped many times, fastened the door handle to the sturdy hook where Pullman had kept the padlock, holding the door shut in place of the broken bolt.

Flames licked up the door, engulfing the wire so Libby couldn't reach it. She wheeled to run for the bucket of water, but remembered that Scab had dumped it on the fire that morning. She turned around and around, her hands outspread and trembling before her, scanning the clearing for something that would help her. The wind that had aided in keeping her hidden was now her enemy, whipping at the flames and goading them to devour the buildings more rapidly. All at once she remembered the hatchet Roach kept by the wood-pile behind the small shack.

She bolted to the rear of the shack and skidded around the corner, one arm up to shield her face from the blistering heat. The wood-pile was blazing like a torch, but the stump Roach chopped the kindling on was a few yards away, and hadn't caught fire yet. The hatchet was stuck in the stump, gleaming with the reflected glare of the flames. She dove for it, and raced back to Pullman's shack.

She swung the hatchet into the flames, chopping with all her strength at the wire holding the door shut. It seemed to take a hundred strokes, but finally she broke through the last strand. Gathering her courage, she kicked at the door, thrusting her foot through the flames and sending out a shower of sparks. The door flew open.

The fire had not spread inside the shack as quickly as it had outside; it flashed through Libby's mind that Slater's men must have doused only the outside with kerosene, and she felt fervently thankful. Smoke poured through the cracks between the boards, filling the shack, but the flames licked through in only a few places.

Scab lay motionless on the plank floor. His face was streaked with dirt and blood, and the eye Libby could see was swollen shut, but the fire had not touched him.

She leapt over the low tongues of flame that still flickered across the threshold, and ran to crouch beside him. She grabbed him by the shoulders and shook him. "Scab!" she grated out, her throat raw from smoke; "*Scab!* Get *up!*" – but there was no response. She darted to the cot and yanked the pillow off it; carrying it to the door, she fell to her knees and used it to smother the flames across the threshold, then left it on top of the hot, charred wood there, hoping it would keep Scab from getting burned when she dragged him through the doorway.

The door had swung back against the wall, and flames were beginning to spread from it to the rafters. The smoke was less dense near the floor, so she crawled back to Scab and pulled at his limp body, inching him across the boards to the doorway, bracing the pillow in place with her feet as she dragged him over it. He was heavier than it seemed anyone so lanky could possibly be. The heat was excruciating, and sweat dripped off her, causing her hands to slip in their grip on him, but after what seemed like

The Birds of the Air | 141

an age she managed to haul him out of the hellish oven of the shack and into the surging night air.

She had dragged him about half the distance to the fire pit when, to her delirious relief, he began to stir and cough. He spat blood onto the ground and, leaning on her heavily, managed to get to his feet and stagger alongside her to the edge of the clearing farthest from the furnace blast of the flames. There he collapsed, his head and shoulders propped against a tree trunk. Libby peered into his battered face. His good eye was open, but frighteningly unfocused, drifting about aimlessly. "Scab!" she said, shaking him a bit, "Scab! Are you all right?" His eye closed again, and she thought he had slipped back into unconsciousness, but after a moment he mumbled something she couldn't make out. "What?" she said, leaning close; "I can't hear you!"

"Thought I told you to stay put." The words came out in a rasping whisper from his split and swollen lips. He coughed and spat blood again, then raised a halting hand to his jaw. His body began to jerk oddly, and Libby was afraid he was having some sort of a fit, but after a moment, unbelievably, she realized he was laughing. He bent and spat something into his hand, then held it out, wavering, for Libby to see. "Looks like them sons-a-bitches got their tooth after all."

CHAPTER ELEVEN

THROUGHOUT THE LONG night Libby huddled at Scab's side, terrified that Slater and his men would come back. Scab never spoke again, or seemed more than half-conscious, and she was horribly afraid he would die. Early on, she braved the heat to retrieve their belongings from the little cellar, and spread one of the blankets over him, folding the other to put under his head. She held his water bottle for him to drink from, then found Roach's handkerchief still in her pocket, poured water onto it, and tried to clean some of the blood from his face. Some of it seemed to have come from his nose, the rest from splits on his cheekbone – where Slater's cane had struck him, she guessed – and his lips. He kept spitting blood from the lost tooth as well, until he sank back into unconsciousness.

After that, she sat beside him, watching the shacks burn, for what seemed like so many hours that she could hardly believe the sky showed no sign of growing lighter. At first she was afraid the

The Birds of the Air | 143

fire would spread to the forest. She divided her attention between peering down the path for the return of Slater's men, checking to make sure Scab was still breathing, and scanning the underbrush to make sure the fire wasn't spreading. But the damp bottomland woods resisted the sparks the wind whipped into them, giving off at most a few sulky flickers of flame that soon died in wisps of white smoke. After a while the capricious wind died down, and she felt less worried about the fire. When the shacks had been reduced to smoldering black skeletons, she could keep her eyes open no longer, and fell asleep sitting up, propped against the tree with one hand on Scab's shoulder.

When she woke, she saw only the green, dew-jeweled swords of grass blades, so close to her eyes that they loomed enormous. Blinking, trying to shake off the haze of sleep, she was confused at first to find herself outdoors. One of the blankets had been thrown over her. Lifting her head, she saw what remained of the shacks: nothing more than heaps of charred wood and ash, with a few blackened studs still spiking up toward the pearl-colored dawn sky. The air was still, and smoke drifted up from the wreckage undisturbed. The clearing reeked of burning, and the foliage nearest to where the shacks had stood was scorched and withered.

At the sight of the ruins, fear flooded back, and she turned quickly to check on Scab; but though the other blanket was still there, he was gone. She scrambled to her feet to scan the clearing, but he was nowhere in sight. She was fighting sleep-dazed panic, wondering whether Slater's men could have come back and taken him while she slept, when he came limping stiffly along the path from the creek, carrying the water bottle.

He had washed his face in the creek, removing the rest of the blood. His left eye was still swollen shut; the whole left side of his face was the color of a nearly-ripe plum, and he moved like a person five times his age. The instant Libby saw him, she raced across the clearing and flung her arms around him.

"*Ow!* Cut it out, ya dimwit!" he rasped. He staggered a bit and shoved her off, but not before giving her a rough pat on the shoulder. "Think I got a couple ribs broke."

He was unsteady on his feet, and allowed her to help him to one of the logs – now pocked with black marks where sparks had struck it. He sank down, rested his arms across his knees and laid his forehead on them. "Can't seem to see straight," he said in a husky croak. "Guess them bastards musta damn near busted my brains out."

Libby told him all that had happened after Slater struck him. He still seemed a bit disoriented, and she wasn't sure how much he took in; but when she told him how Slater's men had shut him into the burning shack, and about her terrified struggle to get him out, he raised his bowed head for a moment to look at her, his battered face unreadable.

She told him about her fear that the men would come back; he nodded and tried to stand, but swayed and sank down again. "Sorry, kid... don't think I can travel just yet." He glanced at the ruin of Pullman's shack. "I don't guess they'll be comin' back. Most likely they figure they finished the job on me; an' I told 'em Pullman has your sis, so they know *you're* no use to 'em now. " He raised a hand to his face to shade his good eye, as if the light hurt him. "Think I might hafta lay down a while longer."

Libby helped him to cross the grass to the place where he had lain before, and he lowered himself painfully onto the blanket. "Now kid," he said, his cracked voice stern, "don't go wanderin' off. There's some food in the pack. Anyone comes around here, you get out a' sight. Best no one knows you're still here, now

The Birds of the Air | 145

Pullman ain't around." Then he closed his good eye again; but at least, this time, he seemed only to be sleeping.

Drained and forlorn, she dug in Scab's knapsack and found some biscuits and some leathery strips of leftover bacon. She ate a bit, leaving the rest for Scab, then wandered around the ruins of the shacks. She could see some of the tin dishes and the cook-pots, blackened, scattered half-buried in the ashes near where the lean-to had stood; she found a long branch on the ground, and used it to dig them out, dragging them into a sooty jumble on the grass. As she was poking the branch into the smoking ruins to see if there were any more, she heard a metallic *thunk,* and felt the end of the branch strike something hard and solid under the ashes. She tried to sweep away the charred wood over it, but it was at the very end of the branch's reach, and it was difficult to get leverage. The wreckage was still smoking, too riddled with live coals for her to get any closer, so she gave up and tossed the branch aside.

She lay down on the grass beside the pile of tinware, and stared up at the brilliant blue sky. What would happen, she wondered, if Scab still insisted on taking her home when he got better? Would she have to try to slip away from him? And then what? Her mind worried at the thought until, exhausted, she fell asleep on the warm grass.

She awakened in the afternoon, her stomach knotted with hunger. Scab was still asleep, and she didn't want to eat the rest of the food in the knapsack and leave none for him. She fetched the water bucket and dove into the bushes around the edge of the clearing, pushing through the more forgiving branches to find the vicious-thorned blackberry vines and gingerly rob them of their fruit. Most of the berries were red and sour, not nearly ripe, but she ate them anyway, putting every other one into the bucket for Scab. It made her think of times when their mother had sent her and Maisie out to gather blackberries for pies, and how sharply she had spoken to Maisie for eating the ripe ones instead of putting them in her bucket; the memory pierced her more painfully than the thorns.

After she had gathered all she could reach, she wondered if she dared go to the creek and wash herself. Her skin and clothes were covered with soot, and she felt sweaty and filthy from her struggle in the fire. The afternoon was hot, and she longed for the cool water on her scorched, scratched skin.

She gathered a handful of small sticks and used them to write a message to Scab, forming letters with them on the blanket she had used the night before: *went to creek*. Then she crept, barefoot, up the path to the creek trail, and peered cautiously along it toward the jungle. She saw no one, so she darted across and slipped down the bank into the creek.

She waded upstream to the pool where she and Roach had rinsed out clothes – a gravelly basin a couple of feet deep, edged by rock outcroppings. She dug in her pockets, pulled out the photo of Maisie, Scab's razor and jackknife, her father's pocketknife and the little glass vial, and placed them carefully in a depression on the top of one of the rocks. Then, gratefully, she submerged herself in the cold, clear water, clothes and all. She washed herself as well as she could, rubbing her skin, her hair and her clothing vigorously, wincing at the burned and scratched places. When she finished, she sat submerged to her neck, letting the current wash over her and carry the traces of the last miserable day and night away from her downstream.

She gazed at the little glass vial where it glinted fitfully in a shifting spot of sunlight. She thought of the woman who had given it to her, and how she had spoken of John Fuller. Reaching

The Birds of the Air | 147

for the vial, she frowned at the liquid inside. Pullman had said it was Fuller who sent the tramp to steal Maisie, but now Scab said it was Pullman *himself* who had sent the man, and that Pullman worked for someone called Jaeger. What did that mean about Fuller? *Had* he sent the woman? Did he even know about Libby and Maisie? Who was he?

"*Jesus*, kid!"

Scab's hoarse voice startled her so that she almost dropped the vial into the water. She looked downstream and saw him standing in the creek, holding a branch to steady himself.

"You near gave me a heart attack. Thought I told you not to wander off!"

Libby struggled to her feet, dripping. "I left you a message!"

He shook his head. "Don't read so good." He lowered himself stiffly onto a stone, unbuttoning his soot- and blood-covered shirt. "May's well see what I can do with this." When he stripped off the shirt to wash it in the stream, the bruises covering his shoulders, ribs and back were so dreadful that Libby felt dizzy and nauseated. She sank back down. "Scab – I'm so *sorry!*"

He glanced at her. "What for?"

"It was *my* fault you had to go out there!"

"Don't know how you figure that. Ain't many people can resist a callin'." He wrung water from the shirt over his red-and-purple back, then gave her his ghost of a smile, even harder to discern than usual on his swollen, one-eyed face. "What *I'm* thinkin' – if you hadn't a' pulled me out a' that shack, I'd be part a' that pile of ashes right now."

Libby gazed downward for a moment, then answered his smile with a watery one of her own.

"Pass me my stuff there," he said, rising painfully and reaching out a hand for his knife and razor, "and let's get on back and figure out somethin' to eat."

SCAB WAS STILL plainly in bad shape, but his mind seemed clear, and his eyes no longer had the drifting, unfocused look that had so frightened Libby the night before. He inspected the food from the pack, and the unripe blackberries she had gathered, and shook his head. "Gonna hafta scare up more'n that."

Slater's men had burned all the firewood, so he set Libby to combing the edges of the clearing for more; then, with another stern warning to her not to wander, he limped off toward the jungle.

He returned in the late afternoon, an old flour sack in one hand and a pair of dead squirrels dangling from the other. "Bought this stuff off some a' the 'bos," he said, flopping the sack down. When Libby opened it, she was relieved to see three good-sized potatoes, an onion and a few carrots. The squirrels, she knew, were from his snares. He directed her to build a fire with the wood she'd found, and to see if she could find the skillet in the ashes. He went to clean the squirrels at the bank of the creek.

Libby wondered if the metal thing she had felt beneath the wreckage might be the skillet. She retrieved the branch and prodded the ashes until she felt the thing again, but it seemed to be stuck: no matter how hard she pushed, she couldn't get it to move. When Scab returned with the skinned squirrel carcasses, he found her still struggling with it.

He scanned the ruins, and dragged out one of the blackened panels of corrugated metal that had formed the roof of the shack. Standing it on end, he let it fall so it bridged the smoking wreckage between him and the spot Libby had been poking at. He walked across and kicked away the larger pieces of charred wood. "It ain't the skillet," he said. "Run break off three, four willow branches, 'bout this long" – he held his hands a foot or so apart – "and bring 'em here." When Libby came back, he had kicked away the rest of the smoldering coals. He took the branches from her and, using them like a broom, swept the remaining ash aside.

The thing underneath was a hinged iron lid of some kind, eight or ten inches square, flush with the dirt that had once been under the floor of Pullman's shack. There was no lock or latch on the lid, but when Scab touched it gingerly, he pulled his hand back. "To hot to open easy yet," he said, "and it's gonna be dark soon. Let's find that skillet; we'll see if we can open this later on, when it's cooled down some."

When they had found the skillet beneath a charred beam, and had finished cooking and eating, Scab pulled his tobacco pouch from his pocket. "Well, kid… you ready to go home now?"

Libby wilted a bit at the question, but she set her face in a determined scowl. "*No.*"

Scab's hands froze in the middle of rolling his cigarette. "Kid, I sure hope you're jokin'."

She hung her head and took in a shaky breath. "Scab… I know it was looking out for *me* that got you hurt so bad." The thought tightened her throat, and she had to pause until it loosened again. "And… I heard you talking to Pullman the other night, when you said it could have gotten you all *killed*, getting me away from those men. So… I understand if you don't want to help me, but –" she nerved herself to meet Scab's gaze – "I still have to find my sister."

He made a scornful sound, and went back to rolling. "And how you think you're gonna do that – by askin' them stiffs in the jungle to help you? That what you were plannin' to do when I caught up with you yesterday?"

Libby dropped her head again, and nodded.

"Kid, where the hell you think them three we met on that train was headed? All you know, they could still be right here in this jungle. And what about them stiffs been comin' around to get orders from Pullman, and seen you here? You think they don't know Pullman's took off out a' here?" He ran a hand over his battered face. "You got no *idea* what some a' these sons-a-bitches is like once they get liquored up."

"I didn't know what else to do," Libby said humbly.

"Shoulda damn well come *with* me when I *told* you to," he growled around the cigarette, striking a match to light it. After a moment, though, his shoulders bowed. "I wasn't really gonna leave you on your own," he said, his eyes on the fire. "I was just tryin' to spook some sense into you." He snorted. "Shoulda known better."

Libby gathered her courage. "Scab... I *can't* go home without Maisie. It's my fault she's gone; I was supposed to be looking *after* her. I should've been watching closer; I should've taken her into the house the minute that man showed up. And..." Her voice wavered, then came out more softly... "she's Mama's favorite."

Scab gave another snort.

"It's true." Libby kept her eyes on her hands, twisted together in her lap. "I heard Mama tell my aunt one time, when they thought Maisie and I were asleep. She said she just couldn't help it... she said she felt real bad about it. I kind of felt sorry for her." She glanced up; Scab was looking at her, the scornfulness gone from his face. She dropped her gaze again, embarrassed. "It's not like I'm sneaking around listening," she said. "It's just, our house

The Birds of the Air | 151

is small, and our bedroom's right next to the kitchen. Sometimes I have trouble sleeping."

Scab sighed. "Well anyway, it *ain't* your fault she's gone. It's that fella Stubby's fault, that changed her, and Pullman's fault, and Jaeger's." He was silent for a few seconds, frowning down into the smoke that rose from his cigarette; then he spoke in a quieter voice: "… and mine."

There was a soft sound from the ruins as some charred board collapsed, and he glanced toward it. "No matter what else we do, we gotta get out a' *here*. Can't think of no reason why Slater's crew'd come back, but you never can tell. And I don't trust some a' the rest a' these stiffs 'round here, with Pullman gone."

Libby frowned. "Haven't you been here *before* when Pullman was gone?"

Scab laughed, a grim puff of smoke. "Plenty a' times. Just not with *you* around."

"But – why would any of the men around here bother *me* now? Pullman's already got Maisie. There's no reason anyone would still want my..." she faltered, suppressing a shudder. "My... teeth, or blood, or anything."

Scab bowed his head; after a moment he shook it. "Kid, just *listen* to me for once, okay? It's nothin' to do with your sis; it just ain't a good idea, you bein' in the same camp with some a' these bastards."

Libby slumped forward, all at once so tired that even her bones felt weak. "Okay."

The last of the twilight had faded, and the two of them sat staring into the flames, listening to the sounds of the evening insects. Fireflies flickered around the edges of the clearing like sparks left over from the burned-out fire. When Libby got up the courage to speak again, her voice came out hesitant: "Scab?"

"Yeah?"

"*Would* you help me find my sister?"

Scab made no response for a moment, then let out a breath with a sound as if he were blowing out a candle. He got to his feet stiffly, took one of the blankets and spread it a little way from the fire. "Let me think about it," he said. "Why don't you get some shut-eye. I wanna head out a' here early tomorrow, whatever else we do."

Libby was willing; she felt exhausted in spite of her long sleep that morning. When she had curled up in the blanket, she said, "You think you're well enough to travel?"

"Sure I am."

She looked at him, doubtful. "But you're all beat up. You have broken *bones*!"

He snorted, dismissive. "I been beat up worse'n this before." He started back toward the fire, then paused and turned. "And kid – when you heard me talkin' to Pullman the other night? You heard me wrong." The firelight behind him threw his face into shadow. "I never said you coulda got *us* killed. I was tellin' Pullman, we never shoulda brought you here. I was tellin' him, *we* coulda got *you* killed."

HE WOKE HER in the still, deep-blue hour before dawn, when the first birds had just begun their sleepy songs. He had already built up the fire and reheated the leftover food, and the two of them sat eating for the last time in the clearing. Libby watched his face, anxious for some sign of his decision, but suspecting it would be unwise to press him. He chewed gingerly, and she guessed the place where the tooth had been knocked out hurt him. The bruises had darkened, and he looked, if anything, worse than he had the day before, but the swelling had gone down enough that his left eye was visible, white and coal-black amidst the purple around it.

When they had finished eating, he held out a hand. "Let me see that glass thing again." Libby dug the vial from her pocket and handed it to him; he examined it narrowly, holding it up to the firelight. "So you really think this come from John Fuller?"

"I think so. That lady who gave it to me talked about him."

Scab rose and paced a bit, his hand rubbing the back of his neck. At last he stopped and looked down at Libby. "What you gotta know, kid, before you start this thing: Jaeger... he ain't like Pullman or Slater. Folks say he don't need no blood, or bone, or nothin': they say he can kill you just by *lookin'* at you. Prob'ly a load a' horseshit, but –" he shook his head, looking unhappy; after a moment he squatted down stiffly in front of her. "Pullman says Jaeger's got good reasons for what-all he gets up to. I don't know nothin' 'bout that, but one thing I *do* know: there's plenty a' men like Slater an' Pullman – the kind that's got some push a' their own – that'd sooner walk into a grizzly's den than cross ol' Jaeger. And – you try an' get your sister back? – that's just what you'll be doin'." He held up the glass vial between them. "So you gotta be *sure*, kid: you *really* wanna try this?"

Libby swallowed. She felt unfit and ignorant, but she tried to meet Scab's gaze steadily. "I don't *want* to." Her voice wavered and she tried to firm it up. "I just... *have* to."

Scab lowered the vial and looked at it for a moment; then he shook his head again. "Them sons-a-bitches musta beat every last lick a' sense out a' my head." He raised his eyes to Libby's. "OK, kid. I know where Pullman's headed. We'll go on down to Seifert, an' see if we can catch a ride there."

Libby launched herself at him, throwing her arms around his

neck and nearly knocking him into the fire. "*Thank* you, Scab! Thank you, thank you!"

"Cut it out, kid! Get off before you choke me to death." He stood up, extricating himself, and frowned down at her. "Now don't get your goddamn hopes up. There ain't one chance in a hundred we're gonna have any luck with this. We ain't likely to get there before Pullman sends your sis on to Jaeger, for one thing. An' even if we do, I got no idea how we're gonna get her away from him." He sighed, and ran a hand over his battered face. "But… we'll see what we can figure out."

She nodded, trying to look solemn, though the joy and relief bubbling up inside her made it almost impossible. He squinted down at her for a moment, and she feared from his expression that he was going to change his mind; but then he gave a rueful tilt of his head – more expressive, she thought, of exasperation with himself than with her – and held the vial out to her. "Here; take this – and *don't lose it.* Roll them blankets up, and put the little cook-pot and a couple a' cups and spoons in that flour sack: you can carry 'em. Might need 'em if we hafta camp out."

As Libby was gathering the tinware, she remembered the iron lid they had found. She fetched Scab back to the place; the lid had cooled, and he pried it up with his jackknife and opened it, dirt and ash falling aside. Underneath was a small, cement-lined compartment set into the ground. Libby leaned forward to peer around him as he reached to lift out what was inside.

It was a jar, with a metal lid tightly screwed on, and some kind of cloudy liquid inside. Scab lifted it into the dawn light; something grayish-pink and rubbery-looking floated inside. Scab cursed quietly, and with a sick jolt, Libby saw.

The pinkish thing was a human ear.

It looked to be coated with some gray-white scum, which

was peeling off here and there in floating flakes; she stared at it in horrified fascination.

Scab turned the jar, and Libby saw that something had been sewn to the reverse side of the ear with large, coarse black stitches. At first, she could only see a sort of gelatinous pink cloud floating behind the ear. But protruding from the other side was something grayish-white, about the size of the yolk of a hard-boiled egg, looking as if it had once been spherical but was now crumpled in some places and bloated in others. Scab turned the jar farther, and Libby's stomach clenched when she saw the dark iris and pupil, opaque gray-blue under a milky film. "What *is* it? I mean…"

Scab turned it back again, examining it. "Some kinda conjure rig." His tone was grim. "Don't know exactly what it's for, but…" he trailed off, squinting over the treetops to the west.

"What?" Libby prodded. Her eyes kept being drawn to the thing in the jar, even though she didn't want to look at it.

Scab made the candle-blowing sound. "Nothin'. Just wish we woulda found this last night, an' got rid of it before —" he glanced at her, and seemed to stop himself at the sight of her face. "We'll just leave it like we found it; prob'ly nothin' to worry about." He lowered the jar back into the cement enclosure and shut the iron lid again.

"Did Mr. *Pullman* put that there?"

Scab shook his head. "Musta been Jaeger. He's the one had these shacks an' all built; musta put it down there before that." He ran his fingers over the pitted surface of the iron lid. "I don't guess Pullman ever even knew this was here."

The skin on Libby's back felt as if it was moving on its own. "How do you think he… *got* them?"

Scab only shook his head, but he didn't look happy. He

stood up, and prodded Libby to do the same so they could cross back to the edge of the wreckage. "Let's get the hell out a' here before every stiff in the jungle wakes up. I don't want some nosy 'bo sendin' word to Pullman we headed off two days late an' in the wrong direction."

When they were packed and ready to leave, though, Scab paused at the head of the path to gaze back into the clearing. Libby turned as well, to see what he was looking at. She saw nothing except the old buckets and washtub, the doused firepit, and the charred, smoking ruins of the shacks. She looked up at Scab, puzzled.

He gazed for a moment longer, then dropped his eyes. "All right. Let's get on out a' here." And he turned and led the way down the trail toward the river.

CHAPTER TWELVE

SCAB, STIFF AND obviously hurting, couldn't move at his usual swift pace; even so, they made their way through the jungle before sunup, without seeing anyone. When they reached the river, he turned south, continuing downstream past the point where they had turned off when he first brought Libby there. The land sloped more steeply down to the banks, until they were walking in a deep ravine, dense with brilliant green scrub-growth higher than their heads. A narrow, hidden footpath cut through it – a continuation, Libby supposed, of the one they had taken before – and Scab led the way along it.

When they reached the railroad bridge that marked the edge of Seifert, Scab stopped and looked Libby up and down. "Go wash your face an' hands." When she came back from the river's edge, he dug an old cloth flat-cap out of his knapsack. "Put this on, and stick your hair up underneath it." Libby did as he instructed, though the cap was too big and the bill kept threatening to slip down over her eyes. "Now," Scab said, bending down to peer under the bill into her face, "anyone asks, you're my little brother. *Brother*, got it?" Libby nodded, feeling her face flush a bit: Scab must be as aware as she was that her skinny, flat-chested figure would present no obstacle to the pretense.

"We're on our way to meet up with our folks, workin' out west," he went on. "Anyone asks your name, you tell 'em you're called –" he squinted down at her – "Chigger."

Libby nodded again, trying to look serious and not to keep beaming. Her elation and relief that Scab hadn't left her kept swelling up in her chest, so that it was hard to remember they still had an impossible task ahead, and no idea how to begin it.

The town of Seifert looked larger and more prosperous than Gilson, where they had stopped on the way down to the jungle. By the time they had made their way through its outskirts and onto the main street, the earliest businesses were opening. The signs on the shops were a bit faded, and some of the awnings worn, but the buildings seemed well-kept. People went in and out, ringing little bells on the doors of the grocer's, the butcher's, the cafe. It reminded Libby of her own town, and she felt a pang of homesickness.

Scab stopped at a dry-goods store and bought a cheap cotton shirt to replace his bloodstained one. The woman behind the counter eyed him with pinch-mouthed distaste, and took his money gingerly, between thumb and forefinger, as if it might be infested with lice. Libby glared at her, on the point of asking her why she looked like she'd sucked on a lemon, but Scab took her arm and towed her unceremoniously out of the store.

He changed his shirt in a nearby alleyway, and Libby winced when she saw how black the bruises on his body had become. He stuffed the old shirt into his knapsack, even though there were

The Birds of the Air | 159

trash bins close by, and Libby remembered the torn bit of cloth Slater had burned to make his calling to her.

They stopped in a grocer's shop, where Scab put two cans of sardines, a small tin of crackers, and a box of matches into a wire basket. At the candy rack he added a five-cent Baby Ruth bar. The balding grocer, like the woman in the dry-goods store, kept a distrustful eye on him, but he handed him a bag of Bull Durham tobacco – also five cents – from behind the counter, and took his money without comment.

Outside, Scab led the way out of the business district, toward the west end of town. "Where'd you get all that money?" Libby asked, and he glanced down at her with his faint half-smile.

"Think I work for ol' Pullman for nothin'?"

He reached into the grocery bag, fished out the Baby Ruth bar and handed it to her. Libby offered him half, but he waved it off. "Maisie loves these," she said, and tears threatened to rise into her eyes again. *Scab was right*, she thought, disgusted. *I AM the biggest bawl-baby.* She swallowed down the lump in her throat with the candy. "Scab?"

"Yeah?"

"Where we goin', exactly?"

He nodded toward the west, in the direction they were walking. "Gonna see if we can't hitch us a ride to the pick-up house."

"What's the pick-up house?"

"Spot outside a' Portersville, where we meet up with Jaeger's people, pass them kids over to 'em." He lifted a hand a bit, a cautioning gesture. "But *remember*, kid: there ain't much chance your sis'll still be there. We lost a day foolin' around the jungle, and another on accounta' that run-in with Slater's crew. And Pullman's got the car." He glanced down – checking, Libby thought, whether she was taking what he said seriously – before he went on. "But... if Jaeger's pick-up man got hung up, and maybe couldn't come right away... or if Pullman wanted to stop off someplace..." he shrugged. "That's why I figure it's best we try to hitch a ride. We could be all day waitin' for the right train; this way I reckon we got at least a *chance* a' gettin' to the pick-up before Jaeger's man does. Not a very good chance, though, kid."

"Well... what'll we do if she's *not* there?"

He gave his short laugh. "Might as well ask what we're gonna do if she *is*. Pullman'll be there, and we gotta figure some way to get her away from him." He hitched his knapsack up, wincing a little as though the movement hurt him, and thought for a while. "I was s'posed to meet him an' Roach there, after I took you home," he said at last. "Guess maybe we could hide you somewhere. I could tell 'em I took you home, then just wait till they go to sleep, an' take your sis on out a' there – that's *if* Pullman don't figure out I'm lyin', and *if* Jaeger's man ain't picked her up yet. Then, before they figure out she's gone, we gotta try to get out a' range a' what-all Pullman'll do to try to get us back." He gave her his slight smile again, wry this time. "That don't sound too hard, does it?"

Libby heard the sarcasm in his voice, but still she felt a glow of hope. She smiled back at him, but then her question pushed itself forward once more, like a dogged cloud in a blue sky: "But... if he *has* picked her up?"

"Well then... I guess we try to figure out where Jaeger takes them kids. Got no idea how. Reckon we're gonna hafta figure it out as we go along."

"Scab," Libby said, when they had walked for a while in silence, "who *is*... Jaeger?"

Scab's voice was grim. "I told ya: he's a dangerous son of a bitch, and he's the one collectin' all them kids."

Libby frowned. "But… it doesn't make sense. If you and Pullman, and Slater and his men, all work for *Jaeger*… then, why did they try to take me *away* from you, and get my – my tooth?"

Scab looked uncomfortable. "Well… Jaeger pays good money to anybody can deliver one a' them kids to him, and like Pullman told you, there ain't that many of them kids around." He glanced down at her, almost apologetically, she thought. "Guess that son of a bitch Slater got wind a' what happened with you an' Stubby, an' how Pullman brought you down here to try an' call your sis back. Slater figures, he gets your tooth, calls your sis first, and *he* gets the money for her, 'stead a' Pullman."

Pays good money. Libby had to re-swallow the lump in her throat. "Oh."

Scab sighed. "Kid… I owe Pullman. I reckon he prob'ly saved my life. So… I always just done what he told me, and didn't ask no questions." He was silent for a bit, and when he spoke again he didn't look at her. "Never really thought about none a' this before." His voice was quiet; Libby had to strain to hear him over the whir of insects alongside the road. "Never really got to know no one from any a' them kids' families, before." Then he did look at her, and she thought she could see where someday he would have lines around his eyes like Pullman's. "What I mean to say… I'm sorry, kid."

She dropped her gaze, embarrassed. "It's OK. You're helping me now."

They walked without speaking for a while, past widely-spaced houses at the edge of town, with fields here and there between them. Finally Scab broke the silence with the clipped breath of his laugh. "Tell you one thing: ol' Stubby better hope he don't cross paths with Pullman any time soon." He glanced down at her with a smile more unmistakable than any she had seen on his face before. "All this trouble, just 'cause he couldn't get the best a' one little bitty ol' girl."

SCAB TOOK THEM to the highway that led out of Seifert toward the west, and began trying to hitch a ride. There wasn't much traffic, and the few vehicles they saw passed them by without slowing.

"Hope I ain't been a damn fool, tryin' to hitch 'stead a' catchin' a freight," Scab said. "Shoulda thought about lookin' so rough, the way Slater's boys worked me over. Folks'll think twice about pickin' up someone looks like they been fightin'."

Libby hadn't thought of this either. She looked at him, trying to see him as a stranger would. He did look terrible. "What if we don't get a ride before dark?" she asked, anxious.

He shrugged. "We'll make camp along here somewhere. One a' these dry irrigation ditches'll do to sleep in, an' to keep a fire out a' sight from the road, if we want one. But this ain't helpin' our chances a' catchin' up with your sis any."

They continued walking and thumbing all morning, with no luck. Libby was so exhausted that it felt like the noontime shadow pooled beneath her feet was dragging at them with every step. Scab wasn't faring much better. His limp had grown more pronounced, and when they paused to rest at the edge of a wide wheat field, Libby heard his breath catch with pain as he slipped off the knapsack. She collapsed beneath the roadside tree in whose shade they had stopped, and Scab lowered himself painfully to the ground beside her.

"I never knew there were this many miles in the whole *state*," she said, taking off her shoes and rubbing her feet mournfully. "I don't know if I can walk any farther."

"Yeah... maybe we oughta find someplace to sleep for a while." Scab sounded glum. "Reckon we shoulda just gone to the damn freight yard." He shook his head as he fished out the crackers and a can of sardines. "Sorry, kid. Didn't think it out clear. Guess my brain was still rattlin' around from gettin' kicked in the head."

"It's OK." She tried to think of something more to say, but she was dispirited herself, and they ate without talking. Cicadas whirred noisily in the tree above. The sun was coming into its early-summer heat, and the air was sleepy with the scent of green wheat and warm dust. A flock of blackbirds, startled up by something from their midday rest, flew in an undulating ribbon over the field.

Looking out toward the rippling skein of birds, Libby noticed an odd movement among the wheat stalks, far off in the field beneath them. The wheat was only about knee high, and it looked as if something was moving through it, toward the place where she and Scab were sitting. There was something odd about the disturbance in the wheat, and as it drew nearer Libby realized what it was: the parting of the stalks was a good foot-and-a-half wide, and looked as if it would have to be made by a largish animal – certainly one large enough to be seen above the tops of the wheat stalks. Libby could see no animal.

She stared hard, trying to figure it out. "What's that?" she asked Scab, pointing.

Scab, facing toward the road to watch for cars, turned to look over his shoulder. He was still for a moment, squinting. Then, with an odd, flat matter-of-factness, he rasped out one word: "*Run*."

He grabbed Libby's arm, pulling her to her feet and out onto the road. "Wait –" she cried, "what about our –"

"Leave it!"

He raced along the shoulder of the road, pulling her behind him so fast she could hardly keep her feet beneath her. She turned reflexively to look back, but he yanked her arm. "Don't *look – RUN!*"

She faced forward, still running. Something ahead caught her eye, and she pointed. "Scab!"

He looked, and cúrsed: another swath of movement was cutting toward them through the wheat, up ahead and to the right of the road. He veered to the left, pulling her with him. She watched the movement in the wheat with dread, her vision jolting with the pounding of her feet. Whatever was parting the stalks moved as swiftly as a fish through water; she could see there was no way they could outrun it. She heard Scab curse again and, following his gaze, saw the wakes of two more of the things, arrowing toward them through the taller wheat growing on the left side of the highway.

Scab stopped short in the middle of the road, and pulled his razor from his pocket. "You keep goin', kid," he said, shoving her with his other hand. "*Run!*"

But Libby balked, looking wildly around at the approaching swaths. They were nearing the edges of the wheat fields now; if the impossible thing she suspected was true, whatever made them would soon bear down on her and Scab completely unseen. "What are you –" she began, turning back to Scab, and then broke off at what she saw: Scab, his eyes closed, taking two deep, rapid breaths, and lifting the open razor toward his own throat, his movement swift and unhesitating. She saw just in time to grab his arm, hanging on it with all her weight to drag his hand down. "*Scab!*" she cried, and then screamed "*NO!*" as he reached around her to switch the razor to his other hand.

The Birds of the Air | 165

A loud noise blared from the road behind them, and she jumped, crying out. She thought the pursuing things were upon them, but she didn't dare look away from the open razor, from her hands scrabbling to grasp Scab's wrist. But the noise came again, and Scab lowered his arm. She recognized the sound this time: it was the hooting bray of an automobile horn. There behind them on the road, an old Model T truck idled, its engine wheezy, smoke belching from its tailpipe. When she looked around for the things in the wheat, there was no sign of them. A man smiled from the cab of the truck, his arm cocked casually out of the driver's side window. "You kids need a lift?"

IT TOOK LIBBY a long time to think clearly again after she and Scab had piled into the cab of the Model T. While Scab was hustling her around the truck and shoving her through the passenger's door, all she could do was stare back at the places where the things in the wheat had been. She was sure they had come out of the fields and become untraceable, and at any moment would leap on her and Scab and do whatever awful thing they meant to do to them. The expectation crowded everything else from her mind; as soon as she had scrambled onto the seat she grabbed Scab, pulling him in with all her might, causing him to wince as she gripped his bruised arm, and as she leaned across him to claw at the door, trying to help him slam it shut.

Once they were safe – she hoped – inside the truck, she was distantly aware of some interaction between Scab and the man about Scab's knapsack: Scab saying to leave it, and the man insisting on backing up the truck, getting out and picking it up himself. He retrieved the knapsack, Libby's shoes and the flour sack, and tossed them into the back of the truck – without incident, though Scab watched him with wary intensity, and Libby with the nightmarish dread that the unseen things would at any moment drag him down. He also brought the bedroll, which he passed across Libby to Scab when he returned to the driver's seat.

When the man put the truck in gear and they moved off down the highway, Libby's mind shifted from immediate terror to confusion and shock. She turned to stare up at Scab, her mouth open for a good few seconds before she could get her voice to come out. "What were you—" she began, but Scab gripped her arm, hard and surreptitiously, and she fell silent again.

"You ain't thanked the man for givin' us a lift yet, Chigger," he said, fixing her with a pointed stare.

Struggling to gather her wits, she turned to look up at the man. "Th-thank you, Mr... "

"Just call me J.D.," the man said, glancing down at her with a smile. She received a vague impression of affability, and an idea that he looked to be about her mother's age, but she couldn't keep her mind focused. Images kept interposing themselves: the trails in the wheat hurtling toward them, the unfaltering arc of the razor toward Scab's throat. *What happened? What happened?* her mind kept repeating, and it took all of her will not to say it out loud.

As a distant backdrop to these thoughts, she was aware of Scab and the man exchanging pleasantries, of Scab telling the man the prearranged lies about who they were and where they were going. He was talking as if everything was normal, but she could hear a faint tremor in his voice, and knew that he, too, was still badly shaken.

She began to shake uncontrollably, and Scab unrolled the blankets, wrapped one of them around her and folded the other across his knees for her to rest on. He put an arm around her, holding her firmly: an effort, she dimly realized, to hide her trembling from the man J.D., but comforting nonetheless. She heard distantly, without attention or interest, Scab telling the man that his "brother" wasn't feeling too good, but she lost track of their conversation after that. Before long she fell asleep, as much from a need to escape the images and questions in her mind as from exhaustion.

She was awakened by the truck rattling to a stop. When she opened her eyes, she saw it was late afternoon; the truck was parked in the gravel lot of a little restaurant with a neon sign that said "EATS". The man, J.D., had gotten out, and was ambling toward the chrome-and-glass door beneath the sign.

Scab shoved at her. "Get up, kid; can't feel my legs."

She sat up, groggy and bewildered at first, then gut-struck by the memory of what had happened. "*Scab –*" she rasped, but he tossed the blanket off her and flung open the truck door.

"Hush – not now."

He yanked his cap, which had come askew while she slept, back down on her head, and inexpertly shoved some stray hair up under it. "Come on."

She put on her shoes and they joined J.D. at the door; he held it open for them, ringing the little bell inside. He was built like Scab, tall and lanky; he wore a gray fedora, tilted slightly back on his head, and a blue cotton work shirt with the sleeves rolled up. Looking up into his face, Libby noticed there were long, deep grooves on either side of his mouth; she couldn't tell whether they had been drawn there by laughter or by grief. "Feeling better?" he said, smiling down at her.

She nodded dutifully. "Yes, sir."

She followed Scab into the restaurant. J.D. came in after, taking off his hat, and they settled at a table. Her reply to J.D.'s

168 | L. H. Arthur

question had been untrue: she felt sick and shaky, wrung out in the aftermath of terror. She couldn't imagine eating, and dreaded the questions she was sure J.D would ask her, and the lies she would have to come up with to answer them.

But J.D. asked no questions at all. When the waitress came with menus, he waved them off – after a penetrating glance at Scab – and told her that he and Scab would have fried chicken. *Scab can't read,* Libby remembered with a small jolt of renewed surprise. *I wonder if J.D. could tell?*

J.D. measured her with his clear-eyed gaze. "I'm thinking maybe Chigger here still isn't feeling up to eating," he said. "How about a milkshake for you, Chigger? Strawberry, maybe?"

Libby felt her clenched stomach relax a bit, and gave him a relieved smile. "Yes, sir."

Somehow or other, J.D. seemed to handle the conversation so that Scab and Libby didn't have to keep digging up lies to keep their story afloat. He talked with Scab about fishing – calling him Joe, a name Libby guessed Scab must have fabricated while she was asleep – and he teased Libby good-naturedly until, to her amazement, she found herself laughing. *He knows we're not telling him the truth,* she thought, *but he doesn't want to embarrass us.* She felt a surge of gratitude at the realization.

When J.D. paid the bill, and they followed him back to the truck, the sun was almost touching the treetops. He went around to the tailgate, let it down, and dragged a leather grip onto it. "I believe I've got something here...." He opened the grip, dug around inside it, and pulled out a small, black-and-yellow tin box. "Here we go. Come here a minute, will you, Joe?"

Libby felt Scab tense beside her, instantly wary; J.D. must have sensed it too, because his voice took on a note of gentleness, as if he were coaxing a wild animal. "Joe, I can see how much

The Birds of the Air | 169

those ribs hurt you. I think they might be broken, son. I just want to check whether there's one floating around loose in there; if there is, it could puncture a lung, or some other organ."

Scab remained taut as a stretched wire, but after a few seconds he took a couple of shuffling steps toward J.D. Seeing them facing one another, Libby was surprised to notice that J.D. was half-a-head taller. "Lift up your shirt a little," he said, and with some hesitation Scab did so. J.D. probed his bruised skin with extreme gentleness, but still Scab winced and took in a sharp breath.

"Yep." J.D. let Scab's shirt back down, the lines deep at the sides of his mouth. "Cracked, but not broken off. Just be a little careful; they should heal up in a month or two. Gonna hurt like hell for a while, though." He handed Scab the black and yellow tin. "Hold onto these and try to take a couple every four hours or so. They'll help with that toothache, or whatever it is, too."

Scab held the tin up to examine it, and Libby saw it was aspirin.

"Try to take deep, slow breaths once in a while, even though it hurts." J.D. gave Scab a rueful grin. "And – I know you're not gonna do this, but it might be a good idea to take it easy on those cigarettes for week or two. That cough's gonna be no picnic for a while."

Scab had relaxed a bit, but he looked embarrassed by J.D.'s concern. He mumbled thanks and shoved the aspirin tin into his pocket. Libby wondered how J.D. had known about Scab's tooth. She hadn't seen Scab light a cigarette since J.D. picked them up, either, but guessed he had smelled the tobacco on Scab's clothes. "Are you a doctor?" she asked, looking up at him curiously.

He laughed and laid a hand over Scab's cap on her head. His laugh was the exact opposite of Scab's, open and relaxed. "No,

Chigger, I'm not a doctor. Just been around, is all." He turned and, taking hold of Scab's knapsack and the flour bag, dragged them onto the tailgate beside his grip. He looked at Scab. "You sure this is where you want to get off?" he said. "I can take you to wherever your folks are; no trouble at all."

Libby looked at Scab in surprise. Were they in Portersville already, then?

Scab took their belongings in one hand, then held out his other for J.D. to shake. "Thanks, Mr. – J.D.; sure do appreciate it." He glanced at Libby and indicated with a nod that she should retrieve the blankets from the cab. "Think we'll just get off here though; it's close."

Turning back with the blankets, Libby saw J.D, still holding Scab's right hand, put his left one kindly on the side of Scab's neck – a fatherly gesture she expected Scab to pull away from, and was surprised when he didn't. "Sometimes the hard road's the only one that'll get you where you want to go, huh, Joe?" J.D. said, smiling down at Scab. His eyes, Libby noticed, were the same color as the weathered felt of his fedora. He turned to her and moved his hand to her head again, giving it a small, friendly shake. "You take care of your big brother, now, hear?" he said, smiling.

"Yes, sir."

She felt a pang of real sadness, watching him wave and drive off. It was only when the truck had disappeared around a bend that she realized she hadn't thought of the terrible events in the wheat fields for a good half-hour. She looked at Scab, about to say something, but forgot what it was in astonishment: Scab was swiping his sleeve across his face, angrily dashing tears from his eyes.

The Birds of the Air | 171

SHE DIDN'T DARE ask Scab any questions for some time after they left the restaurant. His mood was black as he led the way through the empty streets of the little town J.D. had brought them to; she could feel a bitter anger radiating from him like the heat from the smoldering ruins they had left behind in the jungle. She had a feeling his anger had to do with whatever emotion had overcome him outside the cafe, but she couldn't help going over all she had done and said, worrying that something might have made him angry with her.

Finally, as the late-afternoon shadows lengthened to lie in long stripes across the streets, she could bear it no longer. The brief respite J.D.'s kindness had brought was over, and her mind seethed with anxiety and confusion. She took a long breath and spoke up, testing the waters: "So – this is Portersville?"

Scab glanced down at her with a scowl as fierce as any she had ever seen on his face, but he gave a curt nod.

She waited until she judged enough time had gone by, then ventured, "How far to the pick-up?"

He didn't look at her again. "'Bout another mile an' a half."

She waited longer, gathering her courage, before attempting the questions she really wanted to ask him: "Scab –"

But he turned on her, his face and voice so ferocious that she stumbled backward a bit before she realized she was doing it. "You *talk* too goddamn much, you know that?" He took a step toward her, looming over her, his fists clenched at his sides. "Can't you shut up for five goddamn minutes and let me think?"

The unfairness of it stung her into fury of her own; as he started to turn away, she flung herself at him and shoved him hard, forgetting about his broken ribs until she saw his hand jerk up to his side, his bruised face contort with pain. She didn't care. "*No,*" she yelled, lifting her fists to pummel at him, but stopping herself before he grabbed her wrists with his upheld hands. "I've *been* quiet; I've been quiet *plenty.*" She glared up at him. "I want to know what's going on, and I want to know *NOW.* I'm *sick* of people lying to me, and not telling me things." Her voice was shrill with anger. "What *happened* back there? What were those things in the wheat fields?" She jabbed a finger toward his pocket; "And what were you doing with that *razor?*"

Her anger had tempered Scab's somewhat, though his scowl was still in place. "I was just... takin' *care* a' things, OK?" He kept his hands raised warily. "Them things in the wheat – it was some a' them field-walkers, all right? That's what the 'bo's call 'em, anyway. Same as we seen that first night, and later on in them fields near the river. Just, you can't always see 'em, 'specially in daylight." He lowered his hands, keeping a cautious eye on her. "And – OK, I didn't tell you the truth before: I *do* know what happens if they catch up to you." The rest of his anger seemed to drain away as he spoke. "I was just – takin' *care* a' things. 'Cause them walkers...." He rolled his head back and made an exasperated sound. "All right; sit down a second." He lowered himself stiffly onto the curb; Libby sat beside him, still glowering. "Roach told me this story, long time ago," he said, looking at the ground between his shoes. "This buncha' 'bos, maybe five, six of 'em, was camped out together one night, someplace up north. They got to drinkin' 'round the fire, an' a couple of 'em seen a walker off in the distance. Don't know if they was drunk, ign'rant, or just plain stupid, but they kept starin' at the damn thing till it started after 'em. By the time it caught up with 'em there was more with it – or maybe it was more all along; Roach said it's hard to tell with them things." He looked down at Libby, his gaze drilling into hers. "Only *one* a' them 'bo's got out a' there alive to tell what happened. And what he said was, it wasn't them field walkers killed the other five: they *killed each other.*" He looked away again. "You see now, kid?"

After a few moments, she thought she did.

Her eyes, looking up at him, flooded with tears, and she bent over and buried her face in her folded arms. The tears took hold of her as they had on the day Pullman had taken Maisie. "I'm sorry, Scab," she sobbed. "I'm sorry I yelled at you. I'm sorry I hurt your broken ribs."

Scab laughed, and it sounded more like a real laugh than any she had heard from him before. "That's OK, kid," he said, "I can take it." He put a gruff arm around her shoulders for a moment, giving her a little shake as J.D. had done.

"What *are* those things? Why did they come at us like that?" She shuddered as the picture of it rose again in her mind. "You said they only come after you if you look at them, but I *wasn't* looking at them – I promise! They were already coming when I first saw them!"

"I know. I ain't never seen 'em do that before." His voice was grim, and he hesitated before speaking again. "I don't know exactly *what* they are. Pullman's got some fancy name for 'em. You just see 'em around sometimes, an' usually they just mind their own business. I think the reason they come after us this time... well, I think it might be on accounta' that conjure buried under Pullman's shack. I reckon if Jaeger put that thing there to keep tabs on Pullman, it mighta' ended up keepin' tabs on *us*, too." He rubbed his battered face wearily. "I think maybe he knows about us tryin' to get your sis back. Hate to say it, kid, but... I think we mighta' got Jaeger's attention."

CHAPTER THIRTEEN

SCAB TOOK THEM straight through the town of Portersville to its northern edge, then continued north on a wide dirt road. As the sun set, and twilight began to deepen into darkness, the lighted houses alongside the road gave way to fields, which Libby kept a fearful eye on. "Will they come back, Scab?"

"Don't know. I'm hopin' we lost 'em when J.D. picked us up."

The cooling air was sweet with the scent of wheat and young corn; a mockingbird sang somewhere, and frogs croaked in the irrigation ditches. Libby felt almost angry at the peacefulness of it all, as if the sky, the evening, and the untroubled creatures were all lying to her. The voice of the evil tramp on the train rose in her mind: *most folks walk right on over and don't never know what's underneath.*

She was bone-weary, but she trudged on without complaining. At last Scab turned left onto a narrower dirt road, which passed between the fields toward a dense patch of woodland. "Is the pick-up house in there?" she asked, pointing to the woods.

"Yep," he said, sounding as tired as she felt. "I reckon I can hide you in one of the sheds behind it; don't nobody ever go in those. I'll leave you hid there, sneak off into the woods and come back down the road, like I'm just gettin' there." He glanced down at her, teasing; "Hope you ain't afraid a' rats."

She swallowed, unable to smile. "No," she lied.

It was full dark when they entered the woods, and she grabbed onto Scab's knapsack, as much for comfort as to aid her in staying close to him. The air was damp and mossy-smelling, shrill with cricket songs. Before long, she saw a light glimmering ahead, through the black silhouettes of the branches.

The light shifted gradually to their right as they followed the road, but soon the road came to a dead end, and a gravel drive angled off it toward the light. Instead of turning into the drive, Scab slipped past it and turned into the woods alongside, pulling Libby with him. "We gotta stay out a' sight," he whispered. "Just follow me, quiet as you can." She nodded and crept after him, their steps muffled by drifts of damp dead leaves. Scab pushed his way cautiously through the branches, holding them aside for her, so none of them cracked or even rustled loudly. Before long, she could see a narrow house huddled at the end of the drive, the dark trees pressing in around it. *Maisie might be in there,* she thought, and her heart beat faster.

The light she had seen shone from a single electric bulb over the porch. She could see the gleam of a parked automobile, and a glow on the trees behind the house, as if light was shining from some window in the rear.

As they crept past the lit and curtained window in back, Libby saw small outbuildings behind the house: a disused henhouse, an old privy, and some kind of storage shed. Scab slipped through the trees like a shadow, heading toward the henhouse. Libby cringed at every twig that snapped beneath her feet as she followed, thankful for the loud chorus of the night insects.

When they reached the rear of the henhouse, her tense breathing eased a bit. Scab forced open the rust-stiffened bolt on the door, and they crept inside.

By the dim diffusion of the house light, filtering through the chicken-sized entrance to the hen yard, Libby could just make out the rough plank floor and the shelved laying boxes, still containing dusty remnants of straw. Scab unrolled the blankets and gave them to her; she spread one on the floor and sank onto it, exhausted.

Scab sat with his back to the wall and rolled a cigarette. As soon as he lit it, he started coughing, almost silently, and Libby saw his hand go to his side.

"You ever take any of that aspirin J.D. gave you?" she whispered.

"Naw, ain't got around to it." He dug in his pocket for the tin.

"How come you smoke those cigarettes, when they make you cough so much?" she asked, watching him swallow the aspirin with water from his bottle.

"'Cause I get mean if I don't."

Libby took the bottle when he offered it, and managed a half-hearted smile. "You're mean anyway."

He let out a startled, smoke-filled breath of laughter; this got him coughing again, and he doubled over, holding his side and trying to keep quiet. Libby started laughing – the helpless, half-hysterical laughter of exhaustion – and had to struggle to remain silent as well. *We're acting like a couple of little kids playing hide and seek,* she thought, *like this is all a game.* She wondered if they had both finally lost their senses.

When her laughter had subsided, she lay down and wrapped the blanket around her. The picture of the trails in the wheat kept rising in her mind, and the knowledge that Maisie might be near made lying there doing nothing feel almost unbearable. She cast around for something to distract her, and turned her face toward the glow of Scab's cigarette. "Scab – you said Pullman saved your life, one time. How did that happen?"

He was quiet for so long she thought he wouldn't answer; then, when he did, his hushed words seemed to have nothing to do with her question: "Did you know I'm part colored?"

She thought about this, confused. "*Part* colored? And part white?" She made out his nod in the dim light, and frowned, puzzled. "I didn't know colored people and white people ever got married."

He made a scornful sound. "Gettin' married ain't got nothin' to do with it. My ma's mother, she got raped by some piece-a-shit white bastard; few months later, my mama come along."

Libby's confusion was only compounded. She didn't know what "raped" was, but something in Scab's tone kept her from asking. After a moment, not knowing what else to say, she murmured, "No... I didn't know."

"Well, them sons-a-bitches that like to beat the hell out a' colored folks never seem to have no trouble tellin'." He drew on the cigarette, and in its orange glow his grim, battered face looked like something from the posters of the scary movies Libby's mother wouldn't let her and Maisie go to see. "Ended up in a freight car with a few of 'em one day."

"What happened?"

"'Bout what you'd expect. They beat the ever-lovin' shit out a' me, then tossed me off the train when she was doin' thirty, forty miles an hour." He gave another short laugh. "Couple of 'em was bleedin' pretty good before it was all over, though. Don't remember nothin' else till a few days after. Woke up at Pullman's place – not one a' them jungle camps; a house he was stayin' at then, outside a' St. Louis. Had some bones broke, an' about half the skin on my right side took off. Pullman said he was just drivin' by, saw me layin' there next to the tracks. He took me home, got a doctor, took care a' me till I healed up. Been workin' for him ever since."

Libby lay silent, not knowing what to say. After a while she murmured, "Roach told me something... something about your family –"

Scab shifted sharply against the wall. "That ol' bakehead can't hardly *breathe* for talkin'." He stubbed out the cigarette. "I oughta get goin', kid."

"OK, but – I wasn't gonna –" Libby peered through the dark, trying to make out his features. "I just wanted to say... my dad kind of left me, too. He was a signalman, for the CB&Q? And – my Grandma told me, he made some kind of mistake, and it... well, some people died. So... a little while after that, he went out to his workshop with the hunting rifle, and..." She trailed off, feeling somehow ashamed to say out loud what he had done. "You know what I mean?" she finished lamely.

"Yeah. I know what you mean."

She sighed, relieved. "Anyway... I just wanted to tell you that."

"OK, kid." He reached a hand across the space between them and gave her shoulder a rough pat. "Get some sleep; I'll head out now," he whispered. He took the rest of their food from his knapsack, left it on the dusty floor with the water bottle, and slung the knapsack over his shoulders. "Just keep quiet, and stay

The Birds of the Air | 179

hid in here till I come get you. Don't know how long it'll be; if your sis is here, I'll hafta wait till they're asleep to sneak her out. Just be patient, and *stay put.*"

Libby nodded, and watched as he slipped out the door. She slid over to the little chicken door and lay on her stomach to see what she could see though it, feeling like a very much dirtier and more miserable Alice, stuck in a Wonderland that promised to be both nerve-racking and mind-numbingly dull. She could see very little through the opening: the wire-fenced hen yard, a strip of graveled driveway alongside the house, and the crowding trees, all ghostly in the diffuse light from the house. There was no sight or sound of Scab.

She sighed and rubbed her eyes; she felt chilled and half-starved. She slid back across the floor to her blanket, wrapped herself in its scratchy folds and fished some crackers from the tin. When she had eaten them she lay down, hoping to sleep, but her thoughts were restless and anxious. Her body felt too small to contain both the hope that Maisie would be here and the fear that she wouldn't. She lay trying to pick out any sound of Scab's return from among the noises of night-speaking creatures for what felt like an hour or more. She stared up at the dim, cobwebbed beams of the ceiling, trying to find other things to think about, but every thought that came to her frightened and overwhelmed her: the nightmare flight from the things in the wheat field; what Scab had told her about the men who beat him on the train; the ominous word "rape" he had used about his grandmother; what they would do if Maisie wasn't there, and what they would do if she was.

She began to think she could hear a furtive scratching at the henhouse door, as if some small creature was trying to get in. She turned to look, and when the motion of her head seemed to take an incalculable time, she realized she was dreaming.

She fixed her gaze on the bottom of the door, and saw it moving back and forth, a fraction of an inch out and then back again, as if something was pulling on it but having trouble getting it open. At last a narrow crack appeared between the door and its frame, and she watched with torpid dread as something pushed its way in. It was small – not much longer than her hand – and pinkish-red with streaks of white here and there. It turned a headless stub of neck toward her, as if it could see her with it, and started to crawl toward her on the stumps of its legs, and she recognized it as one of the skinned dead animals from Scab's snares in the forest. The knowledge that she was dreaming didn't prevent horror from swelling in her chest as the thing made its way across the dusty floorboards, moving spasmodically toward her; she couldn't make her body move, and was trying to force a scream past some painful constriction in her throat, when she was jolted awake by Scab's voice, raised angrily outside.

"I *told* ya, I sent her back home."

Dazed with sleep and the clinging horror of the dream, she jerked upright, then remembered where she was and slid across the floor to look out the chicken-door again.

Scab stood in the dim porch light at the edge of the driveway, some way off near the front corner of the house. Roach stood beside him, looking unhappy; his gnarled hands clutched a rifle, pointed at the ground. A few paces away, Pullman stood scanning the forest and the outbuildings, his back to the other two.

Scab was still talking. "Slater's crew come around, and then we seen that conjure-jar, and I was scared to keep her around any longer, so I put her on a bus home. Bought the ticket myself, the money I saved." Pullman ignored him. "Shoulda done that

The Birds of the Air | 181

four days ago, you ask me," Scab went on. "I told you then: we shoulda sent her home soon as we got her *back* from them sons-a-bitches."

Libby realized he was trying to distract or stall Pullman, and was speaking loudly so she would hear him, but she didn't know what she should do. Should she try to sneak away, run off? What had happened to make Pullman suspect she was here? She was shaken by the sight of the rifle, and worried for Scab; and if she did sneak away, she didn't know what she would do afterward. *Scab said to stay put,* she thought. She lay still and watched.

"Come on, fellas," Scab said, his tone coaxing now. "Don't know who's been handing you this horseshit, but they got it all wrong."

"Quiet, you ungrateful whelp," Pullman growled, and Libby saw him dart a fierce glance at Roach. "Keep him quiet, or I'll shut him up myself."

"Now Scab, don't make things no worse than they already are," Roach said, sounding miserable. "Better listen to ol' Pullman and hush up."

Scab paid no attention. "We never shoulda—" he began again, but instantly Pullman swung around and struck him backhanded; when she saw the blow strike Scab's already battered face, Libby cried out before she could stop herself, then clapped both hands over her mouth.

Pullman's eyes fixed on the henhouse immediately. "Libby," he called, his tone stern, "It's time for you to come out now." He kept staring as if his gaze could pierce the wooden wall; Libby fought the impulse to cover her eyes with her hands, as if she were a little child who thought such an action could conceal her. "Come now, Elizabeth," Pullman said; there was an edge of something more than sternness in his voice this time, and Libby felt behind her eyes the uncanny tingling sensation she had felt in the shack on the night he had left. "I don't want to have to compel you, and I don't want to have to hurt your foolish young friend here anymore."

Libby saw Scab spit on the ground – maybe bleeding again – and his voice came rasping: "Goddammit, Pullman, she *ain't out there.*" As she watched, Pullman closed his eyes for a moment; she saw his jaw muscles clench, and his head duck down a bit, his chin angling to one side in a way that struck her as dangerous. He turned and took a step toward Scab, and Libby found herself pounding on the wooden wall of the henhouse. "Stop it!" she screamed; "Don't hit him anymore! I'm coming!"

Through the little opening, she saw Pullman and Roach turn toward her, but Scab dropped his head, looking beaten in a way he hadn't after Pullman hit him. "I'm coming!" she yelled again; she turned and raced out of the henhouse, and back toward the driveway.

As soon as she rounded the corner, Scab lifted his head. "Run hide in the woods, kid! They ain't gonna do nothin' to me. Get on back to town and get the police to take you home!"

Libby slowed to a walk, but she ignored Scab and continued along the drive until she stood in front of Pullman. "Please, Mr. Pullman." Her voice quavered. "We just want my sister. Please – just let us have her, and let us go. I won't say anything to anyone, I promise, I *promise!*"

Pullman gave her a grim smile. "I'm afraid you're a little late, my dear." He glanced at Roach and nodded toward the house: "Take her inside."

"Come on, sis," Roach said.

Libby looked at Scab; his head was lowered again. "We'll be

along," Pullman said. "I just want to talk to your... *paladin*, here, for a moment."

Roach put a gentle hand on her shoulder, and she went with him, glancing back often at Scab and Pullman.

Inside, it smelled like bacon and eggs cooking, and Libby's stomach grumbled in spite of her anxiety. "You want somethin' to eat, sis?" Roach said.

Libby looked up at him. "He won't hit Scab again, will he?"

"Aww, naw, sis – don't worry." Roach gave her an unconvincing smile. "He's got a temper all right, but he's over it now. They'll be in in a minute, just like he said."

The house was old, its interior dark. The musty scent of disintegrating fabric and wallpaper lurked beneath the smell of cooking. Roach laid his hand on her shoulder once more and tried to lead her through the bare entry hall, back toward the lit kitchen she could see at the end, but she pulled away. "What did Mr. Pullman mean, a little late?"

Roach looked even more unhappy. "Well, sis..." he dropped his gaze to the floor and rubbed the back of his neck. "I reckon what he means is... Simms, Mr. Jaeger's carrier? He already come, picked up your little sis." He darted a wretched glance at her face, then dropped his eyes again immediately. "He come this afternoon; she might even be with ol' Jaeger by now."

Libby stared at him for a moment, then leaned against the chalky wallpaper and slid down to sit on the floor. She thought she would cry, but she didn't; instead she just stared into the space between the wall she was leaning against and the one opposite, seeing nothing and thinking nothing.

She was distantly aware of Roach shifting miserably, moving the rifle from one arm to the other; he peered down at her, seeming uncertain what to do. She only half heard him as he went on. "One a' Jaeger's people seen you an' Scab in Seifert, an' when Simms come, he told Pullman about it. Pullman was awful mad; and we was both worried sick, 'cause Simms said –"

The door opened and Pullman came inside, pushing Scab ahead of him and breaking off Roach's one-sided conversation. Pullman paused for a moment when he saw Libby on the floor; then he shut the door. "All right," he said, his voice grim, "all of you, into the kitchen."

Libby looked up at Scab as Pullman propelled him past her, but he didn't meet her gaze. Roach went after Pullman, and Libby dragged herself to her feet and followed.

The kitchen held a large stove, an icebox, and a table surrounded by six ladder-backed chairs. As Libby entered, Pullman pushed Scab down onto one of the chairs. "Sit down, Elizabeth," he said, in a tone that allowed for no argument, and Libby shuffled to the table and sank onto the chair next to Scab's. "I'm going to make a telephone call," Pullman said. "I want you two to stay right there; I'll deal with you in a moment." He stalked out of the kitchen; Libby heard a door shut in the hallway and, after a minute or so, the indistinct sound of his voice from another room.

Roach leaned the rifle in a corner near the stove, and lit the burner under an iron skillet. "I reckon you two must be near starved," he said, but neither Libby nor Scab answered. Soon Pullman's uneven steps sounded in the hallway. "Now," he growled as he entered the kitchen, "what in the bloody hell did the two of you think you were playing at?" He stationed himself across the table from Scab and Libby, leaning toward them, his hands gripping the backs of the two chairs opposite, his eyes blazing like the blue gas-flame under Roach's skillet. "Your *disobedience* is evident, and *you*, at least –" he glared at Scab – "should have recognized the foolishness of your *intentions*." He turned his glare on Libby. "Now – and only after *extensive* persuasion, I might add – I drag out of Scab the particulars of this attack on the two of you by khatojana. Are you trying to get yourself *killed*, Elizabeth? Or get *Scab* killed? Do you still not comprehend the danger of meddling in these affairs?"

Libby felt anger kindling in place of the numb despair that had gripped her in the hall. "*You're* the one who put us in danger – me *and* my sister!" she cried. "You took us away from home; you *lied* to me, and you stole my sister, and I'm not going home until I get her *back*."

Pullman slammed his open hand onto the tabletop, making her jump. "I've *explained* to you, Elizabeth, that this is the best thing *for* your sister. I gather Scab has told you about Mr. Jaeger. Well, he has devoted all his formidable skill, intelligence and resources to the well-being of children like Maisie. He has created an entire infrastructure for the sole purpose of protecting and educating them; he has dedicated his life to finding them and keeping them safe from John Fuller. You asked me, the other day, what would happen if you and your sister went back home. What do you *think* would happen, Elizabeth? Your mother is a woman alone. She has none of the knowledge or experience needed to care for an extraordinary child such as Maisie. Do you really think *she* would be able to protect your sister from John Fuller? Or develop her gifts to their full potential?"

Libby could think of no response to this, and a hard knot of dread began to form in her stomach, like a poisonous pod threatening to disperse its seeds all through her. She shoved it down with all her inner force, and met Pullman's burning gaze with one of her own. "Why should I believe you? You lied to me. And anyway, even if all that stuff you're saying was true, why would you *steal* Maisie? Why wouldn't you just tell our mother? Why wouldn't you talk with *her* about what Maisie needed?"

"Because that doesn't *work*." Pullman struck the table again on the last word, but less forcefully than before; then he drew a long breath, as if to summon his patience. "Libby, I understand how cruel this seems to you, how wrong; but, as difficult as it may be for you to believe, we have good *reason* for the methods we use. We know from centuries of experience – some of it unspeakable – that *secrecy* is the only sure protection for people like your sister, Mr. Jaeger, and myself." He ran a hand over his face. "I do owe you an apology, though. Scab and Mr. Jaeger are right: I should never have brought you into all this. It was a breach of that imperative of secrecy, and it's led to nothing but trouble. But after that imbecile Stubby allowed you to free your sister..." He sighed. "I knew it was a risk, but I couldn't bear the thought of the child trapped in that transmutation, never to be found or restored. I had *hoped* that, with your help, we could recover her within a day or two, and then return you to your home, gambling on the likelihood that no one would believe your story. I should never have chanced it. Mr. Jaeger is very unhappy with me, and I can't blame him."

Libby slumped, elbows on the table, and dropped her head into her hands. "How do I know if *anything* you say is true? You've lied to me about *everything*! You told me it was John Fuller who sent that man to take Maisie, but it was *you* all along! You said you wanted to *help* me, when you just wanted to steal my sister!" She met Pullman's gaze with a tearful glare. "How do I know it's this man John Fuller my sister needs to be protected from, and not *you*? How do I know there even *is* a John Fuller? I've never seen Maisie do anything different from other kids. You could

The Birds of the Air | 187

even be lying about her having these – *abilities.*" She dropped her eyes. "Just like you lied when you said you'd help me."

"And what conceivable *reason* would I have to do that? *Think,* Elizabeth. The necessity for my previous deception is perfectly clear; I've explained it to you. But what *possible* motivation could I have to lie about your sister's abilities? Why would I go to all this trouble, just to burden myself with a perfectly ordinary – no, with *two* perfectly ordinary – little girls? With times as they are now, parents are abandoning their *own* children!" He gestured toward Scab, and at the edge of her vision Libby saw him stiffen. "Do you imagine I'm running some sort of *business*? Stealing mouths to feed, and trying to sell them to people who can't even feed the children they already *have*? Is your mother wealthy, like the Lindberghs, that I would come up with this elaborate scheme to kidnap her daughters?" His eyes drilled into Libby's. "These abilities *exist*; you've *seen* them. The fact that a child of Maisie's age hasn't shown evidence of them yet means nothing. If you possess any intelligence at *all*, it should be perfectly apparent to you that my actions – and Mr. Jaeger's, and Slater's – make no sense in any context other than the one I've described to you. And as to John Fuller... out of necessity I have had to misrepresent certain things to you, Libby, but believe me, John Fuller is not one of them. The threat he poses to these children is all too real."

Scab shifted in his chair, his face hard. "Seems to me like your *boss* is the one goin' around threatenin' *kids*," he said, indicating Libby with a slight, impatient movement of his hand. "We found that hex-jar a' his, an' next thing you know we got walkers comin' after us."

Pullman's gaze, turned back to Scab, became icy. "Ah; our gutter Galahad lets his voice be heard. *My* boss, is it? You're awfully sanctimonious all of a sudden. Shall I recount for our young friend some of the business *you* have undertaken in exchange for Mr. Jaeger's money?"

Scab's eyes dropped to the tabletop, and he bent his head a bit, as if Pullman's gaze held a heat too intense for him to face. Libby saw the muscles of his jaw tense.

Pullman sighed; a little of his anger seemed to leave him, and he pulled out one of the chairs and sat down. "You've no idea what you're talking about, Stephen. That *fhaireoir* – that… *watcher*, or 'hex-jar', as you call it – is a tactic of John Fuller's. Mr. Jaeger has discovered others like it once or twice, at other outposts, and questioned the builders until he discovered which men Fuller had bribed to place them there." He leaned back. "And this brings us to the matter at hand: Mr. Jaeger was – of course – *not* the one who sent those creatures after the two of you. One way or another – most likely through that *fhaireoir* – Fuller has found out about Libby, and it would seem he considers her a threat: an outsider who has enough knowledge and motivation, or so he believes, to put his own operations at risk of discovery." He fixed Libby with his glare again. "And Elizabeth, let me spell this out for you plainly, since you seem determined to close your eyes to the facts: this danger would not end if you were to retrieve your sister and go home. If Fuller wasn't aware of your sister before, he *certainly* is now. The next time a stranger comes to capture Maisie, it will be one of *Fuller's* agents."

"Whose fault is that?" Scab said, his voice bitter, but his head still bent.

Pullman's gaze looked as if it might burn through the boy's forehead. "And what would *you* have done in my place, Stephen? Just left the little girl trapped in that form, for however long she survived? Tell me this: who was meant to be –" But here,

Scab flinched visibly, and his eyes shot up to meet Pullman's. Whatever Pullman saw in his look, it seemed to cause him to relent a bit; he left his sentence unfinished, and bent his own head for a moment, trying, it appeared, to reign in his anger. At last he spread his fingers in a gesture of concession. "I'm afraid Scab is right, in part... my rash actions have put you in grave danger, Libby, and may even have increased the danger Fuller poses to your sister – *if* he didn't know about her before." His gaze turned to Scab again, hardening. "However, had *you* obeyed my instructions –"

Roach came to the table, a plate of eggs and bacon in each hand. "Aw, boss," he said mildly, "Sis here prob'ly wouldn't a' been no safer at home, once ol' Fuller got his mind set on her."

Pullman turned a black scowl on him. "Unless, you old fool, it was the idiotic plans these two made after we *left* that caused him to *decide* she was a threat."

Roach nodded, but held out the plates a bit. "Let 'em eat somethin' now, huh boss? They must be starved."

Pullman continued to scowl, but assented with a wave. Roach set the plates in front of Scab and Libby, and in spite of her anger and misery, Libby attacked the food ravenously. Roach poured coffee from a pot on the stove, and set steaming cups in front of Scab and Pullman. "Don't scold 'em no more, boss," he coaxed. "They've had a rough enough time already."

"Sit down and be quiet, you old busybody, before I pick up that rifle and shoot you where you stand," Pullman growled; but he sipped the coffee and didn't berate Scab further. Roach only smiled, got a cup for himself, and took a seat at the end of the table.

"Mr. Jaeger believes Fuller has fixed those khatojana on

you, specifically, Stephen," Pullman said. "I've heard talk of such things being possible, but I've never seen it done."

"Wh-why would he *do* that?" Libby asked.

"Come on, kid; thought I explained all that." Scab bowed his head, propping it between his clenched hands, elbows on either side of his plate. One of his legs bounced up and down in a rapid, restless motion that reminded Libby of her mother's sewing machine. "Fuller sent them walkers after us, on *purpose*, to make it so... so I'd...."

"So he'd kill you," Pullman finished for him flatly.

"But... *how* could those things make him..." Libby's throat felt as if there were a stone lodged in it, and she couldn't finish her question.

"The khatojana enter the *minds* of those they utilize, Libby. *Possession*, people used to call it, in less complacent times. These particular khatojana were sent to enter *Scab's* mind, to goad him into murdering a selected target: you. Apparently John Fuller feels that one little girl's awareness of our activities is enough of a threat to warrant this kind of..." his face darkened before he spat out the word... "barbarism. And... it's because of *me* that you possess that awareness." He stared into his coffee for a moment, then rose abruptly and crossed to a cabinet. Taking a bottle with no label from a shelf, he sat down and poured a bit of the contents into his coffee cup. Roach took the bottle when he offered it, and poured from it into his cup as well.

"What'd ol' Jaeger say?" Roach asked.

"He's going to call me back. He believes he may know of a way we can get the khatojana off Scab's trail."

Scab looked up. "But – we *lost* 'em, didn't we?"

"Not permanently, I'm afraid," Pullman said. "Neither Mr. Jaeger nor I, of course, have had any dealings with such creatures, but Mr. Jaeger has read and heard a great deal about them. It seems not every person is a suitable candidate for possession by them – though if Mr. Jaeger knows the reason for that, he didn't convey it to me. He believes that Fuller somehow determined that you were not only a *convenient* vessel for his purpose, but a *serviceable* one, as well, and targeted you for that reason. He suspects the creatures won't stop tracking you until the task Fuller has set them is accomplished – or until he calls them back himself. In fact, he was rather surprised they haven't caught up with you again already."

Scab raked both hands through his hair, stopping halfway to clutch his head as if he were trying to hold it together. "What if I get *out* a' here? Go off somewhere, away from the kid?" He pushed his chair back, looking ready to leave the house on the instant.

"No, lad. They'd likely be able to drive you back here – or to Libby's home, or wherever she chanced to be."

Scab looked stunned; the bruises stood out starkly on his ashen face. "Reckon maybe I had the right idea out there on the road, then."

Libby's mouth dropped open, but before she could protest, Pullman gave a quiet chuckle. "Let's wait to hear Mr. Jaeger's plan before we resort to anything as melodramatic as all *that*, my boy," he said. "We have a bit more time for thought than you had on the road there. Mr. Jaeger believes there is a way we can cast the khatojana out, and send them back to Fuller in such a way that he will believe they have accomplished what he sent them to do." He lifted his eyes to Scab. "But in order to do that, my boy... we'll first have to let them in."

CHAPTER FOURTEEN

BEFORE SCAB AND Libby had finished eating, the telephone in the parlor rang. Pullman went to answer it, and spent a good half-hour shut up in the room. From the kitchen, Libby could hear the occasional rumble of his voice, but he seemed mostly to listen. When he came out, he held several small sheets of paper covered with penciled notes; he looked grim, but not, Libby thought, hopeless.

The first part of the plan was to restrain Scab. "Roach and I are going to be too busy with preparations for a while to keep watch on you," Pullman told him, "and there's no way to predict when those creatures will catch up with you again."

Only the basement proved secure enough to meet with Pullman's approval. He found a dusty toolbox, dug out a screw-driver, and removed the sturdy sliding bolt from the back door in the kitchen. Taking the bolt to the hallway, he screwed it onto the outside of the basement door. Roach carried one of the kitchen chairs down the creaking basement steps, and set it under the single hanging bulb. He took down a bottle of water, and found an empty bucket – "Case you need to take a leak," he said to Scab, apologetic.

Libby watched from the top of the stairs, mournful, as Scab lowered his bruised body stiffly onto the chair in the tomblike room. "Wait!" she said when Roach reached the top of the stairs and prepared to bolt the door. She raced out to the henhouse and retrieved the blankets, then ran back and started down the stairs to take them to Scab, but Roach stopped her. "You go on out, sis. I'll take 'em down to him. Better safe than sorry." When she still lingered, he put a kindly hand on her shoulder, but spoke firmly. "We gotta do this, sis. Not just to keep *you* safe; Scab bein' locked in here could make the difference between him gettin' bad hurt or not; might even make the difference between him livin' *through* this or not."

Libby gaped at him, shocked. "What do you mean?"

Roach looked at her hard. "Weren't you *listenin'*, sis?" He glanced down the stairs, then drew her back a bit from the open door. "We got no *idea* when them things might turn up. If they get here before Pullman's ready, and get hold a' Scab, won't be no way to stop 'em – except by stoppin' *him*."

LIBBY HELPED ROACH stack a large pile of firewood outside, near a ring of soot-blackened stones a little way from the front of the house. Roach cut some kindling and laid a fire in the ring, but didn't light it. The woodland night still held the last of the spring coolness, and he fetched a quilt from one of the bedrooms, gave it to Libby, and bent to look her in the eyes. "I need you to wait outside now, sis. I don't want you comin' in that house before Pullman or I say. We got some business we gotta attend to without no interruptions."

When he had gone back inside, Libby wrapped the quilt around her and lay back on the grass. The leaves stirred above her, picked out by oblique light from the porch bulb. Night insects sang, and after a while she dozed.

She had disjointed, feverish dreams for a while, often half-waking. At last she slipped into a deeper sleep, and in her dream she found herself back in the parking lot of the restaurant. She was standing beside J.D., near his truck, waiting for Scab, Pullman and Roach, who were inside the building. She looked to see if they were coming, but instead of the little café with the "EATS" sign, she saw Pullman's shack standing there, burning.

She ran to try to open the door, but it was sheeted over with flames, and through them she could see the padlock snapped shut in the hasp of the bolt. The fire burned fiercely, scaling the walls and rising above the roof. Panicked, she raced around to the little window. Its glass had broken; through the jagged hole she could see more flames, and beyond them Pullman, Roach and Scab, trapped in the far corner, their faces contorted with pain.

She stood weeping, not knowing what to do, and found J.D. by her side again. He was smiling down at her, untroubled. "Use *that*," he said, pointing toward her hands. Looking down, she saw she was holding the glass vial the woman had given her in the clearing. She frowned up at J.D. in confusion; even dream logic told her the tiny amount of liquid in the vial would never put out the towering flames. But he pointed again, insistent: "Hurry."

Not knowing what else to do, she obeyed him, twisting off the little cap and throwing the few drops of liquid toward the blaze.

It looked to her as if the heat evaporated the liquid before

The Birds of the Air | 195

it even reached the flames, but in the next instant the fire had vanished completely, leaving the shack charred and scorched but still standing. "Kid!" she heard Scab's voice calling; "kid!" And then she was awake, lying on the grass under the trees.

"Looked like you were havin' a bad dream," Scab said. He stood near the fire-pit, a kitchen chair slung in his hand. The shirt he had bought in Seifert was gone; he wore a sleeveless undershirt instead, and Libby could see the shadow of Jaeger's mark on his chest through the thin ribbed cotton. Roach stood at his side, holding the rifle.

Libby blinked at them and sat up, still shaken from the dream. "What are you doing?"

"Almost time," Roach said. "Gotta get ol' Scab here ready."

Scab carried the chair to a young tree a couple of yards from the fire pit. The tree's trunk was about as big around as Libby; he set the chair down with its back against it, facing the pit. Roach followed; he laid the rifle on the ground and pulled a coil of sturdy cord from his pocket.

Scab dug his knife and razor out of his pockets and handed them to Roach, who tutted and shook his head. "Shoulda thought to take these from you before," he said, sliding them into his own pocket. "Must be gettin' old."

When Scab had settled himself on the chair, Roach bound his wrists tightly, joining them together with a short, doubled length of cord behind the tree. "Ain't you got nothin' stronger'n that?" Scab asked, scowling over his shoulder.

"Aw, don't you worry – this here's plenty strong enough to hold a skinny little ol' kid like you," Roach said; but, seeing the solid-looking muscles in Scab's arms, and remembering the strength with which he had restrained her during Slater's calling, Libby didn't feel so sure.

Roach crouched by the laid-out fire and lit it, then turned to Libby. "Now sis, we got a couple things to finish up inside. You keep this fire goin' for me. And I want you to *stay away from Scab*; ain't no tellin' when them things might show up. If anything happens before we come out, you holler for us, you hear?"

Libby nodded, and Roach returned to the house.

Scab slouched on the chair, his long legs splayed and his head dropped forward. Libby thought at first he was trying to sleep, but when she looked more closely she could see the firelight reflected in his eyes. She sat on the ground a few feet from his chair. "Too close," he said brusquely, and she looked up, startled, to see him frowning down at her.

She moved a couple of yards from him and sat back down, hugging her knees to her chest. "Scab... are you mad at me?"

He glanced at her, and some of the fierceness left his face. "Naw, kid, I ain't mad at you. I'm just... scared a' what might happen."

Libby nodded. "Me too."

He was silent for a while, frowning down at the ground between his feet. "Kid," he said finally, "no matter what them walkers make it look like, I want you to know it ain't *me* wants to hurt you."

Libby nodded again and tried to smile.

Roach and Pullman were a long time coming out. After a while Libby got up and put more wood on the fire. Scab allowed her near for a moment to take the tobacco pouch from his pocket and – sending her to her old spot a little way off from him – coached her through several failed attempts at rolling a cigarette before she was finally able to produce one that held together. She placed it between his lips and lit it for him; after that he gestured with his head for her to back off, clenching the cigarette at the corner of his mouth while he coughed after his first inhalation. He grimaced in pain at the cough.

"Does it hurt your ribs, sitting like that?' Libby asked, hovering.

"Naw, I'm OK."

"Your hands all right? Is it too tight or anything?"

"I said I'm OK, kid. Now get on back away from me."

"Scab," she said after she had settled herself on the ground again, "I'm sorry about all this."

"Will you quit sayin' you're sorry all the time? It ain't your fault."

"I guess. But I feel like it is."

"That's just 'cause you're a kid. That's what kids always think." He tilted his head back against the tree trunk, holding the cigarette in one side of his mouth and talking out of the other. "When I was a kid, I always kinda figured it was my fault when my dad worked me over, even if I didn't know why he was doin' it. If he started in on my ma, or one a' my little brothers or sisters, I'd get so mad, I felt like I coulda killed him. But when it was me… I mean, I'd get mad all right, but I always just figured it was somethin' wrong with *me* made him do it." He breathed a laugh – a less bitter-sounding one than usual, though Libby couldn't imagine why. "Sometimes I even figured it was somethin' wrong with me made him get after my ma, and my sisters and brothers." He shook his head. "That's just how kids are, I guess."

"Scab… I know it's not a good time to ask, but… what's gonna happen after this? Will Pullman try to take me home?"

Scab snorted. "Try? Hell no; he's gonna *take* you home, like I shoulda done after he left. You know what he said to me after you an' Roach went inside earlier?"

Libby shook her head.

"He said I was a damned fool, lettin' a little ol' shirttail girl talk me into doin' somethin' that was liable to get us both killed. An' he's right."

"But Roach said it wouldn't have helped, even if you took me home. And my sister —"

Scab broke in: "Maybe Pullman's right about that too, kid. Maybe she *is* better off with Jaeger. She ain't like us regular folks; you took her home, she'd prob'ly just grow up mean and mad, 'cause she never got to do what's in her to do."

Libby scowled. "How can it be *right* to steal a kid away from her family? You're talking as crazy as Pullman."

Scab gave his short laugh again. "Maybe so, kid." He was quiet for a bit, his eyes fixed on the fire without seeming to see it. "I really did have a little brother called Chigger," he said at last. "His real name was Charlie, but he wasn't no bigger than a little ol' bug, so we always called him Chigger."

Libby turned her head quietly to look at him; his talking like this made her feel she ought to be still and silent, as she would if a wild animal wandered near to her in the forest. "How old is he?" she ventured after he had said nothing more for a while.

"Aw... he ain't around no more." Scab's voice was barely louder than the evening breeze that twisted the smoke off into the woods. "He died a' the diphtheria when he was about three. Guess he woulda been... nine, ten years old by now. Been what — seven years? — an' I still think about him near every day." He was quiet for a long time, and Libby sat silent too, not knowing what to say. Then he gave another cough and tilted his head to angle the stub of the cigarette upward. "Would you come get this damn thing, kid? It's fixin' ta burn me."

Pullman and Roach came out as she was tossing the stub into the fire. Both were without jackets, shirtsleeves rolled up;

when Pullman turned to close the door, Libby saw that his shirt clung to his back, dark with sweat.

Roach held the rifle in the crook of one arm. In the other hand he carried a stand of some sort – a tall, spindly little marble-topped table Libby hadn't noticed in the house, maybe a washstand from one of the bedrooms. Both men looked grim and haggard, and Libby noticed, as Pullman drew near to the fire, that his face was pale, his forehead beaded with sweat. He carried a black leather bag that looked like the one the family doctor carried back home, and when he set it on the ground near the fire, Libby saw that his left hand was wrapped in a makeshift bandage: not the old one from when he had cut his palm with Scab's razor, but a new, larger one, stained with fresh blood.

He opened the bag and took out a metal bowl, similar to the one Slater had used back in the jungle, but slightly larger. Roach leaned the rifle against a tree a little distance away, then set the stand by the fire. Pullman set the bowl on top of it. "Very well, children," he said, "we're ready to begin." He fixed each of them with a stern stare. "Now, before we start, I want to make one thing clear: this is a desperate undertaking. It could potentially cost any or all of us our lives. These creatures are not to be trifled with; yet, of course, out of necessity, that's exactly what we're attempting to do. So I want you all – and you especially, Libby – to obey *exactly* and *immediately* any directions I give during this procedure. Do you understand?" Libby and Scab nodded; Roach said "Yes, boss," looking a little ill.

Pullman fished from his shirt pocket the folded pages of notes he had brought out of the parlor earlier, and a pair of steel-rimmed spectacles. "Libby," he said, "I want you over there, to my right, on the far side of the fire from Scab. You'll be responsible for keeping the fire burning. Keep it high; we'll need its light." He nodded to Roach. Roach took a tin cup from the bag, used it to scoop up some hot coals from the fire pit, and tipped them into the metal bowl. "All right," Pullman said, "everyone keep quiet now." He stood over the stand, squinting at the paper. Spreading his good hand above the bowl, he began to murmur in a language Libby couldn't understand. The firelight flickered over him, casting his monstrous, wavering shadow onto the front of the house. Libby peered at the bandaged hand that held the papers, wondering what was wrong with it. Scab sat hunched in the chair, his body tense and his head a little lowered.

Without pausing in his unintelligible speech, Pullman nodded at Roach again, and Roach took two jars from the bag. He uncapped one and held it ready until Pullman put out a hand for it. Pullman, still muttering, poured a small amount of clear, colorless liquid from the jar onto the glowing coals, and Libby expected the coals to die. Instead, brilliant yellow flames sprang up from the bowl; they burned fiercely for a few moments, reaching almost as high as Pullman's hand, then began to die down. Roach took back the jar and exchanged it for the other, which appeared to contain some slightly viscous black liquid. Pullman fell silent, holding the new jar and watching the flames intently until they had shrunk to little more than the height of a candle flame; then he doused them with a bit of the liquid. When the firelight shone through the residue on the side of the jar, Libby saw with a clenching of her stomach that it wasn't black, but a deep red.

Pullman drew out his handkerchief again and, using it to take up the bowl, crossed to Libby. He dipped his thumb into the paste the flames and liquids had left behind, and raised it to her forehead; Libby had to stop herself from shrinking back. He drew a line with the warm, gluey stuff, from her hairline to the bridge of her nose, then dipped his thumb again and drew a horizontal line, bisecting the first. He spoke one word: "*Skeldus.*" Up close, he didn't look well at all, and the hand that drew the lines on Libby's forehead trembled.

He repeated the same process on Roach, and then on himself. The mixture left a sooty, reddish mark in the shape of a plus sign.

Pullman handed the bowl to Roach, who dumped the remainder of the paste into the nearby bushes. "Right," Pullman said, "that's the ward done. That should keep the khatojana from entering the three of *us*."

He moved back to the little stand, and stood gripping its marble top for a few seconds, head lowered. "All right. Elizabeth, put more wood on the fire. Everett –" He beckoned to Roach, who wiped the bowl out with his handkerchief, replaced it on the stand, and dumped another scoop of glowing coals into it. Libby put another dry branch on the fire and it leapt up, wild as a starved thing, its light rippling like orange water over the trunks of the trees around them.

Pullman moved to where Scab sat rigid, one leg jittering with the sewing-machine motion again. "All right, my boy," he said, laying his unbandaged hand on Scab's shoulder. "Just be brave, as I know you always are. It will all be over soon." Scab nodded slightly, not raising his eyes.

Pullman returned to the bowl, spreading his hand above it again. He spoke, this time in some language filled with ugly guttural sounds. Roach took a small tin from the bag; when Pullman sprinkled whatever it contained on the coals, Libby had to cover her nose at the horrible, dead-animal smell it produced. Again flames sprang up, but this time their color was the deep brownish yellow of old urine.

Pullman, still muttering, nodded to Roach. Roach fished a

small paper-wrapped parcel from the bag; Pullman took it and untied the string that secured it. He opened the paper, took a deep breath and loudly spoke two words – "*kwimid jūz!*" He tipped a light-colored, cylindrical object from the paper into the flames. For a second Libby thought it was some sort of thick, pale worm or caterpillar. When her mind registered what it really was, she realized with a jolt of horror what was wrong with Pullman's hand.

She felt a poke at her shoulder and jumped. "The fire, sis," Roach whispered. The dead branches they were using for firewood burned quickly, and the flames were sinking again. She swayed a bit as she crossed to the woodpile, feeling lightheaded, but she steadied herself, grabbed another branch and tossed it onto the fire.

As the flames leapt up once more, she paused, her attention captured by an odd sound high in the nearest trees. It was a bit like the sound of a katydid: a series of clicks, following one another in succession. But this was different from any katydid call Libby had heard before. The clicks started out at a slow tempo, then grew more and more rapid. As she listened, the source of the sound seemed to change position, circling through the trees just outside the reach of the firelight, and even sweeping across the gap where the house stood, as if whatever made the sound was flying or leaping with impossible swiftness through the branches and the air between them. The speed of this apparent motion increased with the rapidity of the clicks, and more sets of clicks joined the first one, until Libby and the men were surrounded by a frenzied, bewildering vortex of sound.

Then, in an instant, it stopped.

Pullman had quit murmuring; he, Roach and Scab all stared motionless, like Libby, up into the branches. The woods around

The Birds of the Air | 203

the narrow house were silent, save for the crackling of the fire, for about the space of a half-dozen heartbeats; then – so suddenly that Libby jumped like a startled cat – a thunderous flapping of wings exploded from all sides at once: every roosting bird in the forest around them burst into the air, and flew away into the dark above the canopy of leaves.

She turned in bewilderment toward the others, meaning to ask them what was happening, but the words died in her throat.

The khatojana had arrived.

CHAPTER FIFTEEN

IT WASN'T SCAB she noticed first, but the faces of the two men looking at him.

Pullman's face held grim resignation – the expression, Libby imagined, of a soldier facing battle. The look on Roach's face was one of pure dread. Both of them were staring toward the place where Scab sat; Libby turned her eyes to see what they were looking at.

At first she could see nothing different about Scab, except that he seemed to have relaxed. The tension had left his body; he sat loose-limbed on the kitchen chair, his head hanging down so she couldn't see his face well. Then he lifted his head slowly, and she saw that his face had relaxed as well. Beneath the bruises, all the marks of pain, wariness or anger had been smoothed away, and she felt a small jolt of shock at how young he looked without them.

Then his gaze rose to meet hers, and she saw his eyes.

The Birds of the Air | 205

It wasn't that there was any conspicuous change in them; they were still the same coal black, shadowed in the firelight under his dark brows. It took Libby a moment to grasp what was different: something below the surface, whatever it was behind Scab's eyes that made him look like himself, was gone. The black of his irises had become flat and depthless; his gaze was perfectly blank, lifeless-looking. For one disconnected moment, the face of Maisie's paper doll flashed across her mind.

"Hey, kid," he said, "think you could come over here an' roll me another smoke while we wait for these damn things to show up?" His voice sounded normal, and his familiar faint half-smile crept across his face. Libby felt confused, then cautiously relieved, thinking she might have been mistaken, that it might be just the angle of the light that made his eyes look strange.

"Don't move from that spot, Elizabeth," Pullman snapped. Libby drew in a quick breath, realizing she had automatically begun to take a step toward Scab, and she pulled back. Pullman said sharply, "Everett!" and Libby saw Roach make a startled motion, then begin to dig feverishly in the leather bag.

"Aw, come on, fellas," Scab said, in the same jollying tone he had used when he spoke to Slater's men in the clearing. "I ain't fixin' to hurt no one. I just need a smoke, is all. The kid there learnt how to roll 'em real good." His dead black gaze remained on Libby, and one eyelid slid down with dreamlike slowness in a wink.

Roach, scrabbling in the bag, came up with a small empty jar, not much bigger than his thumb, and set it on the stand beside the metal bowl. The flames in the bowl were dying down, and a smell of roasting flesh had spread through the clearing. Libby felt ill when she realized what it was coming from.

"All right, then." Scab's tone was one of mock regret. "If

I was you, though, Pullman, I'd think twice about all this. If I was *you*, I'd be askin' myself just what I stood to *lose* over this little snip a' misery." He indicated Libby with a movement of his head. "I mean, besides your fuckin' *finger*." A different smile slid across his face now: a grin like nothing Libby had ever seen before, stretching much too far toward the sides of his head, and not reaching his eyes. "You keep causin' trouble like this, it won't be just a finger – or a *leg* – you lose," he said, his eyes on Libby though he was talking to Pullman. "One a' these days, the boss is gonna get a bellyful of it. One a' these days, he's gonna string you up in his cellar an' take you apart, one little piece at a time." He laughed, and the laugh wasn't his own either, but a sound like a muddy cough that made Libby feel as if icy water was running between the skin and muscles of her back.

Pullman pulled his knife from his pocket. "Quickly, my dear," he said to Libby, beckoning. Libby went to him, and mechanically held out her hand. Opening the knife, he made a swift, shallow cut across her palm; she winced at the sting of it, but held her hand steady.

"Funny thing is, that little ball-buster *there* is takin' you apart, too – one little piece at a time: chippin' away at the one thing you can't stand to lose – the one thing worth more to you than your sorry life."

Scab had leaned slowly forward in the chair until his bound arms were stretched at a painful-looking angle behind him. Libby dragged her gaze from him, and saw that Pullman had flung the knife aside and taken up the empty jar, letting her blood drip into it. But with an impatient shake of his head, he threw the jar aside as well. Snatching up his notes from the table, hauling her behind him with a hard grip on her wrist, he circled behind the tree Scab was tied to.

"You *know* it deep down, I reckon," Scab said. He was pulling on the cords that held him now, causing them to creak against the bark of the tree. "You got it pushed down and covered up pretty good, but it's *somewhere* in that cagey ol' head a' yours. Here you give up blood an' bone an' skin an' flesh, but all the time, you *know* I'd be doin' you a favor."

Pullman drew Libby's cut hand forward and passed it over Scab's bound ones, smearing her blood across them. Scab's hands remained relaxed; beneath the slight wetness of her blood, they felt dry and hard, unnaturally hot.

Letting her go, Pullman held the papers to the light, read off more words from them in the rough-sounding language, then murmured hoarsely, "May the blood be taken for the deed."

"You're in a kind of a bind though, ain't ya?" Scab went on. "Little bitch keeps takin' what you need, wearin' it down, chippin' away at it. But if you step off an' let *me* handle things – if you get even one little *whiff* of an idea you didn't do all you could to stop me – you lose it sure enough, don't ya? No wearin' or chippin' about it."

Pullman, dragging Libby behind him, returned to his place by the stand. "Now, to get rid of the bastards," he muttered, and scanned the piece of paper feverishly, blinking sweat from his eyes. He pulled his handkerchief from his pocket again, but he didn't use it to wipe his face; instead he pressed it to Libby's palm, soaking up the blood still seeping from the cut; then he pushed her back to a spot a little behind him, his hand brusque and peremptory on her shoulder.

Scab turned his head slowly, and fixed his eyes on her again; the dead black of his irises seemed to suck in all the light from the flames and reflect none back. "Don't fret, though," he said, still speaking to Pullman. "I'm fixin' to bail you out. You just do whatever it is you gotta do. Ain't gonna make no difference to me: I'm still gonna take care a' your little problem there." He panted a bit as he spoke, and Libby saw that he was straining forward harder, increasing the pressure on his bonds; sweat gleamed on his skin, and the muscles and tendons stood out sharply beneath it.

Roach had been feeding twigs into the bowl, coaxing the flames up again. He stepped back at Pullman's curt nod; Pullman held the bloodstained handkerchief above the flames. He began to speak loudly in a different-sounding language: "*Per virtutem sanguinis virginis mando tibi....*" He lowered the handkerchief into the flames, and they leapt up and changed from orange to yellow to an uncanny snow white.

There seemed to be no effect on Scab. "I shoulda let them fellas on the train have her, saved us all a whole hurtin' world a' trouble. Now I gotta take care a' things myself." He turned his black-void eyes to Roach, and the unnatural smile spread across his face again. "*You* could do it. *You* could help your ol' buddy Pullman out." His voice was growing harsh and breathless, and his body had begun to tremble with effort. His arms were wrenched back at a horrible angle; from her new position behind Pullman, Libby could see the cords biting cruelly into the flesh of his wrists. "All you gotta do, just cut me loose." He nodded toward the pocket where Roach had put his weapons. "Just cut me loose, and put that razor in my hand."

Libby sank into a crouch, sick with fear – not only for herself, but for Scab, as she saw blood beginning to seep from beneath the cords around his wrists. Even with her hands pressed to her ears, she could hear his joints cracking. He kept on talking, his words rasping out between jagged breaths, filtering past the shield of her hands: "Put that razor in my hand... an' give me...

thirty seconds… *ten* seconds… shit… give me *five* seconds… an' we'll none of us hafta bleed… or sweat… or fret over this little bitch –" his eyes turned back to Libby, and the inhuman grin widened – "ever again."

Pullman growled out a curse, tossed the papers to the ground and bent to grab Libby's hand again, swiping his thumb across her palm to coat it in her blood. Taking two strides to Scab, he grasped his hair, wrenched his head back, and swiftly drew the same plus-sign on his sweating forehead that he had drawn on the rest of them before. He spoke again, in a tone of command: "*Praecipio tibi ut exeatis!*"

Libby held her breath, waiting to see if this would work, but the only thing that happened was that Scab began to twist his shoulders back and forth, still pulling with all his strength against his bonds. She realized he was rubbing the cords back and forth against the rough bark of the tree in order to fray them. His eyes remained locked on hers, but he laughed the muddy laugh and spoke to Pullman: "Gonna hafta do better than *that*, you old fraud."

Scab's joints cracked as loudly as the fire; sweat ran down his skin in rivulets. Libby heard a deep, sickening *pop*, and all at once his right shoulder slumped oddly, a little knob of bone protruding against the flesh above it. She started at a louder noise to her right, but it was only Roach, throwing more wood onto the fire. "They're liable to kill him, boss," he said, his voice quiet but tremulous. A small, miserable sound escaped Libby, and tears blurred her vision.

Pullman stood for a moment, his good hand grasping his forehead, the fingertips digging in. Then all at once he wheeled and reached directly into the hot coals in the metal bowl, causing Roach and Libby to cry out. His bandaged hand came out holding a charred, blackened sticklike thing. Turning to Scab, he held it before his face with one end in each hand, and broke it in half, thundering out another strange word: "*AMACH!*"

Instantly Scab collapsed, half-on and half-off the wooden chair. His head and upper body lolled to one side, slack; his eyes were closed. The damaged shoulder pulled back grotesquely, the knob above it looking as if it would burst through the skin. Libby was shaking so hard that each breath she dragged in was chopped into a chain of ragged gasps, but after staring at Scab's limp body for a moment, she struggled to her feet, legs unsteady beneath her. "Are they gone?" she managed to whisper, inching forward to Pullman's side. "Is his shoulder broken? Can we untie him now?"

Pullman looked down at her, and a touch of surprise found its way through the pain and weariness in his face. "I regret having called you ordinary, Elizabeth Barnett." He placed his good hand on her shoulder. "No, I don't believe it's broken; only dislocated. When I feel confident that the khatojana are definitely gone, we'll cut him loose and replace it."

"Oughta do it while he's out, if we can," Roach said, appearing at Pullman's other side. "Gonna hurt like a sonofabitch." He shook his head, his wizened face grieved. "Sure has been through it, poor kid."

"Yes, well, he should have done as I told him," Pullman growled, but his irascibility sounded more automatic than genuine. "You two stay back." He moved to Scab and squatted stiffly near his limp form; Libby noticed the gentleness of his touch as he put a hand to the boy's bruised face, lifting it so he could look into it, and she remembered with a sense of unreality the blow he had struck him that evening. After a moment he used one thumb to lift Scab's eyelid, and peered at the eye underneath. "Right," he said, straightening; "Roach, cut him loose. Libby, there's rope beneath the seat of the car; bring it to me."

Libby turned quickly to obey, but found herself staggering, her legs still rubbery with the aftereffects of her terror. She steadied herself as best she could and hurried to where the car was parked, just around the corner of the house, its unlit headlights peering from the darkness like round, frightened eyes. Jerking open the door, she felt under the seat until she found the coiled length of rope, and took it back to Pullman.

Roach had cut the cords holding Scab, and Pullman was laying him on the ground near the woodpile. He directed Libby to add wood to the fire again, to supplement the light from the weak porch bulb. She stepped over Scab's outstretched arm to the pile of firewood, and threw on more branches.

Pullman lifted Scab's shoulders, looped the rope around his body just under his arms, and tossed both ends to Roach. "Now," he said, sounding exhausted, "all I need from you, Everett, is counter-tension. I'm going to pull on his arm to replace the shoulder in the socket; I want you to hold onto the rope and pull back, just enough to keep him from sliding toward me." On one knee beside Scab's limp body, Pullman took hold of his right arm and carefully extended it straight out; then, gradually, he started to pull on it. Libby, crouched back out of the way, found her hands fisted in front of her mouth. Her stomach knotted at the sight of the tension on the damaged shoulder, and she was thankful Scab was still unconscious. Roach braced himself, crouched beside the woodpile, holding the rope taut. In a moment, there was another low popping sound, not as loud as the one before. "There it is," Pullman said, relaxing his grip on Scab's arm. "It'll be sore for a while, but it should be all right." Roach dropped the ends of the rope and straightened, and Libby lowered her hands, letting out breath she hadn't realized she was holding.

"Libby," Pullman began – but that was as far as he got. Libby, turning to him, saw a confusion of motion that resolved itself into sense only after Pullman lay on the ground, eyes closed, blood seeping through his gray hair. Scab, flinging aside a thick dead branch that Libby remembered adding to the woodpile, was already on his feet. He started toward her, swift and purposeful as a diving hawk, the inhuman grin back on his face. Libby turned and ran.

The only refuge she could conceive of reaching before Scab caught her was the car. In the nightmarishly long moments it took her to get there, she caught a glimpse of Roach, still bending over Pullman's inert form, his eyes wide with astonishment and confusion. As she rounded the corner of the house, she saw with a jolt of despair that the car windows were open. There was no time to get herself in and close them. She threw herself onto her belly and began to scramble underneath the car, but before she had gotten halfway, she felt Scab's strong hands grasping her ankles.

He dragged her out from under the car with one rapid, merciless jerk, causing her shirt to ruck up so the gravel scraped her belly painfully. As soon as her head was clear of the car, she felt a viciously hard grip on her arm, and, crying out from the pain of it, was yanked upright. By the time she fully grasped that he had caught her, he had lifted her off her feet, pinning her against him, her back against his sweat-soaked body. One of his arms encircled her ribcage, crushing her arms against her sides; his other arm was locked around her throat, elbow under her chin. He wasn't choking her; only holding her head in place as he spoke, his voice a rough, ragged murmur at her ear. "Remember earlier, kid, when you asked if I was mad at you, and I said I wasn't?" She felt his arm tense a bit, tightening against her throat just slightly. "Well, you know what? I lied."

Her gaze reeled wildly, looking for Pullman, for Roach. She could see neither of them. She kicked and struggled, but her arms were utterly useless, pinned to her body so tightly that they might as well have been fused to it, and her feet, trying to kick out backwards, had neither strength nor leverage to do any damage. She cried out again, hoping one of the men would hear, and felt Scab's arm tighten a bit more against her throat.

"Matter of fact," his ragged whisper went on, "you make me *sick*." His arm was tightening steadily now, beginning to make her lightheaded, to make it hard for her to breathe. She fought with all her strength, as she had on the day when the tramps had taken her, and again felt the horror of finding her utmost efforts completely useless.

There was a sudden wrench that felt as if it would break her neck; rolling her eyes to one side, she saw Scab's boot land a savage blow to the body of Roach, who was flung backwards onto the ground, the branch he was holding – the same one Scab had used to strike Pullman – flying from his hand. Without slackening his grip on Libby, Scab took a step forward and landed a brutal kick to the side of the little man's head; Libby had a second's view of Roach doubling up, his arms wrapping around his head, and then Scab retreated with her farther back into the narrow space between the house and the parked car, and she couldn't see Roach anymore – couldn't see anything but the rough gray wall in front of her.

"Spoiled little house-baby like you," Scab said, panting. "You ain't never had to worry about *nothin'*, your whole life." She could feel the breath of his whisper against her cheek, could smell the tobacco, wood smoke and sweat on him, a mix of scents that until this moment had been comforting. "Always had a place to live, clothes to wear, folks lookin' out for ya." He tightened his arm further, and it became for the first time terrifyingly difficult to get enough air. "You ain't never been starvin', or freezin', or beat bloody an' pukin' 'cause you stole a couple a' spotty apples, or 'cause you was too little to lift a fifty-pound feed sack."

He tightened his grip a fraction more, crushing Libby's windpipe until she was no longer struggling to get free, but instead thrashing and straining open-mouthed simply for a tiny thread of air, like a fish flopped up on a riverbank.

"You ain't never been a little kid comin' home to find out your whole goddamned family took off and left *two fuckin' things behind*: a bucket with the bottom rusted out, and *you*." He tightened his arm again, and the impossibly tiny amount of air she was able to drag into her lungs was cut in half. The edges of her vision were beginning to fill in with black snow, and the far-away pinwheel feeling crept over her, making her feel as if all this was a dream.

"And you come whinin' to *me*? Cryin' to *me* 'cause you were too fuckin' stupid to look out for your baby sister, and your *mama doesn't love you best?*" At his last words, Scab's voice roughened from the harsh whisper to a snarl. The steel-bar pressure of his arm against her throat increased a fraction more, and that was it: all hope or possibility of breath, of survival, was cut off as completely as the possibility of escape had been. She was no longer struggling, and he let her back down to the ground, sinking with her until they were both on their knees. "Things're so goddamn rough for you, huh?" he said. "I shoulda done everyone a favor and put you out a' your fuckin' misery a long time ago. Don't you *get* it, kid? Everybody tries to act decent, and pretend, but ain't a *one* of us – your daddy, your mama, Pullman, me – didn't wish we could be shut of you from the first time we laid eyes on you."

Even through her terror and the agony in her lungs, his words struck into her like his spinning knife had struck into the shack back in the jungle, and tears finally sprang to her eyes – not because of the pain, or the terror, or even the words themselves, but because of whose voice it was that spoke them.

"Let 'er go, Scab."

It was Roach, sounding shaky but determined, his words reaching Libby from very far away.

"Let 'er go, right now."

With a movement that seemed to take a whole minute, Libby's eyes turned from the rough surface of the wall in front of her to see Roach, hazy and distant, sighting down at them from the far end of a rifle that looked a mile long. He stood beside the front fender of the car, just out of Scab's reach; his weathered face was anguished, wet with tears, and the sign Pullman had drawn on his forehead was smeared with sweat. "*Please,* pardner," he said, his voice cracking. But Scab's grip didn't slacken, and Roach didn't fire, though Libby could see now that the rifle was pointed straight at Scab's head. A thought drifted into her fading mind: *he has to choose between us.* It seemed fair enough to her that he should not pull the trigger, that he should choose to let Scab live instead of her. He and Scab were friends. She was nobody – just some thoughts in a dying body, about to become not even that.

Scab had turned a bit toward Roach, shifting her position as well, so she could see more than just the wall of the house; but the blackness at the edge of her vision was creeping inward, obscuring Roach, the rifle, her surroundings. The only thing bright enough to break through was the fire in the distance behind Roach, still high from the last armload of branches she had put on it – because, as it turned out, it didn't take very long at all to die.

The sight of the fire brought the trace of a memory drifting up –

Use that.

– a trace just barely distinct enough from the darkness now suffusing her mind to be recognizable as anything at all –

Use that.

A fire.

J.D., beside the burning shack.

The vial: "Use that."

She could no longer tell what was happening outside her body and her blood-throbbing head, but she could feel, past the shrieking agony in her lungs, that Scab had let her limp arms loose when the two of them had sunk to the ground. She put forth a huge effort, gathering the last threads of her unraveling consciousness, and was able to move one of the arms, lift the impossibly remote hand on the end of it, and slide it into the pocket that held the vial. Sustaining the effort, not quite remembering why she was doing it, she managed to pull the vial out, lift her other hand, and unscrew the lid. In the last instant before the darkness engulfed her completely, she summoned every remaining grain of her dissolving self to the task, jerked up her arm, and threw the contents of the vial over her shoulder and into Scab's face.

CHAPTER SIXTEEN

THE NEXT THING Libby was aware of was Pullman's voice, sounding weary and subdued: "... and you have no idea what was in it?"

She opened her eyes and saw a shadowy bedroom, lit by one small electric bedside lamp. Her throat hurt badly; the skin on her belly burned. Her right hand smarted and, lifting it, she saw that it was bandaged. She lay propped on thin pillows, atop a narrow bed pushed into a corner. Pullman was seated at her bedside, on one of the kitchen chairs. The washstand that had held the metal bowl outside stood next to him, now supporting a china basin in which Roach was wetting a cloth to clean blood from Pullman's head.

"Ah, there she is," Pullman said, his voice softening. "How are you feeling, my dear?"

Libby swallowed painfully. "My throat hurts." Her voice came out in a harsh croak. As her mind began to clear, she stiffened and jerked herself to a sitting position, staring past the two men. "Where's Scab?"

Pullman lifted his good hand in a soothing gesture. "It's all right, my dear. The khatojana have gone."

"And... Scab?"

"He'll be fine; he's sleeping now."

Libby's tension eased a bit, but she drew her knees up under the sheet and wrapped her arms tightly around them. She looked at Pullman and Roach for a moment, then bent her forehead to her knees and dissolved into helpless tears.

Pullman moved from his chair to the edge of the bed and drew her to him, awkwardly but kindly. It was a long time before she was able to stop crying. Roach fetched fresh water in the basin, wet a clean cloth, wrung it out and handed it to her; she buried her hot face in its soothing coolness. "You'll feel better now, sis," he said. "Just needed a good cry, I reckon."

Pullman returned to his chair; he looked ashen. "I am *so sorry*, my dear. I was a *fool* to think I could manipulate those creatures – a bungling hack like myself." He ran his bandaged hand over his face; Libby saw that it was the smallest finger that was missing. "I *grievously* underestimated their strength and cunning, and I'm afraid Mr. Jaeger overestimated my abilities, as well. We put you – and Scab – in terrible danger."

"It... it's OK." Libby had to try more than once before she could push the words from her sore, swollen throat. Roach handed her a glass of water, and she drank gratefully. Her voice worked a little better when she tried again: "You were just trying to help us." Her eyes fell to Pullman's bandaged hand and tears blurred them again. "I'm... sorry about your finger."

"Ah, well –" Pullman held up the hand and looked at it – "I seldom used that one anyway." He gave Libby a haggard smile;

The Birds of the Air | 219

she thought from the set of his face that he might be suffering from one of his headaches, as well as from his injuries. When her eyes followed his bandaged hand back down to his knee, she saw that the rifle lay on the floor beside his chair.

"What... what *happened?*"

"How much do you remember, my dear?" Pullman asked.

"I remember Scab hitting you, and... and choking me. Roach tried to stop him, and then..." she looked at Roach – who had fetched another chair and was setting it down next to Pullman's – and noticed for the first time that he had a large lump on the side of his head, where Scab had kicked him. She grimaced, trying to remember what had happened afterward.

"Do you remember *this?*"

Pullman slipped two fingers into his shirt pocket and pulled out the vial. He held it out to Libby, and she took it. The tiny lid was gone; when she saw the empty air inside, where the liquid had been, tears prickled the backs of her eyes again. "Yes," she murmured.

"Is Scab correct in telling me that it came from John Fuller?"

Libby hung her head, but nodded. "I... think so. The lady who gave it to me talked about him."

Pullman sighed and rubbed his forehead. "Well, we can certainly be thankful that you had it, wherever it came from. Roach tells me whatever was inside that little flask cast out the khatojana when nothing else would."

"Sure did," Roach said, a ghost of his old gleefulness in his voice. "Made a sound like when you leave the gas on too long in the oven, and then you light it: WHUMP!" He pantomimed an explosion with his hands – "and there was somethin' that looked like..." he gazed toward the ceiling, searching for words... "like if you was to blow real hard on raindrops that was stuck to a windowpane, so they'd all shoot off in differnt directions. Only instead of raindrops it was... *shadows*, like, and they all shot off away from Scab. And then they was gone, and the two a' you fell down like a couple a' empty gunny sacks."

Libby clutched her knees more tightly to her chest. "What... what if they come *back*?"

Pullman looked grim, and infinitely weary. "Yes – I'm afraid we have quite a few unpleasant 'what ifs' to consider. I've been trying to reach Mr. Jaeger, but there's been no answer."

"What do we do if they come back?"

Pullman shook his head. "My dear, at the moment, I have no idea."

THEY WERE ALL exhausted, but none of them felt like sleeping – except for Scab, who lay in another of the house's dark rooms, lost in something that looked deeper than sleep. He had regained consciousness only briefly, Roach told Libby, since the khatojana had gone, awakening for a few minutes after Roach and Pullman had carried him to the narrow bed. Libby peered in from the hallway; she felt worried for Scab, but after she had seen him there, she found it easier to stop her incessant, nervous glancing toward the door of whichever room she found herself in.

They went to the kitchen, and Pullman sat down at the table. He kept the rifle close, leaning it against the tabletop; Libby tried not to think about the reason for this. She sank onto a chair across from him, pulling her feet up onto its edge as if something beneath the table might grab them.

Roach cooked eggs and bacon, which seemed to be the only food they had in the house, and made coffee for himself and

The Birds of the Air | 221

Pullman, into which they once again poured what Roach called "shine," from the bottle still sitting at the center of the table. The three of them made a silent, half-hearted attempt at eating, but none of them seemed to have much appetite.

Before long, Pullman pushed his plate away and took up the empty glass vial from the table where Libby had set it. "Libby," he said, "I want you to tell me about this flask, and the woman who gave it to you. You say she spoke about John Fuller?"

Libby nodded. "She said she had a message from him for me."

"And what was the message?"

Libby frowned, trying to remember the woman's exact words. "She said Mr. Fuller said... that I shouldn't believe everything I hear, and that... if I needed him, I should just call."

Pullman and Roach exchanged grave glances.

"And what did she say the liquid in the flask was for?"

"She said it would change Maisie back – make her a kid again. She said I should put it on her when none of you were around. And she said after Maisie was changed, we should sneak off and go into town, so the police or someone could take us home."

Pullman looked at Roach again. "What do you think?"

"Bind and draw, I reckon."

Pullman nodded wearily. "That's what I think as well. Libby, why didn't you tell us about this?"

"I tried, but I *couldn't* – at least, I couldn't tell you or Roach. The woman said I wouldn't be able to, and she was right; every time I tried, my mind kind of... slipped sideways, and I forgot what I was going to say."

"And why didn't you do as the woman told you?"

"I never had a chance. You came back with Maisie, we ate, you took me into the shack and then –" she couldn't help the reproachful note that crept into her voice – "you took Maisie away."

Pullman leaned back, his chair creaking. He let out a tremulous breath, and he and Roach exchanged another glance – both looking shaken, Libby thought, as if something terrible had been narrowly avoided. She looked from one to the other. "What?"

"I can't be certain, Libby," Pullman said, "but I believe that was another attempt on Fuller's part to get 'hold of your sister." He turned the vial in his fingers, looking at it as if it were some sort of poisonous insect, harmless only because it was dead. "These children are becoming harder and harder for him to find, as Mr. Jaeger and his agents gather more of them to safety. Fuller is resorting to more desperate and devious methods to fulfill his need for them. I believe that, rather than restoring your sister to her proper form, the philter in this flask would have constrained her to fly directly to Fuller, had you done as the woman directed."

Libby stared at the tiny container, appalled.

"Why ya think it done what it done to them walkers?" Roach asked, curiosity mixing with dismay in his voice.

"Perhaps it simply did to them what it was intended to do to Maisie: came into contact with them through Scab, and sent them back to Fuller." Pullman set the vial down in front of Libby. "Extraordinarily good fortune for *us*."

There was a quiet shuffling at the doorway from the hall; turning, Libby saw Scab standing there, steadying himself with a hand on the doorjamb. Before she could think, she found herself springing from her chair, knocking it over behind her; she stopped herself only when she had scuttled nearly to the far corner. Looking back, hands still clenched in panic, she saw Scab's face go pale beneath the bruises, and a look came into his eyes that made her feel she would give anything not to have

The Birds of the Air | 223

reacted as she had. Yet she couldn't seem to force her body to move toward him, back to her place at the table.

Scab dropped his eyes. "Oh – y'all are eatin'," he mumbled. "I'll go on outside to smoke."

Roach scoffed. "Ain't no need for that. Sit down. You hongry?"

He jumped up to head for the stove, but Scab shook his head. "I'll just go on outside," he said with the briefest flicker of a glance toward Libby, and he turned and disappeared into the dark hallway.

Pullman and Roach both turned to look at Libby. "You do understand it wasn't *Scab* who wished to harm you, don't you, my dear?" Pullman asked gently.

Libby nodded, having to blink back tears yet again. "I'm sorry... I just... couldn't *help* it."

Pullman rose from his chair. "I'll go and speak to him."

Roach grasped the barrel of the rifle where it leaned against the table: "You – you want this?"

Pullman shook his head. "You keep it... and keep it close." Taking his pipe from his pocket, he left the kitchen.

Roach set Libby's chair upright. "Come on, sis – set back down," he said.

Libby moved back to the table and slipped into the chair. "I'm sorry, Roach. I didn't mean to make him feel bad. But... Mr. Pullman says we don't know if those things might come *back*."

Roach sat down opposite her and nodded. "Yeah, I get ya, sis. But ol' Pullman'll keep a sharp eye on Scab. An'... hate to say, but... if them walkers come back, or some others, it ain't necessarily gonna be like the last time, when Fuller set 'em on Scab specific. If that stuff you threw on Scab really sent 'em *back* to Fuller, I reckon he'll hafta send 'em out again; could be he'll set em' on someone *else* next time. Could be any *one* of us. Could even be *all* of us." He shrugged. "Just depends on whether they really got sent back ta Fuller, an' how much Fuller figures out. If we're *lucky*, maybe he'll just figure them walkers done the job already, and that'll be the end of it. But, to be honest with ya, sis, I don't reckon that's too likely."

"How do you think Mr. Fuller found out about me, Roach?"

Roach drew his coffee mug closer and gazed into it thoughtfully. "Could be a lotta ways. Could be, like Pullman said, that conjure-jar was his. Them things're like spies; they make it so the one that put 'em there can see an' hear what's goin' on, any time he's of a mind to. Or it could be somethin' ordinary, like havin' some stiff or other snoopin' around the jungles. He could even have got to one a' them 'bo's that work for Jaeger, or even for Pullman – paid 'em off for information." He shrugged. "Or it could be some kinda Seein', like what Pullman does to find them kids. Ain't no tellin'."

Libby's eyes were drawn fearfully toward the dark window. "Does he... see us now?"

Roach shook his head, regretful. "I just don't know, sis. Wish I could tell ya somethin' to make ya feel better, but I don't wanna lie to ya."

Libby felt a stab of resentment – *NOW you don't want to lie to me?* She pulled her gaze from the window and turned it on Roach's face. "Why do you *do* it, Roach? Why do you and Scab help Pullman steal kids from their families? Even if what he says is true, it's not *right* – not to do it like *that*."

Roach couldn't meet her gaze; his shoulders drew in, as if he wished he could make himself disappear. "Sis – ya gotta understand: fellas like Scab an' me, we wasn't never brought up nice like how you been – or even like Pullman. Ain't nobody ever taught us to think nothin' about what's right or wrong. Fellas like us, all we ever learned to think about is, what's it gonna *take*? What's it gonna take to get somethin' to eat today? What's it gonna take to keep from freezin' tonight? What's it gonna take to sleep someplace where you don't get woke up by a billy-club bustin' your head? Or not to hafta be scared day an' night a' gettin' robbed, or knifed, or... worse?" He bowed his head, gripping his coffee cup with both hands. "I know it ain't no excuse. All I'm sayin', when Pullman come along and offered money, an' food, an' pertection, an' a place to stay, well... we just done what he said and didn't think too much about it." He glanced up again. "Not till we met you, anyhow."

"You mean... you just stole all those kids and never even thought about whether Jaeger and Pullman were *right* or not?"

Roach's wizened face looked grieved. "I shouldn'ta, sis, I know it now... I shoulda at least thought it through, tried to figure it out for myself. But, until *you* come..." he shook his head miserably. "That's what I been tryin' to explain to ya. Everything I was talkin' about – the money, the food, not havin' to be scared no more – that was all comin' from *Jaeger*. You seen how we live, compared to them other stiffs in the jungle. You seen how them tramps on the train shut up and let you alone, once Scab showed 'em Jaeger's mark." He rubbed the back of his head, wincing when he accidentally touched the lump Scab's boot had left. "Things was so much *better* for us than before. An'... your sis was the first one ever got away. We ain't never had to fool with no kinfolk before. It was easy just not to *think* about it; just to kinda say at the back a' your mind, 'well, Pullman knows best.'" He dropped his hand, palm up, on the table. "And besides, all I ever seen was just little ol' brown *sparrows*." His eyes met Libby's, pleading. "When they don't *look* like kids, it ain't that hard to talk yourself into thinkin' they *ain't* kids."

Libby rose; circling the table to Roach's side, she crouched down, reaching to take his hand in both of hers. "Roach, you have to help me. We *have* to find Maisie; I have to get her *back!*"

Roach dropped his head and began to shake it, blinking repeatedly, turning his face away as if it hurt him to look at her. He tried to pull his hand away, but she held it tight. There was a sound at the doorway again, and Libby turned sharply, but it was only Pullman. He frowned at her, but seemed not to have the energy to get angry. "Libby, I thought we were past all this. There's only one safe place for Maisie, and that is in Mr. Jaeger's care." He crossed to the table, pulled out a chair and sank into it, looking ill and exhausted. "Why don't you go and get some sleep now; Roach and I need to talk about what we're going to do next."

Libby scowled and shook her head, though she felt as exhausted as Pullman looked. "I want to stay."

"Very well," Pullman said, a bit of the growl back in his voice. "Please yourself, as you always do. But Roach and I have serious matters to discuss, and we have no time to soften them to spare the feelings of a child."

Libby slid onto a chair and slumped there, elbows splayed on the table and head in her hands. "I don't need anyone to soften anything. I just want everyone to tell me the *truth.*"

"The *truth,* Elizabeth, is that if you hadn't launched yourself at that incompetent fool Stubby those many days ago, and broken open that cage, you and your sister would both be safe right now – not to mention the rest of us." Pullman sighed. "I don't suppose I can blame you, though."

FOR AN HOUR or so, Libby sat at the table with her head

cradled on her arms, listening as Pullman and Roach went round and round the problem of what to do next without seeming to come to any decision. Twice Pullman went to the parlor to try to reach Jaeger by telephone again, but got no answer. The second time, he came back with an armful of books, which he spread on the table and began poring through. Roach looked on but didn't pick up any of the books himself, and Libby wondered if he, like Scab, was unable to read.

"There's gotta be some kinda pertection, case them things come back – somethin' that'd keep 'em away," he said.

Pullman turned a page, blinking bloodshot eyes. "There's no harm in looking, but I'm not hopeful."

"Why can't you just do that thing again," Libby asked, raising her head from her arms; "those marks you made on our foreheads?"

Pullman and Roach both looked at her as if they were surprised to recall that she was there. Pullman gave her a grim smile and held up his bandaged hand. "I can only spare so many fingers, my dear. Those marks were made with blood from this amputation; it was only a reckoning of that magnitude that could have afforded me even the meager control I was able to exercise over those vile creatures – if indeed I exercised any control over them at *all*." He turned his gaze toward the open window and the dark, insect-buzzing night beyond. "To be honest, I wonder now whether my attempt to summon them accomplished anything at all, except to show them the way to you and Scab, which seemed to be for some reason hidden from them for a time."

Roach turned in his chair and craned his neck to try to see down the hallway. "Where *is* that kid, anyway? He still out front?"

Pullman rubbed at his eyes with his good hand. "I'm afraid he's gone."

Libby's head jerked up. "*What?*" She glanced at Roach; he looked stunned as well.

"He asked me not to tell the two of you right away; he said he 'didn't want no fuss.' What happened this evening... well, it was too much for him. He said —" Pullman's voice caught, and he cleared his throat. "He said he remembers it — *all* of it; that he'll never be able to forget it. And... he said he can't continue to do the work he's been doing for Mr. Jaeger and me. He no longer wishes to be associated with us." He poured whiskey into his cup, downed it in one swallow, then finally looked at them. "It wasn't anything to do with the two of you — he especially wanted me to tell *you* that, Libby."

This time, Libby managed to leave her chair without knocking it over, but she was through the kitchen door before Roach and Pullman could rise, and out the front door by the time the sound of their calls reached her ears.

CHAPTER SEVENTEEN

IT WAS HARD to remember how it had felt to be afraid of walking alone in the woods, only three nights before when she had crept down the trail toward the noisy group of hobos. After all that had happened since then, the mild darkness of the spring night and the ordinary sounds of frogs and crickets seemed peaceful, even comforting. When she heard the sound of Pullman's automobile approaching along the road behind her, and the trees around her began to reflect the faint, ghostly glow of its headlights, she slipped into the undergrowth without hesitation, hid there until the car glided past, and then walked on.

In the black dark beneath the trees, she had to find her way by the feel of the road under her feet. She was tired – more tired than she had been in almost two weeks of constant anxiety and exertion – but she hurried along as quickly as she could. Before long she had to hide for another minute or two, as the car approached on its way back to the house, but as soon as it was gone she struck out again.

When she emerged at last from the shadow of the woods, the moonless sky seemed bright by comparison. She stopped and stared at the empty stretch of road before her; her exhaustion settled onto her more heavily, an invitation to hopelessness. Then a memory struck her – something Scab had said – and she turned to her right and set out along the margin of the field there, walking the narrow strip of ground between the ends of the corn rows and the border of the woodland. Before long she reached a dry irrigation ditch, which also came to an end at the edge of the woods. She looked along it toward the spot, a half-mile or so away, where she remembered seeing it pass beneath the road she and Scab had travelled on their way from Portersville. About halfway between the road and where she stood, she saw the flicker of Scab's fire, far-off and tiny, as if some orange star had fallen to the bottom of the ditch. She slid down the bank and headed toward it.

When she drew close she had to pause, taking shaky breaths, until she was able to fight down the animal fear that rose in her at the sight of Scab. He sat, hunched and tense-looking, in a hollow scooped from one side of the ditch, not moving, not even smoking, though a cigarette slowly burned itself out between the fingers of his right hand. He didn't appear to see her in the darkness beyond the firelight, or to hear her footsteps in the soft dirt.

When he did look up, the sight of her seemed to jolt through him like an electric shock. He was on his feet in an instant, his sudden motion startling her in turn, causing her to jump. He held up a hand, warning her not to come any closer. "Kid – what're you *doin'* out here?" he cried. "Ain't you got no sense at *all?*" He looked as frightened as if the khatojana had succeeded and he were seeing her ghost.

"You have to come *back*, Scab! You *can't* leave!"

He seemed stunned speechless for a second, and she realized it was the first time he had heard what his attack had done to her voice. He bent quickly to pick up his knapsack, and she saw that his hands were shaking. "Kid, you gotta get *out a'* here," he said. "What if them walkers was to come back right now? You gotta get on back to the house, quick as you can. And you oughta lock all them doors an' windows." He slipped the knapsack onto his shoulders, then scooped up his bedroll. "I shoulda kept on goin' an' got out a' town, but I was near worn out."

"But you promised to help me get Maisie back! You *promised!*"

"I didn't promise *nothin'*, kid. Said we'd give it a shot, that's all." Hurriedly he kicked dirt over the fire, smothering it, and the starlit dark closed in. "Sorry it didn't pan out," he said, his voice unsteady. "Sorry for... for everything."

He turned to start off along the ditch toward the road, but Libby, pressing down her fear, darted around the smoking remains of the fire and grabbed his arm, as she had on the trail in the jungle before. She pulled at him with all her strength, as if she could drag him the whole way back to the house. "*Please* don't go, Scab!"

He shook her loose, but she grabbed him again and clung like a tick. "I don't *want* you to go!" she said truthfully, and then – lying – "I'm not scared anymore!"

"Well then you're a goddamn *fool*," he growled, jerking free once more and rounding on her, seeming suddenly enraged. Panic needled through her, and she couldn't help stumbling back from him.

"Didn't Pullman tell you?" he said. "*I remember.* I remember *everything*. I remember *hurtin'* you – tryin' to *kill* you. And you know what?" His harsh voice wavered and he broke off and bowed his head for a moment, then lifted it to fix her with a gaze she could barely stand to meet. "I *wanted* to. Not just because of the walkers; part of it was *me*. I told you it wouldn't be me wantin' to hurt you, but it *was*. There was a part of me *hated* you: hated you for all you had that I never did – hated you enough to want to *kill* you."

She felt his words strike into her, not even causing pain for the first shocked seconds, but only the sense of grievous damage, and the certainty of pain soon to follow.

He took a step closer, not trying to keep her at a distance anymore, and she could feel fury and misery coming off him like heat. "An' I'll tell you somethin' else," he said, his face hard and pitiless: "I was *there*, that day Stubby changed your sister. I was teachin' Stubby the job. He was new; that's why he balled it up. I was watchin' from them bushes, the whole time. I *gave* him that hexed candy to give to your sis."

Libby's face felt like stone; her tongue felt like a stone in her mouth. When she was able to stir it to speak, her damaged voice sounded stony, too, like gravel scraping through a drainpipe. "Make it *right*, then," she said. "Make it up to us. Help me get her back."

Scab flung up his hands and turned to take a few furious strides away from her, then doubled back, his eyes burning, coming at her so fiercely that she had to steel herself with all her will to keep from stumbling backward once more. "Don't you understand, kid? I *CAN'T*. That's the whole goddamn point. I *can't make it up,* what I done to you."

Libby stared up at him, unable to think of anything more to say. He glared back for a moment; then the ferocious rigidity

The Birds of the Air | 233

seeped out of his posture, and he bent his head. "Sorry, kid. I ain't goin' back with you, so you might as well get it out a' your head," he said, and Libby heard the truth of it in his voice.

He started to turn away; but he paused, dug in his pocket, and pulled out the razor. "You ain't got no more a' that stuff Fuller sent you," he said, not meeting her gaze. He held the razor out to her. "I want you to hold onto this, and I want you to promise me – to *promise* me, kid – that you'll keep your eyes open, an' if anyone comes at you – *anyone* – you'll *use* it. Keep it hid till the last minute, then –" He drew a thumb down the side of his neck, just under the jaw. "Right there. *Hard.* Will you promise me that?"

Libby stared down at the razor, its wicked blade folded into the mother-of-pearl handle. She swallowed hard and nodded.

Scab shook his head. "*Say* it."

"I promise," she said, and took the razor from his hand.

He nodded. "OK, kid. See ya around." Now his voice, too, was hoarse. "Make sure you get straight on back to the house, quick as you can. An' – tell them two ol' lunkheads to do a better job a' lookin' out for you." Then he turned, slipped into the night, and was gone.

PULLMAN SEEMED TOO relieved to be angry when she stumbled back into the house. Roach ran a hot bath for her in the tiny upstairs bathroom, gave her another clean shirt of Pullman's to wear, and washed her clothes in the kitchen sink, hanging them to dry in front of the open door of the lit oven.

After all this was done, Pullman carefully locked all the doors and windows, and then insisted that he and Roach be locked in

234 | L. H. Arthur

the basement for what was left of the night, in case the khatojana came back.

Libby watched, uneasy, as he and Roach lugged blankets and narrow mattresses from two of the house's four bedrooms down the basement stairs. Pullman unloaded the rifle, left it in the kitchen, and took all the cartridges with him. At the head of the stairs, before he followed Roach down, he turned to Libby. "If either of us knocks in the night and asks you to let him out," he said, "*don't do it*. Wait until morning, when we're all awake and can keep an eye on one another."

"But… Roach said those things might get into *any* of us, if they come back! Or *all* of us! What if – what if Roach or you hurt each *other*?" Another, even more frightening idea leapt into her head. "Or what if they make me kill *myself*?"

Pullman shook his head. "It's not in the nature of these creatures to provoke suicide. *That,* at least, we needn't worry about." Pullman ran a hand wearily over his face. "I realize this is by no means a foolproof solution, my dear. I have no idea whether any of the three of us are susceptible to possession; I have no idea if the creatures will drive Scab back here. But frankly I'm too exhausted – and too limited in my knowledge of the ways of these creatures – to think of any better plan tonight. If we all make it through till the morning, I'll try to reach Mr. Jaeger again; meanwhile, we'll just have to do what we can, and hope for the best. Shoot the bolt; if you hear Scab calling, or hear anyone trying to break into the house, slip out the opposite side, as quietly as you can, and run into the woods and hide. Otherwise, let Roach and me out when you wake up in the morning." He turned and started stiffly down the stairs. "Or if the house catches fire!" He added, joking, but Libby remembered her dream and felt chilled by his words.

When she had bolted the door, she went to the room she had awakened in earlier, and sank into a dreamless, exhausted sleep.

She woke, with a sickening start, to the dim green morning light of the forest filtering through the windows. The sound that had awakened her came again: a heavy knock on the front door. She shot upright, her heart pounding and her eyes instantly wide. Scrambling out of bed, she ran into the hall, pulled back the bolt on the cellar door and opened it. "Mr. Pullman!" she said in a loud whisper; "Mr. Pullman! There's someone at the door!"

Pullman had apparently heard the knocking as well; he was already halfway up the stairs, pulling his suspenders over his shoulders. "Go back into the kitchen, Elizabeth," he murmured, his face grave. "Be quiet and stay out of sight."

Libby obeyed. She heard Pullman open the door, and his voice giving a guarded greeting: "Euphonious; what brings you back?"

BACK– the word leapt out from the others, snatching Libby's attention. *Maybe it's Mr. Jaeger's carrier!* She felt almost faint at the thought that Maisie might still be with him.

The man made some answer Libby couldn't hear over the footsteps of Roach, who had come up the stairs to join Pullman in the hallway. She heard Pullman saying, "All right; let's go into the parlor. Roach, would you start some coffee please?"

Roach mumbled assent, and Libby heard the parlor door close, and Roach's steps heading toward the kitchen. His hand was already making a silencing gesture when he entered the room. He added an emphatic shake of his head, then went to the stove to make the coffee.

Libby sank down to wait, sitting cross-legged just inside the kitchen doorway. After Roach had made the coffee, carried three cups into the parlor and shut the door again, she rose quietly and listened for a moment, then crossed, silent on her bare feet, to the back kitchen door. She turned the lock as quietly as she could, and slipped out.

Pullman's shirt couldn't keep out the morning chill, and she shivered as she crept along the side of the house. Simms's car was parked in front; it was a big sedan almost identical to Pullman's. She peered around the corner toward the front door, then crossed to the car and stepped onto the running board. She looked through the glass of the window, cupping her hands around her eyes, her heart pounding with the hope of seeing Maisie inside. The car was empty.

She heard the knob of the front door turning, leapt from the running board and raced back to the side of the house, where she crouched behind Pullman's car, peeking out. Pullman and Roach came into view; with them was a thin colored man of about Pullman's age. "We'll be along as soon as we can pack up," Pullman was saying. The man gave a curt nod and climbed into the car; as he started the engine Libby turned and hurried back along the wall.

As she quietly closed the back door, she heard the front door opening. "Libby!" Pullman called, and she went into the hall where he and Roach stood by the open parlor door. "I want you to get dressed as quickly as you can," Pullman said, "and gather any belongings you have. We need to leave here immediately. We're going to Mr. Jaeger."

IN THE BEDROOM she had been using, Libby pulled on her blue jeans and shirt, still damp along the seams. She retrieved the worn picture of Maisie, her father's knife, and Scab's razor from the drawer of the bedside table, and put them in her pockets. The empty glass vial stood on the table; she picked it up and looked at it for a moment, then shoved it in a pocket as well, and went to look for Roach. She found him outside, loading two small suitcases and Pullman's black bag into the trunk strapped onto the rear of the car. His face was drawn and anxious.

"Roach… why are we going to see Mr. Jaeger? Is he going to help us with those… walker things?"

"Hope so, sis; but Simms brought word a' more trouble, too. We'll explain to ya in the car, once we get goin'; we gotta head out quick as we can. You got everything?"

Libby nodded.

Roach fished in his shirt pocket, and handed something to Libby; it was a small linen bag, about the size of an acorn, closed with a drawstring long enough to wear as a necklace. "This here's to keep them walkers away; go on an' hang it around your neck. Jaeger had Simms bring the directions, an' the stuff to make it with, so's Pullman could fix it up."

Libby looped the string around her neck. The bag had a sort of sharp, herbal scent, with a metallic undertone.

"Now don't open it – that'd break the conjure," Roach said. "An' *don't take it off* – not till we get to Jaeger's place. Ol' Simms, he says them walkers can't come within fifty feet a' that thing; but it only works for maybe ten, twelve hours. So we gotta get goin', soon as we can. Once we get ta Jaeger's place, we won't hafta worry about them walkers; he's got it fixed so they can't get in there."

Libby held the little bag, examining it. It had no markings; the string it hung on was made of twined red cotton. She felt half-melted with the relief of having it: the knowledge that the khatojana might return had been like a pressure on her mind, holding her body in constant tension, wearing her out with fear and the necessity for constant vigilance. Every time the men had come into view, her eyes had darted anxiously to theirs, dreading to see the flat blankness she had seen in Scab's eyes.

Roach picked up the rifle, which he had leaned against the side of the car, and laid it across the floorboard just behind the front seat. "OK, sis – you get in the back seat here, an' wait for Pullman and me; we'll be out in a minute. Don't touch that gun – it's loaded."

He turned to start toward the house, but Libby touched his arm. "Roach... will Maisie be there?"

"Don't know, sis. Guess we'll see when we get there." He patted her shoulder, then hurried back inside.

Libby stared blankly after him; her lack of sleep, the shock and grief of the day before and the sudden flurry of activity made her feel a bit dazed, but the idea that Maisie might be where they were going kindled a spark of excitement even through her weariness. She missed Scab with an acuteness that felt like physical pain, and missing him made her realize how much she missed her mother and Maisie. She climbed into the back seat of the car, pulled Maisie's picture from her pocket and sat gazing at it. When Pullman and Roach came out, she didn't trust her voice to ask any questions; the only thing keeping her from giving way to tears again was the hope that Maisie might be where they were going.

The men slid into the front seat, Pullman behind the wheel. Once they got under way, Roach turned, one elbow over the seat-back. "Simms come to tell us there's trouble all over – wasn't just you an' Scab." He rubbed the back of his neck, his anxious gaze roving the passing woods. "Jaeger wants us to head on over to his farm, 'cross the state line, where he runs things from. Didn't wanna give us directions over the phone: seems Fuller's been gettin' information some way or other; he's been able to

The Birds of the Air | 239

find out where a buncha' Jaeger's posts are, an' he's been attackin' 'em. Simms said some a' Jaeger's folks been killed already – like that fella Stubby, that changed your sis." He shook his head. "I'm worried sick about Scab. Reckon if he's on his own he might be OK, but if he's in a rattler with some other 'bos, or jungled up somewhere, ain't no tellin' when Fuller might pitch one a' them walkers into some stiff or other, an' –"

"Everett," Pullman said quietly, and Libby saw that he was watching her in the rearview mirror. He glanced at Roach and gave a slight shake of his head.

Roach looked startled, then self-reproachful. "Oh – I'm sorry, sis! Didn't mean to scare ya. I'm sure ol' Scab'll be just fine. He knows how to take care a' hisself, ain't no doubt about that." He glanced at Pullman. "But – we're gonna take a quick look around town anyway, case we might be able to find him."

Libby didn't feel reassured; her heart contracted with fear that was becoming miserably familiar. "So… you think Fuller might send some of those – walker things – to try to kill *Scab*?"

Pullman met her gaze briefly in the rearview mirror. "We haven't any compelling reason to believe that, Libby. All Simms said was that khatojana had been sent to a few of Mr. Jaeger's outposts, and that some of his people have been killed. Now that Scab has left Jaeger's employ, he may well be safe. He won't be likely to return to any of the posts, at any rate." He hesitated, and a note of apology entered his voice. "However… I'm afraid we don't dare send *you* home yet, my dear; not until I'm able to consult with Mr. Jaeger and determine whether Fuller is likely to be a continued threat to you."

Libby found herself scanning the forest like Roach, even though she knew Scab wouldn't be there. She wished they would find him in Portersville, and that the news of the attacks would persuade him to go with them to Jaeger's farm, but she didn't think it would happen. Her earlier question came back to her mind, and she leaned forward in her seat. "Will my sister be at Mr. Jaeger's farm, Mr. Pullman? Roach said he didn't know."

Pullman shook his head. "No, Libby. Often there are two or three children there, waiting to be placed with foster parents, but Simms tells me that Mr. Jaeger has arranged to take all children directly to their new homes, or to temporary safe houses, until we are able to determine whether Fuller has discovered the location of the farm."

At the words *new homes*, Libby felt a wave of heat rise to her face. "Well... what you said before? It doesn't matter whether Fuller's still after me or not: I'm *not going home without my sister.*"

"Libby, how long will you refuse to accept the truth?" Pullman's voice took on a bit of its testy growl. "Has even yesterday's experience failed to convince you of the fact that Maisie will never be safe at home?"

"We'd figure something *out!*" Libby cast around wildly for some idea that would make Pullman's assertion false; after a moment, a possibility struck her. "If Mr. Jaeger can protect Maisie somewhere else, why can't he protect her at *home?*"

"It doesn't work that way, Libby; and I have enough on my mind at the moment without trying to explain things you are evidently determined not to understand. I want you to sit back now, and stop plaguing me with questions."

Libby sat back in her seat, and scowled out the window, blinking hard, squinting when the shadows of the woods gave way to the morning sunlight that flooded the farmland. The fear that Pullman might be right about Maisie kept growing bit by bit, creeping outward from that initial seed of dread, no matter how hard she tried to resist it. She could think of no argument against his declaration, and her mind kept running into dead ends as she searched for one. *But we can think of something,* she kept telling herself. *There has to be some way. I'm just too tired to see it right now.*

"No one's allowed to just take someone's kids away," she muttered at last, keeping her eyes on the passing fields, trying to keep the quaver from her voice. "Not unless their parents are *beating* them, or *starving* them, or something like that."

She said it half under her breath, but Pullman heard her anyway. "But that's just what people like your mother *are* doing, Libby – don't you see?" he said. "Not *knowingly*, of course; but with their ignorance and their narrow, conventional thinking, they are *starving* these children of what they need to fulfill their potential! They are stultifying their minds, crushing their spirits, suppressing their very natures; and *that*, Libby, is a worse form of mistreatment than any mere physical beating." Pullman's voice was impassioned; his eyes in the mirror burned. "And it's not only the *children* who are being robbed; it's the rest of humanity as well! Imagine people with abilities like Mr. Jaeger's – or even such modest abilities as my own, or Slater's, had we received adequate instruction – in positions of leadership throughout the world: people who would have the wherewithal to establish peace and order, to educate and enlighten. As soon as enough children like your sister have been brought to adulthood with the proper training, they will no longer have to keep their existence secret. They will no longer have to hide their true nature lest the ignorant strike out in fear against them. They will be able to create, at last, the world mankind has always dreamed of!" He shook his head. "No, Libby – it's not Jaeger and myself who are the criminals; it's those who fear the unknown, and therefore unwittingly subvert the fondest aspirations of humanity!"

Libby leaned her forehead against the glass; her throat hurt, and she felt too exhausted to argue anymore. Scab was gone, and Maisie wasn't in the place where they were going. Pullman was immovable, and she had no reason to hope Jaeger would be any less so. She remained silent until the fields and farmhouses began to give way to the houses at the edge of Portersville; then she roused herself to ask, "Mr. Pullman, where *is* John Fuller? I mean... where does he live?"

"That's something we would all like to discover, my dear. We see his servants – human or otherwise – from time to time, and we see the effects of his actions, but no one in our organization has seen Fuller himself for many years; nor has anyone been able to determine where he keeps himself."

Libby frowned, puzzled. "Then – how do you *know* all these things about him?"

"From Jaeger," Roach chimed in. "He's known Fuller purty near all his life. Heard tell they even used to work together."

"At one time, they were friends," Pullman said, "but John Fuller had an insatiable hunger for power, and when he refused to listen to Mr. Jaeger's remonstrance regarding his methods of attaining it, Mr. Jaeger was forced to end his association with him. He used what channels of information he could devise to keep himself informed of Fuller's activity, and as the reports became more and more dreadful, eventually Mr. Jaeger realized he had no choice but to take action: to oppose John Fuller in any way he could."

"Why hasn't Mr. Jaeger *stopped* him, then?"

Pullman gave a short, mirthless laugh. "For the same reason you couldn't stop Slater's men from beating Scab: Fuller is, quite simply, the more powerful of the two. Mr. Jaeger's hope has been that by working in secret – disguising the children in transit,

The Birds of the Air | 243

employing agents who are able to move about unremarked, carefully guarding the information about where the children are placed – he will be able to save as many as possible without having to risk an outright confrontation, which at this point he couldn't possibly win."

Libby thought about this. "Is it stealing all those kids' power that makes Fuller stronger than Mr. Jaeger?"

"I don't know, Libby. But if it is, that's all the more reason to save every child we can from falling into his hands, isn't it?"

Libby shifted uneasily in her seat, the dread pressing up in her again. This answered her question about Jaeger protecting Maisie at home, didn't it? If Fuller was more powerful than Jaeger, then the only way to protect the children was secrecy. What if Pullman was right? What if Maisie really *could* only be safe living with someone besides her family?

What if, to save her, they had to lose her?

THEY DROVE AROUND Portersville for half an hour or so, scanning the streets for Scab, and Libby waited in the car near the freight yard while Pullman and Roach looked there for him, but he seemed to have blown out of the little town like smoke, leaving just as little trace behind. Reluctantly they gave up, and took the highway heading west out of town. At first they seemed to outstrip the climbing sun, but later, as it went into its downhill slide, they lagged behind it. Pullman wouldn't allow Libby to enter any restaurants or other places where people gathered. Toward midday he and Roach bought sandwiches and bottles of soda at a roadside café, and brought them out to the car where she waited. Later, along a lonely stretch of highway, they stopped for gasoline – which Pullman called "petrol" – at an isolated station, deserted except for a lone attendant.

The day was warm with the promise of the coming summer, and the woods and fields along the highway were so green they scarcely looked real. Libby had heard adults talking with relief about the wet winter and spring, after the dry year before and the frightening droughts in the states to the southwest. They had spoken with optimism, encouraging one another in hope that, in this year of Mr. Roosevelt's inauguration, everything would begin to turn around. Even the weather, they said, was cooperating in bringing an end to the hard times. Remembering those overheard conversations, Libby realized a dizzying shift had taken place in her view of the world. Before, it had seemed as if the adults around her knew all that was necessary to know – that they could be relied upon to guide her through the mystifying world they inhabited, and to prepare her to take her place in it. Now she had seen other worlds hidden beneath the one they knew – worlds of which her mother and her teachers and the sheriff's men who had searched for Maisie were completely unaware, even though knowledge of them was crucial for the protection of their children. Pullman and Roach were no different, she realized: they knew the underworld through which they moved, but they didn't understand the simplest things about the wider world outside it – such as the obvious truth that children belonged with their families, and that it was a terrible wrong to steal them away. It began to seem as if *she* understood the broader reality more fully than any of the adults she knew, and this made her feel as if the ground and sky had suddenly switched places, leaving her with nothing solid to stand on.

Scab could have helped her; he had no allegiance to any particular idea of the world – he simply acted upon what he

The Birds of the Air | 245

saw before him. But he had left her on her own. *All right,* she thought, *then I'll do it on my own. I'll figure it out myself.* With an effort she turned her weary mind to consideration of what she should do when they arrived at Jaeger's place. If Maisie wasn't there, she would have to find out where she had been sent. She would need to look for some kind of clue, which would mean trying to get away from the adults, so she could search without interference. If she was able to find out where Maisie had been sent, she could seek help from the authorities: surely when Maisie had reached her destination, she would be restored and recognizable. Libby could tell the police where she was, and they could see for themselves that she was the little girl missing from Schillerton. Then they would call their mother, and she would come and take them home.

And then what? the hateful dread whispered in her mind. *Will you be able to watch her every minute? Make sure she never, ever talks to any stranger who might be Fuller or one of Fuller's people? What about when you're at school? Or sleeping at night? Will you try to get Mama to help you protect her? What will you tell Mama – that an evil magician wants to steal Maisie away?*

A wave of despair rose in her chest, pressing up into her swollen throat. She wanted to sleep forever and never think about any of this again. *I'll figure it out later,* she thought; *maybe at Mr. Jaeger's place I can find out something that will help me.* She curled up in the small space on the seat beside the luggage to try to sleep, but when Roach saw her he leaned from the front and moved the bags, setting them carefully over the rifle in the small space on the floorboard, so she could lie down across the back seat. He spread his jacket to cover her, and sleep spread its temporary darkness over the longings and fears that chased one another along the twisting paths of her mind.

She was awakened a long time afterward by Roach's hand on her shoulder. The sun shone into the driver's side windows, only a couple of handbreadths above the horizon. They were no longer on the highway, but driving north on a wide unpaved road. Fields of green alfalfa stretched on either side, and the sweet scent of them drifted into the car's open windows. "Wake up, sis," Roach was saying; "we're here; we're at Jaeger's farm."

CHAPTER EIGHTEEN

JAEGER'S HOUSE WAS approached by a long, tree-lined drive between the alfalfa fields. A metal gate blocked their way when Pullman turned off the road, but Roach got out and unlocked it with a key he fished from his pocket. Libby wondered if he and Pullman had always had the key, or if Simms had given it to them that morning.

The drive ran for a good quarter-mile, angling a little to the north of the low sun, its dust-and-gravel surface striped with the diagonal shadows of the tree trunks. At its end it opened into a graveled parking area beside a wide lawn. The house stood on the far side of the lawn, white against a backdrop of dark, towering trees: a comfortable-looking clapboard farmhouse, large but simple in its design, with a wide veranda encircling it.

Another car stood in the parking area; it might have been the one Simms had been driving, but Libby couldn't tell. Pullman parked theirs beside it, then fixed Libby with a stern gaze in the mirror. "All right, Libby: I don't want to hear of you badgering Mr. Jaeger about your sister. The discussion about that is over. I know you must understand by now that we know what's best for Maisie." Libby must have looked stubborn, because his voice sharpened. "Mr. Jaeger has more important things to think about now, Elizabeth. He has to find a way to keep *all* the children safe from Fuller; that's *including* Maisie. If I hear of you pestering him, I will put you in this car and take you someplace safe and out of the way: Roach can mind you until this crisis is resolved. Do you understand me?"

Libby dropped her eyes. "Yes, sir."

"Good." Pullman glanced out the car windows. "It would appear we're the only ones here." He looked at Roach. "That's odd."

Roach shrugged. "Depends what ol' Jaeger has in mind."

Pullman nodded, but still looked perplexed.

When they had unloaded the bags and started across the lawn, the front door was flung open and a young man came out. "Colin, Everett!" he cried, sounding pleased and relieved. He had a slight accent, different from Pullman's. He descended the steps and came out to meet them. "Thank you for coming on such short notice." His face became grave, his voice more subdued. "I don't have to tell you we'll need all our capacities to deal with this situation. I'm very much afraid that –" he cut himself off, looking at Libby. "And this must be Libby." He bent slightly in an almost-bow as he shook her hand. "A pleasure to meet you, young lady. I am so very sorry for all the hardship you've endured. Here, let me take that bag."

Libby glanced in confusion at the other two, as the young man took Pullman's black bag from her hand. Surely this couldn't be Jaeger? He looked to be only ten years or so older than Scab.

The Birds of the Air | 249

But Pullman's answer removed any doubt: "We'll be more than happy to provide any assistance we can, of course, Mr. Jaeger."

Jaeger extended his right hand to shake Pullman's, then returned his gaze to Libby. "I hope you will accept my heartfelt apology for the criminal behavior of Slater and his men toward you and your friend Scab. I'm afraid with all that's been going on in the past several days, my attention was elsewhere, and I failed to discover what they were up to in time to prevent it. That's no excuse, of course – those men are in my employ, and I take full responsibility for their actions. I can promise you that what Pullman did to them is mild in comparison to the response they can expect from me when I find them."

Libby dropped her head, not knowing what to say, but Jaeger went on without waiting for a reply.

"I'm afraid things will be awfully dull for you around here. Mr. Pullman and I have serious business to attend to, as I'm sure you know. But my housekeeper, Mrs. Vogel, will take care of you, and get you anything you need." He smiled down at her, and Libby felt herself blush a little: he was very handsome, and it made her feel shy. " I hope you won't mind," he said, "but I took the liberty of sending Mrs. Vogel to town to get some clothes for you. Mr. Simms told me he had the impression you could use them when he saw you sneaking out to look into his car." His smile took on a faint tinge of playfulness, and Libby felt her blush deepening.

"Where are the others?" Pullman asked.

"Ah – well, I haven't asked any of the others to come, Colin." Jaeger laid a hand on Pullman's shoulder. "Let's discuss it over dinner, shall we? Mrs. Vogel's been keeping it warm, and I'm afraid she'll skin me alive if I don't get you all into the dining room within the next three minutes." He winked at Libby, smiling.

Mrs. Vogel, when she appeared in the entry hall to meet them, looked less likely to skin someone alive than any person Libby had ever seen. She was a round, rosy-cheeked, grandmotherly woman with bright, kindly eyes; she spoke to Mr. Jaeger in a language that sounded to Libby like a softer-edged version of the one Pullman had used to summon the khatojana. Mr. Jaeger answered her in the same language, and the old lady nodded. "I'm afraid Mrs. Vogel doesn't have any English," Mr. Jaeger said to Libby, "but I'm sure you two will be great friends."

Mrs. Vogel smiled at Libby, and held out a hand to her. Libby took the hand, which was soft and dry as sifted flour, and Mrs. Vogel led her toward the back of the house, clucking and talking as comfortably and incomprehensibly as an elderly hen. They passed a door, on their right, through which Libby saw a long table set with blue-and-white china; but Mrs. Vogel led her straight back into a big kitchen, bright with late-afternoon sunlight, and, positioning her firmly in front of the sink, handed her a bar of soap and a clean hand-towel. When Libby had washed her face and hands to Mrs. Vogel's satisfaction, the old lady herded her into the dining room, following close behind with a steaming soup tureen.

The men were already seated around the table, but Jaeger gave Libby a welcoming smile and rose courteously to pull out a chair for her. "What I am concerned about," he said, returning to his seat, "is the concentration. If there are even four or five of us here at one time..."

"Yes... I see what you mean." Pullman frowned down into the soup Mrs. Vogel was ladling into his bowl. "And you're fairly certain he doesn't know your location here?"

The Birds of the Air | 251

Jaeger shrugged. "Fairly certain, but I can't be completely sure. It all depends whom he's gotten to. And of course that's another reason I don't want everyone here." His expression was grim, and Libby could see from the fine lines around his eyes and mouth that he was older than she had at first thought. "I can't even be sure of my crew chiefs. Frankly, Colin, I can't really even be sure of you and Everett. But –" he glanced at Libby in a way that clearly held some meaning, though she couldn't discern what it was – "there are reasons to believe that the two of you can be trusted."

Pullman and Jaeger continued to talk, but Libby, trying to gather her courage, lost track of what they were saying. She stirred her soup, blinking against the steam, not daring to look up lest she meet Pullman's gaze. "Mr. Jaeger," she said, interrupting, "where is my sister?"

"Elizabeth!"

Pullman's voice was somewhere between a bark and a growl, and at the upper edge of her vision Libby could see him glaring at her. She heard Roach, who was seated across from her, shift nervously, his chair creaking. But when she worked up the courage to lift her eyes to Jaeger's face, he looked grieved rather than angry. "Don't snarl at her, Colin," he said. "Of *course* she wants to know where her sister is; I would wonder what was wrong with her if she *didn't* ask!" He turned toward her. "But – I'm sorry, Libby: I cannot tell you where Maisie is." His green eyes were tinged with gold, the color of late-afternoon sunlight on leaves. "I'm sure Mr. Pullman has explained the situation to you, about John Fuller, and the threat he poses to certain special children like your sister. But there's another consideration, as well, which you may not have taken into account: the threat to your *own* safety. You see –" he faltered, glancing at Pullman. "I – don't want to frighten you, but – if you were to discover where your sister is, don't you see what terrible danger that would put *you* in?"

Libby frowned a bit, not understanding, and Jaeger went on, his voice gentle: "Libby – John Fuller would do anything to find these children; he is *desperate* to acquire more of them. And – as much as I hate to say it about a man who was once my friend – hurting you, or your mother, to force you to give him information... I'm afraid that falls well within the lengths to which he would be willing to go."

Libby stared at him, stunned. He was right: she had never before thought of this possibility, but now that he said it she was shocked by how obvious it was. The thought of herself or her mother being tortured terrified her, but an even deeper fear rose like icy water inside her, as her mind formed the exact thought that Jaeger's gentle voice next put into words: "Imagine how you would feel, Libby, the anguish you would suffer for the rest of your life, if it was *you* who told John Fuller where to find your sister."

She didn't take in much of the men's conversation after that. Mrs. Vogel brought some sort of roasted meat and vegetables, and she mechanically ate a little when they were placed in front of her, but her mind darted back and forth like a creature in a cage, trying to escape the growing conviction that Maisie would truly never be safe at home. Only one thing struck through her racing thoughts: a change in Jaeger's tone, a lowering of his voice as if he feared that Fuller might be in the next room, listening. "The records," he was saying; "all my files on the children: their names – former and current – their addresses, ages, the names of their foster parents, their health and educational records. I'm very much afraid it is *those* Fuller is after." He stared at his barely-touched plate, not seeming to see it. "It's *vital* that I keep

The Birds of the Air | 253

in contact with the mentors, keep track of where each child is living, monitor his or her well-being and progress. I don't want to destroy them unless it is absolutely necessary, but... " he lifted his eyes to meet Pullman's... "we *cannot* let Fuller get hold of those records. If he ever gets his hands on that information, he will be able to find *every child we have ever placed.*"

WHEN DINNER WAS over Mrs. Vogel took their plates – clucking mournfully over how little they had eaten – and brought ice cream for Libby, and coffee for the men. When she had gone, Jaeger turned toward Libby. "We adults are going to need to talk in private for a while, my dear; but before we do, I'd like to ask you some questions, if I may."

Libby blinked, surprised out of her unhappy thoughts. "Okay."

"Mr. Simms tells me you have had some contact with one of John Fuller's people."

Libby had seen little evidence of the Jaeger who, according to Scab, so terrorized anyone who crossed him; now, as he fixed her with his gaze, she glimpsed the hint of steel behind the sunlit green of his eyes.

"Not only that," he said, "but you were *given* something: a liquid which proved effective for driving away the khatojana?"

Libby dropped her eyes. Though it seemed she had been given little choice, she still felt a bit ashamed of having kept the meeting with the woman secret. "Yes, sir," she murmured.

"And why didn't you tell Mr. Pullman, or Roach, about this?"

"I tried to, but I couldn't. I'd just – *forget*, sort of, before I could do it. The lady said that's how it would be; she said I wouldn't be able to tell anyone about it."

"But you were able to tell Scab about it."

Jaeger's gaze was so penetrating that Libby almost felt he must be able to see her thoughts before she put them into words. She hadn't thought before about why she had been able to show Scab the vial, when she hadn't been able to show it to Roach or Pullman, and she felt, uncomfortably, that this inconsistency made her story sound like a lie. She thought about it for a moment, and then said, "Well... maybe it was different, telling Scab? Maisie was gone by then, so... maybe it didn't matter anymore?"

Jaeger nodded, seeming to accept this. "Pullman told me what the woman said about the liquid restoring Maisie." He closed his eyes and rubbed his forehead, looking angry and tired. "To deceive an innocent child into causing harm to someone she loves." He dropped his hand and looked at Pullman, and the steel in his gaze unsheathed a bit further. "We've got to put a stop to this, Colin, once and for all." Turning back to Libby, he laid a gentle hand on hers where it rested on the table. "We can be very thankful that Mr. Pullman took Maisie away from there before you did what that woman asked. That philter was never meant to restore Maisie. I feel certain Pullman was right: if even one drop of that liquid had touched your sister while she was free of the cage, it would have sent her flying straight to John Fuller."

Libby couldn't meet his eyes. "The – the lady seemed so *nice!*"

Jaeger's mouth crooked in a bitter smile. "Of course. No doubt that's why Fuller recruited her. A kind face, a reassuring voice: what better tools for manipulating a child?"

Libby hung her head. "I guess I was stupid. I'm sorry."

Jaeger shook his head, impatient. "Self-recrimination is nothing more than poorly-disguised self-pity, Libby, and we have no time for that now. You're a child; you are inexperienced, so

The Birds of the Air | 255

you were deceived. The important thing right now is your sister's safety, and the safety of the other children. Now: what made you think to throw the liquid in that vial onto Scab, to drive out the khatojana? The woman didn't mention anything about that, did she?"

A bit stung by Jaeger's reproof, Libby felt herself flush, and sat up straighter. "No, sir."

"So – what made you do it?"

"I... I had a dream." Libby closed her eyes, trying to remember. "Before the khato... khatojana... came. There was a fire, and the man who gave us a ride to Portersville was there, and he told me to throw the stuff in the vial on it. So I did, and it put the fire out." She opened her eyes and looked at Jaeger. "I don't know why, but when Scab was choking me, I remembered the dream and..." she shrugged. "It just seemed like that made me think of it."

Jaeger looked even more grave than before. "And have you had any other dreams like that, Libby? Dreams that caused you to do something in your waking life?"

Libby considered for a moment. "I don't think so."

Jaeger looked at Pullman. "What do you make of it?"

"I don't know." Pullman shook his head. "Obviously it wasn't Fuller."

Libby looked from one of the men to the other. "*What* wasn't Fuller?"

Jaeger turned back to her. "Someone *sent* you that dream, Libby; it was a message from someone – someone who not only knew what Fuller was planning, but also knew what effect the liquid in the vial would have on the khatojana."

Pullman stirred suddenly, a spark of recollection lighting his face. "The day Slater's men abducted Libby, I was alerted by a conduction of some sort." He gave a wry smile, wincing at the memory. "Rather like a shotgun blast to the head. Still, it allowed us to find Libby before she was harmed. Perhaps it came from the same source!"

Jaeger pressed a knuckle to his upper lip and stared at the tabletop. After a moment he looked up, and Libby saw a cautious hopefulness in his expression. "Maybe we're not alone in this after all!" When he looked at Pullman and Roach, some of the hopefulness seemed to be transmitted from his face to theirs. "It's only conjecture, of course, but... maybe we can take some encouragement from the possibility as we go forward: it *almost* seems as if... as if there's someone close to Fuller who's working *against* him!"

Jaeger asked Libby more questions, having her describe the woman who had given her the vial, and tell again the story of the attack in the wheat fields. By the time she finished answering, the late-spring sun had long set and she was growing tired. She tried to stifle a yawn, but Jaeger noticed immediately. "I'm sorry, Libby," he said; "I've kept you too long; I know you must be exhausted." He called toward the kitchen, saying Mrs. Vogel's name and some words in the other language. Mrs. Vogel appeared, smiling, and held out a hand to Libby. Jaeger rose as Libby stood up from the table. "Thank you for your help, Libby. We'll be discussing ideas about how to deal with Fuller tonight, and it's possible things may change, but right now I should tell you that my plan, as it stands, will require Mr. Pullman to leave with me for a while. You'll be staying here with Roach and Mrs. Vogel; they'll take good care of you, and Pullman and I will return when all this is over. Then hopefully, if all goes well, it will be safe to return you to your home."

Libby stiffened, the watchwords of her determination form-

The Birds of the Air | 257

ing in her mind: *I'm not going home without my sister.* But she found she couldn't speak them this time; she was too tired and too uncertain. She said a subdued goodnight to the men and followed Mrs. Vogel from the room, feeling so bone-weary that the effort of climbing the stairs seemed almost more than she could face. Halfway up, though, a thought struck her with the sudden, all-transforming flash of a lightning bolt: *But – they're going to STOP Fuller, once and for all – that's what Mr. Jaeger said!*

She couldn't believe she hadn't realized immediately what Jaeger's words would mean for her and Maisie and Mama. The hope that had been drained from her sprang up again, swelling so powerfully that she could imagine rays of it shining like sunlight out of her ears and eyes, startling Mrs. Vogel as she led the way into a pink-tiled bathroom. Libby watched as the old lady ran hot water into a claw-footed bathtub, and nodded and smiled when she gave her a clean towel and a white cotton nightgown, but her mind was racing, following new possibilities. She was glad when Mrs. Vogel bustled out – taking Libby's dirty clothes with her, along with the little bag-on-a-string – and shut the door behind her.

Should she ask Mr. Jaeger? Should she tell him about her realization, try to convince him to let Maisie come home after the threat of Fuller was eliminated? She frowned, sinking into the warm, lilac-scented water, and shook off the thought. No doubt Mr. Jaeger had already considered the idea. Even without Fuller, there was still Jaeger's and Pullman's conviction that children like Maisie needed special upbringing; she didn't feel confident she could convince them otherwise.

But what if she could *find* Maisie, as she had planned in the car, and somehow get her home? Mr. Jaeger seemed to be a reasonable man. Surely, once he saw the depth of Libby's desire and determination, once he realized Maisie didn't *want* to leave her family, he would have pity on them and leave them alone. *I'll write him a letter,* she thought, *asking him to let us be. I'll leave it here when I go to find Maisie.*

But first she had to figure out *where* to go – to find clues, as she had planned – and in this, too, Mr. Jaeger's dinner conversation had provided her with the direction she needed. She knew what to search for now; she only needed to figure out how to do it without being caught. Turning it over in her mind, she missed Scab even more keenly, wishing for his guidance, his companionship and his canny assurance.

At dinner, she had felt like she could barely keep her eyes open, but now her new hope sent excitement crackling like electricity along her nerves, and she knew she wouldn't be able to sleep. Her mind buzzed with impatience to initiate her plan, so after Mrs. Vogel had shown her to a pretty bedroom with small pale-yellow roses on the wallpaper, she waited until she heard her footsteps recede down the stairs, then pushed aside the covers and rose quietly. She had taken Scab's razor from the pocket of her jeans and concealed it in the folds of the nightgown, in case Mrs. Vogel might think it inappropriate for a young girl to have. Now, having no pocket to carry it in, she hid it beneath her pillow. Then she opened the door of her room as softly as she could, crept out into the hallway, and closed the door again behind her. Her room was near the head of the stairs, and she could hear the men's voices, still coming from the dining room. *Good.*

She turned to look down the hall. All the doors were open, except for the door to her room and one at the far end of the hall. The rooms were dark, but Mrs. Vogel had left the hallway lights

The Birds of the Air | 259

on; she thought she could see well enough by the glow they cast through the doorways.

The first four rooms she checked seemed to be guest bedrooms; all the drawers and closets were empty, as were the spaces under the beds. She found Pullman's suitcase and his black bag in one bedroom, and Roach's brown tweed-printed cardboard grip in another, but she found nothing else. The fifth room was the bathroom, which she had already been in, but she entered it again to check the cupboard shelves and medicine cabinet. She knew it was an unlikely place, and she wasn't surprised to find only clean towels and toiletries. After that, the only room left to check was the one with the closed door, at the end of the hall, which she thought must be Mr. Jaeger's room. As she touched the doorknob, though, she heard the men's voices growing louder, leaving the dining room and approaching the foot of the stairs.

She froze for a couple of seconds, staring down the length of the hallway as heavy masculine footsteps sounded on the treads. The doorway to her room was near the head of the stairs; she couldn't get to it without the men seeing her. After a moment's thought, she ran, silent on her bare feet, into the bathroom. She softly closed the door, switched on the light, and turned on the tap, running water into the sink. Mrs. Vogel had given her a new red toothbrush, which she had already used, but she retrieved it from the shelf in the medicine cabinet where she had left it. Then she pressed one ear to the bathroom door and covered the other with her hand, so she could hear over the sound of the running water. When she heard the men reach the top of the stairs and begin to make their way along the hallway, she turned off the tap, opened the bathroom door and, turning off the light, slipped out into the hall, holding the toothbrush.

All three men stopped short and looked at her, surprised.

Jaeger glanced at his wristwatch. "Still awake, Libby?" His voice held the gracious concern of a good host. "It's been a long time since you came up. Is anything wrong with your room?"

"No, Mr. Jaeger... it's nice, thank you. I was just having trouble falling asleep, and then I remembered I forgot to brush my teeth." She held up the toothbrush as evidence.

Mr. Jaeger frowned a tiny bit, and for a moment Libby was afraid he could tell she was lying. Then he indicated the toothbrush with the lift of a finger, "Why don't you just leave that in the bathroom, Libby? You're going to be here for a while, you know."

Libby looked down at the toothbrush, taken aback. "Oh – okay."

After she had put the toothbrush back, the men bid her goodnight without further comment, but when she glanced down the hall from the door of her room, she saw that Jaeger was watching her with a meditative look on his face.

She went to her bed and lay awake, listening. She heard the men saying goodnight to one another and going to their bedrooms. For a while after that, she heard Roach, who was in the bedroom next to hers, moving around. When those noises stopped, she listened for a long time, and heard nothing but the sounds that drifted through her open window: the chirping of crickets, the far-away barking of a dog, and the song of a wakeful mockingbird. She pushed the covers back again, rose from her bed, and crept out of her room and down the stairs, wincing at every creak of the floorboards. At the bottom she stood still to listen, but the house remained silent.

Stealing along the downstairs hallway, she passed the door to the dining room, a leftover whiff of Pullman's pipe smoke reaching her. She didn't think the dining room or the kitchen likely places, so she headed toward the front of the house.

There were only two other doors off the hallway, one on each side. The door on her right stood open to a large sitting room; she turned into it. A row of tall windows, looking out onto the veranda at the front of the house, let in the glow of a light that had been left burning over the front door. Libby turned slowly to scan the room.

Sofas and armchairs congregated around a yawning fireplace across from her, and more stood around the massive wood cabinet of a radio against the wall to her right. She searched the room carefully, reaching behind and beneath all the furniture, squeezing every cushion and pillow, but she found nothing.

The energy that had welled up with her newfound hope was beginning to wane; her mind was growing fuzzy and her eyes heavy, and she thought she would continue her search another night. Maybe, after Jaeger and Pullman were gone, she might even find opportunities to search parts of the house in the daytime. She crept into the hall, but stopped when she saw the closed door just across from her. She stood for a few seconds, the thought of the soft bed in the yellow-rose room pulling at her, but she couldn't resist taking at least a quick look. She crossed the hall and opened the door softly.

As soon as she saw the room beyond, she wished she had searched it before the sitting room. This room was dimmer than the other, its draperies heavy and almost completely closed, but she could see enough to tell that it was some sort of study or office. She could make out a large wooden desk, and bookshelves lining the walls; it looked like a place that might take her hours to search thoroughly. She glanced behind her into the hallway and listened to make sure the house was still quiet. Maybe she would just close the door for a moment, turn on the light and take a quick look around.

She closed the door as silently as she had opened it, then felt along the walls until she found the light switch and flicked it on. When the room sprang to visibility, full of the deep, rich colors of polished wood, patterned rugs and leather book bindings, she realized it would more likely take days than hours to search. She began to scan the spines of the books that crowded the shelves, starting at the right side of the door as she turned to face it, and working her way along the wall. There was nothing that looked likely on that wall, nor on the upper shelves of the adjacent one, but as she scanned lower, her eyes sweeping the shelves near the floor behind the desk, she saw a row of volumes that looked like ledger books: tall and leather-bound, with no titles on the spines.

She skirted the desk quickly and crouched behind it, pulling at one of the tightly-wedged volumes, having to rock it back and forth to work it out from between its neighbors. The light was dim near the floor, and when she had worried the volume free she stood, intending to place it on the desk to examine it. But instead, as she turned, she jumped like a startled cat and let out a small yelp, dropping the ledger to the floor: the door to the study stood open, and Jaeger leaned against the jamb, arms folded, looking at her with a faint, rueful smile on his face.

"So... *you're* Fuller's spy," he said.

CHAPTER NINETEEN

LIBBY STOOD FROZEN, staring at Jaeger from behind the desk. For a long moment she couldn't speak; her heart hammered, yet she felt as if all the blood had drained from her head.

When Jaeger saw the effect of his words, he seemed a bit alarmed. He lifted a hand: "No no, Libby – don't be frightened! I'm only teasing you!" His expression had become penitent, but there was a trace of laughter in his voice. "I'm not planning to turn you into a toad just yet." He gestured toward the ledger she had dropped. "Is that what you were looking for? The children's records?"

All Libby could manage in response was a mute downward glance. She realized her mouth was open a bit, her breath coming through it in jerky gasps, and she clamped her jaw shut.

Jaeger gestured toward the ledger again. "Go ahead." Libby stared at him for a moment longer, then bent slowly and picked up the heavy volume. Laying it on the desk, she hesitated, raising her eyes nervously to his, but he gave her an encouraging nod. With her fingers still trembling a bit, she opened the book. The first page was filled with lines written in a firm, masculine hand, and in spite of Jaeger's discovery of her, she felt a thrill of hope. Bending closer, she scanned the page, then looked up at Jaeger in confusion.

"It's in German," he said, a faint, rather sad smile lingering on his face. "Not much of an encryption, I'm afraid: even someone who doesn't read the language can still read the names and addresses." His voice became gentler. "And I'm sorry, Libby, but that's why you won't find these here again."

Libby's hands tightened on the book. "But... Mr. Jaeger... after you and Mr. Pullman stop John Fuller, then Maisie *could* be safe with Mama and me! And – I know you and Mr. Pullman think she wouldn't be happy with us, but she *would!* I *know* she would!" She raised her eyes to meet his again, pleading. "Couldn't Maisie come home with me – *just* Maisie? I'd never tell anyone about any of this, I *swear. Please*, Mr. Jaeger?"

The faint lines emerged around Jaeger's eyes and mouth. He crossed the room to stand on the other side of the desk, and slid the ledger around to face him. "Libby... I try to be hopeful – and I *am*, to a degree – but... to be honest with you, in spite of what I said tonight, I can't imagine we will be able to stop John Fuller completely – at least, not any time soon. He's just too powerful."

Libby stared up at him. She felt again the terrifying shift of her inner landscape, the east-for-west, down-for-up realization of how vastly more helpless adults were than she had ever imagined. *Even him... even Mr. Jaeger!* she thought, and felt as if something were collapsing inside her.

"Right now," he said, "we're like... like a handful of hornets,

The Birds of the Air | 265

attacking a bull. Yes, we have our stings, and – who knows? – if there were two or three hundred of us..." He shrugged. "As it is, I'm afraid the best we can hope for is to hide as many children as we can, until the eldest of them can begin to help us in our efforts to defeat Fuller – and that will be some while. I only began planning this entire operation ten years or so ago, and it was at least two years before we were able to find and place our first child. And Libby, Fuller's strength is always growing." His expression became so grim that it sent a chill through her. "It's going to be a very close thing."

"But... if you don't think you can *stop* him, what are you and Mr. Pullman going away to *do*?"

Jaeger met her gaze; a touch of the steeliness returned, cooling the sunlit green of his eyes. "Just what I said, Libby: try to keep the children hidden from him – all the children we can, for as long as we can." His eyes drifted to the closed drapes, as if he could see through them and out into the dark world beyond. "He has some new source of information; he's never been able to find and attack so many of my people in so short a time before. As dreadful as it is to say, it's fortunate that, so far, he's only hunted down people on the fringes of the organization – people who have no knowledge of where the children have been placed. But if any of us who *do* know fall into his hands... well, I wouldn't even trust *myself* to be able to withstand him, if he ever got hold of me." His gaze turned to Libby, and he seemed to pull himself back to recollection of the question she had asked. "It's a – what do they call it in the pictures? An *ambush*, Libby." He gave her a bleak smile. "Pullman and I will meet with a few of my other key people, at one of our outposts some distance from here. Our gathering in one place – that sort of concentration of power – will be like a beacon to Fuller: he'll know exactly where we are. And that's what I want. I'm hoping to *draw* him there – I'm hoping he'll follow the beacon and seek us out, believing he can overpower us and force the information he wants from one of us. And..." he paused, and let out a breath that was half laugh, half sigh... "I'm hoping he'll be wrong. I'm not fool enough to believe we can destroy him. I'm only hoping that, between all of us, we can strike at him hard enough to weaken him for a while – buy ourselves a reprieve from these attacks. And that we can all get away. If not –" he dropped his gaze to where his hand rested on the ledger. "Well... we can't allow ourselves to fall into his hands alive."

Libby's breath caught audibly, and his eyes returned to her. He looked tired and a bit disheveled, she noticed – his necktie loosened, a lock of bronze-colored hair falling over his forehead. "I'm telling you these things, Libby, because you've been dragged into all this – which I *never* would have allowed, had I known about it beforehand – and now everything we do affects *your* future, as well. And – I'm afraid I have more hard news for you." He ran a hand through his hair, pushing the wayward lock off his forehead, but it fell right back again. "If we *don't* return, I'm afraid the only safe course will be to assume Fuller still poses a threat to you, personally. Because of that, I've taken steps to protect you in that eventuality. If we... if... things turn out that way, I've instructed Mr. Simms to take you to the people who are caring for Maisie. I'm dreadfully sorry, Libby, but… now you've come to Fuller's attention, it may be too dangerous for *you*, as well as Maisie, to return to your home; if Pullman and I don't make it back, you'll have no way of knowing for certain." His face was sorrowful, and his voice took on an almost pleading note: "At least you would be with your sister!"

His words buzzed around like insects inside Libby's head, and before they had even begun to settle, he closed the ledger.

"What I'm going to ask you to do now, Libby, is to return this to its place, go back to bed, and promise me you won't try to find these records again."

As he spoke, the sound of his voice seemed to change; it sounded more distant, as if he were speaking to her from the far end of a long corridor. All at once, the strange tingling began behind her eyes, as it had twice before. She felt unsteady, as if the floor were tilting under her. She closed her eyes and shook her head, trying to shake off the tingling, grabbing onto the edge of the desk to keep from tipping over.

It seemed as if her eyes were shut for hardly longer than a blink, but when she opened them again, Jaeger was somehow standing right in front of her, on her side of the desk. The ledger was in his hands, and he held it out to her. "I had meant to remove these to a safer place anyway..." He smiled down at her – from a long way off, it seemed, though he was standing so close – and a bit of the teasing note returned to his voice. "I just didn't realize I needed to do it *tonight*."

Libby reached for the book, but for some reason it was difficult to gauge its distance from her; at her first attempt to take hold of it, she grasped only air, and she had to focus her eyes on it fiercely before she was able to take it from him. The weight of the volume dipped her arms down a bit; the pebbled leather felt cool against her fingers. She gazed at it, agonized: her final chance of finding Maisie lay within this book, or in one of its mates on the shelf. She tried to marshal her scattered thoughts, to come up with some argument that might convince him to change his mind. She could think of nothing. There seemed to be no other choice, so she turned unsteadily to replace the book where she had found it; but when her gaze dropped to the shelf where it had been, she stopped short and glanced back at Jaeger in confusion. She crouched down, scanning the shelves to the right and left, then above and below.

The other ledgers were gone.

On the shelf where she had seen them, a set of Shakespeare's works now stood, bound in pale-green linen. Libby stared, and reached out to run her fingers over the woven surface of the spines. There was a gap in the set where a volume was missing, and as she stared at it she noticed suddenly that something felt odd about the book in her hand. Looking down, she saw she no longer held the leather-bound ledger, but another cloth-bound volume of Shakespeare belonging to the set on the shelf. She opened it; the words were printed, not hand-written, and she read a few of them silently:

For when my outward action doth demonstrate
The native act and figure of my heart...

She looked up at Jaeger with wonder and a touch of fear; then she closed the book slowly and slid it into the empty space. When her fingers left it, her whole body seemed to wilt, as if contact with that physical manifestation of her hope was the only thing that had been lending rigidity to her bones. For the first time the conviction forced itself upon her: even if she burst her heart trying, she would really, truly never be able to recover her sister and take her home. It gave her the horrible feeling she had had when the tramps in the forest had pinned her down, when Scab's arm had been locked around her throat: the unbearable collision of desperate need with utter helplessness.

When she stood, the dizziness came back more strongly, and she had to grasp the edge of the desk again. A wave of nausea swept over her, and tears flooded her eyes; she felt too defeated and exhausted to imagine what she should do next.

Jaeger looked alarmed again, and placed a hand gently on her shoulder. "Come and sit down for a bit. Would you like me to get you a glass of water?"

Libby shook her head, but allowed him to steer her around the desk to one of the leather armchairs. She sank into it and leaned over, bending her forehead to her knees as her mother had taught her to do when she felt dizzy. She was gripped all at once by a searing longing for her mother; sudden sobs jolted through her body, and tears slipped between her fingers, falling in droplets onto her nightgown.

Jaeger pulled another armchair near and sat facing her. "Libby, I'm truly sorry it has to be like this. I *do* understand how painful this is for you." His voice sounded genuinely grieved. "I'll admit that, like Pullman and Roach, I've been coward enough to avoid any contact with the family members of the children we've gathered before now – and not only for the sake of security. I've shielded myself from firsthand experience of their pain, because I was afraid that if I witnessed it, I wouldn't have the strength to do what I know is necessary. But I want you to know I would *never* cause you or your mother – or *any* of the families of these children – all this heartache, if I could imagine any other way."

He sat silent for a while as she wept; then he drew a deep breath and spoke again. "I'm going to tell you something, Libby – something not even all the people working for me know. I realize it won't make the separation from your sister – or your mother, as the case may be – any easier to *bear*, but maybe at least it will make it easier to *understand*." He paused for so long that Libby thought he had changed his mind, but at last he went on. "As important as the safety of your sister and the other children is to us, it's not the only thing at stake – not the only thing we're fighting for in what we're doing here." His tone was so grave that Libby lifted her face to look at him. He took a handkerchief from his pocket and handed it to her. "Have you ever wondered just *why* John Fuller is so intent on gaining all this power?" he asked. "What he wants to *do* with it once he has it?"

Libby felt too drained to think, and too hopeless to care, but his gaze held her, and she forced her mind to take in his question. After a moment she shook her head.

He gave a half-shrug. "Power is like money: there's very little benefit in *having* it if you don't *use* it. What motivates John Fuller – what his long-term plans are – I can't say or imagine. But I *have* been able to discover some of the ways he is using his stolen power *now*." He leaned forward, resting his forearms on his knees. "I'm afraid there's a terrible time coming, Libby. Some of us have seen it, and have discovered that Fuller, and others like him, are working to bring it about. A war is coming – at this point, *that* at least is inevitable. This war, and the horrors associated with it, will make the Great War seem almost sane by comparison; and it will introduce to the world a force for destruction that..." he broke off and closed his eyes, giving a short, sharp shake of his head, as if he wished to physically break his mind free from whatever he had been about to say. "The point is, Libby, we *need* these children, *desperately* –and not just for some idealistic utopian purpose like the ones Pullman is always going on about. We need them to ensure the very survival of the human race – or at least, of all that makes the human race *worthy* of survival. And we *must* keep them safe from Fuller and his associates: it is, in part, the power these people have stolen from the children that is enabling them to accomplish their purposes overseas. Now they've sent Fuller and a few others here, to the United States, to provide them with *more* children. But that's not their only purpose here." His gaze grew fixed and haunted, no longer focused on Libby. "They mean to do the same things in *this* country that they've been doing in Europe. They want to encourage the same sort of spiritual sickness *here* that they've been inciting in certain places overseas. If they succeed in doing that, the outcome of this war..." he raised a hand to rub at his eyes. "Well, it doesn't bear imagining." He lowered his hand and looked at Libby. "Can you understand what I'm telling you?"

Libby's stunned gaze remained on him for a long moment before she realized he was waiting for a response. She hadn't understood everything he said, but enough that she swallowed hard and nodded.

"It's too late for us to stop most of the suffering and destruction that will take place overseas, but that makes it even *more* crucial that we prevent our adversaries *here* from succeeding in their objectives – not only for the sake of this country, but for the sake of the entire world." He reached to rest his fingertips lightly on her hand. "And Libby, what happens with children like your sister may very well be the determining factor in all this."

Libby swallowed again. "But... why didn't Mr. *Pullman* tell me all this?"

Jaeger sat back and shook his head. "I've categorically forbidden any of my people who know about these things to speak of them. Knowledge of the future is an explosive thing; there are few who can possess it without catastrophic results, and *none* who can possess it without peril." He sighed. "I shouldn't have told you what I have, of course; but I can't bear to see you suffering without trying at least to help you understand the reasons. I hope it helps, Libby, if only a little. And one thing I promise you: if the three of us survive the hardships to come, I'll make it my personal responsibility to see that you and your sister *will* meet again."

Meet again.

Libby knew Mr. Jaeger was trying to be kind, but the words filled her with a sickening misery. *Meet again* – after years and years had gone by, when she and Maisie were grown up, strangers to each other? Go home, in the meantime, to the mother who could hardly stand to look at her, and confess that she had failed her once again? Live through all those years, just her mother and her in the dim, shuttered house – endless, silent evenings measured out in the ticking of the parlor clock? Or – more unbearable still....

Jaeger was rising from his chair, one hand extended toward her to indicate that she should get up as well – should accept that the conversation was over. Instead, she reached out and grasped his arm, holding onto it tightly with both hands. "*Please*, Mr. Jaeger – you don't understand! You don't know how much *we* need Maisie." Her eyes were riveted on his face; she could feel them burning. "I do understand what you said, but – it's *different* for us, for Maisie and Mama and me." She faltered, struggling to find words. "Mama – my mother – she *already* lost our dad. He... he did it himself. And since then – even before I lost Maisie –" She let out a sharp breath of frustration: the dread she was trying to express seemed too huge to fit through the door of her mouth. With a distant surprise, she realized it had been with her for a long time. She saw her mother's dim, musty bedroom as it had been before she left, her mother's tangled hair just visible beneath the covers. "Mr. Jaeger, if she loses Maisie too, I'm afraid... I'm scared she's going to do what *he* did!"

She searched his face; he looked more stern than before, but she thought she could see traces of sympathy. He gently disengaged her hands from his arm, placing them on her lap as if they were small, importunate animals; then he sat down opposite her again. He leaned back, regarding her for a minute or two as if he were considering, and she had to dig hard into the flesh of one hand with the nails of the other to keep her hope from bursting out in more words. "We're on a razor's edge, here, Libby." he said finally. "I told you it would be a close thing, and I wasn't exaggerating. We're already having to take children from their homes at younger ages than we would prefer. Our foster-parents are few, and the number of children they work with precludes them from giving very young ones the time and attention they require. If I were to let you take Maisie back, she would have to be replaced *immediately*; that means some boy or girl even *younger* than she would have to be located, and taken away from his or her family – taken away *too* young, before they have the foundation a stable, loving family provides in early childhood. Would you want to be responsible for doing that to another child, another family? Would you really be willing to shift your own hardship onto someone else, just so *you* don't have to bear it?"

Libby hung her head; her cheeks burned, and she couldn't meet Jaeger's eyes, but after a few moments she let out a mumbled word, half in shame and half in defiance: "Maybe." She twisted her hands together and stared with hot eyes at the twining red and blue leaves of the carpet beneath her feet. "It's not just for *me*; it's for Mama, and Maisie. We've had enough trouble already. Why is it more fair for *us* to be sad, than for somebody else?" Her voice just sounded miserable now, and fresh tears slid to the ends of her lashes.

She heard Jaeger shift in his chair; looking up, she saw him pull at his loosened necktie, untying it altogether. He looked haggard and exhausted. "All right," he said finally, and there was defeat in his voice. "I guess I was right all along – to avoid the families. It's just as I thought: I'm a weakling." He straightened, his gaze pinning hers. "I'm not promising you *anything*, Libby: you need to understand that. But what I *will* do... " he rose and reached into his waistcoat pocket, pulling out a small key. Circling the desk, he unlocked a drawer and took out a tin container, like the one Libby had seen in Pullman's trunk. When he had pried off the lid and pulled back a layer of excelsior, Libby took in her breath. Dozens of small sugar birds filled the tin, white as captured snow, each a replica of the one the man Stubby had given to Maisie, except that these were pure white, without the reddish-brown spot that had marked Maisie's bird between its outstretched wings. Jaeger lifted one out, set the tin on the table and came back around the desk, holding the bird in his fingers. "I won't mince words, Libby," he said. "I think you'll regret your attitude about this. But I'm going to let you choose your position for yourself." He held up a warning hand as Libby rose hastily from her seat. "I'm *not* saying for certain that Maisie can go home with you. All I'm doing is formalizing *your* position on the question: that is, I'm asking you to affirm that, should we locate a child with whom Maisie can be replaced, you would choose to *make* such an exchange." His eyes on hers were grave. "It would be your choice – your responsibility." He drew a small folding knife from his trouser pocket and held it out to her. "It would be *your blood*, Libby, that would accomplish the transformation. Do you understand?"

Libby gaped at him. An icy tingling flowed from her scalp down the length of her spine. Quickly, and with all her mental force, she shoved down the certainty that the tingling feeling was horror, and that horror was the only fitting response to the concession Jaeger was offering her. She squeezed her eyes shut tightly

The Birds of the Air | 275

for a moment, drew in a deep breath, and reached to take the knife from his hand.

HER THOUGHTS, AFTER Jaeger had sent her back to bed, hissed and crackled like a radio not tuned to any station. Questions cycled through her mind – questions that had formed even before she left Jaeger, but which she hadn't dared ask, for fear of his taking back even the provisional concession he had made her. Did he know of a way to keep Maisie safe from Fuller if he *did* allow her to go back? Would it mean that they would all have to move somewhere else – somewhere Fuller wouldn't find them? Would he convince her mother to do that, and if not, would Libby be able to? And, most importantly: after all his talk about the urgent need to recruit as many of the children as possible, had he really meant what he said, or had he just offered an easily-revocable fragment of hope, to keep her from causing trouble until he could get rid of her? She had no answers for any of these questions, and the hope of regaining Maisie and the fear of losing her clashed like opposing waves, creating a roiling chaos. Beneath this turbulence she could feel something else, as well – something trying to rise, like a creature drowned but unquiet.

She stared at the moving shadows of branches, cast on the ceiling by some outdoor light, and listened to the night insects. The mockingbird seemed to have gone to sleep. Her throat hurt, and her finger stung where the knife had pricked it. She put it in her mouth, and was stung anew, this time by the memory of how unkindly she had often scolded Maisie for the same action. She expected a scalding flood of remorse, expected to cry again, but her eyes remained dry. She wondered if maybe a person was allotted only so many tears to cry in one lifetime; if so, she thought dully, she had probably used all of hers in just the past few days.

Eventually she began to slip fitfully in and out of sleep. Once, as she was sinking down into a restless doze, she was jerked awake by what she thought was a sound from outside: the scuffling noise of a struggle, and a furious, hoarse, quickly-smothered cry. She stiffened and raised herself to an elbow, listening intently, but she could hear nothing more, and thought she must have dreamed the sounds.

At last, when a solitary robin in the predawn darkness had begun its monotonous, chirruping song, exhaustion dragged her down into a deeper sleep. She didn't wake again until the sun was already halfway up to its highest point in the sky.

When she rose from her bed and glanced into the dresser mirror, she felt distantly taken aback by how different she looked from the image of herself she held in her memory. She was thinner, wilder-looking, scratched and scorched and insect-bitten; her neck showed traces of bruising and strange, tiny blood-red specks beneath the skin, and her face held an unfamiliar seriousness. With her fingers, she tried halfheartedly to comb the tangles from her hair, but a creeping feeling of antipathy toward the person in the glass began to rise like nausea inside her, and she turned away quickly and stripped off her nightgown to change.

The three dresses Mrs. Vogel had bought for her hung in the closet, stiff and unfamiliar. She felt a sudden, foolish longing for the jeans and shirt Roach had bought her in Seifert. They reminded her of being with Scab, and of the time when she had still believed they would be able to get Maisie back. *I might still get her back,* she thought, trying to cheer herself, but with the thought came the memory of what she had done to secure that possibility, and instead of hope she felt the creeping sickness again.

She pulled on a white cotton slip that lay folded on the dresser, and chose the dress that had pockets – a simple, short-sleeved, red one, with tiny black-and-yellow flowers printed on it. It was a little large for her, but she tugged it over her head and buttoned it. Mrs. Vogel had placed her sister's picture, her father's pocketknife and the glass vial on the nightstand. She put the first two objects into her pockets, then lifted the little vial and looked at it again. There seemed no reason to keep it, yet she felt reluctant to throw it away. After a moment she put it in her pocket, as she had the day before. She fished Scab's razor from under her pillow, and slipped it into the pocket with the vial; she didn't suppose she needed it here, but she had promised him she would keep it with her, and having it gave her a small thread of comfort.

She looked at her worn, dusty shoes, but left them on the floor of the closet and went barefoot into the hall. The rooms Roach and Pullman had slept in were empty, the beds made and the curtains and windows open. She drifted down the stairs, aimless, still feeling exhausted, and met Mrs. Vogel bustling through the downstairs hall. The old lady hustled her into the kitchen and set milk and hot oatmeal with honey in front of her. Libby ate what she could, mostly to escape as soon as possible from Mrs. Vogel's fussing. She appreciated the old lady's kindness, but Mrs. Vogel rattled on incessantly in what Libby supposed must be German, and the effort of nodding and smiling in response to the incomprehensible flood of words made her feel even more exhausted.

When she had eaten as much as her knotted stomach would allow, she thanked Mrs. Vogel and rose to take her dishes to the sink, meaning to go and find Roach and Pullman. But with an exclamation of what sounded like self-reproach, Mrs. Vogel crossed the kitchen to a tin mail-caddy hanging by the back door, took a folded sheet of paper from it and handed it to Libby. It was a note from Jaeger; Libby sat down at the table again to read it:

Dear Libby –

I've sent Pullman and Roach into town to pick up some supplies we'll need, and I have some errands to run myself. I'm not sure whether I'll see you again before we leave; if not, please make yourself at home until we get back – or until Mr. Simms comes to fetch you. It will probably be best if you stay fairly close to the house. If you see anyone you don't recognize around the farm – aside from the groundskeeper, Mrs. Vogel's husband Hans, whom Roach or Mrs. Vogel will point out to you – please stay well away and let Roach know immediately.

If you need anything, Mrs. Vogel will be happy to provide it, although you may have to engage in some pantomime to make her understand you.

I realize, Libby, that the things I told you last night are an awful burden for a young girl to bear, but I have confidence in your courage and character. You are as extraordinary in your way as your sister is in hers. I feel that in the difficult times to come you too will have an important contribution to make. Try to keep your spirits up. It has been a pleasure meeting you, and if all goes well I hope to see you again.

– Jaeger

She folded the page and laid it on the table. After thanking Mrs. Vogel again, she went out the back door, onto the covered veranda.

The Birds of the Air | 279

Mrs. Vogel soon followed her out, carrying a wide, shallow bowl made of blue china. She spoke some cheerful, incomprehensible words, pointing a finger in an arc toward the trees behind the house; then she called out in a high, singsong voice. She set the bowl down on the boards of the veranda floor, and Libby saw a little lake of milk inside it. Mrs. Vogel called again, and, with a flurry of answering calls, a trio of half-grown kittens rippled into view from beneath the shrubbery at the edge of the trees. They flowed like gravity-defying liquid up onto the porch, and situated themselves at exactly equidistant points around the bowl, lapping greedily. Two were orange tabbies – the kind Libby's grandmother called marmalade cats – and the third was a calico. Libby felt her spirits lift a bit at the sight of them.

She sat on the boards to watch them, and Mrs. Vogel smiled down. After a moment she spoke a string of words that contained Mr. Jaeger's name, but Libby, looking up at her, shook her head. Mrs. Vogel said Mr. Jaeger's name again, then folded her arms and glared at the kittens with her face contorted into an exaggerated frown that made Libby laugh. Looking pleased at her reaction, Mrs. Vogel glowered even more fiercely at the kittens, impersonating Jaeger, then stomped around in a small circle on the boards, fists clenched, wearing the fearsome frown and startling the kittens so that they froze and stared up at her for a moment with saucer eyes. Libby laughed again; Mrs. Vogel smiled, pointed to the kittens, and put a finger to her lips, eyebrows raised. Libby smiled and nodded, and Mrs. Vogel bustled back into the kitchen.

Though the day was overcast, it was already growing hot, and after the kittens had finished the milk they washed their faces and lazed in the shadow of the veranda. They were at the lanky adolescent stage where they looked like young cougars, rawboned and almost as flat as rugs when they stretched out on their sides to cool themselves against the boards. Libby petted their dusty coats for a while, but thoughts of the night before crept back upon her, making her feel harried and restless.

She left the kittens and walked along the veranda, making the circuit of the house. In the front, she saw that both the Fords were gone from the gravel parking area; when she got around to the back again, the kittens were gone as well. A warm, fitful breeze started up, blowing steamy near-summer rainclouds across the sky, tossing the branches of the trees behind the house. The trees grew thick enough almost to make a small forest; peering into them, Libby saw a striped canvas hammock between two trunks. She drifted toward it and, as small warm spatters of rain began to spit from the sky, climbed into it and lay down. The scattered droplets didn't reach her under the trees, though they raised a sweet, vivid scent from the grass and earth where they fell.

She lay staring up at the swaying branches, listening to the ocean-sound the wind made among them. The sound was soothing, but unwanted thoughts circled the edges of her mind like predators. What would Scab say, she wondered, if he heard all the things Jaeger had told her? If he knew about the agreement she had made with him? What would Pullman or Roach think of her if *they* found out, after all the times she had told them they were wrong to take the children from their families? She tried to concentrate on the idea of Maisie coming home, of their lives going back to the way they had been; but the ghost of another child, a boy or girl even younger than Maisie, taken from another family, kept haunting the edges of her mind. *It's GOOD for them,* she told herself. *They need to be with someone who can teach them – that's what Pullman said.* But another part of her scoffed: *and if you believe him, why don't you want that for Maisie?*

The Birds of the Air | 281

Hoping to escape her thoughts in sleep, she closed her eyes; but almost immediately, a bone-chilling wail startled them open again. It took her only a second to recognize the sound: the banshee-cry of one cat in a standoff with another, carried by the gusting wind from someplace on the far side of the trees. She closed her eyes again, intending to ignore it, but the cry came once more, rising to a blood-curdling shriek, and she sighed and struggled out of the hammock, meaning to find the scene of the battle and chase the combatants away.

As she made her way through the trees, she began to glimpse something through the shifting gaps in the branches: a building she hadn't noticed before. As she drew nearer, she marveled at the size of it, and at the square-cut stone it was built of: it looked more like a hospital or a big-city library than like any building she had ever seen on a farm. The trees grew close around it, brushing its eaves with their branches. On its east wall, facing her as she approached, three concrete steps led up to a pair of massive, windowless metal doors. All the windows she could see on the ground floor were covered by heavy shutters. She felt a slight stirring of curiosity beneath her weariness, and nearly climbed the steps to try the doors, but the feline howling was coming from behind the building, so she continued along its north wall, following the sound.

Rounding the corner, she startled the originators of the disturbance: at the foot of a row of large metal trash barrels, some distance from the back of the building, two of the young cats she had seen on the porch stared up at her, both tensed, ready to run. One was the calico, who held in her mouth some brownish thing – not a mouse, but something that splayed out in an odd way and made her look, comically, as if she had sprouted a moustache. Once she had taken a quick look at Libby – and evidently judged her not to be a threat – she turned away again, flattened her ears and continued to growl at one of her orange brothers, who crouched a short distance away, apparently intent on stealing her prize.

Frowning, Libby crept closer, trying to determine what the calico had. Her approach apparently aroused the cat's suspicion that Libby had designs on her treasure as well, and after a final clench-jawed yowl, she disappeared into a tangle of buttonbush behind the barrels, carrying her prize with her. Whatever that prize had been, it was so chewed and bedraggled that Libby couldn't identify it, though she felt she *ought* to be able to – that it was something so familiar to her thoughts these days that it should be more recognizable than her thin, glum face had been in the mirror that morning.

The wind had quickened, scattering the sparse raindrops and raising a continuous, murmuring roar in the branches, but a metallic rattle cut through the sound, drawing Libby's attention back to the marmalade cat. Having given up on stealing from his sister, he had leapt to where the calico had evidently gotten her plunder: The metal lid of one of the trash barrels was askew, leaving a gap big enough for him to slip into. He stood on the lid of the neighboring barrel, the fur along his back blown into shifting ruffles. From there, he eeled with some difficulty through the gap, and reappeared with his own treasure, which was in much better condition than his sister's.

It was a sparrow's wing.

CHAPTER TWENTY

AT LIBBY'S APPROACH, the orange cat leapt into the bushes, following his sister. Libby shoved the lid off of the barrel he had been in. When she looked inside, it seemed at first that her brain was somehow disconnected from her eyes – as if they were joined by some faulty telegraph line that had shorted out. For a long moment, no matter how hard she stared at the contents of the can, she could make no sense of it.

When that moment passed, she felt sick with longing for it to return.

The barrel stood as high as the middle of her ribcage, and was bigger around than her arms could have reached if she had tried to embrace it. Its interior was blackened, as if it was used for burning trash. It was filled with sparrow's wings – wings only – up to about a foot from its rim.

She stood stunned for a few seconds, and then, as the implications of what she was seeing threatened to take shape in her mind, she recoiled from them and took refuge in action. She reached over the edge of the barrel and plunged her hands among the small, feathered fans of the wings. As she looked at them more closely, she realized they were in fact only dried flesh and feathers: all the tiny toothpick bones had been removed from them. They were as light as dry leaves and moved aside easily; a sickening smell of dead things rose as they stirred beneath her touch. They did not, she discovered with queasy relief, fill the entire barrel, but lay only in a layer two or three inches deep on top of old newspapers, cans and other ordinary trash. Lifting the lids, she checked the other two barrels and found them both empty. She turned back to the first barrel, fished one of the wings out, and shoved it into her pocket with the picture of Maisie.

The isolated drops of rain were quickening into a light shower as she raced back through the trees and around the side of the house toward the front yard. "*Please*, Mr. Pullman, be back! Please, *please* be back!" she murmured to herself as she ran. But when she rounded the front corner of the house, the parking area was still empty.

On the way back she walked slowly, staring at the rain-spattered ground in front of her. Now it was her thoughts that raced, but she fiercely blocked their passage toward the meaning of her grisly discovery. She turned them instead to what she should do next, and they all ended up in the same place: inside the stone building.

As she approached it, she scanned the grove of trees around it carefully, but saw no one. The continuous murmur of the wind-tossed branches made her jumpy with the thought that she wouldn't hear if someone approached; she kept turning her head to peer over her shoulder. She climbed the steps and tried the big double doors, but they were locked. She felt an odd, faint

The Birds of the Air | 285

thrumming when she touched them; it reminded her of the slight quiver of electricity she had sometimes felt between her fingers and the metal of her mother's sewing machine.

She circled the entire building, prying at the shutters on the windows. None of them would budge, and they offered not the smallest gap for her to look through. A smaller metal door at the back of the building was locked tight as well, its tiny window too high for her to see through. She could feel the same faint thrumming in every surface she touched on the building, whether wood, stone or metal. It felt unnatural, as if she were touching some repellent living thing, and she kept her contact with it as brief as possible.

At ground level along the south side of the building she saw the long, narrow horizontal oblongs of basement windows. These had no shutters, but they were immovable and their glass was painted over from within, so that she didn't dare break one for fear someone might be on the other side.

Backing away from the building, she noticed that the second floor was smaller than the first, squatting in the center of the supporting lower story with a pitched strip of slate-shingled roof all around it. All the second-floor windows she could see presented the blank blind-man's stare of drawn shades, but none were covered by shutters. At the rear of the building, she spotted one shade that hadn't been pulled quite all the way down.

She circled the building again, her hair dripping, her wet dress beginning to cling to her legs. This time she was searching for the right tree: one that had both a low branch that she could swing herself up onto, and a sturdy limb overhanging the strip of first-story roof closely enough that she could lower herself onto it without making too much noise.

She found three different trees with the second kind of

branch, but none with the first. She ran back to the metal barrels and, ignoring the one that contained the wings, took the lid off the empty barrel beside it, and rocked it until she managed to tip it over. She rolled it to the nearest suitable tree, a thick-trunked oak with an almost horizontal limb overhanging the roof. She tipped the barrel upside down, with its open end on the ground and its bottom providing a reasonably stable platform from which, once she had scrambled onto it, she was able to reach the lowest branch of the oak and haul herself, dripping and rust-stained, up onto the rough bark.

Glad of her bare feet, she climbed to the overhanging limb, then edged out along it until she was above the roof. The drop onto the wet slate shingles cost her a moment of panic when her bare feet slipped a foot or so down the slope of the roof, but she fell to her hands and knees, managed to stop her slide, and crouched there, heart pounding, until she could calm her ragged breath.

Walking as softly as she could, crouching low and peering down often through the trees to make sure no one was watching, she made her way to the back of the building. Staying close to the wall, she crouched to peer beneath the partly-open blind; then, seeing no one, she pressed her ear to the window, listening for any sound. She listened for a long time, and though she felt the faint thrumming against her ear, she could hear nothing.

The windows were metal-framed, the tall kind that opened like French doors. Peering through the glass, Libby could see the latch inside. She fished her father's knife from her pocket, opened its blade and tried to work it into the crevice, but there was a lip inside that wouldn't allow it to slip all the way through. She thought for a bit, and then, quickly unbuttoning her dress, slipped it off over her head, careful not to spill her belongings

The Birds of the Air | 287

from the pockets. Crouching in her damp cotton slip, she wrapped the dress around her elbow and crooked her arm to hold it in place. She pressed her ear against the window again for a moment, then drew back her arm and drove her cloth-wrapped elbow through the pane closest to the latch.

From outside, in the gusting wind and rain, the noise of breaking glass didn't seem too loud. Nevertheless, she held her breath and listened before she unwrapped the dress from her arm and pulled it back on, shivering at its clamminess. Then she reached through the broken pane, turned the latch, and opened the window. She told herself that anyone who heard the window breaking would have yelled or come to look, and – after taking in a shaky breath – pushed the shade aside and peered around it.

She saw a small, shadowy room with a tall work-table at its center, surrounded by several high stools. Glass-fronted cabinets lined the walls. The room was deserted.

As softly as she could, careful of the glass, she climbed onto the sill and let herself down to the floor, closing the window behind her. The shade blocked out much of the light, but she could see that the table held a small set of scales, a wooden case of little different-sized weights, and one of the cup-like things with grinders in them that Libby had seen pictured on the signs of drugstores.

The broken window blocked out more of the noise of wind and rain than she would have thought possible; the room seemed unnaturally silent, except for the sounds of her own movements and a soft, irregular ticking or tapping whose source she couldn't identify. She began to scan the cabinets, searching – because of what she had seen in the barrel – without allowing her mind to bring the object of her search into clear focus. When she had checked every shelf and found only jars, bottles, and metal implements whose purposes she couldn't guess, she crossed to the single door, opened it a crack, and peered through.

Outside she found a corridor, lined with more closed doors. It was dark, apparently lit only by the gray seepage of daylight that managed to filter around the edges of the drawn shades she had seen from outside, and then through the cracks beneath the doors. When she stepped out of the doorway – her bare feet silent on the polished floor – she could hear a humming sound, pulsating slightly, as if some sort of motor was running some-where. She crept a step farther, her breath trembling, her eyes darting among the shadows. She kept imagining that the wing in her pocket was moving; it felt like a living presence, a con-stant tug at the margins of her attention. She shook her mind free of it, closed the door behind her softly, and crossed to the door opposite.

The room beyond was similar to the one she had just left, except that the cabinets in it had solid metal doors, with no glass in them. She opened the first one, straining her eyes to scan its dark interior. She heard no sounds of life, but searched all the shelves carefully nonetheless. Her reason for doing so kept trying to break into her awareness, like a far-off screaming, but she refused to acknowledge it.

The dimness slowed down her search, and she summoned courage to switch on the overhead light. Its glare was more unnerving than the dark, making her feel as if someone unseen were watching her, but she was able to check the cabinets quickly. They contained only what appeared to be medical supplies: glass-and-chrome syringes, great curved needles, rolls of gauze. Several shelves held trays containing more strange metal instruments: oddly-shaped blades, curved tongs, pointy things like icepicks, a small, shiny saw. When she looked into a hinged case and discovered spools of thick black thread, the horror she and Scab had found in the conjure-jar leapt to her mind, and she jerked her hands back as if she had opened a box full of spiders.

The next room was similar to the first two, but contained a steel table. It looked a bit like a doctor's examination table, except that it had no cushion – only a depression like a small rain gutter running around its surface near the edge, leading to a drain at one end. Libby thought it was the sort of table a mortician would use to work on a dead person – she thought she had seen something like it in a book or a newsreel – until she noticed the heavy leather restraints attached to its edges. When she saw them, she stumbled backward from the room, into the throbbing hum of the corridor. She had to fight off a wave of dizziness and nausea before she was able to force herself to reenter the room and continue her search.

The fourth and fifth rooms she opened were windowless and small, almost closets. The fourth contained only cleaning and maintenance supplies, and the fifth – though its walls were covered with garish mauve wallpaper in a pattern of leaves and vines – was empty except for a hanging bulb and a single wooden chair, sized for a very small child. Libby scanned these rooms quickly, listening always for sounds of anyone approaching. Over and over she jumped at creaks and shifting shadows, and had to steel herself to go on; but when she opened the door of the sixth room and flicked on its lights, her legs nearly buckled beneath her.

It was another small, windowless room, long and narrow like a shoebox. The air inside was thick with an odd, pungent smell, and though the humming sound was no louder, she thought this must be its source: she could feel the vibration of it in her chest and jawbone. When she flipped the light switch, no overhead bulbs lit up as they had in the other rooms; instead, light sprang upward from glass panels set into metal-framed shelves lining the walls. The light rippled on the ceiling after passing with an eerie underwater glow through the objects that stood on the shelves: row upon row of clear glass jars, each filled with colorless, slightly cloudy liquid. Floating in each jar, like some kind of nightmarish sea creature, was a monstrous thing horribly familiar to Libby: the tissue-shrouded globe of a human eyeball, bound to the rubbery, fungoid crescent of a severed human ear by the same crude black stitches that had joined their grisly counterparts in the jar she and Scab had found in the clearing.

As she stared, stunned motionless, a couple of the nearest began to move in their jars, turning with a swaying, sporadic motion. At first their movements looked random, accidental; but others joined in the gradual, bobbing rotation, and when Libby realized that, one after another, the eyes were all stopping with their silvery, opaque irises fixed on her, she let out a smothered cry and staggered back from the door, her hands covering her mouth.

For a few moments, shock cast a dreamlike haze of unreality over her mind, but as it faded she realized – with a rush of blackness at the edges of her vision – that she would have to look into the room again, to make sure what she sought wasn't there in the dark corners beyond the shelves. She couldn't imagine being able to do it. Could Jaeger *see* her, if those things could? How many of them were in there? Forty? Fifty? Which – if the mates to the horrors in these jars were hidden elsewhere, like the one she and Scab had found – would mean... would mean...

It'd mean that son of a bitch woulda had to kill forty, fifty people – that, or just left 'em hacked up an' blind.

It was Scab's voice, speaking in Libby's head. She knew she was only imagining it, but Scab's presence, even imagined, restored some of her courage. Crouching in the dark corridor, her back against the wall and her forehead on her clenched fists, she answered him in her mind: *I know it, Scab. And I know why I have to look inside that room – and every room in this horrible place. I know what those wings in the trash barrel mean.*

Jaeger lied to me.

She squeezed her eyes shut, pressing her courage further.

Maybe even Pullman and Roach are still lying to me. Maybe even you *were.*

And whether just one of you is lying, or you all are, it still means the same thing:

Maisie might still be here.

It took what seemed like ages for her legs to feel steady enough to carry her back to the doorway. She approached it with her eyes lowered, reaching out to find the doorjamb with her hand. She had stumbled away too quickly to close the door. Imagining Scab beside her, she took a trembling breath and raised her eyes.

She noticed with a spasm of revulsion that all the ears were turned toward the open door now, and realized for the first time that her fear had been wringing small sounds from her with every breath. She clamped her jaw shut, silencing herself, and scanned the room as swiftly as possible, making sure Maisie couldn't be hidden there, even in her tiny bird-form. The second she felt certain, she backed out, slamming the door – then cringing at the noise it made – before she could see the monstrosities in the jars complete the slow rotation they had begun again as soon as she returned to their line of sight.

She had to stop, bending to prop her hands on her knees, until she could slow her breathing and feel blood returning to her face. The length of time she had been in the building unsettled her more each minute. The fear of being discovered weighed on her like a constant physical ache, and the muted humming had begun to grate on her nerves as if it were the wail of a fire alarm. She silently berated herself, urged herself to get moving, but the number of rooms still to be searched threatened to overwhelm her with despair. She straightened, clenched her jaw, and ran to the next door.

It was locked.

She tried again, rattling the knob, but it wouldn't budge. She gave up and moved to the next door, but it was locked as well. With a choked cry of frustration she slammed her palms against it once, then ran to the door across the corridor. This one opened.

At first she thought the room beyond it was deserted, as all the others had been. She flicked the light switch, but it remained strangely dim, and, looking up, she saw that someone had removed the bulbs from three of the four light fixtures, leaving only the one nearest the door in place. There were more metal cabinets against the walls, each tall and wide enough that a grown man could have stood inside. She went quickly to the nearest, opened it, and saw shelves containing more mysterious supplies: small bottles filled with liquids or powders; thin, hollow metal cylinders that curved at one end; coils of rubber tubing.

She had to fetch a stool and stand on it to check the top shelf, where she found a number of odd-looking glass bottles, lines and numbers embossed upside-down on their sides, wire arcs like bucket-handles attached to their bases. She pushed them aside to look behind them. As she did so, she heard a sound: a long, low-pitched, rasping hiss that flashed the image of a monstrous snake across her mind. She whirled toward it, knocking one of the bottles to the ground. Scarcely registering the crash of breaking glass, she peered into the dimness at the far end of the room, her eyes stretched wide.

The sound came again, longer and louder this time, and she was able to locate its source: a tall, narrow cage of some sort, its thick steel or iron frame supporting heavy mesh of the same metal. It was oddly shaped, with the panels that formed its sides protruding past its front. She could see why she had failed to spot it when she first entered the room: two of the large cabinets, standing against the wall to the right of the door, had screened it from her view.

The frame of the cage was bolted to a sturdy grating, which was in turn bolted to the wall. The mesh of the panels was heavy and dense enough that, in the poor light, Libby couldn't make out what was inside. It seemed clear, though, that whatever creature was making the noise was securely trapped and couldn't get out to harm her. She climbed down from the stool, careful of the glass, trying to peer through the mesh into the interior of the cage. She couldn't imagine Maisie making the sound that had emerged from that shadowed space, but the cage was taller than a man and perhaps a foot-and-a-half wide and a foot deep: more than large enough to hold a little girl, though Libby's mind shied from the horror of the thought.

As she edged forward, her bare foot brushed a piece of the glass, making a chinking sound. As if in response, the hissing noise came from the cage again; this time Libby could almost imagine there were half-formed attempts at words in it.

When she drew near enough to see inside the cage, the first thing she noticed was the fabric: dingy white cotton, like the fabric of a shirt or nightgown, pressed so tightly against the mesh in places that it pushed a bit outward into the gaps. The fabric shifted a bit, pressed out even harder as if with an intake of breath, and then the hissing sound emerged from above it. The sound drew Libby's eyes upward; then her entire body reeled back.

The thing inside the cage was a man.

In the fraction of a second before she bolted for the door, she took in more of the dreadful sight than she would have imagined possible: the mesh pressed against the body on all sides, so that only the head could move; the familiar coarse, black sutures, sealing shut the sagging flaps of eyelids and a mouth-sized gash across the throat; the mouth itself, dry and cracked, stretched wide to emit the horrible, inhuman hissing.

With every thought but escape driven from her mind, she fled almost the full length of the room before the horror of what she had seen even fully penetrated her mind; but when she came within view of the open door, she recoiled again and staggered back from it, heedless of the glass cutting her feet. She stumbled, half-fell, and pushed off from the floor with her hands, choking back a whimper; unable to keep herself upright, she sank into a crouch against the far wall, her hands trembling against her head.

"Hello, Libby."

Jaeger stood in the doorway.

He leaned against the doorjamb as he had when he had caught her in the study, his smile not rueful now, only amiable and a little amused. "I see you've stumbled on my latest donor." He gestured toward the wretched creature in the cage. "Do you recognize him?"

Libby's terror seemed almost to have become a substance replacing the air between her and Jaeger, so that his words came to her muffled, as if she were hearing them underwater. He stood looking at her, smiling, until at last she managed numbly to shake her head.

"You've met him, you know," he continued, his voice as

pleasant as ever. "He's the one who *started* all this – at least, for you and your sister." He left the doorway. "Come on, take a look."

Libby felt a brief flash of hope as he moved, unhurried, toward the horrible cage; for a moment, she almost believed he would leave her pathway to escape unobstructed. As soon as he left the doorway, however, she saw the foolishness of any such idea, and buried her face in her arms with a sob of helpless terror. The weak light of the single bulb had picked out a figure lounging in the corridor, his walking stick resting on his shoulder and a nasty grin on his burned face: Slater.

"Libby."

In spite of the genial tone, there was an unmistakable note of command in Jaeger's voice. Libby couldn't suppress another small, terrified sound as she tried to retrieve, from the frantic confusion of her thoughts, the memory of what it was he wanted her to do.

"Come over here." He stood beside the cage now, and held out a hand toward her, like a father confidently expecting obedience from a dawdling child. She used the wall to push herself up, and somehow managed to cross the room, halting and unsteady as an infant taking its first steps. When she was near enough, Jaeger placed the extended hand on her shoulder; she flinched, but didn't dare to pull away as he drew her even closer to the dreadful cage. "Are you *sure*?" he said, a faintly teasing tone in his voice, and she cast about dazedly in her mind, trying to remember what he was talking about. Her eyes were glued to the floor, avoiding the dreadful sight before her, and with a clenching of her stomach she noticed that the feet of the man in the cage protruded from beneath the edge of the front panel, allowing the mesh to press more tightly against the front of his body. Jaeger tapped on the mesh. "Take a good look. Are you *sure* you don't remember him?"

His tone remained light, but she heard implacability in it, and Slater had come through the door, his boots crunching on the glass. She raised her eyes.

The man in the cage sagged like a propped-up rag doll, silent now except for soft, voiceless weeping sounds. Looking at him, as Jaeger commanded, Libby made a small, animal sound herself, something between a sob and a moan.

The man wasn't very tall; his face wasn't all that far above hers. The eyelids, puckered between the coarse black sutures, sagged over obviously empty sockets, and she saw now that his ears were missing as well. She realized, with a gagging sensation, that she was looking at the answer to the question she had asked Scab, when they had first seen the awful contents of the jar in the clearing: *"How do you think he... got them?"*

Jaeger, smiling down at her, nodded, as if he could read the realization in her face. "The larynx," he said, pointing to the crudely sewn gash across the man's throat, "was strictly due to my own irritability, I'm afraid. Of course, there are less drastic ways to enforce silence, but they require a constant expenditure of energy – slight, but these things add up." He pointed. "You see that tube there?" Libby looked, and saw that where one of the man's arms was pinned tightly between his body and the mesh, a rubber tube snaked in and attached to some sort of needle that pierced his flesh, held in place by adhesive tape. Following the tube with her eyes, she saw that it led upward along the mesh to one of the odd-looking bottles she had seen in the cabinet. The bottle hung upside down by the wire handle; it was half-filled with a yellowish liquid, which dripped through a rubber stopper into the tube.

The Birds of the Air | 297

Jaeger was still speaking, but Libby couldn't follow his words, either because she was too frightened to take them in or because they were genuinely incomprehensible to her. He said something about not having to give food and water to the man in the cage, and a word that sounded like the name of a planet but seemed to mean something horrific about the tube being the only thing keeping the man alive. His gaze on the man was eager, avid. "The medical community won't perfect this technique for decades to come," he said, "or, of course, the other." He waved vaguely downward, and Libby, sickened by even her indistinct suspicion of what he was talking about, saw other tubes emerging alongside the man's trembling legs from under the hem of the dirty cotton garment – like a nightshirt of some sort – that he wore.

"You see, Libby, it's not just the sacrifice itself – the *meat*, I mean; the blood, or bone – that provides the practitioner with the power he needs: it's the *suffering*. *That's* where the real power comes from. The suffering of the victim *infuses* the sacrifice with power. That's why, in spite of the expense and effort required, it is crucial to keep the donors *alive* for as long as possible." He laid a hand on the mesh of the cage, almost caressing it. "I've made quite a study of it: suffering of the mind, the body, the spirit; which proportion of each is most effective when applied to which type of donor. I've made discoveries that have – well, I don't want to sound boastful –" Libby saw with a nightmarish sense of unreality that he actually flushed a bit – "but I really have been able to help to increase efficiency quite a bit for our people in Germany, and I'm hoping to be able to do the same here."

Libby fought against the terror that hummed and crackled like static in her brain, and managed at last to speak: "Mr. Jaeger – please, *please*, won't you give me my sister and let us go? I *swear*, we won't tell *anyone* –"

Jaeger let out a short, incredulous bark of laughter. "I'm sorry, Libby, but that's quite out of the question. Your sister is much too valuable to me – and *you* are, too, in your way." He patted her shoulder. "Now, I need you to pay attention to what I'm telling you; it's important to your future usefulness. Can you do that for me?" When a small, miserable sound escaped her and she tried to pull away, his hand on her shoulder tightened, holding her in place. He gestured toward the cage.

"Right now, I'm studying the effects of what I call RLTI: Radical Long-Term Immobilization." He grasped one of the two mesh panels that extended on each side beyond the front of the enclosure, rattling it a bit. "The cage is adjustable; I designed it myself. It can be expanded or contracted to fit any body-size, from that of a young child, to – well." He gestured at the eyeless, weeping ruin inside. "Do you still not recognize him, Libby? It should really be a bit of a treat for you, seeing him like this." All at once he struck the cage, a sudden, clashing blow that caused Libby to start violently. He chuckled as the wretch inside began to fling his head backward and forward, slamming it against the mesh until it bled, raising a loud hiss like a whispered wail. "This is your old acquaintance, *Stubby*," Jaeger said. "You're the one that *started* all this trouble, aren't you, Stubby?" He turned his gaze to Libby. "You and Libby's young friend Scab."

His brief, cheerful outburst of aggression sent a nearly obliterating wave of terror through Libby, and only his suddenly-iron grip on her shoulder, pressing her to his side, kept her from sinking to the floor. "Stubby's on his own up here for now; we have to watch him closely for infection, after the procedures we've performed on him." He spoke, in a louder tone, to the man in the cage, who had subsided into voiceless, tearless weeping again: "We want you to have a long and productive life with us, don't we, Stubby?" Then he turned his amiable smile back to Libby. "I don't imagine Stubby, here, was the object of your search, though, was he?" He dropped the hand from her shoulder, turned from her and moved toward the door, Slater backing out again to make way for him. At the doorway he stopped and smiled back at her. "Aren't you coming?" His voice took on the good-natured teasing tone again. "Don't you want to see your sister?"

IN LATER YEARS, when she looked back on the nightmare that followed, Libby could never remember the walk from the room where Stubby was imprisoned to the place where the rest of her ordeal took place. In her memory it played like a dream, where one location suddenly becomes another, without transition or explanation. The walk as she experienced it, though, seemed endless. With every step, she had to fight down the primal, animal instinct to run away, and the exhausting persistence of the instinct was not lessened in the slightest by its absolute absurdity: with Jaeger strolling beside her and Slater swaggering behind, any thought of escape was not only foolish, but pathetic.

At last – after passing through more dim corridors, and descending two flights in a stairwell where a rhythmic droning vibrated the walls – they arrived in a long, shadow-filled basement hallway. A dank, stony smell thickened the air, pressing against the back of Libby's throat; caged bulbs hung from the ceiling, each isolated in its own wan pool of light.

Jaeger led the way along the hall, passing several closed doors before stopping in front of one in the right-hand wall. He took a ring of keys from his pocket, unlocked the door and reached inside to switch on more lights, then turned back to Libby. His pleasant smile remained, but he looked at her with an attentiveness that increased her fear to a degree that seemed beyond reason, until she realized it reminded her of the way he had looked at Stubby. "Right through here," he said, indicating with a courteous gesture that she should go first.

For a moment, even her desire to see Maisie couldn't give her the courage to move forward. But Slater stood in the corridor behind her; there was nowhere else she could go. She forced her legs to move, her feet to carry her through the doorway, and saw Jaeger give a slight nod to Slater, who stationed himself outside the door as Jaeger closed it behind her.

The lights Jaeger had switched on shone dimly, shedding small, widely-spaced pools of illumination, some of them at a surprising distance. Where these began to powder away into darkness, Libby could see great pieces of equipment hulking, all of them unidentifiable to her. From where she stood, she could see no place where the light reached the walls; this made the room seem vast, as if its boundaries might be unimaginably distant, or might not even exist at all.

Jaeger threaded his way between cabinets and chests and oilcloth-shrouded shapes that could have been furniture or machines, propelling her before him with a firm hand on her shoulder. He stopped at last in front of some sort of wide structure covered with a canvas cloth. "We don't have many here now," he said. "We sent the last batch overseas last month." He reached up and pulled the cloth away, and the air was filled with the noise of frantic flapping.

The sound of wings.

Tears blurred Libby's eyes as relief flooded through her: *they still had their wings.*

The falling cloth revealed shelves holding row upon row

The Birds of the Air | 301

of birdcages, cube-shaped and about a foot and a half in each dimension. All were empty except two, which held madly fluttering clouds of little birds. Libby pressed her hands and face to the side of the nearest one; her legs wouldn't support her, and she sank to her knees.

"Oh yes – the wings!" Jaeger said, reading her again without difficulty. "Slater mentioned you had found them. Those damned cats; I *told* Mrs. Vogel to get rid of them." He took a small memo book and the stub of a pencil from the inside pocket of his jacket, and jotted a note. "I've got to remember to have Simms or Slater catch those things and drown them." He put the memo book away. "I haven't quite gotten around to clipping this batch yet. Of course, we transport the children in *this* form; it makes it much safer and easier, as you can imagine. But we *have* had a case or two of accidental escape; the amputations not only prevent this, but – for the reasons I've explained to you –actually increase the value of the subjects. Those wings you found outside were from the last group. We keep the bones for our own use here, and discard what's left over."

The stupidity of her brief surge of relief made Libby feel physically ill. "Then, you... you work for John Fuller?"

Jaeger chuckled and shook his head. "No, no – not for a long time now. As Pullman told you, Fuller and I parted ways. Of course, the story I told Pullman was a bit... adjusted. *I* was actually the realist – the one who recognized the desirability of change, and the indispensability of *power* in bringing it about." He gestured toward the birds. "And *this* is where the *real* power is – at least among the procurable sources: in these children of supernormal potentiality. Of course, all that talk of 'enlightening them,' of 'helping them realize their potential,' of 'bettering the world,' is utter nonsense: fairytales I've concocted to enlist the aid of fools like Pullman." He smiled down at Libby. "At this stage of events, it doesn't matter in the least whether they learn to use their abilities or not. Even before they *discover* their abilities – even if they *never* do – the power is in them, ready to be harvested. It's in their heredity, carried down from their parents, grandparents, great-grandparents. It runs in the family bloodlines."

Prolonged terror seemed to be crippling her mental processes; it was hard for her to unravel the meaning of Jaeger's words. When she finally did, they struck her like a lightning bolt; she scrambled to her feet. "Then... take *me*, Mr. Jaeger!" she cried, grabbing his sleeve. "Send Maisie home and take *me*, instead!" She faltered as the horror of what she was saying caught up with her, but she pushed herself on. "If it runs in families, *I* have it too, right? You could use *me* instead of Maisie!"

Jaeger looked down at her, his expression first mildly surprised and then warmed by indulgent amusement. "Don't you think you'd better be aware of what you'd be letting yourself in for, Libby, before you make such an offer?" His voice took on the teasing tone. "You're not forgetting what I told you about *suffering*, are you?" Watching whatever reaction showed on her face, he laughed and laid a hand on her shoulder again. "Come with me; I want to show you something."

Libby pulled back, and he didn't compel her. He dropped his hand, still smiling, and moved away on his own, not looking back. She turned to the birds, peering into the cages, trying to determine which one of them was Maisie. She could see in the light from the bulb overhead that several had blue eyes; others had green, or brown, or black ones. Beyond this they all looked the same. She glanced in Jaeger's direction. He was some way off now, and she imagined herself grabbing the cages and running. But Slater was stationed outside in the hall. She took a last look at the birds, placing her hand on one of the cages, then turned and followed Jaeger.

Jaeger stopped at a door between two pieces of machinery – both still and silent – that looked to Libby as if they belonged in a factory. When he opened the door, she saw a narrow passageway beyond it, and when he flicked a switch, lighting a row of weak bulbs along the ceiling, she saw that the passage extended so far that its end was lost in shadows where the sullen glow of the bulbs failed. Closed doors lined the right-hand wall, spaced no more than ten feet apart, for as far as the dim light reached.

Jaeger moved to the nearest of these, opened it, and steered Libby into the dark space beyond, stepping through the door after her. He flicked another switch, and all of her blood seemed to drain away: there in front of her, bolted to the wall of a tiny, closet-sized room, stood a cage exactly like the one that imprisoned Stubby.

"This is where I plan to begin implementing my program of RLTI on some of the children," Jaeger said.

Some sort of buzzing seemed to be filling Libby's brain, but she could see the devouring intensity lighting Jaeger's eyes again as he gazed at his invention. "I've obtained permission to keep a few of this last group of children to use in my research here. I have *great* hopes for its effect on the potency of the blood." He glanced down at Libby. "That's what we use, you see. These children are far too rare and valuable to take apart piece by piece, as we do with the ordinary donors. Just a few milligrams of their blood per day – once the optimum state of sustainable suffering has been achieved – can provide enough power for the typical work of one of our practitioners in the field. Meanwhile, the children just keep producing more!" He beamed at her. "If my experiments on ordinary donors are any indication, my methods should allow us to command two or three times as much power for every milligram of blood we harvest. And you can multiply that increase by thirty or forty *years*! With just a small daily expenditure of effort on my part to prevent actual *death*, these children should be able to live out nearly their entire normal lifespans here, without *once* setting foot outside these cages!" The wry twist came back into his smile. "Now: your sister will *definitely* be one of my first subjects here. So – what do you think? Do you still want to take her place?"

Libby couldn't stop staring at the horrible cage. She managed at last to open her mouth, but she couldn't make any words come out.

Jaeger chuckled. "Don't worry, Libby: fortunately, you won't need to make any such agonizing choice." He stepped back and closed the door of the tiny room, shutting them both inside. "If it were true that you met the genetic criteria, as your sister does, I would of course keep *both* of you – which, in fact, I will in any case. Ordinary donors like you and Stubby can be quite useful in your way: a finger here, an eye there."

His last words jerked her gaze to him, and she saw that he was again observing her with avid interest. "*You* are more valuable to me than Stubby, in fact: the suffering of *children* – even ordinary children like you – is more potent than the suffering of adults. But as far as our *special* purposes are concerned – those for which we employ your sister and the other gifted children –" his voice took on a mildly sympathetic tone – "you are useless to *me*, Libby, for the same reason you've been a curse to your own mother, and were the death of your so-called father." His eyes glinted like the metal of the implements Libby had seen in the cabinets above. "Do you really believe your… 'father'… killed himself *only* because of that train accident?" He smiled sadly and shook his

The Birds of the Air | 305

head. "Even the accident itself was because of you: it happened on the day he found out." Libby's confusion must have shown in her face, because the sympathy in his voice edged toward pity. "Found *out*, Libby, that you weren't really *his child*." Jaeger's voice was kindly, regretful, but his gaze held only the attentive, clinical interest. "Not only are you not *special*, as Maisie is, but unlike her, you are a mistake: illegitimate and unwanted. *And* you were the cause of your supposed father's death. He found out, on the day of the accident, that your mother had been unfaithful to him all those years before. *That's* why he was distracted; that's why he caused all those people's deaths, and why, ultimately, he found his own life unbearable. And that's why your mother has always hated you. I'm sure you saw it, though of course she would have tried to hide it. It's all very simple." His gaze on her was keen, appraising; he took out his memo book again and jotted a few lines in it. "You see," he said, closing it, "I like to discover all I can about the family history of my exceptional donors; and in this case, my discoveries about Maisie coincided with some interesting discoveries about your mother – and you."

Libby stared at him. She didn't fully understand all he had said – wasn't entirely sure what "illegitimate" meant, and why it meant she wasn't her father's real daughter – but she took in the essence of it, felt it sink to her core, and knew it for truth. She felt as if some needle, like the one stuck into Stubby, had flooded her veins with ice-water, numbing not only her body but her mind – all except one little corner that kept saying *of course! Of course! I should have known.* In that tiny part, there was a distant feeling of something almost like relief – relief at having an explanation, even such a ruinous one, for what she had sensed all her life.

"No, Libby; your value will never be comparable to Maisie's – not to your mother, and not to me. Don't fret, though. As I told you in my letter, you have your *own* contributions to make. The past isn't important anymore. One thing we excel at in our organization is *simplification*; we can *very* quickly reduce a human being from a complex tangle of sorrows, joys, aspirations, beliefs, habits and attributes to a single, simple commodity." He smiled. "That's what Stubby is now, and hundreds more like him – both here and in other places like this around the world. And soon that's what *you* will be." He stepped toward her, giving an apologetic chuckle. "Forgive my running on so. I'm afraid I *am* rather fond of the sound of my own voice. We're almost finished, though, Elizabeth." At the sound of her name, she felt again the unmistakable tingling behind her eyes, and found she was somehow standing right in front of the dreadful cage, with Jaeger's hands on her shoulders. "All we need do now," he said pleasantly, "is get you settled in your new home."

She tried to jerk away, to reach for Scab's razor in her pocket, to run; her mouth was open, as Stubby's had been, but, like him, she was unable to scream, unable to escape, unable even to move. Her eyes were open so wide she could feel the air stir against them, but the tingling surged up behind them – sharper now, like an itch intense enough to be painful – and she couldn't even blink.

Jaeger was smiling down at her, only a foot away, so that she had to roll her eyes – the only part of her that she could move – upward to see his face.

"You see, Libby," he said, "I know what your purpose is. *You* don't, but I do."

CHAPTER TWENTY-ONE

IN YEARS TO come it was his voice – his words – that would torment her most often in her nightmares.

He talked as he lifted her and wedged her upright in the cage. He talked as he adjusted the panels and bolted them into place. He talked on and on in his pleasant, amiable voice, speaking words that blocked off every avenue of hope her panicked thoughts tried to push their way into.

When the panels were secured – pressing so tightly against her on each side that her arms were pinned immovably to her body, so tightly in front and in back that she couldn't expand her lungs to take a full breath – he freed her from the paralysis. He smiled and told her she could scream if she liked – that no one would hear her. When she did scream, crying out for Pullman and Roach, he told her they wouldn't be coming; he explained about the lies he would tell to convince them he had sent her to a safer place.

"No!" she moaned; "They'll look for me! They'll want to see me... they'll want to say goodbye!"

He shook the cage, testing its solidity. "I'm afraid, Libby, that you have a rather pitiable habit of overrating your importance. You're only one of *many* children who have passed through Pullman's hands. And of course I keep him very busy with our 'cause' – him and his hangers-on. I'm sorry to say it, but I honestly doubt you'll ever cross Pullman's mind again." He left the room for a minute or two, and returned with an electric clock, which he plugged into an outlet near the floor. "I'm *very* interested to discover whether the ability to measure the passage of time tends to *increase* or *mitigate* suffering," he explained brightly, placing the clock on a shelf opposite her. "You know, you will be the *youngest* subject I've tried this procedure on so far!" He squinted at a tape with which he was measuring the dimensions of the cage. "I'm especially looking forward to seeing what results it will bring about in terms of *growth*, over the next five years or so. I'm anticipating something like the effects of Chinese foot-binding – though of course on a comprehensive scale."

Her terror had pushed her to a state of near-insensibility when he rapped sharply on the cage, recalling her attention. "We won't be starting with the tubes and needles just yet," he said. "You see, Libby, I have something to *propose* to you." He watched her through the mesh as he spoke, raising his voice a bit to make himself heard above the terrified rasping of her breath. The word "propose" pierced through her panic with a thread of possible hope, and she forced herself to concentrate.

"You see," he went on, "one of my chief interests is the interplay between self-preservation and so-called 'love' – that is, altruism, self-sacrifice, and so on. Your offer to take your sister's place a few minutes ago, for example." He smiled. "I'm quite confident

The Birds of the Air | 309

that, given enough time – in conjunction with enough pain – self-preservation will always win out; however, there are different *kinds* of self-preservation. I'm *extremely* interested to discover which of these is the most powerful – which 'self,' as it were, is perceived by a subject as the most worthy of preservation. So here's what I propose." He reached a hand into a pocket of his jacket. "I'll be checking in on you periodically, monitoring your progress. Each time I come, I'm going to ask you a question. I'm going to ask if you are ready to take your little sister..." he pulled his hand from the pocket, and Libby saw that he held one of the birds, wrapped tightly in a strip of gauze so it couldn't move its wings or legs. Its eyes were cornflower blue. She cried out and jerked against the mesh, but she could only move her head, and only a couple of inches.

From another pocket, Jaeger produced a pair of clippers, of the sort Libby's grandmother used to cut roses, but brand-new and gleaming. "I'm going to ask if you are ready to amputate her wings – yourself." He replaced the clippers and the struggling bird in his pockets. "And, finally, I'm going to ask if you are ready to put her into my hands and walk away from here – forever. If, at any point, you are willing to do these things, I will let you leave this building and this farm, no strings attached." He raised a hand. "Remember, *Maisie* is staying, no matter what! You can save *yourself*, Libby, without worsening her situation in the slightest. You needn't even see her restored to human form! And I give you my word: neither my employees nor I will ever trouble you or your mother again." He held out both hands toward her, as if he were giving her an invisible gift. "The decision is yours. And given how quickly you agreed to my proposal in the study last night, I don't imagine you'll have much trouble making it!" He laughed, then opened the door of the tiny room and stepped out. He was still talking through the narrowing crack, even as he shut the door behind him. "I'll give you some time to think about it. I'll be back to ask for your answer in a day or so – before I take Pullman off on this counterfeit 'mission.'"

IN SPITE OF what Jaeger had said, Libby cried out Pullman's name, and Roach's, as loudly as she could for nearly two hours, until she was hoarse and exhausted. The next hour she spent trying to squirm and writhe, looking for a weakness in the cage, but the mesh pressed into her so tightly on all sides that she could barely manage to move enough to rub her skin raw.

Somewhere in the middle of the sixth hour, she began to cry out again, screaming this time – not only for Pullman and Roach, but for Scab, and even her mother.

By the eighth hour her screams no longer had words, and by the ninth, she had no voice left.

As for tears, they weren't demarcated by the hours; they flowed almost continually. At one point she remembered how she had thought, the night before, that she had wept all the tears it was possible for one person to weep. A laugh like a hacking cough raveled out of her, but she cut it off the instant the sound of it reached her ears.

When Jaeger returned, she was no longer conscious, though whether the oblivion that had overtaken her was sleep or something else she had no way of knowing. She woke to see him outside the cage, writing in his notebook. The clock said 3:25, but she had no idea if it was day or night. Her legs were no longer able to hold her up; it was the agonizing pressure of the mesh against her knees, her forehead and her backside that bore her weight. When she saw him she immediately began to croak, *"Please... please...."*

He looked at her, a half-smile stealing from behind mock gravity. "Are you ready to do what I asked?"

Libby nodded so emphatically that the cage rattled, but the nod was a lie. She meant only to get him to open the cage; even a few seconds outside it would be worth any kind of punishment he might give her for deceiving him.

But Jaeger shook his head sadly. "I don't think you're telling me the truth, Libby. I don't think you're really ready yet."

When he turned to leave the room, Libby discovered that she *was* capable of screaming more, after all – though the noise that came out didn't sound like any made by a human being.

When he returned again she had no idea how many hours or days had passed; she had been in and out of consciousness so many times that the numbers on the clock meant nothing anymore.

This time she rasped out a different word: "*Water.*"

Jaeger smiled, and raised his eyebrows in mock admonishment. "Oh, no, Libby. We have needles for that. Those will be coming soon enough, if you don't accept my offer. I must confess, you've surprised me! I thought you'd agree to my proposal – I mean genuinely, not deceitfully like the last time – *long* before this." He shook his head. "Unless you *do*, though, it'll be the needles, and you'll never eat or drink *anything*, ever again." He narrowed his eyes, appraising, and addressed his next remarks to Slater, whose presence behind him Libby only now registered. Slater held a clipboard, a fountain pen poised in his hand to write down Jaeger's directions, which Libby heard over the sound of her own desperate breathing.

"I'm thinking of introducing some sort of stimulant, to

increase physical agitation and decrease the possibility of sleep," he said. "I suppose I ought to take care of the larynx soon, too; and in about a week we can begin harvesting the teeth." He nodded. "That will do for now."

As Slater capped his pen and left, Jaeger's words gradually sank into Libby's mind, and when she realized that the idea of their cutting out her voice-box and pulling her teeth filled her with *hope* – because they might have to open the cage to do those things – she began to weep.

"From now on, Libby, to avoid wasted time, we'll add a new proviso to our agreement," Jaeger said. "If you tell me you are willing to accept my terms, but then *refuse* after I have released you, I will take your eyes and ears before I return you to the cage. I'm confident that, even at this very early stage, you've been through enough to make them serviceable." He put his memo book away, then pulled from his pockets again the trembling blue-eyed bird and the shining clippers. "Now... are you ready yet?"

WHEN SHE NEXT heard someone approaching, she had been in pitch darkness for an immeasurable time.

After her last refusal of Jaeger's proposal, there had been an interminable blast of icy water, hammering through the mesh from a hose in the grinning Slater's hands. He had turned off the light when he went away, leaving her dripping and shivering in absolute blackness with the sound of water running down a drain in the floor.

After that, so many things had happened that she couldn't keep track of them all: conversations with Maisie, with Scab, with her father; whole weeks or months of escape back to blessedly ordinary life, lasting so long at times that she fully believed

The Birds of the Air | 313

the cage was only a long-ago nightmare. Sometimes, though, in those dreams of freedom, she would realize suddenly that Maisie wasn't there, and remember that it was by accepting Jaeger's proposal that she had obtained her release. After those moments, even awakening in the cage was a relief.

When soft rattling and scraping sounds reached her from outside the tiny room, she had been whispering, for minutes or days, to a small child who seemed to be wedged into a cage next to hers – a child younger than Maisie, whether a boy or a girl she couldn't tell in the dark. She was begging forgiveness from this child, weeping and weeping. It was only when a crack of light appeared – dim, but painfully bright to her starved eyes – that she stopped whispering and began to moan, thinking it was Jaeger coming back.

"Sis?"

It was a quiet call, a stage-whisper, but it was unbelievably, unmistakably, Roach's voice. She realized the light was the moving beam of a flashlight in the dark corridor outside.

"Here, Roach! Help me; please, *please!*"

Though she put all her force into the call, her ragged voice wasn't much louder than Roach's whisper. She put weight onto her numb legs to gain enough leverage to rattle the panels of the cage, then went slack again, nearly unhinged with relief, when she heard Roach say, "Over here, boss!"

"He said – he said—" she sobbed, as Pullman and Roach fumbled with the bolts and removed the front panel. She crumpled forward out of the horrible metal coffin; Pullman caught her and made a hushing sound, but she kept on with her hoarse babbling: "He said you wouldn't *look* for me! He said he told you I was *gone!*"

"Shhh – don't cry, child; we're here now," Pullman said, his own voice hoarse with emotion.

Roach disappeared, and returned with a glass beaker from somewhere; he filled it with water from the faucet Slater had used, and gave it to Libby. She grabbed it and drank until he pulled it away, saying, "Not too much now, sis, or it's liable to come right back up again." She was about to tell him they needed to free the child she had been talking to, but when she looked for the other cage, it wasn't there.

Pullman grasped her shoulders and shook her a bit. "Libby," he hissed. "Listen to me: where *are* they?" At the urgency in his voice, she struggled to marshal her dazed, half-crazed thoughts. "*Maisie*, and the other children," he said, shaking her again. "Did you see where they are?"

She pointed in the direction she believed was correct, and Roach picked up the flashlight from the floor where he had set it. Pullman lifted her in his arms, and they wound their way through the labyrinth of cabinets and mysterious equipment, until at last they found the cloth-covered cages. "Do you think you can stand now, Libby?" Pullman said. She nodded, and he set her on her feet; her legs felt weak and rubbery, but by leaning on one of the shelves she was able to support herself.

Roach set the flashlight on another shelf; Libby noticed for the first time that he held the rifle, as well; he kept watch toward the doorway as Pullman drew away the cloth that covered the cages.

"Oh, no – no, *no!*" he said. There was such horror in his voice that she leaned forward, panicked, fearing the birds – the *children* – were dead; but then she heard the sound of flapping wings.

The Birds of the Air | 315

"Heaven forgive me," Pullman said; "are these the only ones still *here?*"

"We gotta get goin', boss," Roach said quietly, his eyes still on the far-off doorway that led to the long basement corridor. The door stood ajar, and light from the caged bulbs showed through it.

"Yes." Pullman's voice still shook, but he swiftly pulled the two occupied cages from the shelves, holding them, one in each hand, by the wire handles on their tops. "Can you walk, Libby?"

"I... I think so."

Pullman handed the cages to Roach, and took the rifle and the flashlight. As he led the way toward the open door, Libby managed to stumble along behind him, praying that Jaeger had put Maisie back into one of the cages. Her legs began to feel as if hundreds of Jaeger's needles were being plunged into them all at once. Roach came behind her, maneuvering the cages awkwardly through the narrower spaces.

Pullman left the flashlight on a steel table when they neared the door, and took the rifle in both hands. "Wait a moment," he murmured. He edged to the doorway and peered around the jamb into the corridor. "All right." He gestured with the rifle for Roach and Libby to go through, and with a sob of gratitude Libby stumbled at last out of the horrible room.

They covered the length of the corridor as quickly as Libby could manage. Pullman went first up the stairwell, and peered out of it to scan the corridor above, holding the rifle at the ready; then he gestured again for them to go ahead of him.

The corridor was dark, all the doors along it closed. The only light came through a small, steel-meshed window in a distant door at the far end – a yellowish electric glow, flickering with moth shadows: nighttime. Libby recognized the door as the one she had seen from outside, at the back of the building. The corridor separating them from it looked a mile long.

Roach moved quickly toward the door, carrying the cages, and Libby tried her best to make her prickling, nightmare-sluggish legs keep up. Pullman came behind, looking back to watch the corridor to their rear. Roach scanned the doors they passed, wide-eyed, as if he expected one of them to burst open at any moment. His obvious fear, added to her own terror, made the frantic, echoing noises of the birds' wings seem unbearably loud; but the doors remained closed, the corridor deserted, and only the door at the end stood between them and the outside.

They were seconds from reaching it when the terrible things began happening again.

First, the lights along the ceiling flickered to life. At almost the same instant, Pullman's voice thundered through the corridor: "Roach, get the children out! *GO!*"

Turning, Libby saw that Pullman had stopped in the middle of the corridor. He stood with his back to her and Roach, but glared over his shoulder at them with such intensity that it seemed he meant to propel them out the door with his gaze alone.

Far down the corridor beyond Pullman, brightly lit when he passed beneath the electric lights and falling into shadow when he moved through the spaces between, Jaeger strolled toward them.

The sight of him almost sent Libby to her knees.

Pullman roared again – "*GO!*" – and she managed to turn and stumble after Roach.

She heard Pullman growling behind her: "I'm warning you now, Jaeger, you'll not touch them again while I live." The ratcheting sound of the rifle being cocked echoed from the walls; she glanced back and saw that Pullman had lifted the gun to his shoulder. He leveled it at Jaeger, but Jaeger didn't slow his

The Birds of the Air | 317

leisurely advance. Instead, he moved one hand carelessly, as if pushing aside a curtain. With a jerk, the rifle flew from Pullman's hands, and traveled in a straight, hard line to slam against the wall high up near the ceiling. It went off as it hit, and Libby cried out, her hands flying to her ears as it clattered to the floor.

She seemed to lose herself for a few seconds; when she returned to awareness, she heard Roach's voice: *"Come on, sis! Keep goin'!"*

She saw he had reached the door and, shifting the cages, was flinging it open; he looked back, waiting for her. She forced her wobbly legs to move faster, but her eyes kept reeling back over her shoulder. She made out Slater and the man called Simms, both following a little behind Jaeger. She saw Jaeger turn his glance from Pullman toward Roach. Immediately a slamming sound, almost as loud as the report of the rifle, reverberated through the corridor. Wheeling toward it, she saw that the door Roach had opened was closed again. Roach put down the cages and wrenched frantically at the handle, but the door remained shut fast.

Reaching him, Libby tried to help, but even their combined efforts couldn't budge the door. She sank to a crouch with her back against it, her eyes fixed on Jaeger's approach. A moaning sound started in her throat and rose to a choked wail.

Pullman stood perhaps three of four yards away, fists clenched at his sides, facing Jaeger and the other two men. When he glanced over his shoulder and realized that she and Roach were trapped, Libby saw resignation mix with the grief and fury in his face. He turned back toward the men. "You're a sneaking, cowardly liar, Jaeger," he said, "and I'll never forgive myself for the harm –" his voice broke, and he paused for a second, dropping his head, then lifted it again – "the harm I've done by being

318 | L. H. Arthur

foolish enough to listen to you. But I'll stay here; I won't resist you. You can take me apart piece by piece; it's no more than I deserve. Just –" he pointed an unsteady finger back without looking away from Jaeger's face – "just let Everett and the children go."

Jaeger's tranquil smile remained unchanged. "Well! That's a very handsome offer, Colin. Or rather, it *would* be, if the least possibility existed of your being *able* to resist me." He stopped a dozen feet or so from Pullman. Simms had scooped the rifle from the floor, and as he and Slater approached, Jaeger spoke over his shoulder to them. "We'll take them to the Testing Room. I have something there that I want to show my old friend Colin."

The two men moved forward, a malicious grin on Slater's burned face, and Pullman stepped toward them to block their way. Simms started to raise the rifle, but Jaeger waved a hand. "Don't trouble yourself, Euphonious." He shifted his gaze to Libby. "Elizabeth?"

The instant he said her name, Libby felt the tingling sensation behind her eyes again, but this time it was multiplied a thousand-fold. It felt as if a swarm of hornets had entered through her ears along with Jaeger's voice, and was swirling around, buzzing, inside her skull.

And then the hornets began to sting.

She had no idea how long it went on. She didn't know she was screaming until the pain began to subside; only when it had receded enough that it no longer seemed to be the only thing in the universe did she hear her own hoarse shrieks, echoing against the hard, bare walls of the corridor. She clenched her jaw shut, cutting them off. When the pain had abated a bit more and she was again aware of her surroundings, she found herself half-sit-

The Birds of the Air | 319

ting, half-lying on the floor, curled up into a tight ball, with someone's arms supporting her.

Opening her eyes, she saw Pullman's face looking down at her, white and shaken. He was crouched beside her, holding her to him. She looked immediately for Jaeger; when she saw he hadn't moved, she was foolishly relieved, as though he needed to be near her to do her harm. Beyond him, she could see Slater already shoving Roach back down the corridor the way they had come. Someone had given the cages to Jaeger, and the birds were fluttering against the bars. "Bring those two," Jaeger said, and Libby saw that Simms was standing over her and Pullman. He held the rifle in one hand; with the other, he grabbed Pullman's arm and dragged him to his feet.

After that she lost track again for a while, as if whatever Jaeger had done to her had short-circuited her senses. Sights, sounds and sensations came to her in jerky, jumbled fragments, like the broken bits of different motion pictures, spliced together with no order or coherence. And then, when she looked up to see that she was once more approaching the stairs that led down to the basement, for a time there was nothing at all.

When her mind came back to her, she was being shoved, along with Roach and Pullman, through a door into a hugely long, echoing room she hadn't seen before. Jaeger had gone in ahead of them; he flicked a switch, and metal-shaded bulbs hanging from the ceiling flickered to life, their harsh light glaring back at them from a glossy white-tile floor. The room looked to be somewhat longer than the boxcars she and Scab had ridden in, which Scab had told her were forty feet long. It was shaped like an enormous shoebox, narrower than it was long, and the door they had stumbled through was in the middle of one of its longer walls. High on the wall opposite, Libby saw the row of small, painted-over basement windows she had noticed from outside. Beneath the windows stood a number of low metal benches, lined up a couple of feet from the wall as if for spectators; others lined the wall to either side of the door they had entered.

At a nod from Jaeger, Slater retreated into the corridor – where Simms waited, holding the rifle – and closed the door behind him. Libby's eyes fixed fearfully on Jaeger, but he turned away and moved off unhurriedly. He carried the cages toward the end of the room far off to her left, where the only other pieces of furniture stood: an enamel-topped table with a desk lamp on it, and a metal chair. Behind these, Libby saw two narrow doors, also made of metal. The one on the right was secured with a heavy padlock.

The birds fluttered noisily, ricocheting off one another and the cage-bars. Pullman drew Roach and Libby with him quickly, moving them away from the door, and toward the far end of the room from Jaeger. He leaned close to whisper beneath the noise of the birds' wings: "Be ready, both of you. I'm going to try to deal with Jaeger. If it works, I want you to get the children, move the table over beneath the windows, put the chair on top of it and climb out. You may have to break the glass, but get out as quickly and quietly as you can; I'm sure Simms and Slater are still outside in the corridor."

Libby looked up at him, confused. "But – what about *you*?"

"Never mind about me; just be ready." He glanced at Jaeger, who had reached the table and was setting the cages on it. "And when you get out, Everett, don't wait: get the children as far away from here as you can."

He seemed about to say more, but Jaeger had turned toward them, and instead he pushed Roach and Libby behind him. "Where are all the other children I've sent to you, you perfidi-

The Birds of the Air | 321

ous bastard?" he called, raising his voice to make it carry down the long room, sending thundering echoes off the stark walls and floor. He spread out his bandaged left hand to signal that Roach and Libby should remain where they were, and took a few limping steps back toward Jaeger. As he went, he lowered the bandaged hand, and Libby saw something slide from beneath his jacket into it: a knife, glinting in the harsh light – not his pocketknife, but some sort of dagger-like weapon with a long, thin, wicked-looking blade. He held it slightly behind his leg, concealing it, and stopped, facing Jaeger across the expanse of white tiles.

Jaeger was pulling off his own jacket; he tossed it onto the table beside the cages. "They've been sent to where they're needed, to serve the purpose for which you captured them." He turned and ambled toward Pullman, smiling his pleasant smile, one hand reaching up to loosen his tie. "I'm afraid I've been telling you a sort of mirror image of the truth. It is, in fact, *our* organization that has been laying the groundwork for the coming changes overseas. The children you've gathered have been invaluable to our work there. Now it's time to get started *here*. Plenty of fuel for the fire in these not-so-United States, don't you think, Colin?" He chuckled. "I believe there's even more potential here than in *your* godforsaken little homeland." He paused a few yards from the spot where Pullman stood, unbuttoning the cuffs of his shirt to roll up the sleeves. "What we have planned for *this* country will make what happens in Europe look like a church picnic."

As Jaeger spoke, Libby saw Pullman slip his right hand behind his back, to where his left hand held the knife. She winced as he grasped the blade and pulled it, blood-streaked, out of his closed fist. "Well, you'll have no more help from me, you craven son of a bitch," he growled. He made a sudden, swift motion with the bleeding hand, lifting it to his forehead. Libby heard him mumble something, and then he spoke clearly, words she had heard before: *"As to the servant, so to the master."* She saw him whip the knife forward, and expected to see him lunge toward Jaeger with it. Instead, he turned it back toward himself, grasped its hilt with both hands, and plunged its point toward his own chest. She couldn't see, from behind him, whether it made contact; she cried out and started forward, but Roach held her back. It was only when she heard an odd, surprised sound coming from Jaeger, and saw blood spreading like a red blossom on the left-side breast of his white shirt, that she remembered where she had heard Pullman speak the words before.

Jaeger's hands were already flung out, fists clenched tight, his arms extended stiffly in front of his body. Slowly, he began to lower his hands, and though several paces separated the two men, Libby saw Pullman's arms begin to sink as well, strained and trembling. She could see him struggling to raise the knife to his chest again, but Jaeger was too strong for him. She heard Pullman panting more words she couldn't understand, but Jaeger spoke as well, drowning him out. He rapped out a strange word – *"Genug!"* – as if he were reprimanding a child, or an animal. Immediately the long blade flew from Pullman's grasp and went skittering along the floor, leaving flecks of blood in a lizard-trail behind it, coming to rest at Jaeger's feet. Pullman's body went still and rigid; Libby couldn't see his face from where she stood, but his arms were twisted behind him at a painful-looking angle.

Jaeger laughed, sounding a bit winded, but amiable and untroubled. "You'll have to be quicker than *that*, you old rascal." He winced a bit, hand to his chest. "Damned good try, though! A half-inch deeper and we'd both have been done for." He glanced down at the blood spreading across his shirt, and chuckled again.

"Oh – we can't have *this*! If Mrs. Vogel sees it, she will *certainly* succeed where you have failed!" He brushed the edge of his hand over the wet red stain. When his hand had passed, his shirt was a snowy, unblemished white again, and no new blood appeared. He bent, his movements easy and graceful, and caught up the knife that lay at his feet. "Let me show you how it's done, Colin." He turned toward the door to the corridor and called, "Slater!" The door opened and Slater came in; Jaeger nodded toward Roach.

Slater moved forward immediately, striding with his swaggering limp toward Roach and Libby. Libby stumbled backward, but Slater ignored her. He grabbed Roach by the arm and dragged him – struggling, panting, but too slight to break free from his vicious grip – past Pullman's rigid form, to where Jaeger waited.

Jaeger didn't even glance at Roach; his calm gaze remained on Pullman's face as he reached out to grasp Roach's wrist. He pulled it toward him and – with the faint, pleasant smile still on his face – drove the blade of Pullman's long knife to its hilt through Roach's hand.

Roach gave a horrible, jagged cry and fell to his knees; Libby cried out as well. An instant later, though Jaeger had spoken no words, Libby heard a muffled sound from Pullman. Looking to where he stood, she saw that his bandaged left hand, as well as the right, now dripped fresh blood onto the floor.

Roach moaned, doubled over on his knees, his wrist still in Jaeger's grasp. Smiling at Pullman, Jaeger shifted his grip on the knife, and twisted the blade in Roach's hand as a man would twist a screwdriver. Roach screamed again, and a rough cry came from Pullman, sounding as if it had escaped through clenched jaws. Roach's blood spattered the floor, and the drip from Pullman's hand became a thin stream, soaking through the bandage and pooling at his feet.

A wave of nausea rose in Libby, and she sank to her knees. She covered her face to block out the sight of Roach's kindly, cheerful face contorted in agony, but when she heard Jaeger say something to Slater that ended with the words *"to RLTI"*, her hands dropped to the floor, ready to push herself up so she could run. When Slater took hold of Roach, instead of moving toward her, relief flooded through her. The relief was followed by a wave of shame so overpowering that she could scarcely believe there was anything left of her to watch, half-blinded by tears, as Slater dragged Roach from the room.

Simms, who had remained in the corridor, closed the door behind them, and Libby heard it lock. When Jaeger advanced toward Pullman again, she scuttled to the nearest wall – the one beneath the windows. She pressed her back to it, huddling behind one of the benches, and drew her knees to her chest, trying to make herself as small as the bird-children, as small as the tiny spider in her dream: invisible.

Peering out, she saw Jaeger stop, still smiling, in front of Pullman. "I'm truly sorry to lose you, Colin," he said. "I was so hoping to preserve that serviceable ardor of yours; I've gone to a lot of trouble, since this whole Schillerton mess began, to try to keep you in the fold."

All at once he turned his smile on Libby. "Did Colin ever tell you how he lost his leg?" Libby stiffened, ready to run if he approached, but he turned back to Pullman, laughing. "I'm sure it's quite mortifying to you now, Colin, but you must admit it's rather funny. Slater and the others were at least shrewd enough to insist on being *paid* for theirs. But for *you*, it was a noble sacrifice, to save innocent children – from John *Fuller*, of all people!"

He laughed harder, though quietly, raising a hand to his eyes. When the hand dropped back to his side, Pullman dropped as well

The Birds of the Air | 325

– collapsed to his knees, freed from the paralysis. Hunched on the blood-spattered tile, cradling one bleeding hand with the other, he glared up at Jaeger. "You're nothing but a detestable *animal*. No human being worthy of the name would prey upon little *children*."

Jaeger had almost composed himself, but now he slipped back into helpless laughter, as if Pullman had told an unbearably funny joke. "You must be having me *on*, Colin! What creatures prey upon their own young *more* habitually than human beings?" He took a few moments to calm his amusement, then spoke in a gentler tone. "Your naiveté is endearing, Colin, but rather astonishing in a man who has seen as much of the world as you have. I do respect your idealism, and your genuine concern for our young donors. Sadly, however, those very qualities have made you quite useful in causing unimaginable suffering to those you meant to protect."

His words seemed to strike Pullman like stones; Libby saw his body shudder with the impact of them. His head bowed, his shoulders shook, and with a tightening in her own throat she realized he was weeping. Jaeger, standing over him, looked on with interest. He retrieved the memo book from his pocket and jotted in it with his pencil. "Don't blame yourself too much, Colin," he said in a kindly tone when he had finished. "You and I, and our whole operation here, make up only a very small part of the forces mobilized throughout the world by our organization. Had you resisted us with all the same zeal you have unwittingly devoted to our cause, it wouldn't have made the smallest difference to the achievement of our goals."

"*What* 'goals'?"

Jaeger let out a slight, incredulous laugh, as if the answer should be obvious. "Well, *destruction*, Colin. Damage; degeneration; disintegration; dissolution; decay. Death."

Pullman lifted his head to look up at him. "*Why?*"

"Do you really mean to pretend you don't *know*, you old hypocrite?" Jaeger squatted to gaze with pitiless intensity into Pullman's face. "Do you think there's ever a *second* when you aren't completely transparent to me? Do you imagine there is one self-serving motive, one burrowing beetle of cupidity beneath all your sanctimonious posturing, that I am unaware of?" He leaned closer to Pullman, his voice becoming low, confidential, so Libby had to strain her ears to make out his words. "You don't *need* to ask me 'why.' You *know* why. You know it every time you violate the sanctity of a human mind to coerce obedience; you know it every time you cultivate dread in some superstitious hobo to bend him to your will. You knew it when you used your power to revenge yourself on Slater and his men; you knew it when you bullied Libby, there, by striking young Stephen, and you know it *now*." He laid a hand on Pullman's shoulder. "There is *nothing* I need explain to you, Colin, about the utility of violence, and pain, and terror."

He rose and stood for a moment, looking down on Pullman. Libby saw Pullman's head drop between his bowed shoulders; blood kept dripping onto the floor beneath him. She longed to go to him, but her fear of Jaeger was like a physical force pressing her against the wall.

Jaeger slipped the memo book back into his pocket. "As to the greater objective served by these short-term goals," he said, "it varies only in minor detail from the objective of *any* undertaking, by any living being, anywhere. There is only one *genuine* objective in this world: self-preservation." He smiled, lifting his hands as if to forestall some challenge, though Libby didn't see Pullman make any attempt to speak. "Granted, self-preservation as *we* define it is not of the most primitive variety. It's a *continuum* of sorts – beginning with mere survival, advancing through security, to comfort, to prosperity, and culminating in dominion." He shrugged.

The Birds of the Air | 327

"There are forces in this world dedicated to the annihilation of our organization, and of all its members. We mean to frustrate these forces in their purpose: we mean not only to *survive*, but to create the environment most conducive to our comfort, well-being and security. We mean to gain, and to retain, the power to shape the world as we see fit."

"I suppose you mean your execrable Nazi Party?"

"Really, Colin – the *rubbish* you speak!" Jaeger looked as if he were in danger of being overcome by laughter again. "I hope you're not so simpleminded as to confuse the organization I refer to with *those* blustering idiots – or with the Bolsheviks, or the Fascists, for that matter. Although I suppose one *could* call it 'our Nazi Party,' in the sense that a man might say, 'my cigarette lighter,' or 'my flyswatter.'" He smiled down at Pullman. "You're even more naive than I supposed, if you imagine we attach any importance to such trivialities as race or nationality – though I won't deny that those who *do* are nearly as useful as self-satisfied do-gooders like yourself."

Pullman spoke again without lifting his head. "And John Fuller?"

"Ah, yes – John Fuller. Well, I confess I've rearranged the facts a bit in what I've told you about *him*. But – what's the saying here? – I've been 'bending your ear' long enough." He turned and started, unhurried, back toward the far end of the room. "I brought you here to *show* you something, Colin."

Pullman let out a muffled groan, and struggled to push himself to his feet. His face, when Libby saw it in profile, looked nearly as white as the blood-spattered tiles. As soon as Jaeger was far enough away, she left her place against the wall and went to try to help him.

Jaeger paused partway down the long room, and turned. "I

really am so isolated here; I seldom have the opportunity to speak with colleagues who have any vision or education." He waved a hand toward the door through which Simms and Slater had exited. "*Those* two are former vagrants, like your friend Everett; they possess some rudimentary ability, but not an atom of imagination. I might as well try to converse with a pair of jackals. But *you*, I think, will find what I have to show you quite interesting."

Libby held tightly to Pullman, who stood, swaying slightly, with an arm around her. Pullman turned his head to the side and spat onto the white tile, but said nothing.

"You see, I have a particular interest in expanding the usefulness of khatojana, and other spirit-based entities," Jaeger went on, unperturbed. "These creatures can, for the most part, accomplish little of value to us without a physical host, but in the natural course of things, they never retain control of a host for longer than, perhaps, eight to ten hours. I'm speaking here of *full* control, you understand – not mere influence. Now, often we find this length of time sufficient; but in those cases where it's *not*, we're faced with added expense in time, energy and donor resources for re-summoning, re-directing, and so forth." He beamed at Pullman, his face alight with excitement. "But Colin, I believe I've *solved* that problem! I've been perfecting a method by which I can bring about *indefinite* possession of a human host! This will open up entirely new possibilities! Consider: the khatojana can *inflame* – and, to a limited degree, *focus* – pre-existing hostility. They are invaluable in stirring up interfamilial feuds, interracial hatred, class warfare and the like. The klacek also relies on predisposition in the host, and produces a primitive, mindless violence which cannot be directed toward any specific target, though it can certainly be useful in situations where the simple fact of mayhem serves our purposes. The luupainaja can exacerbate a pre-existing, specifically sexual form of cruelty and violence. But *none* of these entities has been able, thus far, to retain a host long enough to prosecute any long-term plan of action." He spread his hands. "Through *my* method, we can choose the most promising hosts, and retain control over them, *and* the entities possessing them, *indefinitely!*" He gave an incredulous laugh, as if he could hardly believe the magnitude of his own accomplishment. "With a single expenditure, we can lock these creatures in place, *collect* them, and use them for our purposes for as long as the hosts survive!"

Pullman was leaning on Libby heavily; he let out a contemptuous breath. "If you're planning to put an end to me, Jaeger, I can only request that you get on with it, and spare me any more of your lunatic raving."

Jaeger looked almost surprised for an instant, as if he had forgotten whom he was speaking to. "Oh, I'm sure you know better than to think it will be as simple as *that*, Colin," he said. His voice had returned to its even, pleasant tone, all the jubilant excitement gone. "But don't worry; I won't keep you from your useful existence as a donor much longer. I must ask you to bear with me for just a little while, though: I suspect what I have to show you here tonight will contribute greatly to your effectiveness in your *new* form of service to our organization. You see, I have my latest subject in the experiments I've been describing, *there*." He pointed toward the door with the padlock. "Right behind that door."

Pullman said nothing, but he began to edge backward toward the opposite end of the long room from Jaeger, leaning on Libby and pulling her along with him. Jaeger smiled and gave a slight nod, as if Pullman had answered him; then he turned and resumed his unhurried progress. By the time he reached the padlocked door, Pullman had backed Libby and himself to within a few paces of the wall farthest from him, and Jaeger looked distant, diminished – almost as if he were too far away to harm them. He took the ring of keys from his pocket and turned one in the padlock.

When he opened the door, Libby could at first see nothing but darkness beyond. Jaeger stepped back and called in a peremptory tone, "Come out now, please." After a long moment, Libby saw a moving shadow sliding among the still ones, and then a figure slouched into view at the edge of the doorjamb – a lean figure in torn clothing, tall, with an odd, hunched tension in the head and shoulders. She heard a desolate sound from Pullman – saw, at the periphery of her vision, his hand rise to cover his eyes – and only then did it break in upon her whose figure she was seeing in the doorway.

"Scab!"

For perhaps a second, she was overjoyed. She tried to pull away from Pullman, but he pushed her back, moving in front of her. She peered past him, still confused, until Scab moved into the light. Then her breath caught, and the import of all Jaeger had been saying struck her with a sickening jolt.

She could see, even from thirty-five or forty feet away, that Scab looked drawn, gaunt, as if something inside him had sucked his skin cruelly tight against the bones and muscles beneath. He was too far for her to see his eyes clearly, but his face looked pale, and she thought she could see new bruises overlaying the old ones. He stood beside Jaeger in the odd, tense posture, and seemed to vibrate with a sort of mindless restlessness that made her think of a malfunctioning machine. His fingers twitched and jittered cease-lessly, and his head made barely perceptible jerking motions every few seconds.

Pullman turned his head and hissed fiercely to Libby over his shoulder, "Stay *behind* me."

Jaeger beamed at Scab – or at the thing inside him – with

obvious pride. He had to raise his voice to make it carry to where Pullman and Libby stood; Libby fought the urge to cover her ears as it reverberated against the hard surfaces of the room, making it sound as if there were many of him: "I've been working on this for several years now. The main problem has been that the *bodies* burn out so quickly – often in a matter of days. But with careful observation and experimentation I've managed to make *tremendous* advances in overcoming these difficulties, in just the past year or so." He laid a hand on Scab's shoulder. "Stephen here is one of the most promising candidates I've come across: young, intelligent, sagacious; a fine physical specimen, and –" he smiled and moved his other hand to indicate the bruises – "no stranger to violence. Given his exceptional suitability as a subject, and the progress I've been able to make with my last few candidates, I believe we can look forward to a lifespan of at least five or six years from him." He patted Scab's shoulder with a proprietary air; Scab seemed no more aware of the touch than if he had been the machine Libby imagined. "I really owe you a debt of gratitude, Colin, for putting him in my path."

Libby heard Pullman make a sound in his throat, as if something was choking him.

Jaeger called out again, now in a playful, teasing tone. "Come now, Colin: nothing to say? *You* chose – with flagrant disregard for my very explicit instructions – to bring this child –" he gestured toward Libby – "into the midst of our operations, exposing our most sensitive secrets to an outsider. So just remember, as you witness this: it's entirely your doing." He turned to Scab. "Stephen: the girl. Take her eyes."

CHAPTER TWENTY-TWO

LIBBY COULDN'T AT first absorb the shock of Jaeger's command; it jolted along her nerves like a lethal surge of electricity, blazing white-hot in the first moment, only to extinguish all thought in the next.

Scab's hand went instantly to his pocket and drew out his jacknife; he flicked it open, at the same time moving forward with the fluid purposefulness of a tiger released from a cage. Pullman shoved Libby backward, his eyes riveted on Scab: *"Go! Back against the wall!"*

Libby darted to the wall behind him, and crouched with her back pressed against it, as far away from Scab and Jaeger as she could get. Pullman stood still, his feet planted firmly, facing toward Scab as if he would make himself a barricade. But after only a few strides, Scab faltered and stopped, still a good twenty feet or more from Pullman. He raised a hand to his forehead, where it hovered, trembling.

The Birds of the Air | 333

Jaeger had moved closer as well, following Scab's advance at a leisurely pace. Now he stopped, a little beyond him, and his smile faded. "Stephen: *NOW!*" he said sharply; but Scab still didn't move. Jaeger glanced at his wristwatch with a faint frown, and drew his memo book from his pocket to write something in it.

The trembling spread throughout Scab's body, and quickly grew so violent that it seemed likely to shake him off his feet. Jaeger moved forward to stand at his shoulder, and looked into his face intently. "Remarkable! Do you have any idea how unusual this is, Colin?" He gave a rueful, incredulous laugh. "What we're seeing here is your young friend actually *fighting* the khatojana. I've seen this happen once or twice before, but *never* for this length of time." He turned to smile at Pullman. "You certainly know how to pick your protégés; quite an extraordinary young man." He slipped the book and pencil back into his pocket, turned back to Scab and barked out some guttural-sounding words in what sounded like the language Pullman had used to summon the khatojana. Scab's head had dropped forward, the hair that fell over his forehead dripping sweat onto the tiles, but at Jaeger's words his trembling began to diminish. His eyes lifted slowly until they fixed on Libby; the stretched grin that had frozen her blood in the forest spread across his face. He took a firmer grip on the knife, then all at once surged forward again. Libby screamed.

In an instant, Pullman's right arm was extended, his bleeding hand held out palm forward, as if to ward Scab off. Bracing his legs, he began to rasp out words Libby couldn't understand. Libby's breath came in terrified gasps; she could see there was no way that Pullman, scarcely able to stand, could block Scab's approach. But at five or six paces away, Scab jolted to a sudden stop – was even thrown back a bit, giving a slight, jerking shake of his head. Libby moaned, close enough now to see the horrible, opaque blankness in his eyes. There was an added strangeness about them, as well – something she hadn't seen before, and couldn't pinpoint at the distance, that made them look oddly unfocused, almost unseeing. Yet his gaze remained fixed on her.

Jaeger ambled forward to stand a little beyond Scab. He folded his arms, looking on with an expression of genial interest, as if he were watching a sporting event.

Scab lunged forward again, trying to break through whatever barrier Pullman had created. The barrier held, but Pullman staggered and almost fell. Libby forced herself to calm her breathing, forced her shaking legs to lift her up, to carry her to Pullman's side. She clasped her arms around him, trying to steady him.

Pullman didn't pause in his muttering, but he put his left arm around her shoulders and leaned on her. Libby saw that he was losing a great deal of blood from the wound in his chest, as well as from the ones in his hands. She looked up and saw his narrowed eyes locked on Scab, but he kept blinking hard, as if to clear his vision. Grim determination was drawn in the lines of his face, but she could see hopelessness beneath, and as soon as she saw it she understood why.

How long?

She felt him slump a bit against her, saw his eyes lose focus for a moment, heard his voice falter briefly before he straightened again and steeled himself to go on.

How long can he hold Scab off? And what happens when he can't anymore?

Jaeger, confirming her despair, gave his jovial laugh. "How long do you think you can keep that *up*, Colin?"

Scab was pacing with the restless agitation of a caged animal, back and forth across the tiles. His dead-looking gaze never left Libby's eyes; the knife jittered in his hand. He paused when she looked up at him, and the horrible grin oozed back across his face. It seemed to edge her mind with the same black void that looked out from his eyes.

She heard Jaeger bark out words in the rough language again. Scab tried once more to move forward, lunging like a spurred horse, and was deflected as Pullman continued his rasping stream of words. Scab's head lowered, weaving a bit, like the head of a snake. His gaze shifted from Libby for the first time, and fixed on Pullman. He gave the knife a slight toss and caught it again, adjusting his grip, and then all at once his arm rose in a quick, smooth, and somehow familiar motion, the hand with the knife flinging itself forward.

Even as Libby tried to recall where she had seen that motion before, she felt a sudden convulsive jerk run through Pullman's body, and his ragged voice was cut off abruptly. Looking up, she saw something protruding from his throat – something so close to her eyes that they couldn't immediately focus on it. Before she could grasp what was happening, Pullman's full weight bore down on her, buckling her body like a blade of grass. He crumpled to the tiles, pulling Libby to her knees beside him.

As she tried to take in what had happened, she saw swift motion at the edge of her vision: Scab, freed from the barrier Pullman had created. He bore down on her like a flood released from a dam, driving away every thought, leaving only the mindless reflexes of self-preservation. She scuttled backward, spider-like, but Scab didn't follow: he made straight for Pullman and fell to one knee beside him, so quickly that Libby's shock-staggered brain lagged behind what her eyes were seeing. As Pullman's hands moved weakly to try to fend him off, he yanked out the thing Libby had seen protruding from Pullman's throat. It was only when he grasped it in both hands and drove it hilt-deep into Pullman's chest that she realized what it was.

Pullman's hands dropped to the floor, their feeble movements stilled. His eyes, blank and vacant as Scab's now, stared up at the ceiling – but Scab's eyes turned to her.

She scrambled to her feet to run, aware of the hopelessness of her flight even as she began it. Scab was upon her in an instant, one hand grasping her arm to drag her to him. He flung her to the floor and pinned her there, his knee across her body crushing her right arm to her chest. She tried to struggle free, to turn her face away, but he gripped her left wrist and pulled her arm up over her head, using it like a clamp to pin her head against his other knee. His eyes were locked on hers, and she could see now what was wrong with them: the irises kept up a minute, continuous vibrating movement, quivering a needle's breadth from side to side in a motion almost too rapid to perceive, like the oscillation of a plucked violin string. He bent closer and spoke the first words she had heard from him in Jaeger's hellish domain: "It's just you and me again, kid." His voice sounded as if mud and gravel and the decay of dead things were whispering in her ear.

His weight on her chest crushed the breath out of her, and he pulled her arm so brutally to keep it tight around her head that it felt as if he would uproot it from its socket. His other hand rose into her field of vision, holding his jackknife, red with Pullman's blood. Her own hands, struggling to free themselves, might as well have been two leaves brushing against him for all the difference they made. All she could see in the whole of the world was the dripping knifepoint moving toward her eyes, and somehow her crushed lungs dragged in enough breath to carry scream after scream from her straining throat. She squeezed her eyes shut, becoming nothing more in body and mind than an agony of terror, waiting for the knife to cut through her eyelid and pry into the space between her eye and its socket, tearing blood vessels and breaking nerves.

But nothing happened.

She dared to open her eyes, and saw the knife point stopped, an inch away.

She heard Jaeger, much closer than he had been before, mumble a curse under his breath, then rap out a command – "Get *back*, I said." Immediately Scab fell back from her, and she scrambled away and pressed herself to the wall again, huddled with her knees to her chest and her face in her folded arms, trembling as if her body would shake itself to pieces.

Jaeger's voice, nearer still, filtered through the sound of her shuddering gasps: "That's unfortunate." There was a pause, and Libby heard movement at the spot where Pullman lay; she tried to shrink even further, tightening her arms around her head.

"A shame," Jaeger went on. "After today, our old friend Pullman would have made an *exceptionally* good donor."

He was silent again for a bit. Libby tried to force herself to think of something that might offer relief, or hope of escape, but her mind seemed shredded, her thoughts swirling like bits of paper in a whirlwind, with one still, frozen point at the center: *Pullman is gone.*

She dared to steal a terrified glance at Scab, and immediately longed not to have done so. He stood only a few steps away from her, toward the wall between the room they were in and the corridor. His right hand still held the knife, which dripped red onto the tile. His body was tight-wound and racked by small jerks and spasms, his opaque, quivering gaze still fixed on her. The hideous grin remained stretched across his face, but it was the tears that streamed unchecked from his dead-looking eyes that made Libby wish she had kept her own eyes hidden from the sight of him.

Jaeger spoke again; Libby's gaze flew to him, and she saw that he was pulling out his memo book as he stood over Pullman's motionless body. "It *is* very interesting, though..." His voice was low but animated; he seemed to be thinking aloud now, not addressing Libby or whatever inhabited Scab. He wrote in the book briefly, then paused and, with his foot, pushed at Pullman's body, moving it slightly as if to make sure there was no life left in it.

All at once, fury blazed up in Libby, exploding inside her with a furnace-blast so powerful that it felt as if the tears in her eyes would boil and rise as steam. Hatred of Jaeger seemed to evaporate all her terror, and as her body tensed to leap on him – to punch, scratch, bite, *kill* him – the memory of Scab's razor, still in her pocket, leapt out in her mind like something pulled white-hot from a forge.

In an instant she was scrambling to her feet, plunging her hand into her pocket as she rose, meaning to launch herself across the floor toward Jaeger. Her other belongings scattered onto the floor as she yanked the razor out; and then the razor was open in her hand, the light of the hanging bulbs gleaming wickedly along its edge.

Jaeger never even bothered to glance up.

Her gaze was fixed with ferocious intensity on his face, and though his eyes never left his memo book she saw a faint, wry smile touch the corners of his mouth. Pausing in his writing for less than a second, he lifted the hand that held the pencil slightly, like a parent silencing an importunate child. Before she even had fully gotten her feet under her, she found herself slammed onto the tiles, the side of her face striking the floor so hard that she tasted blood in her mouth.

She was laid out flat on her stomach, the outstretched hand holding the razor still a yard or more from where Jaeger stood over Pullman. Every inch of her body pressed against the floor so forcefully that she could feel her muscles being crushed between her bones and the tiles. She cried out from the pain of it, but also from the terror that rose again like a tidal wave; the tiny, distant part of her mind that managed to stay afloat marveled at her own foolishness: how could she have imagined that her little candle-flame of fury could evaporate this ocean of fear?

Panting, struggling for breath under the crushing pressure, she rolled her eyes sideways to look up at Jaeger, terrified that he would allow the force he had brought down upon her to crush the life from her. She saw him finish his writing, close his memo book, and replace it in his pocket; only then did his eyes turn to her.

"Such *hatred*, Libby," he said, looking down on her with his pleasant, amused smile. His voice was light, teasing. "You mean to slice me to pieces, eh? It almost makes me want to see what the khatojana would make of *you!*" He stepped around Pullman, and squatted down next to her in his easy, graceful way. "It may surprise you to hear that, after all that has just happened, I'm rather disappointed in your young friend Scab over there. Not because of *that –*" he gestured toward Pullman – "Although it *is* a waste. No, it was what happened *before*, when he managed to fight off the influence of the khatojana for those few moments. Experience has taught me that subjects with such strength of will seldom last long under continuous inhabitation. They never give *up*; they never *relax* – they simply wear themselves away." He turned his appraising gaze toward Scab. "I would have seen it right away if I had looked at him more closely; he's deteriorated a great deal in just the past twenty-four hours. I believe it has to do with the nervous system; it simply burns out, like the filament of an overcharged light bulb. Perhaps I'll just lock him up, and send an entity of some sort into him when I need something done." He gave a half-shrug and turned back to her. "We'll see. The question at *this* moment is what to do with *you*. Having Scab take your eyes was really for Pullman's benefit; I don't actually need them just now." He tilted his head, considering her. "It *is* a bit of a temptation to try you with the khatojana; but I'm also short an excellent donor, now that Pullman is dead. You'll never be as valuable as *he* would have been, of course, but –" he smiled – "there's always my work with *suffering*. Practically speaking I suppose that would be a better use for you." The playful tone returned to his voice. "And you really have caused me *so* much trouble." He rose again, and Libby could only see his feet and legs. "Yes, I suppose it's back to the cage for you. I'll just get Simms and Slater."

His feet moved away toward the door, and Libby struggled again, uselessly, to free herself. The effort wrung another moaning cry from her; panic and despair formed a swelling knot in her chest. In the distant part of her mind still capable of coherent thought, she was again appalled at her stupidity – this time, for ever having thought she would have the strength and resourcefulness to save her sister. Pullman, Roach and Scab had all come to ruin through trying to help her, and she had failed. Her labored breaths turned into sobs. "Maisie!" She managed to cry out, struggling to move her jaw against the pressure of the floor; "Maisie, if you can hear me, I'm *sorry* – I'm so sorry! And you too, Scab, if you can hear me: I'm sorry; I'm so sorry I got you into all this!"

The Birds of the Air | 341

She heard Jaeger's footsteps pause, and then return to her, halting with a slight scuffing sound right in front of her. Opening her eyes, she saw his shiny brown shoes only a few inches from her face; then he stepped back and squatted down again. Libby turned her eyes and saw him looking down at her, his expression lively with interest. "You see, *this* is what I find so *fascinating* – exactly what I was speaking about earlier!" He pointed a finger at her, bouncing it a bit. "Here you are, with nothing left to look forward to in life but year after year of excruciating torment, yet you speak as if you still retain some sense of *responsibility*, or *concern*, for your sister and your so-called 'friend.'" He shook his head. "Now of course, any such sentiment is utterly factitious. Your *natural* mental state at this moment would be no more adulterated by such trivialities than that of an animal caught in a trap. Yet because of the powerful effects of acculturation, your sense of 'self' is inextricably bound up with the idea of being a 'good' or 'moral' person, so that even in this extremity you cling to the modes of thinking that perpetuate that conceit – preserve *that* 'self,' so to speak. Consequently, you have two separate and conflicting forms of the all-powerful drive for self-preservation, within a single psyche!" His green eyes were bright with enthusiasm. "The question that so fascinates *me* is, to what extreme must the individual be driven before he is finally able to free himself from the dictatorial imperatives of society – or at *least* to recognize them for what they are?" He shifted his weight, leaning forward. "To what extreme would *you* have to be driven, Libby?"

He rose and began to pace, walking slowly toward where Scab stood off to Libby's left. Libby, still crushed to the floor, could no longer see his face, but she saw in the movements of his shadow the eager gestures of his hands. "For example, what if I had your *mother* here, as well as your little sister, and I asked you to choose which one would live, and which die? *Or –* " his shadow stopped moving abruptly, and his voice brightened – "Yes! Let's make this a *practical* experiment!" Libby heard his footsteps turn purposefully toward the far end of the room. He moved into her line of sight, heading for the far-off table on which the cages rested. The birds fluttered at his approach; he bent to examine them intently for a few moments, then opened a cage, reached inside and grasped one. He closed the cage again and turned back to Libby, smiling; he gave a slight lift of his chin, and at once the crushing force that pressed down upon her vanished. With a sob of relief, she laid her forehead against the tiles and gulped air, so thankful to be able to breathe freely again that she did nothing else for a time, as Jaeger made his unhurried way back down the length of the room.

"Here's what we'll do," he said when he drew near enough to speak at a comfortable volume. "I have your little sister here in my hand. In *your* hand, you hold the razor with which you tried to attack me just now."

Libby was surprised to realize that this was true; when she tightened her right hand, she felt the mother-of-pearl handle of the razor still clutched in it.

"I'm going to give you a choice, and a certain length of time in which to make it," Jaeger went on. He moved toward her in his unhurried way, and she pushed herself into a sitting position, holding the razor in front of her. He paid no attention, but stopped a few feet away. "The choice is this: either I will crush your little sister to death, here in my hand." He held out the tiny, trembling sparrow, so that Libby could see the corn-flower blue of its eyes. "*Or – you* will take that razor, and slit the throat of your young friend Scab over there, deeply enough to kill him." He shook his head and laughed in mock self-reproach.

The Birds of the Air | 343

"The Directors would have fits if they knew I was risking one of the children like this, but the opportunity is irresistible!" He looked at his wristwatch. "Let's say, two minutes: you make the choice within that time, or I kill them both. Or – no! Let's do it *this* way, so you can see for yourself when your time is running out." He stretched one hand high over his head, holding Maisie with the other, and pushed the metal shade of one of the hanging lights, causing it to swing back and forth – not wildly, but in a moderate, measured arc about two feet long. "When that light stops swinging, your time is up." He lowered his eyes to meet Libby's stunned gaze, light and shadow from the moving bulb ebbing and flowing across his smiling face. "Don't worry; I won't let Scab harm you; he won't even move, should you choose him for extermination." He indicated the light with an upward glance. "Your time has begun, Libby! Make your choice!"

Libby gaped up at him, struck as motionless as she had been under his crushing paralysis. Without any awareness of speaking, she heard her own hoarse whisper: "*Why?*"

Jaeger gave an incredulous laugh, as he had when Pullman had asked the same question. "You're sure you want to spend the time *this* way?" He shrugged. "Very well. I've already explained the obvious reasons to you: the added potency that emotional suffering imparts to donors like yourself; my interest in the conflicting imperatives of the human psyche." He paused, then moved toward Libby, so suddenly and swiftly that he was crouched in front of her before she had a chance to scuttle away. He leaned forward, bending down close, and she squeezed her eyes shut and turned her face away, her whole body going rigid. He didn't touch her, but his voice dropped to a low, conspiratorial tone: "But there *is* another reason – and *this* reason, Libby, will be a secret, just between you and me." He leaned even closer, and

Libby cringed as she felt his breath against her ear. "You want to know why I do these things?" He paused again, as if waiting for her to answer, and when she tried to draw away from him, he gripped her arm hard with the hand not holding Maisie, and held her in place. "It's because it makes me *feel* better, Libby. It *helps* me, being an *agent*, and not just another *sufferer*, of all this pain. I mean the pain that beats down with the heat and glare of that jaundiced star around which we are doomed to circle until the day when it explodes and incinerates us all. I mean the pain dissolved in the water we drink, and joined to the molecules of the food we eat – the poisons that slowly weaken, sicken and kill us, even as we are forced to take them into our bodies. I mean the pain that we invariably, inevitably, and willfully inflict upon one *another* – that others have inflicted on me, and that I am inflicting on you, and will *continue* to inflict, without a *moment's* remission, for all the remaining hours and days and months and years of your wretched existence." All at once Libby jerked and moaned, because his voice was no longer coming through her ear, but from inside her head:

All of the pain, Libby, that has built up, and built up, and built up inside me since the day I was born; the pain that has become more and more concentrated in my blood and nerves and bones, until I am MADE of pain.

As his words pulsed through her brain, the hornet-sting feeling began to unfurl behind her eyes again. She cried out, trying to yank her arm free; the words and the stinging inside her head broke off, but Jaeger spoke in her ear again, almost whispering now: "*Nothing* I could do to you would ever adequately replicate it. And did you ever wonder, Libby..." he leaned even closer, his voice barely more than a breath in her ear. "Did you ever wonder who *made* it like this? Did you ever ask yourself *that*, Libby?" His left hand rose and grasped her hair, pushing her head against his. "Who decided *this* was the way the world would be?"

He let her go and pulled away again, and she opened her eyes and stared at him. He stood up, looming over her, and nodded toward the slowing movement of the light. "Time's almost up, Libby; make your decision. Who will it be – Scab or Maisie?" He paused and pressed a knuckle to his upper lip, as if a sudden thought had struck him, then pointed at her jauntily. "I'll tell you what: I'll give you a *further* incentive!" He gave her the smile she had once thought charming; now it made her stomach clench with such revulsion that she nearly gagged. "I give you my word," he said, "that the one you *don't* condemn to death, I will let go free; I'll never bother him – or her – again."

Libby's vision darkened at its edges, and her knotted, empty stomach heaved again, as if it had something inside it to vomit up. She looked at Scab where he stood near the wall, his shadow reeling behind him like a drunken thing in the light of the swinging lamp. His tense, hunched posture now looked to her like the clenched rigidity caused by terrible pain; the shifting light sent silvery reflections along the tracks of the tears still coursing down his face.

Tears half-blinded Libby's eyes as well; she looked at Maisie's tiny, unfamiliar form, recognizable only by the color of the eyes, utterly vulnerable in Jaeger's hand. She looked up again into Jaeger's smiling face and saw no mercy there. "I can't!" she cried. "I can't do it! I can't choose!"

Jaeger nodded in satisfaction. "Precisely: as I said. Self-preservation." Libby looked at him wildly, uncomprehending, and he went on. "Don't you see, Libby?" The shadows slid across his face more slowly now, and Libby saw with sick dread that the span of their back-and-forth movement was quickly narrowing. "You're willing to let *both* Scab and your sister die, in order to spare *yourself* pain: the pain of remembering the choice you made, through all the years you will spend here with me; the pain of losing the illusion that you are worthy of existence because you are a 'decent human being.'" He gestured toward the light, still swinging, though its arc was now only five or six inches long. "You're sure, now? That's your final decision? Are you ready for me to carry it out?" He lifted Maisie, tightening his grip on her just enough that she began to struggle, panicked, in his grasp.

"No!" Libby screamed, dropping the razor as her hands flew to clutch her head. "Please, Mr. Jaeger – *please!*"

"*Please?*" Jaeger's gaze on her grew very still, the faint lines etching themselves into his face, and Libby saw, with a dizzying sense of disconnection, a genuine, piercing sadness in his eyes. "I can tell you from my own experience, Libby: *never* has a more useless word been invented." He glanced up at the slowing movement of the light. "I'd say you have about thirty more seconds."

Libby moaned; she retched, doubled over by the heaving of her stomach, and this time the bit of water Roach had given her came out onto the floor. Shock and anguish, on top of her physical weakness, seemed to short-circuit not only her thinking but her senses as well; she heard a loud buzzing in her ears, and the darkness encroaching on the edges of her vision had become a sparkling, tingling nothingness. As her hands spread out on the floor to support her, one of them struck something there, sending it rolling into the center of her narrowing field of vision. It was the little glass vial, pulled from her pocket when she had yanked out Scab's razor, cracked from its fall to the floor. The instant she saw it, the voice of the woman who had given it to her spoke clearly in her mind: *John Fuller says, don't believe everything you hear. John Fuller says, if ever you need him, just call.*

The Birds of the Air | 347

Libby squeezed her eyes shut and clenched her fists; she straightened her body and threw back her head. *"Mr. Fuller!"* she cried out, as loudly as she could; *"John Fuller! Help me!"*

PART 3: FULLER

CHAPTER TWENTY-THREE

WHEN SHE OPENED her eyes, nothing seemed to have changed.

Jaeger still stood over her, with Maisie in his hand; Scab still stood twitching near the wall, his shadow barely moving behind him now. Pullman's lifeless body lay where it had fallen, and the bird-children huddled in their cages at the far end of the room. There was no one else to be seen, no sign of any help. Libby saw that the light hung nearly motionless from its cord, and turned her eyes up to Jaeger, despairing. But then she saw his face.

His expression was blank, his slack jaw pulling his mouth a little open. His eyes were fixed on her, and there was astonishment in them, outlandish in the face where she had, until now, seen only absolute self-assurance. But there was something else as well, equally alien to her experience of him, that she couldn't quite identify.

"*Why did you say that?*" he demanded, and his voice sounded utterly unlike itself as well, jagged edges where Libby had only heard glassy smoothness before. When he spoke again, she realized what she saw in his eyes: it was fear.

"Why did you say that? *Who told you to say that?*"

His face was white, whether with the fear or with fury Libby couldn't tell. Her own terror constricted her throat so that she could form no answer, but he didn't wait for one. His eyes shifted to the door that led out to the corridor, and he turned to stalk toward it, Maisie seemingly forgotten in his hand. He stopped near the door and listened, his eyes wide and fixed but not focused on anything in the room. He stood motionless for a long time, and Libby crouched frozen as well, afraid any movement would recall his attention to her and Maisie.

At last he gave an audible exhalation, and ran an unsteady hand through his hair. When he spoke, his words were addressed to her, but his voice sounded as if he were talking to himself. "Well, it won't do you any good. John Fuller has *infinitely* more important things to concern himself with than the circumstances of one meaningless speck in the swarm like *you*." He turned and, with a visible effort, recovered a semblance of his genial smile, focusing on Libby again. He nodded toward the light. "One thing you *have* accomplished, though: you've used up the last of your time."

Libby looked at the light and saw that it hung motionless from its cord. Jaeger gave a short, shaky laugh, watching whatever reaction showed on her face; she could see his confidence returning with every moment. He lifted his free hand in a conciliatory gesture. "In all fairness, though, I *did* run on a bit in answering your question. So since it seems John Fuller won't be joining us, I'm going to be magnanimous and give you one last chance: choose between Scab and your sister within the next five seconds, and I won't kill them both." He began to saunter toward her again; she could see Maisie's tiny form quivering in his grasp.

"Five," he said.

Libby's hands flew out reflexively toward Maisie.

"Four."

She looked at her outstretched hands, and saw their utter, unbearable uselessness.

"Three."

She realized she had dropped the razor, and searched for it wildly, her fingers scrabbling over the floor until she grasped it.

"Two."

Her gaze reeled from the razor in her hand to Scab, and she knew that, even if she had more time, even if she had the rest of her life, she would never be able to do what Jaeger demanded.

"One."

Jaeger squatted down in his smooth, easy way, and held out the hand that gripped Maisie so it was only inches from Libby's face. Libby tried to lift the razor, meaning to slice at Jaeger's arm, his face, his throat, but his free hand grasped her wrist and forced the razor down, and the hand that held Maisie began to tighten.

A breath like a hammer-blow slammed into Libby's chest and seemed to petrify there, filling her lungs like hardening concrete, threatening to rip them out of her with the scream that was rising to her throat. But before the scream could escape, a few things happened.

First, a deep sound, like a soft explosion, struck her ears and vibrated through her bones. At the same instant, there was a shadowing of the light, so brief she wasn't sure if it was real.

Then she heard another sound, from where Scab had been standing. Jaeger rose, slackening his grip on Maisie, and turned to look. Libby turned as well, and her battered mind floundered,

354 | L. H. Arthur

trying to grasp the meaning of what she saw: Scab, crumpled to the floor, his eyes closed and his body as still as Pullman's.

"What – what –?" Jaeger stammered. When she looked at him, he was slack-jawed again, and the fear had returned to his eyes.

There was a sound of commotion in the corridor outside – a short, sharp cry, and the report of the rifle. Jaeger backed away from Libby, gaping wide-eyed at the locked door to the corridor. And then the door opened, and a man walked in.

It was J.D.

Libby stared, unable to believe that her eyes were conveying truth to her brain; she felt her own jaw go slack, like Jaeger's, in astonishment.

J.D. looked just the same as he had when she had last seen him in the parking lot of the cafe – the same old gray fedora tilted back on his head, the same open-collared work shirt with the sleeves rolled up. He smiled at her and gave a nod of greeting, but spoke first to Jaeger: "Hello, Karl."

"You – *you can't be here!*" Jaeger's voice ravelled out shrill and brittle, unrecognizable; he stumbled a few steps backward. "You – you're not *welcome* here; I didn't *invite* you!"

"Libby, there, invited me." J.D. crossed the room to where Scab lay, and squatted down beside him, looking into his bruised face, the lines deep at the sides of his mouth. He put a hand to the boy's head, pushing back the sweat-soaked hair with grieved gentleness, but when he looked up at Libby again, his face held no anxiety. "Your friend will be OK, Libby," he said. "Don't worry."

"These are *mine*, Fuller." Libby could hear the attempt at authority in Jaeger's voice, and the quaver that undermined it. At the name he spoke, she stared at J.D. with renewed amazement.

The Birds of the Air | 355

"You can't interfere," Jaeger rasped. "These children belong to *me* now."

J.D. let out a soft, amused breath. "How do you figure that, Karl?" He stood up and held out a hand to Libby, crooking the fingers a bit to beckon her. She rose at once and went to him, and he took her hand in his.

Jaeger gave a laugh, as harsh as the squeal of a rusty hinge. "Are you pretending that *you're* a fool, or that you think *I* am?" He circled warily toward the center of the room, staying on the far side of Pullman's body. Libby's stomach tightened with fear for Maisie as he swept the hand that held her in a wild arc. "These are all lawful captures." He jabbed a trembling finger toward Scab. "I'm sure you're aware, at the very least, that *that* one bears my mark; he's done my work and accepted my currency; there can certainly be no question about *him*." He swung the pointing finger toward the cages. "*These* made the choice; no one forced them. They were *told* that their acceptance of the instrument of trans-formation amounted to thievery, yet they chose to take it anyway. They were *told* that it was a means of rebellion, and they chose to rebel." He turned his gaze on Libby, and she shrank from it. "As for *that* one," he said, his voice icy, "she's the worst of them all. *So* full of condemnation for the actions of others, yet just look into her mind: bitterness, jealousy, resentment, self-pity. The cruelty she's knowingly inflicted on her mother alone would have made her fair game. But, should any doubt remain —"

Libby saw him slip his fingers into a pocket of his trousers. When he pulled his hand out and opened it, she felt a dizzying surge of nausea: on his palm rested a tiny sugar bird, with a red-dish-brown spot between its wings.

"These have *bound* themselves to us, Fuller." Jaeger's voice was growing steadier, gaining strength. "Every one of them – and the ones overseas as well! All of them have *deliberately* chosen to do harm to others in order to benefit themselves."

J.D.'s calloused hand remained strong and steady around Libby's. "I see the bonds, Karl." He made no comment about the sugar bird, but inclined his head toward the living one clutched in Jaeger's other hand. "Speaking of harm," he said, "I heard you telling Libby that was her sister you have there. You're wrong. That's not Maisie; Maisie's still over there in the cage. That little girl you're holding is Betty Czajka, from Springfield." Libby looked at him in surprise, and saw his gray eyes fall to the little quivering creature, and the tenderness that warmed them. "She loves music. She was learning to play the violin." When his eyes lifted to Jaeger's again, Libby saw something in them that made her think, with a mixture of awe and rekindling hope, that Jaeger was right to be afraid. *He can do it!* she thought. *He can beat Jaeger – he can save us!*

Jaeger, however, seemed only to be gaining confidence. "What difference does it make?" he snapped. "For my purposes they're interchangeable." He slipped the sugar bird back into his pocket and stared at J.D. for a long moment, a kind of amazed exultation beginning to dawn in his face. "I was *right*! I suspected it, but now I *know*! *You can't do anything here*, Fuller! If you could, it would be done already – I know you well enough to be sure of *that*." He shook his head, his eyes wide. "I *see* it now! Don't imagine you can bluff me. When these children bound themselves to us, they tied *your* hands as well! There's too much of *us* in them now – too much of what your kind of power *destroys*. With all that extravagant ability of yours, you can't so much as bind my little finger to save them!"

Libby looked up anxiously into J.D.'s face, but his expres-

The Birds of the Air | 357

sion remained calm. "*Can't* and *won't* are two different things, Karl," he said.

Jaeger made a scoffing sound. "Another pointless distinction. Why should I care what you *could* do, when I know you won't *do* it?" He gave a wild laugh. "It's quite funny, really: the mighty John Fuller, brought to an impasse by the petty misdeeds of such insignificant creatures as these. That's the problem with *perfection*, isn't it, Fuller? It's so very *delicate*. Drop one tiny stitch, and your entire elaborate tapestry unravels."

Jaeger's growing confidence was making Libby more and more apprehensive, and when J.D. let out a sudden, easy laugh, she looked up at him, startled. "I'd almost forgotten how long-winded you are, Karl," he said. "I believe you can spout more bull per second than just about anyone I know."

Libby saw a frown flicker briefly across Jaeger's face, but his exultant expression returned quickly. "There's nothing you can *do* here, Fuller," he said. "Be so good as to take yourself off my property, before you bring death to those you came to protect."

J.D. gave a slight, untroubled shrug. "The way you carry on, Karl, just about *anything* that happened to these kids would be an improvement. And anyway –" he smiled down at Libby for a moment – "death isn't nearly as big a deal as most people think it is. But it's no part of my plans for these kids to die tonight; and you're right: if it comes to a dust-up, they're liable to get hurt." He turned his gaze back to Jaeger. "That's why I didn't come here to fight with you. I came to make you a proposal – the same one Pullman there made: me for the kids. You take me, and let the kids go. That's if you don't have the same objection you had when Pullman offered."

Jaeger made a scornful sound. "You must think I'm an idiot, Fuller." He squinted at him for a moment, the exultation in his

358 | L. H. Arthur

face fading to suspicion. "And anyway, even if you were to make such an offer seriously, perhaps I *would* have the same objection. I told Pullman his offer was meaningless because he was no threat to me; now I could rightly say the same about *you*."

J.D. crooked an eyebrow. "Maybe you could, and maybe you couldn't. But one thing's for sure: I'd be a lot more *valuable* to you than Pullman was." He nodded toward the cages. "And I'd be a lot more valuable to you than these kids, Karl – your, what do you call them? Donors?" His tone as he said the last word made Libby think of the way light glinted off the blade of Scab's razor. "You'd gain more from a drop of my blood than you would out of a year's worth from all the kids you and your controllers have, put together. Multiply that over decades, centuries..." he shrugged. "Think about it, Karl."

Libby felt a growing dread at the direction the conversation was taking. She could see a greedy excitement seeping into Jaeger's face, but he gave a derisive laugh. "And I suppose you want me to let the children go *first*? Dissolve the bonds, so you can attack me without fear of harming them? I'm not a fool, Fuller."

J.D. shook his head. "You couldn't dissolve the bonds, even if you wanted to. But I'm not trying to cheat you, Karl. You play straight with me and I'll play straight with you. If we make this bargain, I'm in your hands; I won't do a thing to resist you." He glanced at Libby. "But let these kids go; they don't need to see it."

The trace of greed in Jaeger's eyes was becoming an avid gleam, but still he pretended to scoff. He made a contemptuous gesture toward Pullman's body. "You must think I'm as stupid as *he* was. You won't do a thing to resist me until the *bonds* are broken, you mean. Once that happens, what's to stop you from attacking me? No, Fuller; the children stay where they are; then at least we retain *physical* control. When I'm confident that you're restrained, I swear on my power I'll let them all go; I'll restore them to their forms and homes, and I'll never bother them again."

J.D. gave a quiet laugh – a single breath, like Scab's. "I think we both know what *that* promise would be worth." He let go of Libby's hand and pressed her shoulder lightly to tell her to stay put, then moved toward Jaeger. "And how do you imagine you'd 'restrain' me, Karl, if I decided not to keep my word?"

All the cocky confidence drained from Jaeger's face; he stumbled hastily backward, one step, then another, even though J.D. was still some distance from him. He lost his balance, threw out his arms to regain it, and the bird – Betty Czajka – burst from his hand and flew about confusedly, finally perching on one of the pipes that ran the length of the room near the ceiling.

J.D. advanced a few more steps, then stopped. "There's no need to swear on anything, Karl – and no oath you could take that I'd put any confidence in. If we reach an agreement, it'll be binding. The minute we shake on this thing, yes, your hold on these kids will be broken. But if I break my word and use my power to resist you, the bond will be restored, no matter where they are."

"Your 'word.'" The scorn in Jaeger's voice couldn't quite disguise the tremor beneath. "That's not good enough, Fuller. The children stay, or there's no deal."

J.D. glanced back at Libby. "All right, Karl. But don't be fool enough to think it'll be anything but my word that holds me. And I'm warning you now: if you break *your* word, and refuse to let the kids go when this is over, you'll never get the chance to restore that bond. Our contract will be broken; I'll be free to act against you, and no 'restraint' you think you've put on me will stop me." He lifted a hand. "And just to be clear: I want *all* the kids. Not just the ones in this building; I mean *all* of them, in this country *and* overseas. Any rights you or your controllers claim over them are transferred completely and permanently to me. You agree to that, we've got a deal."

Jaeger's eyes, feverish now with excitement, wavered a bit. "I don't have the authority –"

"Sure you do. The minute they let you share in their power, they gave you all the authority you need to make a deal like this. All you have to do is say the word; I'll take care of the rest. 'Course, they might not *approve*, but..." J.D. shrugged. "How angry can they be with you, once you tell them you've got John Fuller?"

This was not how Libby had hoped it would be. Her eyes turned miserably to J.D., but not before she saw a grin spread across Jaeger's face, stretching almost as wide as the one the khatojana had pasted onto Scab's; naked greed shone in his eyes, and she would hardly have been surprised to see him salivate. "All right, Fuller," he said. "You've got a deal." He crossed to the door leading out to the corridor; taking the keys from his pocket, he locked it again. He nodded toward the cages. "These, and the girl and boy, I keep as security until we're finished here." He re-pocketed the keys and turned the grin on Libby. "And besides – this will be instructive for your little admirer there."

Libby ducked her head from Jaeger's gaze. Scurrying to J.D.'s side, she pulled at his arm. "No, Mr. Fuller – *please!* He's *lying* – he'll *hurt* you; he'll lock you up, and then he won't let *any* of us go!"

But J.D. gave her his clear-eyed smile. "It'll be OK, Libby," he said, laying a hand on her shoulder. "It'll be scary for a while, but just trust me, and it'll be OK. Now here's what I'm going to ask you to do: I want you to go sit by Scab over there, and cover your ears and close your eyes. I'm going to ask you not to open

The Birds of the Air | 361

them again until it's all over, OK?" He nodded toward the cages. "Maisie and the rest will be all right; they won't take any of it in; Scab'll likely be out for a while, but I don't want you seeing this."

"Well, Fuller," Jaeger said, "are you ready?"

J.D.'s eyes smiled into Libby's for a moment more, then he patted her shoulder and turned to Jaeger. "Yep," he said, sounding as untroubled as if Jaeger had suggested they drive into town. He gave a last glance at Libby as he moved away, nodding toward the spot where Scab lay, and she retreated and sank to her knees beside him.

J.D. halted in front of Jaeger, and the two men stood face-to-face near the door. "You sure you really want to go through all this, Karl?" J.D. said. "It's not too late, you know. You could stop all this, cut your ties with them. You could come back."

Jaeger snorted. "Getting cold feet, Fuller?"

J.D. smiled and, without another word, extended his right hand. Jaeger flinched a bit, looking down; then his eyes returned to J.D.'s, and the greed flooded back into his face. He grabbed J.D.'s hand and shook it.

The instant their hands clasped, Libby felt a tremor in the ground beneath her. The panes in the basement windows rattled, and the lights hanging from the ceiling swung slightly; there was a rumble, almost too deep to be a sound. Libby braced her hands against the floor, and a frightened cry escaped her. She saw Jaeger jerk his hand out of J.D.'s and pull back, his wide eyes on the ceiling. But when the tremor passed and nothing more happened, his gaze dropped back to J.D. He fixed him with a searching stare, and then a slow, delighted grin spread across his face. Libby, glancing at J.D., could see nothing different about him, but Jaeger let out a laugh that sounded both astonished and triumphant. He took several steps, circling partway around J.D., looking at him as a man might look at a car or a horse he had just purchased. "All right!" he said finally; "How shall we do this?"

Libby looked anxiously back to J.D. As her gaze fell on him, his head jolted violently back and to one side, and he staggered as if he had been struck a brutal blow, though Libby had seen nothing hit him. He raised a hand to his forehead; before he could fully regain his balance, another invisible blow struck him, this time from behind, and he fell to his knees, bracing himself with one arm to keep from falling forward. Libby cried out; she began to scramble to her feet, meaning to go to him, but he threw out his other arm and held up a hand to halt her. "*Stay back*, Libby," he panted. Libby heard a crunching, crackling sound from the hand he had extended toward her and, looking at it, saw the fingers crumple like breaking twigs. J.D.'s body went rigid, his breath hissing through his teeth.

"*Mr. Fuller!*" Libby cried, agonized.

"Please, Libby – do as I asked you." With an obvious effort, as if his gaze itself was almost too heavy to lift, J.D. raised his eyes to hers. They were stained red with broken blood vessels, as Pullman's had been before; but Libby could see that, beneath the blood and pain, the calm was still in them. He knelt hunched over, bracing himself with his good hand, the other drawn in to his chest, hanging twisted like a dead leaf. "Everything will be all right."

"Why lie to the child, John?" All traces of fear had vanished from Jaeger's voice; he turned to look at Libby for a moment, smiling. "The unmasking of the world comes to us all, sooner or later. It will serve her much better than *you* have, don't you think?" He brought his hands together in a loudly-echoing clap, making Libby's body jerk. "Well! Let's get started."

THE THINGS THAT happened in the next monstrous hour were so unbearable that they penetrated Libby's mind only in disjointed fragments; but never once, through it all, did she hear J.D.'s voice.

Jaeger went first to the table at the far end of the room. He yanked the long cord out of the desk-lamp, then opened the second door in the wall behind the table, and disappeared into a sort of closet beyond. After a moment he emerged with a large metal washtub, like the one roach had used in the clearing. He carried it to a spot near the high, painted windows, set it on the floor, and came back for J.D.

Libby huddled beside Scab's still body, trembling, unable to obey J.D. and close her eyes. Jaeger, in an obscene parody of solicitude, put an arm around J.D. to pull him to his feet, and supported him, leading him across the room. He steadied J.D. as he made him step into the basin, and propped him up as he threw the lamp-cord over a thick pipe that ran along the ceiling above, stretched J.D.'s arms up above his head and bound his wrists tightly with the ends. When Jaeger withdrew his support J.D.'s knees buckled, and his weight pulled down on the cords, digging into the flesh and causing the knots to creak. His head hung down, but when Jaeger began to rip his shirt and under-shirt from his body, cutting the seams with Scab's razor, Libby saw him put forth an effort and raise his eyes enough to meet hers from across the room. His unsteady, bloodstained gaze was meant to remind her, she knew, but still she couldn't bear to look away; to do so, she felt, would be to abandon him.

It was only when Jaeger began in earnest and she realized – seeing him wield the razor with slow, painstaking dexterity – what he meant to do, that the horror of watching became greater than the agony of not doing so.

After that, for what seemed like an unbelievable length of time, there was only the blackness behind her squeezed-shut eyelids, the hard tiles beneath her, and – muffled but not entirely shut out by the pressure of her hands over her ears – the sounds. She heard the creaking of the cord as it jerked against the pipe, the sound of J.D.'s ragged, tearing breath, and the horrible drumming of his feet when they convulsed in agonized spasms against the inside of the washtub – which Jaeger had placed there, she realized distantly, to catch the blood that J.D. had said would be so valuable to him.

It's finally happened, she thought: *I've finally used up all my tears.* It seemed to be true; her closed eyes were dry and hot, as if grief and horror and despair had at last scorched all the tears from them forever.

She must have either passed out at last, from shock, hunger and exhaustion, or actually slipped into some sort of sleep, because all at once it was over, and Jaeger was pushing at her with one blood-smeared shoe. "Take a look, Libby!" he said. "Look at your hero now!" But she wouldn't; she saw Jaeger's bloody footprints on the white tiles, saw the red wetness covering his hands and the shirt he had said Mrs. Vogel would kill him if he ruined, but she wouldn't lift her eyes to look at the horror that had been J.D.

Instead she looked down at Scab, still lying where he had fallen, his breathing shallow and irregular. She shook him. "Wake up, Scab! We're going. It's over; we're leaving here."

Even as she was saying the words, she knew they weren't true. She had tried to tell J.D.; she had known all along: Jaeger had lied, as he always lied; he would never let them go.

His laughter, therefore, didn't surprise her. "Don't tell me you *believed* all that twaddle I fed to Fuller," he said, mock pity in his voice. "I'm still trying to come to terms with the fact that *he* believed it." He waved a contemptuous hand toward Pullman's still form. "Colin and those other buffoons I have working for me are one thing, but the mighty John *Fuller*?" He bent over Libby, lowering his voice, and the muscles on her back tightened, the skin there feeling as if it would crawl off her body to get away from him. "And *you*, my dear," he said, "should *certainly* know me better than that by now."

He seemed unable to keep still, and soon moved off to pace the blood-spattered tiles, his hands moving in agitated arcs. "Do you remember what I told Colin – that I had given him a mirror image of the truth?" His eyes darted toward her, then away again. "It was *Fuller* who postured himself as some sort of 'protector' – some self-proclaimed watchdog, trying to keep us from acquiring donors. You can judge for yourself how effective he was." He laughed again. "I suppose you thought he was terribly gallant, giving up his power like that. I'm sure *he* thought so too. You were both wrong: he was an *idiot*." He spat out the last word with disgust that sounded close to anger. Libby, unable to keep her eyes from his face, saw exultation there, but also a disorienting resentfulness – almost as if he were angry at Fuller for having been defeated. "And do you know *why* he was an idiot?" He angled back toward her, and she ducked her head, hiding her face against Scab's unresponsive shoulder. "Because he thought he had me all figured *out*, Libby. He thought I would keep him *alive*, like the rest of my donors – thought I would be too greedy to resist the power I could gain by drawing out his suffering indefinitely. And it would have been an *incredible* amount of power. But what need do we have for it now?" His voice quivered with the bizarre bitter-edged elation. "A *fraction* of that power will be sufficient to accomplish our purposes, in a world without John Fuller!"

366 | L. H. Arthur

Libby forced words through her tight throat; they came out weak and hopeless: "But – Mr. Fuller said –"

"*Mr.* Fuller said!" Jaeger straightened and spread his arms, speaking the words loudly, as if to an invisible audience. "What he *said*, little girl, was that if I broke my word, he would be free to take *action* against me." Jaeger bent close to Libby again, and she hunched where she knelt, arms clutched about her, pulling herself in like a snail. She kept her face down, but at the edge of her vision she saw him extend an arm toward the place where she couldn't look, pointing a sticky red finger to where the horror hung from the pipe. "What kind of action do you imagine he'll take against me *now*, Libby?"

He straightened again, and clapped his hands together. "Now: where were we, before you started all this foolishness? Ah, yes." He crossed the room, and when he returned she saw he held Scab's razor in his hand, its blade and handle so uniformly covered with blood that no color but red showed on it anywhere. "Here you are, Libby," he said, laying it on the floor in front of her where she knelt beside Scab. "We'll start again, from the beginning. And I promise you, *this* time, you *will* choose."

Libby stared down at the razor as he started toward the cages, and all at once it was so obvious that she almost laughed aloud to think she hadn't seen it before. Scab had shown it to her; so had Pullman. It had been in her pocket all along; it had been in her hand. And now Jaeger had laid it right in front of her – the key, the door, and the path all in one: escape. All she had to do was reach down and take it.

She heard the flutter of wings, and saw that Jaeger had picked up both cages and was already starting back down the long room toward her, carrying one in each hand. Dropping her eyes to the razor again, she heard Scab's voice in her mind – *Right here, hard*

The Birds of the Air | 367

– and saw him draw a thumb down the side of his neck, just under the jaw. She lifted her fingers to her own neck and felt the place, the pulse like the stirring of some small underground creature beneath the skin. She felt a stab of guilt at the idea of escaping and leaving Scab and Maisie behind in this horrible place. *But there's nothing I can do for them,* she thought; *nothing besides this.* Her breath quickened with fear of the pain, of the finality. *But it won't hurt for long,* she told herself, *and afterward it will all be over. Just do it fast, and do it NOW, before he gets back.*

But when she looked down at the horrible instrument of J.D.'s death, it seemed more than she could do to touch it. Unable to stop herself, though she knew the futility of it, she pled one more time with Jaeger: "*Please,* Mr. Jaeger – *please* just let us go!"

"Really, Libby, anyone would think you're a dull-witted child, and I know *that's* not true." Jaeger had set the cages on a bench beside the door to the corridor, and was crouched down, peering into them. "Ah! *There* you are, Maisie." He opened the door of a cage, reached through the miniature tornado of panicked birds within, and pulled one out. "I'm sure I've spelled it out clearly enough for you to understand," he said, closing the cage door and addressing Libby again. "You will, of course, never leave this place. Not you, not Scab, not your sister or the other children here. Nor will the Directors be relinquishing any of the children in *their* facilities to comply with some ridiculous, illusory bargain John Fuller imagined he made with me."

Libby seemed to feel the words physically; they buzzed through her teeth and skull and down the length of her limbs like a pulse of electricity, burning out in one surging jolt the last of her preposterous hope and foolish hesitation. She took a final deep breath and reached out her hand for the razor.

And then, just before her fingers touched it, everything shifted.

She couldn't have said how she knew it, because everything went together – the walls, the floor, the hanging lights, which didn't even swing, Pullman's and Scab's still shapes, Jaeger, the bird-children and her own body. There was no sound this time, no earthquake-rumble. It was as if some part of her, more integral than her flesh or bones or brain, was for a moment left behind by a swift, sideways movement of the universe, and had to re-center itself within her again.

She looked up reflexively toward what she most feared – Jaeger, still standing ten or twelve feet from her beside the cages – and was transfixed at the change in him.

He was dead-white, so pale he looked incandescent. His eyes were huge and round, making his face look not just young but bizarrely childlike. His gaze was locked on something behind and above Libby.

She twisted her body to see what could have frightened him so, and felt her own eyes go wide as shock surged through her.

Behind her, his level gaze following Jaeger as he staggered back from the cages, stood John Fuller.

CHAPTER TWENTY-FOUR

A ROARING THAT was more a sensation than a sound rose inside Libby's head; she swayed where she knelt and had to catch herself with one hand to keep from tipping over.

J.D. was no longer the horror she had feared to look at when he hung beneath the high windows. He looked as he had when he had first come through the door; even the clothes he wore looked as they had then – untorn, unstained by blood. But when he reached a hand down to her, not dropping his gaze from Jaeger, she slid away from him in a panicky scramble across the floor. When she dared to glance across the room toward where he had been bound, the grisly testimony to Jaeger's butchery still lay, smeared and spattered, across the white tile, but the cord that had held J.D. hung empty.

Jaeger found his voice, choking out one word in a stifled squeal: *"How –?"* Looking toward him, Libby saw him begin to edge toward the door to the corridor. He still held Maisie – if it *was* Maisie this time – cupped in his bloody hands; but just as Libby looked, he let her go and wheeled to grasp the doorknob with both hands, twisting and shaking at it. The door didn't open, and he turned, panting, and faced Fuller with his back pressed against it.

The bird didn't flutter about as Betty Czajka had done, but flew like a tiny arrow, straight across the room, to land on Libby's shoulder. Its feathers were tinged red where Jaeger had held it; Libby put up a protective hand to shield it.

"You – you can't kill me!" Jaeger cried, his voice shrill. "You'll destroy the children!"

J.D. shook his head. "You know better than that, Karl. The bonds are broken." He skirted Scab's body on the floor and began to move, unhurried, toward Jaeger. "But I'm not here to kill you. I'm just here to collect. I'm here for the children."

Jaeger made a strangled sound. He didn't look as if J.D.'s words had diminished his terror, but Libby saw a sort of frantic fury dawn in his face along with it. He edged sideways, toward the cages on the bench. "Y-you can't *have* the children! The agreement is broken! You resisted me; you used your power. Otherwise you'd be *dead!*"

"The agreement is broken all right, Karl. But I'm not the one who broke it."

"*Stay away*, Fuller!" Jaeger's hands darted out like two snakes to grasp the handles of the cages. With the bird-children fluttering in panic, he backed slowly away from Fuller. "I'll kill them *all*, right now, before I'll let you take them." A note of desperation, even of pleading, came into his voice. "They'll take me apart, John – one piece at a time, over years, over *decades* – if they find out what I've done!"

"They know what you've done, Karl," J.D. said, and Libby

The Birds of the Air | 371

heard genuine pity in his voice. "The other children are already on their way here."

Jaeger made an animal sound of terror and misery, and his wild eyes darted around the room as if he expected to see, materializing in one of the corners, whomever it was he feared so greatly. But, seeing J.D. continue his approach, he turned his head to the side and spat onto the floor, as Pullman had done earlier. Libby flinched in surprise as this time, in the place where he spat, a wide sheet of flame sprang up, reaching nearly to the ceiling. The heat of it was so great she felt it from where she knelt.

"I'll burn them alive, John, right in front of you, before I let you have them. At least then I can tell the Directors that *you* didn't get them!" Jaeger's voice was almost a snarl, but when he spoke again the pleading note had returned. "*Go* – take those three, but leave me these. *I can't lose them all!*"

J.D. didn't hesitate in his slow approach, but he lifted the fingers of one hand slightly, and Libby saw the cages Jaeger held dissolve into black sand, which showered to the floor at his feet. At the same instant there came an explosive sound of shattering glass, and every one of the high windows burst outward at once. Like a ribbon of windblown smoke the bird-children flew, calling noisily as they went, through the windows and out into the open air. Libby saw, as her eyes followed them, that a pearly dawn light was just beginning to filter through the darkness outside. Betty Czajka took wing from the pipe where she had perched so long before, and followed the others; but Maisie stayed, a small, warm softness against Libby's neck.

J.D. spoke to Jaeger again. "It's still not too late for you, Karl. You can turn; you can come back to us."

Libby saw the expression on Jaeger's wax-pale face change with uncanny rapidity from terror to fury. "You must be out of your mind, Fuller. Come back to *you*? *You* drove me away; *you* cast me out!" Libby was stunned to see what looked like tears on his face, glinting in the light of the fire. "*You* taught me, *you* made me what I am, and then you *rejected* me."

J.D. stopped, several feet from Jaeger. His back was to Libby, his voice quiet, but she could just make out his words above the crackling of the fire: "You're mistaken, Karl. I've *never* rejected you. The only thing I reject is the ugliness you cling to. *Look* at it." He lifted his hand in a gesture that encompassed the scene of slaughter beneath the windows, Pullman's body, the entire building above and around them with all the horrors it contained. "I saw it when it was only a seed, germinating inside you. I'll ask you again what I asked you then: *leave* it, Karl. Come back to us."

Jaeger's face twisted with contempt. "You need one more bootlicker, do you, Fuller? One more castrated sheep for your flock?" He gave a bitter laugh, but then his scornful expression seemed to slip, and something showed beneath it – a desolation so complete that the mere sight of it seemed to hollow Libby out. "I can't, John," he said. All the contempt had drained from his voice, leaving only infinite weariness. "They've eaten my soul. There's nothing left of me *to* come back."

Without another word, he stepped into the searing sheet of flame. Libby cried out in shock; before her cry had ended, Jaeger's body was consumed, flying up in burning tatters that disappeared before they reached the ceiling, as if he had been made of tissue paper. The flames themselves followed an instant later, evaporating into bright rags that flickered upward and disappeared, leaving no sign of where the fire had been.

A sudden noise, between a moan and a cry, came from Scab. Looking down, Libby saw he had awakened. Fear jerked her muscles taut for an instant before she saw that he was himself again. His eyes, on Pullman's body, held horror and anguish, but not the dead blankness of the khatojana.

Staggering to his feet, he stood over her for a moment with a shaking hand at his forehead, staring at Pullman's still face. He made another, quieter sound of misery, approached the body with unsteady steps, then dropped to his knees beside it, doubled over, his face hidden in his hands.

"Time to go, Libby." J.D. had crossed the room again, and his voice came from just above her, causing her to start. Looking up into his face, she saw tears in his eyes, but his voice was calm and steady. He went to where Scab knelt, crouched down beside him, and put his arms around him, pulling him close. After a moment, Scab's arms came up and clung to Fuller as well, his hands clutching the fabric of his shirt tightly, like the hands of a small child.

THE THINGS THAT happened in the following hours seemed remote and disjointed to Libby, as if her shock-battered brain was no longer able to sort out the jumbled messages of her senses. Somehow they made their way out of the dreadful building and back through the trees to the main house, Libby cupping Maisie gently to her chest, and J.D. carrying Pullman's body as if it weighed no more than Libby. Roach appeared from somewhere – weeping at the sight of Pullman, his wounded hand tied up in a bloody handkerchief – but to her relief Libby saw neither Simms nor Slater. She and Roach supported Scab, who was so dazed by grief and horror, and so weakened by the physical toll the khatojana had taken on him, that he could scarcely stumble along between them.

It seemed as if someone tried to get her to eat something,

but though her stomach was painfully knotted with hunger, the thought of food made her feel ill. She found herself, at some later time, in the upstairs bathroom with Mrs. Vogel, who was clucking away as she ran a bath for her and helped her to get undressed. Libby felt disoriented, thinking that somehow it was once again the night when they had first arrived, until she saw Mrs. Vogel's red eyes and stunned, tear-streaked face. Later still, when she lay huddled under the covers of the bed in the room with the yellow roses – morning sunlight coming in at the window – she heard a man in the hallway outside the closed door, speaking with Mrs. Vogel in German. She suffered a jolt of terror, thinking it was Jaeger, until she recognized J.D.'s voice.

After that there was a period of broken, troubled sleep that felt as if it lasted for days. Half-waking from some awful dream, Libby would will herself to get up, afraid to be alone again on the lawless backroads of sleep with all the horrors that swarmed her mind; but before she could act on her resolution, exhaustion always pulled her back under. Once, hearing voices outside, she thought she sat up to look out the window, and saw pairs of men carrying stretchers toward the front of the house. On the stretchers lay people in a similar condition to Stubby's; all were missing their eyes and ears, and some were missing limbs as well. Later she was uncertain whether it had been real or just another horrible dream.

At last she was jerked fully awake by an appalling realization: she had no idea where Maisie was. Glancing out through the window, she saw the long shadows and amber light of approaching evening. She struggled out of bed and out of her nightgown, and put on one of the stiff new dresses from the closet. Her feet, she saw, had been bandaged where the glass had cut her, though she didn't remember when, or who had done it.

The Birds of the Air | 375

She hurried downstairs and looked into the kitchen, but no one was there. Checking the other rooms, she found them empty as well. The heavy wooden front door stood open, so she slipped through the screen door and out onto the veranda.

The shadow of the house lay stretched across the lawn, and the trees lining the drive cast their own long-trunked shadows far out across the gold-tinged green of the fields. A breeze touched her face, sweet with the scent of alfalfa. Cicadas buzzed noisily, but beneath their shrill drone she could hear crickets beginning to chirp.

"Hello, Libby. How are you feeling?"

It was J.D.'s – Fuller's – voice, coming from the veranda to her left; she turned, startled, and saw him leaned back in a wicker chair, just a few yards off, his long legs stretched out and crossed in front of him.

Her first reaction was a reflexive jolt of dread, and she shrank back toward the door, half-turning to flee before she was able to stop herself. The horror he had become in the basement room, the horror of what Jaeger had done to him, still hung about him for her; and the impossibility of what had happened afterward made her mind feel as if it was teetering on the edge of an unfathomable void.

J.D. seemed to understand, because his voice grew gentler. "Will you sit with me a while?" He nodded toward a porch swing next to his chair. Libby looked at it, reluctant, but when she looked back to J.D. and saw his faint, friendly smile and the easy repose of his body, she felt a pang of longing. In her mind he now stirred up a tempest of confusing, contradictory and terrifying impressions – everything associated, in the past harrowing days, with the name *John Fuller.* But he was also still J.D. – still the man who had rescued her and Scab on the road to Portersville, and had shown such matter-of-fact kindness to them. She had felt almost safe during the brief time they had spent with him, and a part of her wished more than anything that she could go back to knowing him only as J.D., and experience that feeling of safety again.

As she stood wavering on the threshold, her eyes caught a movement on his shoulder, and she realized Maisie was perched there, puffed up like a dandelion head. Relief rushed through her, and at last she took the few hesitant steps along the veranda, and sank onto the end of the swing closest to the door. Gathering her skirt around her legs, she pulled her knees up to her chest and hugged them to her, her gaze sliding out toward the shadow-striped fields.

She felt she should ask J.D. questions – what it was that had happened in the basement; whether he could restore Maisie; when and how they were going home – but she found she didn't want to think about those things. She didn't want to think, or to talk, at all, but after they had sat silent for a while, J.D. prodded gently again: "How are you, Libby?"

"I… I don't know. Where are Scab and Roach?"

J.D. lifted a hand toward the house behind them, causing Maisie to sidle a few steps and resettle her wings. "Scab's asleep upstairs. Roach needs rest, too, but he won't leave Scab. He's keeping watch by his bed up there; he wants to be there when he wakes up."

"Is… is Mr. Jaeger… dead?"

Sadness deepened the lines in J.D.'s face. "He's been walking around dead for a long time, Libby. The fire didn't change that; he's just doing it someplace else now."

The answer seemed to settle with a sickening weight into

Libby's stomach. "Will he...." She trailed off, not wanting to let out the words, as if to speak them would make them come true.

"Don't worry, Libby; he won't bother you again. There's an ocean and half a continent between you and him; and the powers he's enslaved himself to aren't forgiving." He gazed out over the fields to the east, squinting a little, his eyes so far-focused that Libby could almost believe he was looking at Jaeger, wherever he was hiding on the other side of the sea. "He's walking around for the moment, but he won't be for long."

Libby weighed this answer, uncertain whether it made her feel better or not. They sat silent for a while, watching the shadows grow longer. Maisie shook herself on J.D.'s shoulder with a tiny rustle of feathers, and cocked an eye toward a spot where a cloud of gnats swirled, glowing like motes of gold-dust, over a sunlit sliver of lawn. The cicadas, as if at a secret signal, all stopped whirring at once, leaving only the sound of the crickets on the evening air.

A sudden worry clenched Libby's chest. "Mr. Fuller... is Scab going to jail?"

"No, no, Libby. He's not the one responsible for what happened." The sadness shadowed J.D.'s face again. "But he's had a lot of damage done to him – and not just by Jaeger. It'll take a long time for him to recover; and he'll have to make the choice to do it – not just once, but every day, maybe for the rest of his life. If he's willing, I'd like to keep him with me, at least for a while. He has the makings of a fine man – and even a happy one. He just needs someone to show him the way."

"But – what about Roach?"

Affection flooded J.D.'s face, driving out the sadness. "Your friend Roach has a heart in a thousand, Libby. I'd be proud to work alongside him, if he sees fit to stay."

Libby nodded mutely. She wanted to feel relieved, and glad for Scab and Roach, but she couldn't seem to feel anything but a sort of numb heaviness, and the tightness in her chest didn't loosen. "Mr. Fuller," she said, dropping her gaze to the floor of the veranda, "Mr. Jaeger told me something... something about my mother... and why she doesn't...."

Once again she couldn't seem to finish, but J.D. nodded. "Libby, Jaeger and those he works for – they take *pieces* of the truth, and twist them into the deadliest kind of lies." At the edge of her vision she saw him turn his head to look at her, but she kept her gaze on the dusty boards. Her eyes felt seared and dry as two stones in a desert.

"It *is* a fact," J.D. went on, "that the man you knew as your father wasn't blood kin to you, and that your mother did something that caused pain and destruction. But the idea that because of that she doesn't love you? That's just not true."

The old bitterness stirred, the familiar worm-twist almost comforting now inside the clenched fist of Libby's chest. "It *is* true," she said, the words coming out flat and hard. "I *always* knew, even before Mr. Jaeger told me. I just didn't know *why.*"

J.D.'s voice was steady. "Libby... parents aren't the all-knowing, all-powerful beings they look like when you're young. They're just people. Your mother's a *person*, just like you – sometimes strong and generous and admirable, but at other times heartsick, or bewildered, or resentful." He turned his gaze out across the fields, and Libby lifted hers as well. A breeze stirred the alfalfa, making golden ripples across the amber-touched green. "Your mother has had damage done to her, too – like Scab; like you," J.D. went on. "She may *never* be able to love you in exactly the way you wish she could, but that doesn't mean she *doesn't* love you." He looked at Libby again. "*You* have to decide whether

The Birds of the Air | 379

you'll recognize and appreciate the love she *is* able to give you, and whether to give your own love – which isn't perfect either, Libby – in return."

Libby thought about this, but the image of her father in his workshop kept rising in her mind, and the memory of her mother's eyes shifting to one side to avoid looking at her. The old, unbearable pain threatened to rise up and crush her from within, but she discovered something: the bitterness – if she welcomed it, if she let it – could harden her inside, encasing the pain like cement and blocking it off from her, forcing the worst of it down. And as the pain was pressed down she felt a spike of aggrieved anger, like the shoot of some thorny desert plant, springing up in its place, and her words came out resentful: "But – it *hurts*."

"In this world, things are *going* to hurt, Libby."

Feeling her spine stiffen, Libby slid her bandaged feet from the seat of the swing to the veranda floor. "That's what Mr. *Jaeger* said. He said that was *why* he did all those things he did." She looked up at J.D. with her new stone eyes, and a note of accusation hardened her voice. "He said *you're* the one who's supposed to *protect* us."

J.D.'s gaze met hers without flinching. "And you don't think I did?"

Libby felt a pang of shame, and she hung her head, twisting her hands together in her lap. "I know you did... thank you; thank you for coming to help us, Mr. Fuller."

A faint teasing note came into his voice. "I thought I told you to call me J.D., 'Chigger.'"

Libby, her eyes still on her hands, felt herself flushing at the memory of the lies she and Scab had told him, and his graciousness in not exposing them. "Thank you for helping us, J.D."

J.D.'s voice became even gentler: "But?"

She was silent for a long time, torn between the anger and the shame. When she spoke at last, it was barely louder than a whisper. "You... you came to help us – Scab and me – on the road, right when the field-walkers were about to get us. And I think you sent... whatever that was... to Mr. Pullman, so he knew where those men took me in the woods. That dream I had about the fire... that lady in the clearing... even that funny wind the night Slater's men beat Scab up. You..." She felt grief threatening to push back up, and stopped for a moment to gain control of her voice. "You *knew* what was happening to us, didn't you? Not just on the road: the whole time." She didn't wait for an answer, but pressed her hands flat against each other and clamped them between her knees. "In the basement... you didn't *have* to wait till I called, did you? You... you could've come *sooner*." She summoned the nerve to look up again and meet his eyes. "You could've kept Mr. Pullman from getting killed."

His gaze remained steady. "And?"

Her face felt hot. The grief and anger seemed to mix together, swelling up inside her, choking her, and she turned her eyes away, not daring to speak.

But J.D. spoke the words for her: "I could have kept Jaeger from hurting Roach, and Scab, and the children he sent overseas. I could have kept him from caging you, terrorizing you, tormenting you. I could have kept Pullman from ever sending Stubby to your house in the first place. Maybe I could even have kept your father from taking that rifle out to the workshop. Is that it, Libby?"

Libby dropped her head again, but after a moment she nodded.

J.D. rose and held a finger up to Maisie, who stepped onto it agreeably. Holding out his hand, he offered her to Libby; she

The Birds of the Air | 381

took her on her own finger and held her up before her face, stroking the russet feathers on her back. Someone had cleaned the blood from them.

J.D. walked to the edge of the veranda, his hands in his trouser pockets, gazing out where the light on the fields had changed from gold to orange. "Libby – do you remember what I told Scab in the parking lot of the cafe, just before we said goodbye?"

Libby thought for a moment, lifting her finger carefully to transfer Maisie to her shoulder. "You said, sometimes the hard road is the only one that'll get you where you want to go."

He nodded. "We could talk for a long, long time about my reasons for doing things the way I do," he said, "and I sure wouldn't mind doing that, if it would help you; but it wouldn't." He turned back to face her. "Jaeger was right: I am, among other things, a protector. And my protection of you, and of the people you care about... it's like your mother's love, Libby: it might not always be the way you *wish* it could be, but that doesn't make it any less real." His clear eyes searched hers, waiting for what he had said to sink in before he went on. "So... that leaves you with another decision to make." He lifted his hands and, undoing the buttons of his shirt, pulled it back from his lean frame; then he pulled up the edge of his undershirt, and Libby's breath jerked in, so sharply that it hurt somewhere inside the new hardness in her chest.

Extending across his ribs and stomach, as far as she could see, there was nothing but a map of scars: the scars left by what Jaeger had done to him with Scab's razor. Not an inch, not a fingertip's breadth of skin remained unmarked.

Libby stared for a stunned second, then a small sound escaped her throat, and she turned her face to one side.

J.D. lowered his shirt. "You'll have to think back on what

you've seen of me *yourself*, Libby, and decide: decide whether you believe that I care about you – and about the people you love – or not." His gaze seemed to draw hers to it; it was so direct that it made her feel as if she were looking into a bright light. "You'll have to make a choice – one I won't take from you. Looking back at what you *can* understand, you'll have to choose whether you'll trust me for the rest, or not."

The breeze that had stirred the alfalfa touched Libby's cheek and ruffled J.D.'s clothes. As she looked up into his steady gray eyes, she felt a prickling behind her own – not the tingling Pullman or Jaeger had called forth there, but something that felt like the pins and needles in a numb limb coming back to life. J.D.'s face began to blur, his features obscured by dazzling refractions of the orange light behind him, as tears welled in her eyes, burning against their dry heat. "Mr. Fuller – J.D. –" Her voice trembled. "You... you know what I did? Mr. Jaeger showed you... he showed you the..." her words cracked in the middle and broke off.

"You mean this?" J.D. reached into the pocket of his trousers. When his hand came back out and opened, Libby saw that it held one of the small sugar birds. This one, though, had no spot of white left on it; it was entirely saturated, a uniform brownish-red, and the spot where her own blood had stained it could no longer be discerned. As she stared, J.D. closed his hand around it, clenched his fist and crushed it, so that when he opened his hand again there was nothing but a small heap of blood-hued grains. He tilted his hand and scattered them onto the boards of the veranda, then dusted his hands off against each other. "Now," he said, "are you hungry? Do you think you could eat something yet?"

Libby looked up into his smiling gray eyes, and her tears

overflowed, melting the arid stoniness, breaking up the hard tightness in her chest and washing it away. A sob wrenched through her like something tearing loose, and she jumped up from the swing, sending it lurching behind her. With Maisie fluttering, startled, on her shoulder, she buried her face in J.D.'s shirt and wept, and his arms surrounded her and held her tight.

THEY WERE IN the kitchen – Libby eating pork chops and potatoes that J.D. had cooked for her – when Roach came down. His wounded hand had been bandaged; his eyes were red, and he looked haggard and exhausted. He told J.D. that Scab had awakened, and J.D. nodded and put down the skillet he was washing. After he had gone up, Roach sat down across the table from Libby.

The sky above the trees outside the windows had darkened to a deep, bright evening blue, and the electric light over the kitchen table glared harshly on Roach's drawn face. The way he sat – his empty gaze, and the limp purposelessness of his hands on the table – reminded Libby of her mother after Maisie had gone, but he met her eyes with his kindly gaze and gave her a brave attempt at a smile. "Feelin' better, sis?"

Libby nodded, but at the sight of the grief carved plainly in the deep lines of his face, tears rose to her eyes again. Pushing her chair back from the table, she moved to the chair beside him, sank onto it and put her arms around him, bowing her head against his narrow chest. She held him fiercely, trying to say with her embrace what she couldn't say with words. She felt silent sobs begin to rack his body; he returned her embrace, and they clung to each other for a long time. "He wasn't just my boss, sis," Roach said at last; "he was my friend. Only friend I had, 'cept for Scab."

"And me," Libby said.

He broke down again at this, and it was a few moments before he murmured, "Thank you, sis. Thank you."

At last Libby pulled back and looked anxiously into his face. "How's Scab, Roach?"

He shook his head. "He's awful broke up, sis. Don't guess he'll ever get over it. He an' Pullman didn't always see eye to eye, but I reckon ol' Pullman was the closest thing to a *real* dad Scab ever had." He glanced toward the upstairs rooms, his brow knotted. "Hope Mr. Fuller can help him." He was quiet for a while, gazing at one of the windows, where the reflection of the kitchen was beginning to eclipse the black silhouettes of the trees outside. "Who woulda thought it," he said at last; "*John Fuller.*" He looked at Libby. "I never *was* sure ol' Jaeger was shootin' Pullman straight. I reckoned all along Pullman put way too much stock in that bastard. I *told* him, many's the time, but he wouldn't listen to me – and it did him in, in the end, sis." He wiped his eyes. "I just *knew* that snake was lyin', what he said about sendin' you off. Pullman wouldn't believe me – not till I near about pestered him to death. Kept askin' him to get a fix on you, sometime when Jaeger wasn't around, just to be sure, like. He finally done it, just to shut me up." His eyes widened. "Oh, you shoulda seen his face, sis, when he seen you was still around here someplace; it was somethin' fierce. He went straight out to the car to get the rifle, an' we scouted around the place till we found that barrel you'd turned up by that ol' oak tree, an' seen the busted window up top there." He looked scornful. "That bastard Jaeger shoulda known better'n to leave that barrel settin' out there like that."

The memory of the locked doors surfaced in Libby's weary mind. "But – how did you get in?" A preposterous image came to her mind. "You didn't climb the *tree*, did you?"

Roach snorted. "No need, sis. Ain't no door, nor lock, nor wall in the world coulda kept ol' Pullman away from you, once he figured you might need him. That's just the kinda man he was."

LIBBY HAD FINISHED washing the dishes, and Maisie had fluffed up and gone to sleep on a towel bar, when J.D. came down. He laid a hand on Libby's shoulder, but spoke to Roach: "Almost time." Roach's face creased with sorrow, but he nodded, and rose from his chair as J.D. returned upstairs.

"Time for what, Roach?" Libby asked.

"Time to say goodbye to ol' Pullman, sis."

By the time they had gathered on the lawn, the warm night was blazing with stars. Mrs. Vogel seemed to have gone away; only Roach, Scab, Libby and J.D. remained – along with Pullman.

He lay on a narrow marble-topped table that J.D. and Roach had brought out from the house. His hands rested on his chest, the one that was missing the finger on top of the one that Jaeger had pierced; someone had washed away the blood and put fresh bandages on them. His clothes were without bloodstains as well – whether because they had changed them, or because J.D. had done something to them, Libby couldn't tell. His face wasn't slack like a sleeper's; though his piercing blue eyes were closed, he looked to Libby as if he had just shut them to rest for a moment, and would open them any second, look at her, and say her name with his wry smile.

J.D. supported Scab, who was still weak; his eyes on Pullman were stark with shock and misery, and Libby saw tears on his face in the light of the lantern J.D. had given her to carry. Roach stepped forward wordlessly to lay a hand on Pullman's shoulder; after a few moments he lowered his head and stepped back again.

They all stood silent for a while, a rising night breeze stirring their hair and plucking at Pullman's clothing, giving an illusion of movement to his still form. The only sounds Libby could hear were the sighing of the branches and the chirp of the crickets. At last J.D. said quietly, "All right," and stepped toward the table.

"Wait!" Libby said, and handed the lantern to Roach. Fishing in her pocket, she pulled out her father's knife and the picture of Maisie; stepping forward, she slipped them under Pullman's folded hands. Standing on tiptoes beside the tall table, she put her arms around him as best she could, and laid her cheek on the breast of his dark jacket, dampening it with tears. "Thank you, Mr. Pullman," she whispered.

When she had stepped back again, J.D. moved to stand on the far side of the table and, looking down at Pullman, rested a hand on his forehead for a moment. Then he stepped back as well, and a great sheet of fire, like the one Jaeger had summoned in the tiled room, leapt up from the marble top of the table to engulf its silent occupant. The table stood unaffected by the flames, but Pullman's body was consumed in an instant, floating upward in tatters of glowing ash as Jaeger's had done; but this fire didn't disappear immediately afterward. It glowed and crackled for several minutes, sending up cyclones of orange sparks, which the eyes of the four onlookers followed as they drifted up and scattered beneath the still white sparks of the stars. At last the flames, too, leapt up, breaking apart so they looked like a flock of burning golden birds taking wing, and vanished.

LIBBY SLEPT THAT night in the yellow-rose room, with Maisie perched on the headboard of the bed – a much deeper and less troubled sleep than the one of the day before. In the bril-

The Birds of the Air | 387

liant light of sunrise, she was awakened by a rippling, swelling flood of sound. It burst so loudly through the open window that, for a moment, she had the confused idea that the sound itself – and not the breeze that carried it – was billowing the curtains into the room.

Kneeling on the bed to look out, she saw J.D. standing on the dew-silvered lawn below. He was dressed in his usual work-worn clothes, as if he hadn't slept at all, and he was looking up into the branches of the great trees that edged the grass. Following his gaze, Libby saw the source of the sound: the trees were filled with birds, hundreds of them, tiny sparrows lining the branches and twigs, all of them singing as though their little bodies would burst if the swelling exuberance inside them didn't pour out in their voices.

Hurriedly transferring Maisie from her perch on the head-board to her shoulder, Libby dashed to the door of Roach's room next door. Knocking, she called his name, and he answered, "Come in, sis." Opening the door, she saw him standing at his own window, dressed in his baggy brown pants and an under-shirt, his suspenders looped down against his legs.

"What is it, Roach?" she asked, crossing the room to join him at the window. "Is it them? Is it the children?"

"I reckon so, sis."

"But – it's so far!" She looked up at him. "How could they get here so soon? And – their wings!"

Roach shrugged, and for a moment the ghost of his old cheerful smile flickered across his face. "I reckon ol' Fuller helped 'em along a little."

Libby had to cover her ears against the joyous, cacophonous sound that poured from the branches. Looking out at J.D. again, she saw him raise his hands. The noise of the birds trailed off, as if they were an orchestra tuning up and he was their conductor, and when she uncovered her ears the morning breeze carried his voice to her. "It's all over, kids," he said simply, when the last stragglers had grown quiet. "You'll be all right now. Go on home to your families." There was a moment's stillness, and then the trees exploded with the sound of wings – the same sound Libby had heard the night Pullman had summoned the khatojana, but this time coupled with the joyous calls of the bird-children. They rose in a cloud, and swirled over the tree-tops for a few seconds, then began to disperse, flying off in every direction, in noisy streams and clusters beneath the rose-tinted early-morning clouds.

Maisie trembled, but remained on Libby's shoulder when the others burst into the air. Staring after them, Libby heard a sound behind her and turned; Scab had come through the door to stand behind them. He gazed up past her and Roach at the dwindling streamers of birds, and even his drawn, ashen face was touched with wonder.

Downstairs, Libby helped Roach cook breakfast, while Maisie pecked enthusiastically at a pile of bread crumbs they had scattered onto the table for her. They all ate at the table together – even Scab, who, though pale and silent, came downstairs, leaning heavily on the bannister, to join them.

When they had finished eating, J.D. looked across the table to where Libby sat, with Maisie perched on her shoulder. "Well, Libby," he said, "are you ready to go home?"

Strangely, the idea stunned Libby, as if her battered mind had shut out the thought of any future at all. She tried to think of what it would be like to go back to her home, to her old life, carrying with her all that had happened, and couldn't imagine it. She stared back at J.D. mutely.

The Birds of the Air | 389

J.D.'s voice softened. "I know it seems hard to go on from here, Libby, but you'll be all right." He smiled. "I'll be keeping an eye on you and Maisie.

Libby's voice shook a little. "What about you, and Roach, and Scab? Will we ever see you again?"

He smiled. "It's a promise." He leaned back and spoke to all three of them, his expression growing serious. "But... I won't hide it from you: there are more hard times coming – terrible times. The damage that's been done to the world by the powers Jaeger served –" he shook his head, looking out the window; there was sadness in his face, but also the look Libby had seen before – the look that had made her think Jaeger was right to fear him. "Sometimes it may seem like I and my people have been beaten, or like we've given up." He turned his gaze back to them, and the sadness was gone, replaced by an absolute assurance that sent a sort of thrill through Libby, like the water of a pure, cold stream. *"Don't ever believe it."* His face lit suddenly with a smile so untroubled and joyful that it shocked Libby a bit in the midst of such talk. When he turned the smile on her, the cold-water feeling was changed to warmth, as if she were stepping into sunlight for the first time after a long, dreary illness. "And don't ever think the hard times will go on forever," he said. "The road seems long when you're traveling, but when we get where we're going, you won't believe how quick the journey was."

He reached across and put a hand on Libby's where it lay on the table, clasping it with a gentle firmness for a moment. "Right now, though, it's time for you and Maisie to get back home to your mother. This has been an awful ordeal for her, too."

Libby nodded, her eyes cast down. She wondered if J.D. was right, and her mother could really be glad to have *her* home – the daily reminder of shame, the cause of her husband's death. It was almost too hard to believe. A thought struck her – one that seemed at the same time frightening and appealing. "Maybe... maybe *Maisie* should just go back, and I should stay with you, and Roach, and Scab." The minute she said it, the idea made her feel unbearably homesick; but the idea of parting with the three around the table made her feel a sort of home-sickness, too.

"You oughta give your ma a chance."

It was Scab who had spoken; Libby turned in surprise to look at him. Roach, she noticed, looked a bit surprised as well; only J.D. seemed not to find his interjection unexpected.

Scab leaned forward, folding his arms on the table; his black eyes met Libby's, shadowed but steady. "It ain't no triflin' thing, kid – havin' a family."

Libby lowered her head, thinking about it. Maisie shook out her feathers on her shoulder, making a brisk sound like the unfolding of a paper fan, then nibbled at Libby's earlobe with her tiny beak, tickling her until she couldn't help smiling a little and putting up her hand to brush her back. She looked up, meeting Scab's gaze again, and nodded.

THEY GATHERED OUT on the lawn once more, this time in bright morning sunlight. The trees where the birds had perched not long before stood at the edge of the grass like great, silent onlookers. There was a weight of sadness in Libby's chest, but also a fluttering excitement.

She embraced Roach, tears rising to her eyes. "I'll miss you, Roach. I wish..." but she wasn't sure what she wished, so she just hugged him tighter.

The Birds of the Air | 391

He returned her embrace with tears in his own eyes. "I'll miss you too, sis. Reckon we'll meet again someday, though, if ol' Fuller says so."

She gave him a watery smile, then turned to Scab. She put her arms around him gingerly, not wanting to hurt his broken ribs, but he bent and hugged her fiercely, half lifting her from her feet. "So long, kid," he said. "You take care a' yourself, now."

She nodded and looked up at him. He looked worn, marked by grief, but the stark misery was fading from his eyes; she could see a little of his old self starting to return. "I wish..." she said again, her voice quavering... "I wish you *were* my brother, Scab, like we pretended."

He gave her his faint smile. "Me too, kid."

At last she turned to J.D., who stood near on the grass with Maisie on his shoulder. "You ready?" he said.

She looked one last time at Roach and Scab, then nodded.

"OK," J.D. said; he too embraced her. "Goodbye, Libby," he said, holding her tightly for a moment. "Remember, I'll be keeping an eye on you." She nodded, holding him tightly as well. And then all at once she was rising above him, and above Roach and Scab, higher and higher. She felt the crisp sliding of feather over feather on her wings; her sister rose into the air beside her. The three faces below looked up at her, beloved still for a moment, and then beginning to lose significance as thought and identity dropped away, the pull within her becoming all – the magnetic imperative in every cell, drawing her unmistakably and irresistibly toward a single far-off pole: home.

THE NIGHT BEFORE it ended was nothing at all: a fading dream of arrow-swift passage between sailing clouds and the ocean-surge of treetops, of singleness of purpose and knowledge without thought; a dream that vanished in the gray pre-dawn light when they found themselves standing hand in hand on the grass behind their home, blinking themselves human again, gazing at the back porch, where a single light was shining.

THANK YOU FOR YOUR SUPPORT
OF INDEPENDENT AUTHORS!

Sign up here for L. H. Arthur's **newsletter** for updates about future publications:

Find L. H. Arthur on **Instagram**:

Find L. H. Arthur on **Facebook**:

Made in the USA
Monee, IL
27 October 2024

68727114R00223